VEIN PURSUITS

BOOKS BY RHETT C. BRUNO & JAIME CASTLE

The Black Badge Series

Dead Acre (prequel novella)

Cold as Hell

Vein Pursuits

The Buried Goddess Saga

Web of Eyes

Winds of War

Will of Fire

Way of Gods

War of Men

Word of Truth

Standalone Novels

The Luna Missile Crisis

VEIN PURSUITS

RHETT C. BRUNO
JAIME CASTLE

Published in 2023 by Blackstone Publishing
Cover design by Stephen S. Gibson. Typography by Steve Beaulieu

Printed in the United States of America
Originally published in hardcover by Blackstone Publishing in 2023

First paperback edition: 2023
ISBN 979-8-212-27742-6
Fiction / Fantasy / Action & Adventure

Version 1

Blackstone Publishing
31 Mistletoe Rd.
Ashland, OR 97520

www.BlackstonePublishing.com

And throwing down the pieces of silver into the temple, he departed, and he went and hanged himself.

—Matthew 27:5

ONE

Throughout my life, the sound of gunfire has always been an omen of bad, bad things. Whether I'm at the wrong end of it or the right, someone's blood is wetting the earth. Someone's heart's gonna stop. A paltry sacrifice to the God of Death, if there is such a thing.

Hell, it's the last thing I heard in my natural life. That final blast from Ace Ryker's LeMat sending me hurtling into this unlife, where I have the unspeakable *honor* of serving as a Hand of God. A Black Badge. Beholden to the whims and caprices of angels in perpetuity, all to circumvent eternity in the icy torments of Hell.

Gunshots. As common in the West as the caw of a hungry crow. As common as dying of thirst and hunger. As common as impropriety amongst men of ill repute.

Bang!

The revolver next to me went off, lead grazing rock down a ways. A handful of stones were lined up on a cracked and dried-out tree stump. The remaining portion of the spindly trunk had long fallen over into the marshlands.

"Woo-wee. Almost got it," I said.

The widow, Rosa, glanced at me sidelong, those green eyes glistening like a field of fresh grass amid the arid desert sands. However, a threat was there, dancing behind them—a viridescent sky before a tornado. Then, too, there was weariness. Neither of us had found much sleep, though for different reasons. Hers, likely nightmares about the wicked man—a necromancer who took the life of her dear husband—with powers she couldn't understand and I couldn't divulge the truth behind.

Or maybe it was the more recent memory of Ace Ryker in Revelation Springs—another evil son of a bitch responsible for such heinous acts of horror, they were better off buried Hell-deep. Luck didn't seem to follow Rosa, unless you counted me.

For my part, the lack of sleep derived from a sort of emptiness, a great chasm of nothing that existed behind my undead eyelids. My body couldn't feel, so sleep was a remedy for nothing but a spent mind aching for a moment's respite. Never true restfulness. Not anymore.

And, so, with Rosa waking with a startle and me already having been up, staring out at the fog of the southern wetlands, here we found ourselves playing target practice, not wanting to discuss the things eating us up inside.

"*Mierda*! I *was* close," Rosa said.

Her voice was like velvet soaked in honey. Hardly an accent at all, though she wasn't from the States. She'd worked hard for that, to fit into a place where fitting in kept you alive and free.

Her raven-black hair was sleek and straight, shining like bubbling oil. Olive skin appeared smooth from afar, but up close, lines formed at the corners of her eyes, her forehead and cheeks. Just a bit of roughness.

Not in a bad way, mind you. Rosa was stunningly beautiful. The girl could twist a man a hundred ways with nothing but a glance—the kind of lady who bewitched the senses. And trust me, as a hunter of demons and all things otherworldly, I know a thing or two about being bewitched.

She'd taken to wearing all black these days, and I like to think I had some responsibility in that decision. Her sleeves bunched up at the elbows. Gold bracelets jangled on her wrists as she checked the chamber of her Colt five-shooter, twisting her forearm to reveal a tattoo of a serpent slithering around a dagger. I'd known her back when she used to wear dresses like a proper lady, that ink always covered up as best she could. I think these travelers' clothes suited her better.

My horse, Timperina, snorted. The old girl stood next to us, unwilling to lie in the wet dirt. She could be quite the baby. Skittish too, but never when the shooting comes from me. No, sir. Me, she trusts, and the feeling is mutual. I used to call her my only true friend, until recent days.

"That's sure right, Timp," I said. "Close only counts in horseshoes, don't it?"

Rosa scoffed. "If you're so good, you try."

I smirked. For a moment, I got lost staring at her. Sure, that was wrong, I know. She was more than a bit younger than me, considering she was only a girl when I'd saved her and her mama's lives so many years back. Plus, unlike me, she was alive and breathing. The heart in her chest still beat, sending blood coursing through her veins, whereas mine was still as footprints in the snow.

Snapping out of it, I drew one of my Peacemakers in a smooth motion, my eye never leaving her as I cross-fired and sent the rock she'd been aiming for spinning off into the mud.

"Did I hit it?" I asked, knowing full well it was a perfect shot. Always is.

Rosa rolled her eyes. "He always like this, Timp?"

My horse whinnied.

"Love you too, girl." I scratched her behind the ears where she likes it.

Rosa dug into her pocket and slapped down a wrinkled greenback. "One dollar says I get the next one."

I blinked. "You ain't serious."

"Are you in, or are you scared, James?"

James. God, it was so strange hearing that name from her lips. Most folk I met or had the displeasure of knowing simply called me Crowley. Rolls off the tongue and ain't so common. There must've been a thousand Jameses in the West alone, and yet coming from her, it sounded special.

I put down a bill of my own. "Like stealing alms from a blind man."

"Ha-ha." She snapped her revolver's cylinder into place and sighted her target. "Got any tips, cowboy?"

"Don't miss."

I evaluated her stance, muscles relaxed, weight on her front foot, shoulders square. Most women of the times ain't never shot a gun, let alone looked so natural doing so. She breathed out slowly.

"You watching, James?"

"Always." Damn if it didn't come out a whisper.

Jesus, Crowley, get ahold of yourself with the sweet-talking-a-floozy-at-the-saloon business.

Rosa wasn't that kind of girl. But I barely got the word out anyway before she squeezed the trigger and sent a bullet corkscrewing into one of the rocks. It cracked open like a walnut—dead center.

I began to *whoop* in support of her—too soon, 'cause she wasn't done. Not yet. Her aim slowly shifted right. She pulled back the hammer, let it drop, again and again, until the cylinder spun empty, each round hitting one of the stones we'd set up as targets—and believe me when I say they weren't big. Never even heard the gun click dry, neither. She counted five and stopped.

Now, it wasn't a quick draw or anything. Wouldn't win a medal for fast shooting. She took her time lining up those shots. And in a real gunfight, it rarely matters who's fastest but whose aim is truest. A half-second of planning could mean all the difference.

Her face pursed with the gravity of every round expended, and I knew, in that moment, it wasn't a game for her. She'd been fantasizing about the heart of every man who'd ever hurt her or her mama. And considering the gap in her history I was not abreast of, I'd reckon that was a long-ass list.

Had those men been standing there today, I held little doubt she'd have fired just as confidently. Back in Revelation Springs, only a few short weeks ago, she'd been ready to send Ace Ryker to meet God until I stepped in, using the supernatural power of a harmonica I'd earned by putting down a foul Nephilim. Looked normal enough, besides being made from bone of some kind. But when that instrument was played, even with as meager a skill as I possessed, it emanated awful power—enough to ensnare the thoughts of anyone listening and bend their will to that of the player.

Wasn't something I was proud of, but it kept her hands clean and her heart pure. For that, I was willing to do just about anything.

Only when she was done did she exhale and grin.

"I can't tell, 'did I hit it?'" she asked, mocking me.

"You slippery eel," I replied. "Who knew you were a hustler? Worked me good, you did."

She grasped both our dollars. "When will you learn to stop doubting me?"

I looked at her, incredulous. There was doubting someone's ability, then there was witnessing the extraordinary. Even I would struggle to land five perfect bullseyes from this distance, and I was a better shot than most. Learned across two lifetimes of having to be, lest I wind up as worm food.

"Maybe when you put up more than a buck," I said. "You had me in your greasy palm and let me off that easy?"

"What can I say? I have a soft spot for old men." She chuckled.

I joined her, though mine was forced. If only she knew the deeper meaning behind that quip. If only I could tell her. Thing is, the White Throne and I've been on better terms lately, and considering that relationship was forever, I figured I'd be a good boy . . . at least for a little while.

I plopped down on a fallen log I wagered would support my weight.

"Where'd you learn to shoot like that?" I asked.

Rosa sat beside me. Her features grew dark. Stern. "*Mi madre*. After you saved us from Ryker and his boys, she figured it was time. I've been shooting ever since that day. Ever since there was something to shoot at."

"Smart mama you had. Sad thing about it is, I reckon there'll always be something to shoot at. But someone who can handle themselves like that'll be better off."

She nodded and smiled with soberly appropriate diffidence. Then, her gaze wandered off into a thousand-mile stare. "Didn't help Willy."

Her husband. The man she'd lost back in Dead Acre. The man I didn't save and never had the chance to try.

"No. Can't say it did. But that don't mean your mama was wrong."

"It's just weird. I always felt like she and I were running from something. Even after you saved us. We never stayed anywhere long. Like she saw a ghost in every corner, a devil behind every bush, as it were. And then she died, and eventually, I found a man. Settling down seemed like a new adventure. No more needing to shoot."

"Life's full of them," I offered. "You think I thought I'd be here playing babysitter all these years later?"

Rosa laid her hand upon my shoulder. Oh, how I longed to feel the warmth of her skin. Instead, I got nothing. Could only see that it was there.

"*Ya no soy una bebe.*"

I didn't speak much Español, but I got the gist. "She ain't a kid." Right. I harrumphed and stood out of reflex. Now she was just being cruel.

"How times change," I remarked, trudging across the swamp, caking my boots with mud. I reached the end of our makeshift range and spotted one of our targets poking up through the grass.

"Now, let's see if that was just beginner's luck!" I kneeled and dug my bare hands under the stone.

My head snapped back. A disorienting rush flowed through me, and before I knew it, my world shifted . . .

* * *

Creak. Creak. Creak.

That was all I heard, like rope on a docked boat being stretched too far. Then came panic. Didn't belong to me, though. I saw through the eyes of another man, his throat being constricted. His hands—my hands—pawed at what was, indeed, a three-fold strand tightening around my neck, desperate to inch my fingers beneath the hemp for just a hint of air.

My gaze darted around, down, so I could see the sheriff's badge on my chest, then up at the bough of a tree. That very same fallen tree we'd used for target practice, though younger and still upright. Strong and proud enough to hold the weight of a grown man.

"All right, Ace, he's had enough."

A familiar voice spoke, and my gaze wandered down, centering on a group of roughly dressed men standing in the marshlands. Men I knew. In the center was Ace Ryker, the man who'd ended my mortal life and boss of the Scuttlers, the crew I used to run with. Beside him, the one who spoke, was a man as known to me as any . . . me.

"Enough?" Ace laughed. "You hear that, boys? Crowley thinks this traitor should be let off the hook. Or noose, so to speak."

The others laughed too. Even my oldest friend, Big Davey. Dead nowadays, like every one of them, even Ace.

Ace stepped forward. "What'd they pay you to try and sell us out?"

The man I inhabited tried to speak through his choking. "It . . . wasn't . . . me . . ."

"You really gonna lie now, right before Heaven takes you?" Ace cleared his throat and placed a solemn hand against his chest. "'All liars shall have their part in the lake which burneth with fire and brimstone: which is the second death.'"

To hear scripture spoken from such a serpentine tongue made me sick, even then.

"What if it's the truth, Ace?" younger me said, voice a hell of a lot less gravelly. Beard thin and all brown. Actually, being honest, of all the men there, I recognized myself least of all. "Vern's been good to us."

"They always are 'til they ain't." Ace clicked his tongue. "Loyalty is more common in dogs than men. But, hey, what do ya say we leave it to providence?" He looked up to the sky and raised his hands. "Oh, Almighty God, if this man is innocent, let him free of his bonds! Send your leagues of angels. Strike me down!"

Ace closed his eyes. Everyone went silent but for the chattering frogs and my host asphyxiating. Blackness closed around my vision. The panic and the pain gave way to serene calm. Not acceptance, no, but exhaustion. I could sense the poor man's thoughts and tried to determine if he was guilty or not, but his mind was consumed only by the idea of breathing the air he couldn't get.

"Let that be a lesson to you all," Ace said. "Thirty pieces of silver ain't worth it. Never was."

And the last thing I witnessed before the blackness took hold was Ace's shit-eating grin and young Crowley standing right behind him, Stetson pressed against his chest . . .

* * *

I snapped out of my trance, falling on my ass into the mud. Gasping for air, even though in my current state, I didn't need it.

I gaped down. In one hand, I clutched a rock Rosa had shot, along with a rope colored black by the mud. A skull clung to the loop, so old even the maggots had given up, but some remnants of that man must've remained for me to have Divined.

That's one of my gifts as a Black Badge—seeing the final moments of a dead being, assuming there's enough flesh or blood or something left of them to touch—shows me things I'd never want to see. Sacrifices so beautiful even angels would weep. Or mortal terrors that would make ol' Lucifer himself shudder in his hooves. Or a myriad in between.

Thing is, though, no matter what I see, those moments are mine. Forever. They stick with me. Time won't take them away. Time won't even lessen their intensity.

The biggest problem is I experience it all through the victim's eyes and mind. That means I don't always get the full truth, subject to my own subconscious interpretation.

Fortunately for me, if I could consider it fortune, I'd been there for this one.

I stared at the fallen hanging tree. Something must've knocked it over in the twenty or thirty-some-odd years since Ace, myself, and the Scuttlers killed that man for something. I couldn't remember what. Didn't even remember that moment until I saw it.

Just one sin in a long line of them I'd spend eternity atoning for—or until the White Throne grew sick of me.

"Nice moves, James. How's your backside?" Rosa's voice sprang me from staring into the dark, empty sockets of the skull. I let it fall from my hand and glanced back. She was laughing. Must've thought I'd slipped instead of seen ghosts.

"Need a hand?"

"I ain't *that* old," I grumbled. Pushing into the mud with balled fists, it took some deal of effort to raise myself from the soupy earth. The rope came with me, in remarkably good shape for having been there so long, maybe preserved by the mud—a perfectly usable lasso.

And that was when I heard *her*. Her ghostly voice hanging in the humid air, speaking my name in that singsongy way. If Rosa was honey, she was acid.

Though I couldn't feel much of anything physically, her presence brought a deep itch to my scarred chest, like it was lodged in my very soul.

"*Crowleyyyy.*"

Shargrafein. Shar. My angelic handler spoke to me from the little shaving mirror sitting open in the mud. Must've slipped from my pocket, or maybe she willed it there. I don't know. She just appeared in the reflection like burning incense—a wispy, undefined shape.

"To replace the one you so carelessly destroyed," she said,

speaking of my old lasso that had snapped back in the town of Revelation when I'd employed its use against a Yeti—a man possessed by the demon Chekoketh. "Or have you forgotten about your greater purpose? To bring judgment to true evil, not the miscreants of your past life."

"So, Vern *was* guilty?" I asked softly.

"Does that forgive murder?"

"James!" Rosa called, looking all concerned. For me? Who'd have thunk it?

"I'm coming!" I hollered over to her across the way, then returned my attention to the mirror.

"Crescent City nears, and it is time you regained focus," Shar said.

"I'm always focused." Even as I said it, I knew Shar had caught me in a lie.

Rosa and I both had business in Crescent City. She and her traveling companions were kind enough to afford me the time to give the late Deputy Dale—who'd died facing that same Yeti—a proper burial before we departed to the swamplands. Even Shar couldn't stop me from escorting a widow and her soft, posh friends across dangerous roads sure to eat them up. Wouldn't be very Heavenly.

"Does this companionship remind you of those good old days?" Shar asked.

She might not have been wrong. It's incredible what the years can do to the mind. Though I barely look like I'd aged a year, I hardly remember my Scuttler days, apart from the bitter end. If you'd have asked me whether I was here, in this very spot, hanging a man for treachery, I'd likely have thought about it long and hard before saying "no."

"Does it?" Shar asked again.

"Is it so bad to remember simpler things?" I asked.

"To harp on the impossible will only drive you mad. You don't get a family, Crowley. The closest you'll ever have are those same sinners who killed you."

"What kind of angel are you to say such hurtful things?"

"The truth will set you free, Crowley. I am merely a bearer of that particular gospel."

"Better than a ma who drinks, I reckon. Can I call you 'Ma'? 'Cause the way I figure it, family's those who are there for you even when you don't want them to be. And, yeah, here you always are."

"I allowed you this dalliance because you did well in Revelation. But do not push your luck. Rosa is not your friend."

I watched out of the corner of my eye as Rosa started to approach me like temptation itself. Hell, she even had that serpent tattoo. Temptation in a romantic sense, sure, being that I'm a man and she'd become a beautiful woman. But it was so much more. Temptation for a normal life . . . Eggs and sausages for breakfast before milking cows, unwinding at the local, throwing back a few beers with the boys after a hard day. Shit, I'd even consider waking up early to go to church on Sundays at this point. But, alas, those are the whims of the living.

"You've seen what effect time has on mortals." Shar's mist exited the mirror and swirled about the skull, half sunken already. Didn't even know she could do that. "Her, the rest, they'll all pass. And here you shall remain, the servant of a higher power."

"More like slave," I said, soft.

If Shar heard—which I'm sure she did—she ignored me.

"This is their world you protect, but you are not of this world."

One thing about Shar and me is that we can't stand each other. If angels are capable of hatred, she'd be the one to find out. I'm not sure that makes for a good team, but Heaven doesn't seem to care to reassign me a new handler. Maybe it isn't a bad thing since we're so damn blunt with each other. I've never been one for chariness.

And there is nothing I loathe more than when she's right.

"You okay, James?" Rosa asked, her serious voice now coming from directly above me. I caught a glimpse of her eyes and, this time, dared not stare.

"Fine. Just found this is all." I shifted to push the skull down into the sludge to spare her seeing it, then yanked the lasso up. Mud and crust fell off, probably some ancient skin matter too. You know what they say, the object of one man's demise is another man's treasure.

Wasn't sure how, but I could sense the rope had been enchanted like my last one, with the ability to compel hellish beings to feel the White Throne's wrath should I tangle them with it.

"It's in great shape," I said. "Kismet, I guess. Fate. Needed a new one."

Rosa looked disgusted, her nose wrinkling in that very particular way—*stop it, Crowley.*

"I thought you didn't believe in such things?" she asked.

"Well, a man can change, can't he?"

She nodded, but her smile vanished when she peered down at it once more.

"It's falling apart, James. Why not just buy a new one?"

"For starters, you just gouged me of my last dollar. Besides, I like 'em broken in."

I rose, shoving the mirror—and Shar along with it—down into my pocket so I wouldn't be further subjugated by her castigations. Then I secured my new lasso through a loop at my side and dusted off my pants. Rosa tried to take my arm, but I shook her away. Judging by how her expression darkened, she got the message. I didn't need help.

"C'mon, I think it's time we wake the others and get moving," I said, trudging toward the carriage where our travel companions—Bram, Harker, and Irish—slept. "We should hit Crescent City before another nightfall."

"Yeah, you're right," Rosa said, unable to mask her disappointment. She'd get over it. "I'm sick of the bugs." She slapped her arm, crushing a mosquito into a tiny splotch of red.

"Being in the city won't change that much," I told her.

"What are you after in Crescent City again?"

"A little of this and a little of that," I replied. Truth is, I wasn't exactly sure yet. That was the way it usually worked. Shar got an inkling of hellish doings, rumors and whispers, and I was dispatched to play inspector. When I was living, I figured the Almighty had His fingers in every pot, always knowing what His great adversary was cooking. Turns out, it ain't that simple. When God made man, the Devil was at His side.

That's where me and the others like me come in: His Hands where—apparently—He can't, or won't, reach.

Something sinister was afoul in Crescent City, and I'd been sent to smoke it out.

"All right, play coy," Rosa said. "I won't pry."

"I don't aim to be," I said.

"No, really, it's fine. It's none of my business. I'm not your wife."

That was for damn certain.

"I've just . . . heard things about the place, is all," she went on. "Do you really think someone there will be able to help me?"

"Can't say." I sighed. Just couldn't lie to her.

In a place like Crescent City, you either lose yourself or find yourself. The Devil and wicked things have a hold on the place, unlike most regions. Guess it's just easier there, with all the vices.

"If there's anywhere in the world where someone can

help you truly reach the other side, it's Crescent," I admitted. "Though I still don't think it's wise."

Rosa caught my gaze. Her eyes grew wide, almost begging me for more.

"Why?" She crossed her arms over her chest.

"It's unnatural. Mumbo jumbo." I went to keep walking, but she pulled me back.

"You know more about this stuff than you let on, James. I know it. Back in Dead Acre when that *thing* came after me—when he made the dead . . . *not* dead—you alone didn't seem shocked."

I blew a raspberry. "Parlor tricks and men in costumes."

"James," she said sternly.

Again, I sighed. Why couldn't I just walk away from her? "I know very little except to shoot at things hurting good folks like you."

"Liar."

"Never." Taking her by the shoulders, I gave in and stared straight into her eyes, sparkling like hidden emeralds behind a veil of sadness. "It's dangerous stuff, what you're after. This world is full of cheats and charlatans preying on grief—"

This time, it was her turn to shake me off. "That's all I am to you, isn't it? A grieving widow refusing to let go. Pathetic."

"No, I—"

"I know what I saw that day, James," she snapped. "The Devil's work. *El Diablo*. And I know Willy's gone. I know that. But I need to know he's at peace. That that monster didn't curse him forever."

"I get it. I really do. All I'm asking is for you to be careful."

I could practically hear the wheels of her brain revolving as she tried to conjure up a response. In the end, one side of her mouth pinched into the slightest smirk. "That's why you're around. To shoot anyone who hurts good folks like me."

At that, she resumed toward the carriage and left me somewhat speechless. It was true; I had a knack for stumbling upon her in jeopardy and shooting whoever was putting her there. And I'd just told her as much, but was that the only way she saw me?

Like a grim reaper—an angel of death?

As she tramped away, a mosquito landed on my arm. I didn't swat it. I just watched as it tried to drink blood that wasn't there. And instead of engorging itself, it choked on whatever was inside of me and tumbled off my arm into the mud.

Dead.

Cursed forever, indeed.

TWO

Few things are hotter or more stifling than the swamplands outside Crescent City. Felt like swimming through air while my boots squelched in knee-deep mud. Even having Bram's carriage, all that meant was getting stuck once every hour. Luckily, with my inability to feel, getting us free was a cinch. I'm not exactly stronger than average, but you'd be surprised how much strength can be mustered when you're unafraid of injuring yourself.

Though mosquitos buzzed in thick clouds, at least the canopy of trees above served to blot out the baking sun. Wasn't like the heat bothered me none, but everyone else? Had it not been for those tall cypresses, they'd have found themselves like burnt toast after too long.

Stunk to high heaven, too—like something died while eating something dead.

"This is putrid," Harker said.

He was an unimpressive man. Messy hair, even when he tried. As he talked, his corncob pipe bounced on his lips, though I hadn't noticed him smoking it for some time. Guess it must've been some sort of oral fixation.

"That's complaint number twenty-two this hour alone," Bram commented through the sliding window from his seat, steering the cart.

Abraham Stoker. Oddest fellow I've met in a decade, and I've met my fair share of nutjobs. Distinguished as they come and eccentric. Which is a word rich people use instead of bat-shit crazy. Claimed he was scouring the country for supernatural entities. Sticking to well-worn roads was the antithesis of that—hence taking the swampiest routes. Though, they were the faster.

Why any sane mortal would be out hunting such things is beyond me.

"Twenty-three," Rosa argued.

"I'm quite sure it was only twenty-two," Bram said.

"Feck's it matter?" Irish said, swatting a biting bug. Her normally short-shorn, red-as-blood hair had grown wild down to her ears. She was Bram's bodyguard of sorts and did a fine job of it. "He don't shut his yap, I'll swell it up for him."

It was a promise I had no doubt she'd keep with fervor. Really, I think they were all exaggerating. Most of the trip, the small company had been twattling this and that about the affairs back in their home country. Things about Bram's studies and what'd led them to this side of the pond in search of answers. You ask me, they're only gonna find more questions.

"Threats like that are very unbecoming of a lady," Harker said, shrinking away.

"What part of me looked ladylike to ye? Was it the tits or the brawn?"

"I don't know how you put up with this," Harker shouted to Bram, shaking his head.

"Come, join me up front," Bram said to Harker. "Let's discuss the book. I've got grand ideas for some of your artwork in the chapter about the American broods."

Bram pulled the horses to a stop. Timp whinnied. The poor girl was pretty drained. She wasn't used to being all tied up, pulling a wagon. The other two horses did most of the work, but she was spent. Almost made me feel bad for tagging along with them. Except roads to Crescent City from the West were dangerous, filled with brigands, gators, and worse. I couldn't find a good reason—save for appeasing Shar—not to offer extra protection on my way to the same place.

Harker climbed out, giving Irish a look of contempt before ascending to the bench beside Bram. With a crack of the reins, we started up again, and they were at it, arguing about illustrations.

The book in reference was apparently a tome of facts and myths surrounding what Bram called "vampir" in North America and Great Britain. He had far more of the latter than the former, but he swore there were bloodsuckers walking around city streets at night like any ordinary man.

I'd encountered enough of the beasts to know to stay away. Most were feral, taken by bloodlust. Older ones could control it better. And they hid well—partially why I believe him to be a little off his rocker. If a human stumbled across one, he didn't survive to tell a soul.

Thankfully, silence carried us for a spell, giving me time to think. I had a few reasons for journeying to Crescent City—and no, being with Rosa wasn't one of them. Happenstance. Good fortune, if you'd believe it. Just so happened to be Bram's next stop on his crusade, and for whatever reason, Rosa found kinship with the fella. Both futzing around with things they had no business futzing with, I reckon.

"Funny-looking trees you folks have in these parts," Bram turned and commented through the window. "The way they hunch—looks like they're praying."

"Would do them the same good it do us," Irish said, causing Bram to perk up. "That is feck-all."

"You'd be surprised," was all I said.

I've come to accept the existence of a higher power. Still couldn't tell you his or her name, but they're up there, perched on a White Throne, belching out orders to angels. Guess I can't blame the Almighty for ignoring an ex-outlaw like me when Heaven's at war with the powers of darkness. Though I wouldn't mind a bit more instruction from Shar on occasion.

"Ye expect me to believe in all that Heaven, Hell, angel, demon malarkey?" Irish said, spitting each word.

"Don't matter to me," I said. "They exist regardless of what you believe."

"Never did take you for the preaching type, Mr. Crowley," Bram said.

"Shit, I ain't preaching. Just stating the truth." Even as I said it, I realized that was precisely what every street-screaming, Bible-thumping, fire-and-brimstone-calling-down soul would say. "I'm just saying, her belief or disbelief in a matter don't make it any more or less true than some priest in a pulpit."

"To that," Bram said, "I'll agree." He tipped his hat and turned back to the road.

"Bowl full of shite," Irish said under her breath.

Rosa shot me a look that said it all.

It was getting dark, and we were almost there. Though I could imagine everyone was getting hungry and tired.

As if on cue, Rosa spoke up. "I'm starved."

"Now look who's doing the bellyaching," I said, making sure she saw the smile I wore.

I rummaged around in my satchel and pulled out an apple. "It's Timp's, but I'm sure she won't mind."

"Thank you," Rosa said, giving it a bite. Her face screwed

up, and the lack of crunch told me I'd handed her rotten mush. Bit of grace she'd taken my chastisements to heart and refrained from grousing about it. Guess she figured a belly full was better than a belly empty.

"You really believe all that, James?" she said quietly, only to me. I eyed her questioningly. "It's just . . . you're an enigma, really. One moment, you're talking about me avoiding 'hocus-pocus' and 'mumbo jumbo,' and then you're defending faith."

I shrugged. "Funny thing about faith: it goes faster than it comes. Guess my many years have taught me to believe in something, even if I'm wrong."

"And that something is—what?"

A sound in the distance caught my attention. Bram must've heard it too, 'cause the cart rumbled to a stop.

"Hear that?" he asked.

"Yeah," Rosa said. "Sounds like a—"

Then we heard it again.

"Goat," a few of us said at once.

"Might mean there's a farm up ahead," I said.

"In wetlands like this?" Rosa questioned. She would know. Back when she was married and living a peaceful life, her deceased husband came from ranching folk. Most I knew about tilling soil and tending livestock was that they were fine places to raid for some grub in a pinch.

"That would be a welcomed sight," Harker hollered back. "I'd kill my own mother for a bath."

"That's dark," Irish said. "But I'd kill her too, I guess."

Sometimes, it was best to ignore her comments. We started up again, a bit faster now with a new aim in mind, listening intently for the goat's "bah" all the while.

"Wouldn't mind slicin' his neck and firin' his arse over a spit," Irish said.

"I've got bad news," Bram said from up front. "Road's blocked, and there's no going around without getting sunk."

I hopped out of the carriage and took in the scene. He was right. A mighty big tree lay fallen across our path. I could maybe push it aside enough for us to pass, given the time, but that would raise questions I wasn't currently keen to answer. Straining to lift the wagon out of the muck and plowing an eighty-year-old trunk aside were different things entirely.

Bram stepped up beside me. "Think us three men could give it the old university try?"

I glanced at Harker, still sitting on the bench, doodling on his notepad. "I think we'd have more luck with Irish."

"I heard that," Harker said.

He leaped down from the carriage, sliding a bit as he landed. Irish unloaded from the cart, followed closely by Rosa.

I turned back toward the obstruction. Behind me, Harker yelped. I spun just in time to watch him land ungracefully in the swampy water. To his credit, he rose quick, muttering curses.

"My good sir!" Stoker commented, rushing over to him. "Are you well?"

"I tripped," Harker commented, as if that weren't obvious.

I strode over as he slipped endlessly over himself. When I bent to offer aid, I found myself staring at the object of his embarrassment.

Two wide eyes beamed back at me, lifeless and cold. The bloody remains of a goat, the best parts eaten away. I took care not to touch it, having no idea how long it'd taken for it to succumb to so many teeth gnashes, and I certainly wasn't interested in knowing what that felt like.

Next, Harker spotted it, eliciting further curses and exclamations of both shock and horror. "What could have committed such a heinous act?"

"Plenty of gators 'round these parts," I told him. "Now, let's get this tree out of the way before we all end up like our little friend over there."

That caused Harker a visible shudder. Best not to tell him about all the *other* things it could've been. Monsters, demons, a rogue witch coven sacrificing to Satan—the list was truly endless.

"Guess we'll all just give her a shove," Bram said. "Let's go, Mr. Harker. Right here by me. Irish, over there, if you will. Rosa between her and Mr. Crowley. Everyone ready?"

He planted himself, one foot in the swamp, the other on mostly solid ground, and pressed his hands against the tree. I did the same, and the others found their spots shortly thereafter.

"On the count of three," I said.

I lowered my head, pressing my shoulder into the bark. I'd just started to count down when I heard something that was very much not a goat. Bram screamed as he plunged below the swampy waters. Ripples coruscated outward from where he fell. Harker reached down to grab for his friend, and his hand came up wet but empty.

"Bram!" Harker shouted.

Then in an instant, water burst up along with thrashing limbs and flashing teeth. Everything descended into chaos. Rosa pulled her revolver.

"No!" I snapped. "You'll just as likely shoot Bram as whatever that is."

The struggle stopped for an instant. It was like we were stuck between the stuttering ticks of an old broken clock. Everything was still and quiet until it wasn't. Bram's head popped up from the water, gurgling a horror-stricken scream. Then whatever had hold of him dragged him deeper into the underbrush.

Rosa and Irish started running. I told Timp to stay put and slung the rifle off my back. Wasn't sure what we were getting into, but this place had gators the size of wagons. Although they wouldn't require silver bullets, I had my Winchester loaded with them all the same. Better safe than dead.

"Rosa, wait up!" I yelled, lumbering forward.

Once Irish reached Harker, they both followed after the undulating muck. Rosa stayed on their heels despite my best efforts, while I swore under my breath. Not just because she was refusing to heed my warnings. I was receiving a warning all my own.

Someone screamed. Could've been Harker. Could've been Bram. I wouldn't have a chance to find out, for I had my own problems. Bright yellow eyes stared at me from the low-hanging branches. Not just two of them either. Half a dozen pairs blinked, watching me from the inky darkness.

All at once, they lurched forward and into the light. Holy God in Heaven, they were ugly.

No fewer than six vile reptilians launched themselves at me from the trees. Only thing I knew for sure was they weren't crocs or gators. Too small. Sure, they had scales, but they were stark white. And them teeth—long, needle-thin ones. Four legs and a tail was where the similarities ended. Foot-long spikes along the ridges of their spines stuck straight up like ship sails.

I raised my Winchester and blew a hole straight through the mouth of the closest. Black ichor gushed like a fountain behind it, and the beast's dead corpse crashed down with a splash.

Fast as I am, that was the only shot I was getting off before the rest converged on me. I brought the butt of my rifle down like a mallet on another's head. My footing shifted, and I turned to see one of them hanging off my arm, dangling there, teeth deep in my flesh. It made a gurgling, groaning sound, unlike anything I'd heard before.

"Off me, you son of a bitch," I said, dropping my weapon

and grasping at its jaws. Wouldn't you know it, the creature's fellows didn't have any couth or decorum; they kept coming.

The one on my arm wouldn't relent, but I managed to backhand another and send it flying. The raw power that came with a pain-free life likely broke its back.

I had no time to celebrate, hesitate, or even formulate a plan. Reaching for my side, I pulled one of my Peacemakers, tucked the barrel against my parasitical friend's neck, and shot it to Hell. The result was an explosive shower of dark mist.

I shook its carcass free and used my now free hand to liberate my second pistol.

However, when I turned to put down the remaining three, there was nothing. If I had a beating heart, it would've been racing. The benefit of such a condition was that my mind remained clear, and I still had my wits about me. Twirling a slow circle, I skimmed for any sign of danger. Sibilant sounds echoed behind me. I spun—nothing—heard another hiss from the opposite direction and spun again.

These bastards were playing games with me.

A ripple in the swamp caught my eye and I quick fired. Couldn't tell if I'd hit anything, but the water turned a shade darker, informing me I must have. Assuming that one was dead, there were two of these buggers left.

"Come on!" I shouted, taunting the pair to make a move.

They didn't disappoint. I ducked as both dove for my head. They must've had damn powerful legs to catapult themselves so high out of the water. It wasn't as comical as them slamming into each other, but they did connect. And like a leashed dog, they took their aggression out on one another, allowing me a moment to slip free of the fray.

I fired twice. Caught one in the gut, slowing it to near paralysis. The second round bounced harmlessly off the other's back spikes. It whirled, finding a new target for its ire. Emitting a low growl, it stalked toward me. Then I heard something subtle behind me. Was there another creature unaccounted for?

I dropped to a knee in the wet marsh, turned, and nearly fired before realizing it was Irish standing there with a creature in hand, fingers digging between its teeth on both jaws. She gave it a hefty pull and tore the thing down to its hind legs. Dropping the beast unceremoniously to the swamp, she moved toward me.

"Feck you waiting for?" she asked, pulling one of her throwing daggers from a sheath across her chest. With deft movement, she flicked her wrist, and the blade buried itself hilt-deep in the final reptile's yellow eye.

"No!" A shout that sounded like Rosa. Then a shriek that could only be Harker.

"C'mon," I said to Irish. "Let's go."

We sloshed noisily through the muck, Irish calling out for Bram with every step. There was no response.

I tried my luck, screaming, "Rosa!" All that returned was my echo.

We turned 'round a form of a corner, pushing past sharp, wet branches that would've been an inconvenience for anyone but me. The full scene came into view, stopping me cold.

Rosa knelt in the marshland, water up to her waist. Next to her, elevated on a brittle log, Abraham groaned, an agonized look etched on his weathered face. But that wasn't the worst of it. Rosa's eyes were wide and locked on a pair of yellow ones belonging to one of the Hell lizards, only inches from her. One of her hands rested on the grip of her pistol, but she didn't draw with how close it was. Her other was raised in front of the beast. Its teeth weren't bared; it simply stared, head cocked to the side.

"No," Rosa whispered to the beast, firm as iron.

Something held me back from rushing to her aid. Call it

intuition, providence, or God's own hand—I don't need a definition. Not to mention, it might be able to take a chomp out of her face before I got to her, close as it was. All I know is my feet stayed firmly planted, eyes watching.

Irish stirred to action beside me but I held out a staying hand.

"Like hell," she said. Seeing her boss in such straits had her understandably determined to put down the threat. And she could without breaking a sweat.

I didn't blame her, but my feeling persisted.

"Just hold up, dammit," I whispered.

Then the fruition of my inclinations manifested. The reptile, eyes still set on Rosa, backed down. At first, it was a meek step backward. Then it hissed, twirled, and scurried back into the shrubs. I rushed forward to kneel beside Rosa.

"Feck was that?" Irish asked, joining us. I thought she was referring to the way the creature responded to Rosa's . . . whatever that was. But her look, pointed at me, made me realize she was speaking of my insistence that she stayed put. Her ensuing words did the rest of the job. "Ye could've gotten them dead."

I ignored her.

"You all right?" I asked Rosa while Irish ministered to Bram.

"Fine," she said, obviously still shaken from her stare down with the swamp monster. "It had me dead to rights, then . . . stopped. But, Bram . . ."

"I'm fine," Bram said in a tone that sounded anything but fine. "My ego is more bruised than I—"

He winced, and I got my first look at his mangled leg. Blood, tissue, and bone poked through a layer of scummy, muddy water.

"Bullshit," I said. Then I scanned the battlegrounds for Harker. I found him hiding behind a tree. "Harker, here, now."

He wormed his way to us, stumbling over a half-baked apology for his cowardice.

"Whatever, ye fly," Irish said.

"You hurt?" I asked him.

"Nothing a change of britches won't fix," he admitted.

"Good." I placed a hand under Bram's neck, and with the other, I grabbed his legs. "I'm gonna need you to drive the coach."

"I—"

"Ain't gonna argue." I was already beginning to rise with Bram nestled in my arms. "Irish, eyes peeled for more of those things."

"James," Rosa said. "What can I do?"

"You just survived—"

"We all did," she said with all the intensity I've come to expect from her. "What can I do?"

"Fine. Help me get him into the wagon."

The trek back wasn't far, but with Harker stumbling every few feet, it took longer than any of us would've wanted. Bram took the pain with grace, as he did all things, but I could tell he was hurting.

"All right," I said to Rosa, "hop in and guide his head."

Rosa did as I asked, placing her valise beneath his head like a pillow. Then I carefully navigated his lower half until it rested on the bench. Once sure he was as comfortable as possible, I stepped aside and let Irish in. The ladies took the bench opposite him.

A shimmer in the mud caught my attention.

"You're wasting time on these Children," Shar said.

I growled softly, unable to respond without looking like a loon to my companions. Instead, as I strode by, I gave the puddle a good kick and sent Shargrafein's wispy visage back to Heaven.

Sometimes it amazes me that she's supposed to be on the good side of things. How could someone sworn to love and serve humanity decide a dying man was a waste of time?

I shook the thoughts away and rushed to the front of the carriage.

"We still have the problem of the blockage," Harker said, gesturing toward the fallen tree barring our path.

"I know. I know. Hold your horses," I told him.

Throwing caution to the wind, I analyzed the situation. Muck had accumulated on the tree's backside, so pushing in that direction wouldn't be as effective. Instead, I pulled my lasso free and aimed at a thin branch. Finding purchase, I set my feet and poured every ounce of my will into yanking the thing to the side of the road.

I returned to Harker, who sat there, trading glances between me and the tree. I said nothing as I clinked and climbed up beside him.

"Let's go."

"How did you—"

"Must've been hollow," I lied. "Now come on before your friend bleeds out."

No less confused, but at least that got him slapping the leather, and the horses were off. In the corner of my eye, I noticed Rosa watching me with puzzlement. I thought the tree being hollow was a good enough excuse, but then it hit me—it wasn't me baffling her. She was looking through me, deep in thought.

That beast could have torn into her, but it didn't. Her being as enchanting as she was, I wasn't surprised, but the beast wasn't some horned-up man. Still, things like that have a knack for survival. Probably it saw me and Irish, and instinct took over as it realized that one tasty morsel wasn't worth its life.

Either way, I wouldn't complain. Better it be Bram down and bleeding than her.

THREE

We rolled into town under the pale light of a half-moon. Our carriage bounced along the cobbled streets, making enough clatter to stir the dead, as some say. I was grateful that was just a saying. Crescent City is famous for its cemetery . . . a necromancer's playground.

Living people did poke their heads out to watch us pass. But only because we made our way through the quieter backstreets. It was the witching hour, which, honestly, meant very little here. The city was always abuzz with some activity or another, whether it be fishing skiffs coming in or a noisy parade for a funeral. Beats sitting around in church, hearing sobbing. First few times, it really weirds you out to hear cheerful music accompany stories of death.

Sure, you had your usual human debauchery—drinking, fornicating, a total disregard for one's fellows. It was more than that though. In a place with so much stirring, it was simple for real demons and Nephilim to prance about unnoticed. Every year, dozens went missing here in Crescent City, never to be heard from again. To most, it just came with the territory. Bigger city meant more people, which meant more bad things. I knew better. Shar could have me after any number of nocuous entities.

But first, Bram needed help.

"Her place should be right up here," I told Harker.

"Thank heavens," he said. "Remind me to give him a piece of my mind when he's well. Hauling us to such a despicable place . . ." He shook his head.

"Something tells me you won't need much reminding."

We pulled up to a humble cottage on Saint Anne Street. I'd been here a few times over the years. Its owner was an ally when it served her. Though I noticed a few things out of the ordinary.

First, the flickering candles I'd come to expect in the windows were absent. Just darkness and white curtains stained brown with age. Second, the sign that used to hang proudly above the door—the one that read Herbal Healer—was no longer there. Furthermore, the house looked like it went a few rounds with the Devil. Then again, who hasn't? But it worried me the place had gone vacant.

The third thing—though I suppose it might really be a fourth—was the two men nonchalantly standing nearby. To the untrained eye, they might've appeared to be common riffraff having drunk too much, unable to make their way back to their homes. But to my mind, I saw them for what they were.

Dark jackets and pants—overdressed for the heat. Clean, unlike most locals. Gave me the notion they were outsiders, unaware of what it took to fit in. But the way they fudgeled around in the shadows told me they were more interested in concealment than comfort. It also told me they didn't plan to do much in the way of moving.

Pinkertons, US Marshals, local enforcement . . . they were something of the like.

"Pull over here," I commanded Harker.

He took the horses to the side of the avenue, and we made quick work of tying them up. More than once, those men gave us cop eyes, all professionally detached neutrality. I even waved, making sure they knew I saw them as much as they saw us. They turned away, subtle as a thrown brick.

I slipped Timperina a hard-pressed cake and patted her lightly. She looked tired as a coal mine mule. "You rest now, girl. We're done moving for a bit."

I dragged my hand along her back as I made my way to the wagon door. She gave a soft whinny and the other horses joined in the chorus.

"How is he?" I asked, opening it.

Rosa must've dozed off, 'cause she jumped in her seat. As was her nature, she quickly recovered. Her eyes settled on the cluttered buildings and busy streets at my back, and went wide. I knew the look. Probably the first time she'd seen a city with buildings as big as this.

Stacks spewing out black smoke hovered over everything. Clothes were strung from balconies. People hollered to each other just to be louder than a hundred loud things. It's enough to give anybody pause. And it's why I prefer the frontier. Cities . . . they're like living, breathing things. And such things are unpredictable. The trees have neither ears nor tongues, I always say. Normal ones, at least.

"Hanging on," Irish said.

"Good." I turned back to the bench. "Harker, help Irish. Quick. He looks pale as a fear-stricken ghost."

Bram stirred a bit at that but made no comprehensible words.

I gave Rosa a reassuring glance before making my way across the street.

Upon closer inspection, the cottage looked even worse. The

boards were rotting—paint peeled and nearly nonexistent. And the beautiful flowers once planted in the garden were dead and withered.

I knocked lightly three times, worried I might pound a hole through the fragile door. I peered over my shoulder—as expected, the two lawmen perked up.

Why they were watching the place, I couldn't say, but their intent was clear.

When no one answered, I rapped a little harder. And some more.

By now, Harker and Irish stood directly behind me, holding Bram aloft across their forearms. His head lolled as he muttered nonsense.

"He's got fever," Rosa said, hand against his forehead.

"Perhaps she isn't home," Harker said.

"For his sake . . ." I pointed to Bram, " . . .I hope you're wrong."

"Step aside," Irish said, dragging Bram and Harker with her up the step. She slammed her fist against the gray wood door with enough force to send the termites running for cover.

The neighbor's shutters threw wide. "Shut the hell up!" shouted a man with a Cajun accent thick as roux.

"You shut your feckin' cakehole," Irish answered. "Or I'll burn yer house down wit ye inside."

The man looked like he'd been scolded by a church marm and retreated indoors.

"We've got to find a doctor, James," Rosa said.

I gritted my teeth. If there was anyone on Earth that could help Bram, it was—

The door finally cracked open.

Marie Laveau, better known as the Voodoo Queen of Crescent City, greeted us through the gap with a single eyeball. I guess she recognized me since something sparkled in her gaze before the door shut. Rosa gave me a sidelong glance. The sound of a chain rattled on the other side, and the door reopened.

A woman of rich color around seventy years old stood before us, her hair hidden beneath a tall, tightly wrapped mauve cloth. She was old, but her eyes were alive and alert beneath strong, sharp eyebrows. Around her neck and shoulders draped a large snake I knew to be called Damballah. Laveau loved that snake every bit as much as I did Timp.

The Voodoo Queen looked far older than the last time I'd seen her, even her wrap unable to hide the gray by her temples. Me? I looked exactly the same. Though she said nothing about it—ever—I'm sure Laveau had her suspicions about what I was and was gracious enough to never pry. She knew things about the supernatural world that no mortal should.

"Come in, come in," she said, eyes darting behind me at the men across the street. She turned her focus to Bram and the others. "And who is this?"

"We need your help," I said.

"This, I can see. But that was not the question."

I was quick to introduce everyone. Rosa seemed positively drawn to Damballah, while Harker shied far away from the snake.

"And this is Bram Stoker," I said. "Got bit by something in the swamp."

"His noggin's hot as the noon sun," Irish said.

Laveau led us through the sitting room into the central part of the cottage, which was both her main living room and kitchen, with a spot in the corner behind a shade I assumed to be her pot.

"Put him on the bed, quickly."

"The bed" referred to one of several makeshift hospital

berths scattered around the small home. None were occupied. In fact, nobody was around at all. A Voodoo Queen can't be queen without followers, and last I was here, she had plenty. Local folk with a gift or a yearning for dark secrets. Some who just wanted to help her heal but didn't have the education for institutions.

Now, it was only her. Alone. Old. Withering away. Where had time gone?

As Bram was laid down, I caught sight of Laveau's windows. The candles I thought were absent were right there on the sill, flickering. She caught me looking.

"Part of the protection spell cast upon the cottage," she said.

"You're being watched," I said, not a question.

"There is no light without shade," she said offhandedly as she dithered about the cottage.

My eyes darted from side to side. "Marie, where is every-body?"

"Moved on. Dead. Tired of persecution. Everyone except Damballah." She stroked the reptile's head like one would a small dog. "All the strange things coming and going in Crescent City, it is *easy* for blame to fall upon those who do not wish to hide for unexplainable crimes."

"But that—"

"Times have changed, James," she cut me off. "And not for the better."

"Can we focus on Bram not kicking the bucket and gab gums later?" Irish asked.

Laveau gave an agreeable nod and dashed away as fast as her elderly legs would take her.

The place had always borne a queer mixture of voodoo el-ements in stark juxtaposition to paintings of everything from the Virgin Mother and various saints to a large crucifix upon which an effigy of the wounded Christ hung. Just below said cross was a black altar covered in jars of herbs, dried roots, and earthen-colored powders.

Laveau gathered a handful of crushed, browning herbs from a bowl beside a petrified head, slapped her hands together, and wafted the floating fragments toward her face. Then, she made herself busy collecting other items, returning to us holding a stick embellished with what appeared to be bird feathers and bones of origins unknown to me.

"What did this?" she asked, pulling at the hastily wrapped bandages on Bram's leg.

"I truly don't know," I answered.

"Well, if I am to attend to him properly—"

"Was one of these sons'a whores," Irish said.

We all turned to find her pulling the mangled reptile head from her satchel. Not sure when she managed to saw one off.

"My word," Laveau said, breathless. "This is worse even than I thought. Okay, everyone out. I need quiet."

"I ain't going nowhere," Irish said.

"You want him to live, no?" Laveau asked. "Then you go. Now."

I put a hand on Irish's shoulder, hoping to bring assurance. "It's okay. She's good people."

"And leave the grunch," Marie added.

So, that's what this was. A grunch. I'd never encountered one before, much less half a dozen, but I'd heard stories. They've got different names depending on the region. Back near Dead Acre, people told tales of the chupacabra—heinous little beasts that would lure their prey with something like a . . .

"That explains the goat," I said, my mind drifting a bit, considering all the implications.

"Yes," Laveau said. "They did not used to be in the region

but migrated from west of here in recent years. And they do not merely bite; they suck the blood from their victims."

"Like a vampire," Harker whispered, a hint of excitement behind his dread.

Laveau shook her head. "No, no. Nothing like those. Pray to meet none of those."

Harker blinked. "They're . . . real?"

Laveau sighed. "Your friend will live, but I need quiet. Go now."

Irish took a step forward. "Happy to keep my flabber shut, but I ain't leaving Bram with no stranger."

Marie's eyes went dark, and Damballah rose slightly from her shoulder, unleashing a soft hiss. Irish took a small step back, the first sign of backing down I'd ever seen from the woman.

"I said I'd vouch for her," I said.

"No offense, Mr. Crowley," Irish said, "but you ain't much less a stranger than this one. I'll be keepin' put."

I looked to Laveau, pleading.

She nodded.

"I'm staying too," Harker said.

"As am I," Rosa added.

Bram moaned.

"Blessed mother," Laveau said, waving us away. "You can all stay. Just wait in the front room, please."

We emptied out into the sitting room. Damballah swayed toward us as we brushed by. Fascination was etched onto Rosa's face, and her hand slowly reached for her snake-and-dagger tattoo, though I don't think she even realized it.

The front room was cramped, with only three chairs, each one upholstered with a different pattern and torn at the seams. A rotting wooden bookshelf on one side had myriad unmarked texts bearing secrets of the thin line between our world and that above and below. Forbidden texts. On the other side, petrified things in jars like pickles: organs, chicken feet, small creatures—curiosities galore.

Weak flames flickered from about ten or so wax candles already half-length, set in hollowed skulls. But, with the windows magically boarded shut, it was dark.

Harker and Irish took seats without so much as a thought for Rosa and me, though Rosa offered me hers.

"No, ma'am," I said. "Ladies always first. Besides, I've got some things to take care of in the city if I can't be any good here."

"Want company?" she asked.

Truth was, I'd have loved Rosa to come along, but with my line of work, it would just put her in undue danger. Rosa and her companions had their reasons for being in Crescent City, and I had mine. Though admittedly, I had no idea what that was yet. It was high time to find out.

"No, it's late. No time for a lady to walk these streets. And yes, I know you can handle yourself. But all the same, spare my conscience."

Rosa stood and lowered her voice. "James, please. You didn't tell me how creepy it was here."

I grunted. She was right about that. Wasn't that it was a mess, no. Everything—all Laveau's oddities—were neat as a pin. Untouched.

"Used to be more full of life," I admitted.

Rosa gawked at the pickled body parts. "What is she?"

"One who trifles with things no mortal should." I said it as a warning, though I wasn't sure Rosa caught on.

"Yet you brought us here? To a witch?" Guess she hadn't.

"She ain't a witch," I said. "She's got a good heart. She's a healer. But just because she does good deeds with dark mysteries doesn't mean others will. Best not to dig deeper than that."

I moved to the door. Rosa gave my arm a firm tug.

Her voice got even lower. "James, can she—"

Irish made smoochy noises with her lips and interrupted us. "Oh, take her behind the feckin' bushes already, would ye?"

"Irish!" Rosa scolded, cheeks flushing a shade of purple.

A retort got caught somewhere in my throat.

"What? I can smell the musk from here," Irish said. "Sickening. Harker, tell me I'm wrong."

Harker cleared his throat, purposefully avoiding us. "You've got the grace of a bull stomping a field mouse. That mouth will get you into trouble someday."

"At least my mouth's doing somethin'." She made more kissing noises.

"Enough of this," I groaned. "We'll talk later, Rosa, all right? For now, make sure those two don't get into trouble. And try and get some rest."

Her lips twisted, but she didn't say anything more than a soft grunt of acknowledgment. Embarrassment was an excellent way to end that particular conversation. Soonest done, soonest over.

I knew where Rosa was going, wondering just how deep Laveau's abilities went. Places where only those with complete clarity of mind should dare cross, and Rosa, strong as she was, was still grieving.

But what did it mean that she didn't hide her embarrassment like I had?

She shuffled over to the books, running her hand along the spines. Light reading, none of it was. Most likely not written in English.

I left her that way and headed outside. Because unlike Rosa, I *was* hiding. I leaned on a column out front, imagining my heart racing when it couldn't. Why did Irish have to say that? It'd been easy to toe the line with Rosa. To pretend I was indifferent.

Strange how a few simple words out loud can change

everything. And I knew it too. Intuition was never a gift of mine, but in this, I was clear. In a breath, Irish unleashed into the world an impossibility. And some doors, once open, can't close. They just wear down until the wood crumbles and falls off the hinges.

Timp whinnied from her spot on the hitch, taking a break from slurping water from a trough.

"Not you too," I said, giving her a look.

Why's everyone always gotta have it in for me?

FOUR

Saint Anne Street was still and quiet, though nowhere near as garroted with silence as Laveau's place. And—surprise!—the badges still inconspicuously hung around on the opposite side of the street. This time, I noticed some posters on the walls behind them. Not bounties like I was used to. They all had the word MISSING in bold print.

Marie seemed unhappy to have those fellas milling about, which was understandable. What she'd hinted at—that things weren't like they used to be—got me thinking. She and the others in Crescent—voodoo practitioners and traiteurs alike—had mostly kept to themselves. Hell, the Catholic healers wouldn't even get involved unless they were petitioned to do so.

So, what did these boys want? What blame fell at Laveau's feet to drive all her people away? Or had she simply grown old, complacent? Tired of fighting for her way of living. I contemplated striding over there and picking their brains—maybe spilling them. Wasn't quite sure which fate they deserved yet. However, I didn't figure they were going anywhere anytime soon. And for now, I needed some answers.

Marie's little home was so close to her neighbor's I'd wager they could hear each other snore. I ducked into the narrow alleyway and pulled out my small shaving mirror, ready to send a spiritual telegraph to the bane of my existence. I rolled the mirror around in my hand for a minute, wishing I could feel the smooth edges against my fingertips.

In truth, I was just preparing myself for what awaited me inside. I was where I'd been dispatched to be, which meant I'd be hunting something soon. Last time, in Revelation, that something turned out to be a tragedy. An enemy possessed by the demon Chekoketh, who didn't deserve what came to him.

I sucked in a deep breath. My lungs might not have needed the air, but I needed the moment. Except no amount of hesitation would change anything. So, I flipped the mirror open.

For a second, it was just me staring back at myself. The exact face I'd worn twenty or so years ago when Ace Ryker shot me dead for sticking up for an eight-or-so-year-old Rosa and her mama.

"Oh, Shar," I said in a cute little melody as I strolled. She hated the nickname, but I couldn't help myself.

"Crowley, I see you've finally decided to stop playing hero."

"It was on the way," I said. "Besides, it's not like I have the first clue why I'm here. So why rush?"

"You are here because the White Throne bids it so."

"And that's fine and well," I said, "but since I'm aimless anyway, I figured a visit to an old friend wouldn't hurt. Might even save a life."

"For once, you've used that word correctly," Shar said. "The Madame is, indeed, a friend to the Throne."

"Was that something nice you just said?" I didn't even try to hide the shock in my voice.

"Don't mistake kindness for weakness, Crowley. Mortals

like her are always a mere breath from using their secrets for ill means."

"Yeah, yeah. We're all just a coin flip from madness. Now, if you wouldn't mind, for once in my damned unlife, could you just tell me exactly where to go, so I don't end up wandering?"

She spoke, but I didn't hear it. My chest started burning fiercely. More with each step I took. That's the bit of gratitude I get from the White Throne. They could've done anything: goose pimples, a ringing in my ears, but no, they chose searing pain on the chest of a man who otherwise can't feel a damn thing. That burn is meant to inform me about the presence of a hellish entity.

Something wicked this way comes.

And it wasn't out of the ordinary for Hell's minions to come after me. I'd pissed off someone powerful back in Revelation, after all.

"Hold on a second," I said.

"Crowley, would you—"

I tucked Shar back into my duster and followed my instincts until I didn't need to anymore. As I approached a cross alley enclosed by two brick buildings, I could hear it now as much as feel it. A wet sound, like a particularly vile person chowing down on smothered lamb chops—lips smacking, throat gurgling.

I peered around the corner, and the sight stopped me dead in my tracks. Its skin was the color of dried blood. I was unsure if it was due to natural pigmentation or years gone without a wash after its many meals. It was frail and nearly bald, just a few wisps of gray hair poking up from an otherwise smooth dome. I couldn't see its face, though the pointed ears clued me in to what I was seeing.

Whoever that was beneath its fangs only had a precious few moments left on this side of the afterlife, so I acted on instinct and barreled around the corner.

When the vampire sensed company, it stopped.

Hunched over like a dog, its head whipped toward me, showing long, vicious fangs. Its eyes, like golden nuggets, glinted in the wan moonlight.

Thing to know about vampires—feral and uncivilized as they come—is they move in stuttering flickers. By some form of Hell's power, their actions ain't smooth like a human, though human they'd once been. This one moved so damned fast, I could hardly follow. And knowing how close by those marshals were, I figured I had only enough time for a shot before they'd come running. If I drew and missed, I'd lose any chance afforded to me.

It hissed. Such an unnatural sound, like no animal I'd ever heard. The blood in its throat rattled as the air passed, and it bolted upright. I'd tried to tell Bram that his hopes of discovering sentient, intelligent bloodsuckers were all for naught, but he wouldn't listen. He was convinced Crescent City would conjure up some previously unknown version of this mindless beast.

I'll give him one thing, though, it's not often I happen on these things in the city. They prefer to live together in packs—or broods, as we call them. Caves, forest hollows—anywhere the occasional unsuspecting traveler might wind up and wouldn't be missed. But here, in the middle of a crowded city?

They're skittish like deer. To accentuate my point, the beast snarled and bolted before I could even draw iron.

"Get back here!" I took off after it, vaulting over the soon-to-be corpse that was its dinner.

I've got a lot of skills. Some came from hard knocks, some by the teaching of one Ace Ryker. Others still, a gift from my Heavenly benefactors. None of them include rooftop hijinks. So when the vampire skittered up a wall and onto a flat-roofed, one-story building, it gave me pause.

Some juice just ain't worth the squeeze. However, being the

ever-dutiful Hand of God I was, I ran, planted a foot on the sturdy brick wall opposite the building upon which my quarry was in full escape, and shoved off. I gained just enough height to wrap my fingertips around the eave.

Old as these buildings were, the shingles cracked under my weight. Dust fell, obscuring my vision. Finally, I managed to get an elbow over the top and proceeded to pull myself up. By the time I scrambled to my feet, the vampire had crossed two gaps and was heading north. I pursued, my Winchester free of my back scabbard and already taking aim.

As I said, if I were to open fire, I had to be damn sure I was gonna hit the thing. There was even more at stake now than alerting some harmless federal thugs. Wouldn't want a stray bullet losing steam and winding up in someone's living room. Even with the inevitable slowdown, it could still pack enough punch to kill or maim.

I leaped to the next building, then the next, finding my footing despite the slickness of nighttime humidity that'd coated the shingles with dew. That sucker was fast, and worse, desperate to escape. But I had him in my sights.

I said I possessed skills. Shooting deadeye was amongst those abilities. Even before I was resurrected, I could put a plum through a penny at a hundred yards. Thing is, pennies didn't move like vampires.

Just as I was about to pull the trigger, someone below shouted, "Hey, get off there!"

Distracted, I turned my attention to a man waving some sort of makeshift club at me from the street. I put myself in his shoes, seeing a six-foot-two cowboy springing from roof to roof in the middle of the night. He must've thought I was crazy, drunk, or up to no good. More than likely, with my heavy boots and not-so-catlike graces, I looked all three.

I'd only glanced down at the screaming civilian for the briefest of moments, but when I looked up again, the vampire was nowhere to be found.

"Shit . . ."

"You get off my roof before I summon the marshal!" the man warned.

I gave one last frustrated glance at the clear horizon and groaned. "All right, all right."

Returning my rifle home, I carefully negotiated my way back down to street level. The man met me, and he was shouting again before my boots touched the dirt. "What the hell do you think you're doing?"

"Relax, friend. You'll wake the whole neighborhood."

I noticed he was wearing his nightgown and a cute little hat—that was probably exactly what I'd done, stirred him out of bed to find out what manner of animal was thudding along his roof.

His face screwed up, and he looked like a cherry pit on fire. "You'd best give me a good reason not to have you arrested!"

I can be a real son of a bitch when needed, but I saw no value in treating this man with hostility. He'd been minding his own business when I rocked his home. Unlike Shar and the White Throne, I tended to empathize with that kind of thing.

"Just hunting a noisy owl," I told him. "Guess I got a bit carried away. No need to get the law involved, friend. I'm going home. Lost it anyway."

Might not have been owls I was chasing, but my words were true enough. I wouldn't be causing this man any more distress this evening.

He huffed a bit, trying to find his words. "We like our owls just fine around here. Keeps the pests away. Seems they brought one tonight."

"Heard and understood." I tipped my hat. "Apologies again. Have yourself a fine night, sir."

He set off, grumbling back into his cottage, yelling to his wife inside. I only caught the first few words before the door slammed shut. With all the hubbub over, it was quiet enough to hear a mouse piss on cotton.

I hurried back to the alley in hopes I might still be able to save a life even if I couldn't guarantee that vampire wouldn't claim another. The shaving mirror in my pocket rattled, but time was of the essence for that poor soul who'd found themselves at the sharp end of a set of fangs.

When I returned, I found something unexpected. I quickly spun away to make myself scarce when a voice rang out. "You there! Don't you take another damn step."

Rising from a squat beside the victim was a US Marshal with a port-wine birthmark.

FIVE

In addition to the distinctive mark on the marshal's chin, a few other things struck me. One, his suit had too many stitches for my tastes, and their tan color stood out rather garishly against the navy blue of his jacket. It was a show suit more than anything intended for a working man.

Second, he wore a crucifix around his neck like so many do, but it was disheveled and stuck upside down like he'd been running and never took the time to fix it. I may not care much for tradition, but if you're gonna wear the thing, at least have enough pride in it to keep it right.

Lastly—and probably most important—was that he had his sidearm pulled and trained directly on me. I stopped like I'd been asked to do, just about to speak, when a second man appeared at the mouth of the alley.

"No sign of anyo—Who's this?" He, too, pulled his gun, following his partner's lead. He looked like ten miles of gravel road. His face was pockmarked, and I couldn't tell if he had one freckle or a million.

He wore round, gold-coated spectacles that splayed out on

the sides like they were two sizes smaller than his head. A little patch of fur dangled just under his lip, dancing as he spoke.

They circled me like wolves, eyeballing me boot to brow.

"That's what I wanna know," Birthmark said. "So? This is the point you tell us your name and what you're doing so close to this body."

He pointed to the corpse, which I could now see was a young man—about twenty or so. He had a thick head of golden hair. Now I really regretted not shooting that monster.

I put my hands where they could see them. Authoritative types like that sort of thing. Makes them feel powerful. Besides, last thing I needed was for one of them to get spooked and find out how useless their bullets were against someone like me. I'd leave that can of worms tightly shut for now.

"Reckon I could ask you the same," I said.

Doesn't mean I can't get a little fresh with them.

"We're not messing around, *partner*." He said that last word as if somehow mocking me.

"Yeah, you returning to the scene of the crime?" the second marshal asked in a voice that sounded like a crackling campfire.

"I was just out for a little stroll," I said. "Guess I should've taken the main streets."

"Guess so," the partner replied, no lack of scorn in his tone.

"Bit late for a stroll," Birthmark said. He took a few steps toward me, and his pistol didn't waver at all.

"Sleep and I have a bit of a strained relationship. Look, you gonna shoot me for taking a walk?" I asked. "There some curfew I'm unaware of?"

"Mighty well-armed too," Birthmark's partner said, ignoring the question outright. "Especially for a midnight promenade."

I considered my options. It was true. Could likely draw and drop them both before either even pulled the trigger, but then

I'd be left standing in the middle of an alley with three stiffs and no good excuse.

Could also tell them the truth. Though, if I had to put a dollar on it, they'd lock me up for being a few cards shy of a full deck, and I'd still get pegged for murdering this guy. Didn't matter that he was covered in blood and I wasn't. These kinds of lawmen don't generally care about such frivolous details.

Or, I could lie. Pretty sure that's a sin, but I wasn't too sure it mattered anymore, damned as I was. "All right. Fine. You got me. I was hunting owls." Might as well keep the story going in case people talked.

"Owls?" they both asked.

"Taxidermied, they bring in a pretty penny."

They both eyed me like I was the one stuffed.

"Owls?" Birthmark repeated.

"You know, *hoo-hoo*. Birds."

"I know what a goddamned owl is!" he snapped. "Let's say we believe that crock of shit. Can you prove it?"

I smiled internally. "Matter of fact, a gentleman about two streets over just gave me a ration of hate for perching myself on his rooftop. Guess I woke him. Gave him quite a scare. Could introduce you if need be."

They both looked at each other now.

"Mind me asking what happened here?" I said before they could respond.

"None of your business," Birthmark said.

"You'll excuse me if I disagree," I said. "A crime of this nature happening so close to where I'm staying seems to be just that."

"You're staying with the Voodoo Queen, that right?" Birthmark asked.

"I generally just call her Marie, but if we wanna use silly titles, I suppose so."

"You got a sharp tongue on you, you know that?" Birthmark said. "What business you have with her?"

"My own."

Freckles scoffed. He got so close, I could finally see the flesh-toned separation between his marks. "Word to the wise: don't be making friends with the wrong types."

"You know, when I was a boy, I heard someone say a word to the wise was unnecessary. It's the fool who needs advice." I closed the gap between us that barely existed. "And I ain't a fool."

Birthmark stowed his gun and slinked toward me to join his partner. "Well, you'll have to excuse *me* when I say whatever happens in this city is the business of any US Marshal who wants to know."

"That right?" I whistled. "A marshal. Woo-wee. Didn't know I'd stumbled into the presence of greatness. Sorry if I don't bow." I pointed to my hip. "Old war injury."

"You don't look old enough to have fought in any wars."

"That's a mighty fine compliment, Marshal. You ain't so bad yourself."

His lips became a straight line.

"I don't like you," he said. Each word was bitten off at the end.

"Well, that ain't nice," I replied.

"Shut it, roughneck. This ain't the frontier no more. While you're here, you play by my rules. That clear?"

"Crystal. Can I go now, or you wanna arrest me for tripping over the same corpse as you did?"

He seemed to consider the question, eyeing me up and down. "Get the hell out of here!"

I started to walk, but he pressed a hand against my chest. I almost broke it off at the wrist but controlled myself, lightly brushing it aside instead.

"Good night, Marshal."

Birthmark growled, almost dyspeptic with incredulity. He pressed his finger against my chest. "We're watching you. You and your *friend*. We get even the slightest inkling you're involved in this or Senator Cartwright disappearing, and you'll be heading eastbound on the next train out. Got it?"

I tipped my hat to them, and they backed away. When they were almost back to the street, I called out, "Hey! Thanks for the advice."

"Fuck off, cowboy."

I left them at a calm pace. That was a close one. In most towns, you get caught near a body and that's proof enough for a hanging, even if you didn't do a damn thing. But these were trained men from more civilized places. My guess, the body I'd seen wasn't the first to pop up, and they'd just watched my arrival into town.

Missing senator. Bodies. Crimes had to add to a good sum for marshals to travel this far out. The clues were starting to stack up.

I waited until I was out of earshot, then answered Shar before she blew a gasket. She was yammering on about something, but I cut her off.

"Vampires," I said. "That why I'm here?"

"As always, your observation skills astound me," she bristled. "Perhaps instead of trying to kill that beast, you might have followed it and found where the rest are hiding."

"And maybe I'd have known to do that if you told me why I was here earlier."

"As was my intention."

"Well, be faster with your words, Shar. Life's a shootout. You shoot or get shot."

"Do not lecture me about the nuances of life," she said. "*You* jumped the gun, Crowley. But now you have witnessed firsthand the die cast over this infested city. Bodies are piling in the shadows."

"Got it. So, you want me to take out a brood?"

"They are not your concern."

"Oh, you've got to be fu—" I caught my tongue and leaned against the wall. Always games with her. "They're dropping people in alleys, and you don't want them gone?"

"Their fate is inconsequential," Shar said. "That was a youngling. Mostly feral. And when a brood grows bold like this, it means the Betrayer is near."

"Who now?"

"It is from his blood by which all vampires originate. The first to taint their kind. Rarely do they make their presence known, but he is somewhere in Crescent City."

I sucked through my teeth. "Let me get this straight. You want me to take down the Vampire King?"

"In no uncertain terms, yes."

"Well, that's more straightforward than you usually are. What's the catch?"

"It is out of necessity I am blunt. You have never faced an enemy like this, Crowley. Many Hands have tried, over the years, to end the curse. All have failed."

"You son of a bitch, Shar."

"I beg your pardon," she thundered.

"You're plucking at my heartstrings," I said. "A real challenge. You know I can't say no to the chance to be your best."

"You can't say no, period."

"Semantics." I stood tall and straightened my Stetson. "You'll have his heart on a platter. And any other bloodsucking fiend I pass on the way. Any tips on finding him?"

"Power," she said plainly. "Follow power. His brood is extensive."

At that, her form wisped away, and the mirror became mundane once more.

"Follow power?" I grumbled. "You've gotta be kidding me."

A straightforward task and target was a pleasant surprise, only for her to return to her riddles right after. I wasn't shocked. Shar hid her ignorance behind an air of superiority. I wondered if all the angels were the same or if I just wound up with the biggest pain in the ass below the White Throne.

Oh well. I was itching to get started. For real this time. No chance of winding up caught in some conspiracy or having to kill a possessed being who didn't actually mean harm.

Find me a vampire who hasn't murdered somebody in cold blood, and I'll find you a man who hasn't sinned. And murderers, I got no problem killing.

Time to start chucking stones.

SIX

I pushed through Laveau's door and found the sitting room empty. A couple of books were out of order, but nothing else.

Didn't take long to find Irish and Harker. The former lay on the empty bed next to Bram's, her boots kicked off and her legs crossed. Harker's pipe hung from her lips, but she had her chin tucked and was sawing a log.

Harker sat by Bram's side. Before I stepped in, I thought I saw his hands clasped in prayer. He quickly brought them to his lap as he whipped around.

"Oh, it's you," he said.

"Where's Laveau?" I asked.

"You're not even going to ask how he is?"

I studied Bram, under blankets and sleeping as soundly as Irish. Only difference was the film of sweat caking his forehead. What a coincidence it was that he was here in the place where I'd been tasked with hunting vampires—the very creatures he hoped to study up close. Providence maybe. Don't ask me.

"He's alive," I said.

"What a sad sack this country is," Harker said. "Everyone

only interested in themselves. Companions on the road. Strangers next door."

"Hey, I got you here, didn't I?"

He sighed, heavy-like. "Yes, you're right. Sorry, I'm exhausted. Bram, he couldn't wait to get here. Made it our last stop because he felt nothing else would live up to it. That here, in Crescent City, we'd find living, breathing proof of the supernatural. All I see is an old loon toying with herbs and cadavers. No different than our gypsies or so-called shamans."

"That old loon saved his life," I countered, probably more aggressively than intended. Harker didn't mean to insult beings like . . . me. Of their crew, he was the resident skeptic, bound only by loyalty to a friend. What that must be like. Choosing what to do with your life.

"I meant no offense . . . I just . . . I don't see the things he does," Harker said. "This is where he wanted to be. I only hope he doesn't miss it."

"He'll perk up. Laveau works wonders. Just be patient. You can finish here and then finally go home."

He closed his eyes and inhaled deeply. "Home. Wouldn't that be grand. I can't express how I miss a good old-fashioned English breakfast. Just the thought of a nice slice of black pudding has me salivating."

"Coffee not to your taste?" I asked.

He smiled, but it was forced. After another sigh, he leaned back in his seat and plucked his drawing pad from the nightstand. He was midway through an illustration of the grunch attack, depicting Rosa and the foul little beast when it had frozen rather than attacked her.

"Laveau's in her room," he said in passing. "Rosa went to bed, I think."

"I didn't ask," I said.

Irish pulled the pipe from her mouth and tilted her head toward us, eyes still closed. She puckered her lips at me, then snickered under her breath. My fists clenched, then I stopped. This was what Shar had talked about. The camaraderie of a found family of travelers. The constant ribbing and joshing of one another. And you don't joke around with strangers unless you want to get hit.

Maybe I was getting too comfortable running in a crowd.

Harker leaned over and snatched his pipe back, ceremoniously rubbing the button on his sleeve.

I moved past them toward Laveau's room in the back.

My first stop. She knew things she shouldn't. It's never been clear if there's a touch of something otherworldly in her, as I never felt that familiar burn around her. Some beings can hide what they are pretty convincingly. In the end, I think she's really just a practitioner with a kind heart. A mortal, messing with nonmortal things and reaping the benefits and the costs. Alone, scrutinized—such things come to witches who live too long without getting hanged or burned.

I brushed through a bone curtain and into a short hall leading to her bedroom on one side and what I presumed to be a closet on the other. Paintings on either side were inscribed with symbols I needed to learn the meaning of. A side table held a shrine, three candles and a jarred petrified head under a painting of an older woman who bore a striking resemblance to her. Family, no doubt.

Her door was cracked open.

"To reach the other side is a complicated thing," Laveau said, her voice low and intimate.

"But your books—" Rosa began.

"Are books. Not practice."

"But it can be done?"

"Yes. Easier when I had support. However, it can be done. James is correct, though. Such business is dangerous. To actually commune with the dead, not just when crones and charlatans pretend, you open up our realm to anything that might be listening. Or waiting."

By then, I'd stopped near the door without entering. Wasn't right to eavesdrop, but when you're in for a penny, might as well bet the pound as well.

"Like what?" Rosa asked.

"That, my dear, is a question I would rather not answer."

"You won't help me?" Rosa's tone grew sour.

"I did not say that. Only that it has been a long time since I attempted such a thing. The strain it could put on these old bones might be too much."

"I can help," Rosa offered eagerly.

"Oh, you would have to. It is your connection, not mine, which creates the bridge. But I would need focusing agents, perhaps even a host. No risks can be taken."

"Then I'll help you gather everything you need—"

I threw open the door. "Gathering for what?" I asked, acting ignorant.

Rosa popped to her feet, startled, hand falling toward the grip of her gun. A natural reflex from a rough upbringing. Laveau sat on her ratty old sofa with Damballah on her shoulders, not even flinching. As if she'd already known I was there. Wouldn't have doubted it.

"Personal business," Laveau said.

Rosa's shock turned to excitement as she crossed the space between us. "Madame Laveau said she can help me talk with Willy."

"Just like that?" I asked, eyes drifting to Laveau. "Time was when that would cost a pretty penny. Now it's charity?"

"There is not much left to fund, sadly," Laveau said.

"So, you're gonna help Rosa breach our mortal boundaries because, what—you're bored?"

"James . . ." Rosa said.

I ignored her—had to. "You know the risks, Marie. You ain't from some forest coven."

"No. I am merely a queen of nothing. This woman is in need, James. In need of closure. Clarity. A healing of the spirit. Those beds out there are where I mend broken bodies, but you know it is the spirit that endures the deepest pains."

"Would you two stop talking about me like I'm not right here?" Rosa bristled. "We've been over this, James."

"Failed at it too," I said. "Or did you forget Ethelinda in Revelation?"

"She was a fake. You said that yourself."

"I did."

"So, are you saying Madame Laveau is a fake too?"

I gritted my teeth.

"I ain't saying that," I said, keeping my eyes on Rosa, not letting them pass to Marie.

Rosa took my hands, every bit of her pleading. I don't know what it was about all this that made me so uneasy. Sure, her attempt in Revelation went nowhere. And I could see in her face then that failure hurt. Laveau was as real as it gets, but sometimes you put a voice out into the realms beyond, and nobody answers back. What if that happened to Rosa?

"I'm saying, what's the point? He's dead, Rosa."

Her eyes welled up. I wish I'd thought harder about my response, but it came out blunt, as the truth often does. A pot shot from a blunderbuss.

"You think I don't know that?" she said in a harsh whisper.

"That's not what I meant."

"Why are you so against this? I practically had to drag you inside that carriage. Now you just won't even think about it. As if everything we saw in Dead Acre when Willy died was normal when we know it wasn't. I'm *not* crazy."

"You're not," I said. "Just trust me. It's better to leave the dead be and move on."

"Easy for you to say. A roaming outlaw who never got close to anybody or anything. Your own boss tried to kill you. Maybe now I get why."

A dagger to my cold, lifeless heart. I knew I'd pushed her to respond with the same level of cruelty I had, but that didn't mean the blow landed any softer.

"I'm just trying to protect you," I argued.

"And that isn't your job. I wanted you along for this because I thought . . ." Rosa's lips pursed, and she averted her gaze. "Doesn't matter. At least I'm honest, James. You know why I'm here. So why don't you go off and do whatever business it is you need to do and leave me to mine."

She brushed by me, storming out of the room and down the hall before I could get another word out. Not that I knew what to say anyhow.

Was it Shar rubbing off on me? Warning me constantly about what I couldn't have, that made me not want Rosa to chase ghosts? Maybe I was jealous. Jealous that she still loved Willy even though I knew we could never be like that together.

I exhaled and plopped into the seat across from Laveau. "Why'd you have to go filling her head with hope?"

"I put nothing there that was not already present," she said. "I merely offered answers to questions that have plagued her mind for many years."

"Right." The single syllable took on a few more as I drew the word out.

"I invite you into my home, and you dare use that tone with me, James?"

I groaned. "You're right. My apologies. I don't know what it is about her that just gets my yarn all spun up."

"I do. You care." She affected a warm smile. Inviting, like the grandmother I never had. Like I said, as witches and their ilk go, Laveau is decent. Better than decent. Though, to be fair, I'm usually hunting rotten ones and not joining them for teatime.

My eyes rolled. "Not you too, Laveau."

"I mean nothing by it. It is a good look on you, James. When we first met, I was not sure if you were capable of caring for another. So wrapped up in yourself you were."

"I sort of miss it."

She chuckled. "Don't. And I am glad you brought her to me. Crescent City has been infested with untrustworthy souls seeking money or infamy. I will take care of her if she continues down this path."

"I know. You're one of the good ones." I smirked. "You could have told her it was impossible, though."

She eyed me with disapprobation heavy on her features. "You would have me lie to her?"

"If it kept her safe. Maybe."

"I do not suspect it would be so easy. There's something about her. You see it. Her curiosity. Her spirit. Her mind is open like mine was at her age. I believe she can handle the hidden truths of our world."

"Now, now. Don't go looking for an heir in her."

"An heir to what?" Laveau hissed, and Damballah rose ever so slightly from her shoulder.

A brief silence passed between us. The elephant in the room. So much had changed for her over the years and nothing for me.

Wasn't often I saw that side of her. I'd struck a nerve, and I felt it was best to slather some ointment on it before it was too late.

"I met the marshals outside," I said. "Bothersome fellas. A senator, missing here? That's rough."

Laveau drew a deep, beleaguered breath like she'd been holding it in since the war. "The cherry on top, I am afraid. The city grew. Rich folk from out east immigrated. Doctors. The kind of people less grateful for simply being healed than needing to know how it was done. We were easy to blame."

"For what, though?" I asked. "The marshals can ask around. Whether they like you or think you're a devil in disguise, nobody can deny you've been good to this city."

"For everything unexplained. Sicknesses. Disappearances. Death."

"Easy to point fingers when bodies start piling."

Her head bobbed. "It got so bad after Senator Cartwright vanished, I even sent my daughter away. He had a fascination with the occult, you see. About a month ago, he thought it would be fun to show up at my famed doorstep and ask for me to read his fortune. Apparently, slamming a door in the face of a senator was a mistake. He disappeared that night."

I chuckled. "Might explain why you're being watched."

She agreed. "Stayed here so I can help with whatever I can in *my* city. It is hard getting around on these old legs, though. Mostly, none show up for aid anymore anyway. I have not been to Mass in months. Many presume I am already dead."

"Wouldn't that be the day?"

"Such is life." She crossed her legs, and Damballah slithered down onto her lap. Marie stroked its head like a house cat. "Now, you came here for something, James, so just ask."

This was why I liked her. She knew that talking around a point was like bringing a potato to a gunfight.

"Barely a block outside, and I ran into a vampire. Out in the open, sucking a poor man dry."

She didn't look surprised. Just nodded. "They are more brazen than they once were," she said. "And there are more of them. Something changed a few years back. Could not say what. But the werewolves loosened up their hold downtown, and it all worsened. More . . . unexplainable beings were seen."

"What about Roo? Did he kick the bucket?"

"Rougarou?" Laveau shook her head. "Not that I know."

"Well, it just so happens I'm after a vamp. Who knows, if I clean him—could help this place."

"I fear it is too late for that."

"Either way, I'm wondering if you might have heard of a vampire lord known as the Betrayer."

She scratched her wrinkled chin. "You will need to be more specific."

"Wish I could be. I know where there's a nest, there's a breeder, but those in charge usually prefer their children to stay underground, away from the sun and prying eyes. But this is Crescent City. Weird happenings abound."

"I would not doubt the presence of one here, but I am afraid I am a bit out of touch these days. I wish I knew more."

I blew a raspberry. "Ain't a problem. That've been too easy anyway. If you can't point me in a direction, perhaps I could at least buy some silver off you. You know, the rounds you keep for 'contingency.'"

"Not much left in stores," she said with sadness in her eyes.

"I'll take whatever I can get. I'm a little low on cash, but—"

She waved her hand in dismissal. "Take it all, James. Do I look like I have any fighting left to do? You can pay me back by letting me help that grieving woman out there."

"As if I could have stopped you anyway?"

She smiled. "Too true. But yes, take it. I may not be a queen anymore, but I stayed behind here because this is my city. If what you say is true, then we will all be better off with this vampire gone."

I stood and crossed the room, straight to a painting on the other side. Her father: a pale Frenchman, from what I reckon, all decked out in a wig the way those people do. I lifted it off the wall, revealing a niche in the stone. Boxes of ammunition shined, along with a few bars of pure silver. I claimed the bullets but left Laveau the bars.

As I turned, I noticed her staring longingly at nothing in particular, petting Damballah in rhythm. I didn't truly realize until then how old she'd gotten.

"Chin up, Marie," I said, resting a hand on her shoulder. "You ain't dead yet."

"Of course I am not. I would be haunting you." She let out a weak chuckle, then patted my hand.

Our history was short. Barely there, really. But there's something about spending time with another person who just . . . gets it, without anything needing to be said. We both had our demons because of the things we'd known and done. Sometimes, that's enough to form a bond.

"Just promise me one thing before I go," I said.

"Promises only bind the weak," she said.

"All the same. Just don't go starting any spells or nonsense with Rosa until I'm around."

"I believe it is she who will need to make that promise. And I do not sense weakness in that one. Not at all."

"You're damn right about that. Just try to influence her in the right direction for me?"

She nodded.

"That's all I can ask."

"When will you return?" she asked.

"Couldn't say. At least now I've got a good reason to come back."

I headed out the door, understanding exactly what she meant. It was what made her decent. She sought to understand and unravel truths, not control them. And she was the same way with people. Probably why her operation fell apart once other powers rose.

I made my way back through the place. Harker had finally passed out next to Bram. Irish snored even louder. Back in the foyer, I passed Rosa but didn't dare look. She was reading softly to herself, thumbing the pages of Laveau's books.

Part of me wanted to stop and apologize for coming off so harsh. But I think both of us needed some time to stew. Once outside, I checked the cylinders of my Peacemakers.

It was time to go hunting. And I knew precisely where to start.

SEVEN

First stop in my pursuit: the dead house. Or morgue, as some more refined folks have come to calling them. Most towns don't have them, but a city as big as Crescent needs to. Sad truth about the world—a denser population means more bodies, and somebody's gotta sort them before the grave takes them and the priest whispers, "Amen."

Deep down, humanity is just on one long race to the end. Somewhere inside, no matter how happy a person is, we're all just waiting for the sweet release of death. Question is, will we even know when it's come? As someone who bit the proverbial bullet, I can say with assurance I've got no idea what happened during those years I spent on the other side. First thing I remembered after Ace's cold eyes and bullet was staring into Shargrafein's wispy form.

Trumpets blared, dragging me back to the present. Hadn't realized how far I'd walked until a funeral precession nearly trampled me. A few dozen people marched by on their way to the ceremony, celebrating a life. Women in garish gowns, men dressed to the tees, wearing colorful masks—a custom not used elsewhere in the world. Can't say I minded. Why does death have to be so morose? What I've come to learn in my service to the White Throne is that life is a flicker.

You don't cry before you blow out a birthday candle.

They took a seldom-used route to the cathedral, avoiding the obstreperous crowds gathered to celebrate life by different means. It was getting late, but for this time of year, the party had just begun. I halted at the corner of the Avenue of the Holy Cross and waited. It wasn't long before the mortician exited his humble building beside the graveyard and closed up shop.

He checked his pocket watch, then proceeded toward the partying. Couldn't blame him. After what he likely saw all day, something as mindless as throwing back a few and dancing the night away seemed a small comfort.

The morgue was attached to a sheriff's building—a two-story affair I guessed contained a fair number of lockups. I paused at the door around back, checking both ways. Nobody paid me the slightest heed. Why would they? Dead men don't got pockets. Anything inside had been picked clean of valuables long before they were brought in by street rats or peckish deputies.

Made sense the only defense was a locked wooden door. My old life as an outlaw afforded me certain skills, one of which was picking a lock as simple as this one. The tumblers clicked, and I was in. I gently shut the door behind me and relocked it. Easiest B and E I could recall in some time.

I said there was nothing to steal from the cold, naked dead, but that ain't entirely true. The dead . . . they talk to me, show me their memories. Don't mean to, of course. How much easier would it be if bones started rattling off secrets, saving me the trouble of looking? But if older vampires were amidst and catching enough heat for Shar to care, perhaps one of the bodies below had been a meal like that fella in the alley.

A set of stairs descended into a basement, and I stopped at the bottom. Moonlight crept in through narrow, grated windows up near the far ceiling. Twelve tables were arrayed in rows down the stark room, each covered by a cloth. I knew it was chilly as Hell in there without even needing to feel it. Something about the way the cold makes fabric stiffen. Or maybe it was the feet sticking out, skin white as marble.

I considered touching one as I passed the first, but instead, continued on to their upper body and peeled the cover down to just below the neck. Considering it was a young woman, I dared not go farther.

Say what you will about James Crowley, but he's a gentleman.

I whispered my usual Latin prayer and stretched my hand over her face.

"A tenebris ad lucem." Means something like *From darkness to light.*

Though I served angels, I never did quite get used to this part. Felt worse than grave robbing, and I'll admit I'd plucked a few things here and there off corpses, like cash to pay for silver. They wouldn't miss it.

It was one thing to accidentally stumble upon the remains of a hanged man, but Divining the dead in a row like this felt so . . . clinical. Invasive.

Skin touched skin, and my head lurched back . . .

* * *

Waves crashed. It was dark. Only moonlight to show the feet beneath me—my feet. They were completely bare, balanced at the edge of a building on the wharf. Wind whistled, whipping a sheer white nightdress with a red stain around her thigh region. Cold, even though the humidity or stress had the body sweating.

An odd sensation. A rare one. Something I'd forgotten about.

I filtered through thoughts of loss and sorrow but soon came calm. Intense, demystifying calm. No worry about what came next or what the fall might feel like. Just acceptance.

As I inhabit these flitting memories of death, I rarely do more than observe. But this time, I strained mentally against the movement of her legs to no avail. For the tears on her cheeks were dry, and her decisions were made.

A child lost. A broken heart. And a few steps later, a plunge into the icy depths of the gulf. Water flooded her throat, and panic came all too late, as it always does. The will to survive is a primal thing.

The water didn't kill her, even as it choked and filled her lungs. The heavy current tossed her body, and under the water where not a soul could see or help, her head—my head—cracked against a rock.

* * *

I snapped out of the vision, hacking up seawater that never came. It took me a few moments to compose myself, then another as I reached for the phantom pain where her head struck.

I leaned over the table, breathing slowly, still feeling like that girl. I can take death and brutality, but usually, it's got a purpose. A fight. A murder. This was . . . well, a first.

"You save me and not her?" I beseeched the moldy ceiling.

All those dark days when I doubted this unlife of mine and wished it would come to an end, now I felt like a damned fool. How lucky I was to get to wish that, all while complaining about my holy mission—while this poor girl lay here, a barren womb and a dead, broken heart.

I couldn't help but think of Rosa losing her husband and that maybe I'd been too harsh on her.

I never had anyone I'd cared for much. Which meant I'd

never had anyone to lose who'd break me so. Is that despair what Rosa fought against every day? And it wasn't the agony of loss or terror of dying that got me most . . . It was the emptiness.

The cavern in that woman's chest and mind before she took the jump . . .

Left me with a new wish—that I'd left her to be at peace as I slowly lifted the sheet back up to cover her face. Then I looked up and sighed.

On to the next.

* * *

One body at a time, I worked my way through. I had all night. Each glimpse was half a minute or so, but it took me longer than it ought to have.

Divining is a valuable ability, but I always forget how it drains me. Witnessing another's death shouldn't be like turning pages of a book, and it's not. Feeling it . . . that's penance enough if I never suffered a moment in Hell's icy grip. There's no way the White Throne left me numb to all else but the suffering of others without reason. A little on the nose, if you ask me.

But you know what? No one asks me. A Hand of God is just that. We aren't called to be a mouthpiece or a sounding board. Just do the job and shut up. And that's what I hope to do here.

I'd replaced all the coverings as I went. Most of the deaths were commonplace. A few from old age. One, a complication due to a botched amputation. People say life flashes before your eyes when you die, but for these people, their last thoughts were everything from loved ones to all the things they'd dreamed of doing but never did.

A couple died from too much drinking. Hard to believe, but it's true. A young man—his wedding day—choked on his own vomit. Could've done without a sense of taste for that one. Another young man started up with the wrong crowd—threw exactly one punch before getting himself shot. One lead plum straight through the heart.

Courage and long life make shitty bedfellows.

Opium caught one. A veteran from the war, lost a leg and never kicked the stuff. Sad. His last thoughts were merely for more of the thing that killed him. The next one was an older woman. Matronly. Not sure where they found her, but at the time of her death, she wore opulence all over her and lived inside a beautiful plantation house. Servants roaming the halls. Big bed. That kinda place. Would've made old Reggie Dufaux proud.

Her husband ascertained she'd been sleeping with the stable hand and throttled her with his own two hands after hanging the man—a detail I saw, but no one else knew. The two lay like the lovers they were, side by side on the table, both their faces beaten and bloodied beyond recognition. A family affair. Might've rearranged their features after their deaths. However, if the mortician's notes could be believed, the culprit—concerning which, they still had no leads—had the bodies dumped in the city to get lost amongst the rabble.

That was where I spent some extra time. Reading notes. Taking notes. Took a bit to search through cabinets for a writing implement.

"You're wasting time again," Shar said as I unlatched a locker containing a mirror and a straight-edge razor. I guess the mortician didn't always have the luxury of going home, so many dead passed through these parts.

"It'll only take a minute," I grumbled as I kept rummaging.

"Curious, you think your time holds such significance."

"You're the one always griping about wasting it."

"The truth you should cling to is that your time is borrowed. Your life is not your own, James Crowley."

"So I've been told. Listen, ain't it my duty to help when I can? 'Love thy neighbors' or some shit?"

"A dead man is no neighbor."

"You say that when you're down here." I slammed a cabinet shut. "Last I checked, everyone up in those clouds of yours is dead."

"And these Children have found refuge in their new homes, their new bodies." She continued speaking, her ominous, smoky form flicking around the many reflective surfaces in the room. "Their corpses are empty vessels awaiting the moment they enter the ground and become a sumptuous repast for crawling critters."

"Well, woe is for the living," I said, still searching lockers. "What kind of angel doesn't care about the truth of a killer?"

"On the contrary, Crowley, I care a great deal. Have you not heard, 'vengeance is the Lord's.'"

"You'll have to forgive me, but I'd rather see them suffer than trust it's happening behind closed doors. Look at that woman's face," I said. "I know where the bastard who did that lives. Saw his face because of the powers the White Throne entrusted me with. If I don't do something about it, who will?"

"He will receive his judgment by Heaven, not his peers."

"Like you said. I ain't his peer," I reminded her. "I'm a goddamned Hand of God."

"Watch your words. A Hand has no true need for a tongue."

See? Be seen, not heard. That was why I preferred to refer to myself as a Black Badge. Seemed more appropriately unimportant.

I found the pencil the mortician used to label the identities of each body beneath a half-eaten beignet. Thing had flies all over it, yet I still wished I could taste the pastry.

"There. No time at all. What did I tell you?"

Taking a tab, I wrote down HUSBAND CHOKED HER in big capital letters, then returned to her corpse and pinned it to her chest by staking it through the pencil. She wouldn't feel it.

I could hear Shar asking if that made me feel better, even though she hadn't.

It did.

Not that the wife hadn't sinned by sleeping with another man, but there are other ways to handle such things. Like I said, I'm a gentleman.

"Shar, unless you plan to offer any useful information, I got more work to do."

This time, no answer came.

* * *

It'd grown darker down there, the moon rising higher and farther away as night pressed on. More than ten Divinings observed so far, and nothing out of the ordinary. As if any death should seem mundane.

It made sense, though. There was a reason most people had no idea my side of the world even existed. If a whole city was wiped out by demons and monsters, humanity might just begin to think them more than a myth.

Not that things like that don't happen, mind you. Sometimes dark magic does dark things. Where do you think the Mayans disappeared to?

But that's just it. Supernatural incursions like that tend to leave little or no witnesses. They become tall tales or the ravings of lunatics who lost their minds from grief. I always wondered what might happen if the unnatural things I knew to be real became known by all. It'd probably be the end of society as we knew it. Mortals are like that, after all. Like Bram. I wasn't exactly sure what his plan was, writing this book on vampires, but he was a fine example of what the world at large would be reduced to. If they discovered new creatures or beings, they'd be desperate to find them, explain them. To control them or wipe them out.

They'd lose, of course. Guns can only go so far.

Bye-bye, food source for vamps and Nephilim and whatever else. Bye-bye, toys for demons. It's a delicate balance I'm part of preserving. Most monsters don't crave war. They need humans like we need horses or cows.

I approached the next man—an older fellow. His cane had gotten caught in some loose stone, and he tripped. That was that. He was just walking along, thinking about lunch, when slip-crack. No fear or longings. Life is that fragile.

And then, just like that, I was on to the final corpse. I pulled the cloth down to find a middle-aged gentleman. A bit gaunt but more or less average. Good hair. Strong jawline. The only abnormal thing about him was his mouth was already sewn shut. Maybe they were getting him ready for presentation and didn't have time to bring him to the parlor. I don't know.

I stopped by his head and took my time. Didn't bother whispering any Latin since, after the first few bodies, I was pretty sure I'd gotten my point across. Shar might call this a waste of time, but I'd solved one double homicide. Hard to argue with results.

"See you on the other side," I said to the body before grabbing his shoulder and entering his mind . . .

* * *

My vision blurred. Thoughts were scrambled. The man I inhabited was very clearly inebriated. Unlike those poor fools I'd Divined earlier, he had just enough in him to feel good and not die of something stupid. I could get used to staying here. Nothing like unwinding both brain and body, chugging toward the bottom of a barrel.

And I wasn't alone.

We were naked as the day we were born. Sitting on the edge of a red satin sheet draped over a mattress that looked fit for a queen. Gold, frilly tassels, a shower of translucent veils hanging from an oaken canopy.

And my vessel—sporting equipment to be envious of—was hard as a sailor in a whorehouse. Caught me off guard.

The woman sauntering toward him had pale skin and sharp features, eyes dark as the devil at midnight. Hair too. She had an old-world look to her, and the puffy scarlet dress she wore may as well have been donned at some French king's ball. Heels made her tall, intimidating, and judging by my host, that wasn't an issue for him.

"They say there's nobody like you in this house," the man said.

"Ils parlent sincèrement, mon amour," *the woman replied.*

"Keep talking fancy like that, doll."

He gave her a slap on the side of the thigh, a bit too high and hard for my taste. She grinned something fierce, then pulled a string on the back of her dress, and it cascaded down porcelain skin to her feet. She wore nothing underneath, not even a brassiere.

"Tu veux ça?" *she asked, voice mellifluous like someone practiced in such arts.*

He grasped her by the hips, fingers digging gouges in her flesh, but she didn't budge. Instead, she pushed him down with unexpected strength, so his back was flat on the mattress.

"So that's how it's gonna be, huh, honey?"

"You get what you pay for," she said with a thick French accent.

And he had paid. A lot more than any average woman of the

night should cost. A price only a wealthy man could afford for a few hours of distraction.

She mounted him—me—and in that moment, I experienced the full touch of a lady, which I hadn't known in decades. I lost focus—he did—or both of us. If Divining was always like this, I'd ditch Shar and shack up in a cemetery.

I knew my time in this memory was coming to an end quickly, but how? What'd he die of, pleasure?

She arched her back, breasts dangling over him. My host could barely contain himself as she leaned in for a kiss.

And then it happened.

A shimmer caught in her eye. Already dark eyes became solid, black orbs. Thick veins coruscated down from the sides of her lips to her throat. Her formerly delicate jaw went wide, unhinging like that of a snake, and in it grew needle-thin fangs.

Before I knew what hit me, she kissed me hard and bit down on the back of my tongue. Pain rushed through my mouth, along with the taste of iron. I panicked and tried to kick her off, but she held me down with the force of a rail worker despite her slight frame. And all the while, she kept riding me like I was a wild horse she was trying to break.

The confusion of pain and pleasure had my host paralyzed. Finally, logic returned. He slapped. Punched. Whatever he could do as blood rushed out of his lower regions and into her mouth. Pulling free, he turned to the side, moaning and unable to speak from his cloven tongue. Blood disappeared onto sheets the precise sanguine shade.

I faced a baroque-style golden mirror on top of an old dresser. In it, the reflection of my host squirmed on the bed, all by himself. No sign of the woman at all.

But she wasn't gone. "Reviens vers moi," *she said.*

If his heart hadn't been racing before, it was then. Sobered him up fast. She clutched his head on either side and pulled his lips back to hers to continue her meal. His heart thumped against his rib cage, terror inducing a fatal heart attack as she fed . . .

* * *

"Get off me!" I think I shouted, but I lisped from what just happened to my tongue in the memory. While it seemed like a lot, it all occurred in less than a minute. Mounted by a vampiric seductress, killed as they made love. I'd never heard of a vamp feeding with such gratification. Not just on blood but on stilted emotion.

Hell, I've never seen one feed with such clarity of focus either. In all my days, the broods I'd faced were unthinking, singularly minded beasts.

"Jesus, he's alive!" a voice blurted, I think in my present. Everything remained a bit of a fog. And while I staggered back from shock, my body was suddenly thrust in another direction by an unfelt force. Shells clattered. I looked down. A chunk of my side and clothes were blown onto the corpses.

I peered back at two grimy-looking fellas with leathery skin standing a few feet away, perturbation plastered on their faces. Rotting yellow teeth. Black coats with more holes in them than a block of cheese.

Scavengers, ruffians. Whoever they were, I knew the type.

"Now hold on a sec—"

A shotgun flashed and struck me on the other side. The corpse table slid back from the weight of me. My hand dipped toward one of my pistols. I couldn't say why these hicks were in a morgue, but they'd pissed me off too much to get a chance at mercy.

Another gunshot pierced the serene silence of the room.

My world suddenly turned sideways. I'd memorized the grip and draw of my pistols long ago, even before I lost feeling as a Black Badge, but the gun never came. No part of me responded. Suddenly, I was lying on the stone floor, my head facing a way it shouldn't have been able to, considering where my body wound up.

EIGHT

"*Merde. Merde. Merde.* I think he's dead," one of my assailants said. Now that it was quiet, I recognized Cajun accents.

"You think? Head's hanging on by a got damn thread." The other chuckled and kicked me, causing my view to shift.

I gazed straight up at the underside of one of the metal tables. The reflection was murky, but I pieced it well enough together after hearing what was said.

"Hanging on by a thread" was no exaggeration. The shotgun had blown through more than half my neck, leaving my head lolling off to one side from a severed spine. All my nerves were cut off, explaining why I couldn't move a thing except my eyes.

"It ain't funny," the first said. "This ain't the job."

My arm was lifted by one of them, then dropped with a thud. Then the ingrate took my jaw and puppeted my mouth. "You shot me, mista," he said like a poor English beggar. I could've chomped his fingers off, but it didn't seem wise, being as exposed as I was.

"I said it ain't funny, Demars."

"He look like a doctor?" Demars spat a wad of something

inches from my eyes. "Nah. Some grave-robbing scoundrel who no one'll care about."

"Sounds familiar."

They both cackled. "We'll load him up with the other. That greedy mortician won't ever have to know. And he can scrub out the blood."

I heard the short, stout one—the one not called Demars—shuffling around me, then I was heaved up. He grunted a few times as he got me up over his shoulder.

"Light for his size," he exhaled.

My head swung to and fro like a pendulum. Demars—the skinny one—scraped his foot across where I'd been.

"Weird, I don't see no blood," he said.

Right, he wouldn't. Because running through my veins is no more than stray air and dust, though sometimes I like to believe it's ash. More biblical that way. Hands of God, reborn as we are, don't bleed.

"That's 'cause you can't see in the dark," the one holding me remarked.

"This ain't funny, Nello," Demars said.

"It's a little funny," Nello said.

"Don't smell none either."

"Just hurry up, for Christ's sake. I said he ain't heavy for his size, but that don't mean I wanna stand here holding him. Besides, someone might've heard them shots. Mortician said the marked body's a girl. Washed up in the gulf last night. All bloated. No one's claimed her yet."

Demars moved away from where I'd been and started checking beneath each table, holding his hat so it didn't fall. One by one, he went through, similar to how I had, but somehow their intentions were far more sinister. If only I could get my new lasso around them.

"Here it is!" Demars shouted, slapping the table. "An X. That's gotta be it, right? Woo-wee, she's fresh." He pulled the cloth down to get a look at her naked body beneath. It was the young woman who'd thrown herself to her death after losing a child. If my brain was connected to my fists, they'd have balled unconsciously.

"Bet she looked mighty fine, too, before the bloat," he added. "Even with it . . ."

"You got something wrong in the head," Nello said.

"You know you wanna peek."

"No way. No how. I like my ladies how I like my oysters. Alive."

They snickered again as I was carried over. Demars fully lifted the cloth away, and Nello dumped me down on top of her. The way I was twisted with my dislodged head, I stared right into her serene, dead face. Heaven protect these men if they tried something with this poor girl besides laying her to peace.

Then the cloth went back over us, and it was pitch black. Wheels rolled, rumbling over stone. A door unlocked.

"Hold that end."

"Watch it."

Then I heard a cranking sound I assumed to be some kind of lift used to get the bodies down here. Another door opened, and by the light pouring in, my eyes adjusted. It was still dark beneath that covering, but part of my gifts allows me to see quite well in near-darkness.

My head bounced as we were pushed somewhere. The eerie quiet of the morgue was replaced by the din of Crescent City nightlife: horse-drawn carriages screeching, men and women carousing, drunks pissing.

The cloth was momentarily peeled back, and in the silver moonlight, I watched as myself and the dead woman were slid into a secret compartment beneath a food cart with a sign up top that said OYSTERS: FRESH SHUCKT 3¢ EA.

Stunk like it too.

No level of muted senses could mask the wretched stink of seawater and brine. I'd never been a fan, though I'd never felt the need to live by the water. Men are meant for the land if you ask me. But visit any pub around here, and oysters are practically thrown at you. Snotty things always had challenged my intestinal fortitude.

And that was that. A trapdoor shut behind us, the cart rumbled on, and we were being smuggled across the city for God knows what.

I couldn't hear the men masquerading as oyster shuckers over the noisy cart. Just muffled voices and a few low cackles. I could tell when the wheels transitioned from rolling on cobblestone to dirt. It was smoother, but for natural divots here and there.

It wasn't a brief journey, but I didn't mind. The longer they left me be, the more time for the gash in my neck to heal, thanks to Heaven's blessings upon my unliving body, and I'd be right as rain again. I hoped. Truth was, I'd never had my head blown off before. Part of me always wondered just what extent of damage my body could take before it failed to reassemble itself.

I'd lost digits, chunks of flesh—all those returned with a vengeance. But a whole head? It was a good sign I wasn't unconscious at this point, but would I be forced to live, unable to move, with my head hanging off my body like some kind of trampled-over dandelion?

My mind whirled, contemplating my mistakes. I knew better than not to lock doors behind me when I Divined. I'd made myself damned vulnerable—wait. I *had* locked it. I remembered that. These men had been *granted* access.

What was it they'd said? The mortician marked the girl's body? There wasn't much more I could've done differently to avoid this predicament if the morgue master himself was in on this little grift. Perhaps if the White Throne didn't feel the need to make me experience every ounce of the dying's sufferings, I might've reacted faster.

At least I'd gotten far enough to see what I needed to. That vamp wasn't some monster. She was highborn for sure—something I'd only heard talk of and never witnessed firsthand. And intelligent enough to be sadistic. Shar had mentioned the Betrayer being male, but a vamp that pure ought to be able to lead me to her kin.

The room she'd holed up in could've been the bedchambers of any Victorian house in Crescent City, but as I focused back on the memory, I recalled hearing lots of voices outside the door. Moaning too. And it didn't sound like the bad kind.

A brothel, perhaps? That's right, she'd mentioned him getting what he paid for. There were more than a few whorehouses in Crescent—famous ones even. No way of knowing which it might've been, but there were far fewer of them than private homes. That narrowed things down. Finding her was my best option.

"*Follow power*," as Shar so vaguely put it.

This vamp certainly had it.

A particularly violent bump smacked my head against the roof. Worked out well for me. I was no longer staring at the poor dead girl, and it squeezed together the gap in my neck, which would only expedite my healing.

There was a tapping noise. My own finger against the metal table. I couldn't feel it, but my will was returning. Saints and Elders, what a surprise those two bastards were about to be in for. Would be nice if Shar could summon some of her

Heavenly wrath to get me out of this bind, but as usual, I was out for myself.

* * *

The call of crows rang clear. We were outside the city limits. How far, I couldn't be sure. But suddenly, the ride got unexpectedly steady before it abruptly stopped. I could move my arm at the elbow by now. Only a matter of time before all the little nerves and veins and what-have-you sealed themselves back together, and I was ready to drive Demars's and Nello's teeth through their assholes.

Voices grew louder as the trapdoor below the cart fell open.

"Rough couple of corpses," Demars said.

"Just help me dump them out."

The men strained, the cart tilted, and the young woman and I went tumbling off the table and out onto smoothly paved stones. Bright moonlight illuminated everything around me now, and I could finally get a sense of where they'd taken me.

We were in front of an old plantation, and I do mean old. Abandoned, by the looks of it. The fountain in the center of the turnaround didn't spew water and was instead overwhelmed by encroaching vines. The walls of the main house were no different—cracked windows, busted doors, and not a lantern or candle in sight.

Trees dotting the long driveway in the opposite direction had long since died. Now withering husks with bare boughs danced on a light breeze like naked skeletons. Weeds grew everywhere. This place hadn't been tended to for a decade or more.

Started to wonder if somewhere deep inside this mansion awaited the red room where that vampire seductress had claimed her prey. Had she come for me for snooping already? Their kind were known to be fast, and our entry into Crescent City wasn't as subdued as I'd have preferred, thanks to the grunches and all the eyes on Laveau. The more untoward and unsavory portions of society were bound to hear about new arrivals.

My head still stuck as I healed, I watched the two shuckers approach the front doors. It was a tall entrance—taller than the men—painted white at some point like the rest of the trim. The paint was all peeled now, and lichen grew like cancer. Standing there, at the stairs on the front porch, all their giddiness and bravado melted away.

"You go," Demars said.

"No, you," Nello retorted.

They pushed each other like children until Demars decided to suck it up and grasp a bronze knocker carved in the shape of a fleur-de-lis and gave a few quick raps. Blackbirds cawed and flapped away, causing Nello to scurry back down the stairs to the circular driveway.

"Goddammit, mother fu—"

"Shhh. Quiet, you!" Demars chided.

A mail slot flipped open.

"Leave her," a deep voice said from the other side. A few bills flittered out. I wasn't sure what denomination.

The shucker swallowed audibly. "We . . . uh . . . got two, actually. Caught a man robbing the dead. So . . ." He stood quietly as if waiting for an answer.

"So, we should be paid for two," Nello barked, regaining confidence. "And then some for his weapons. Could've made a mint on them back in th—"

The door shook. "You will be paid as agreed upon!"

"That ain't fair," Nello said, only a bit deflated. "It's supposed to be easy. In and out. We ain't killers like you folk."

"And yet, you killed, then brought that trouble to our doorstep."

A dark hand jutted through a hole in the door, grabbed Demars by his skinny arm, and pulled him against the wood. He sniveled in fear.

"Do you not understand how this works?" the voice asked. "Crescent City belongs to us. Leave, or we will show you exactly how replaceable you are."

"Any chance we—"

"Leave!"

Demars was pushed back, crashing into Nello. They scampered away, then stopped to crawl back to collect the money on the ground. Slipping and skidding across the porch, they fell over each other in the race back to their cart, too terrified to even consider taking my guns. Lucky me.

Then, from the thicket all around the property, small figures emerged. Children, all of them, throwing rocks at the shuckers as the men started yanking on the cart, not bothering to look where they were going. One wheel ran over my leg and hip, causing me to roll so I could only see the plantation exit.

"Tell me again why we agreed to this, brother?" Demars asked.

"Cash. Protection. Now, c'mon!" Nello growled.

"Yeah, yeah, I know." Demars paused for a moment and looked back at me and the naked girl. A fleeting wave of grief crossed his features.

I knew the look. Some rewards have too high a price. I learned that the hard way working with Ace Ryker.

Cash doesn't mend a broken soul.

When they were gone, the mansion's door squeaked open on rusty hinges. Heavy feet slapped across the stone. I desperately willed my head to turn, but I wasn't whole yet.

"That'll be that, children," the voice said. A choir of groans followed. "Take them."

All at once, the pitter-patter of a dozen feet clattered toward us.

The young woman's body slid away first, thudding up the steps amid giggles. Then my world raced by as I followed. Nobody even bothered to heave me up onto a shoulder, just dragged across the ground like a sack of garbage.

Up I went, inside the derelict mansion. The whole thing was in disrepair. Made Marie's place look like a palace. A chandelier had fallen in the foyer, little crystal shards left where they'd shattered. The kids dragged me right through them, stopping only to readjust their grips.

Light shimmered in the reflection of one of the glass fractals.

"This is what happens when you dawdle," Shargrafein said, her imprecise form flowing from one bit to the next.

I nearly spoke, not sure if I even could. However, if I had, I'd have immediately blown any chance of figuring out where these people were taking me without causing a fight.

After getting jerked around, I found myself staring straight up and through the lofty ceiling where a gash revealed a silver-lined moon. A painting of whatever family had owned the place was torn above the grand antebellum staircase, one side of the two treads totally collapsed.

Must've been quite the tale, whatever happened here—slave revolt, maybe. Maybe caught on the wrong side of a property feud. The place would have been better off razed, but it ain't cheap these days, purchasing land like this. Plus, this is Crescent City. Abandoned home with some sort of gang squatting in it, creepy trees on the way in, kids by the dozen just milling about?—city folk would be frightened it was haunted.

If only they knew what kind of things really lurk in the dark.

"Two-for-one special thanks to those morons," someone said. As my body was dragged by children, I caught glimpses of larger shadows moving. Nothing more.

"Boss'll be happy," said another.

"I don't see why we're being so careful anyway. Got a city full of prey."

"You know why. That senator vanishing opens up more eyes than usual."

"Let 'em come. Then we can feast for ages."

"Boss hears that, you're dead."

"You gonna tell him?" No answer. "Thought so."

Besides these two and the kids still hauling me along, the house seemed empty.

"We got him," one of the voices said. "Go on ahead."

Immediately, my limbs collapsed to the wood floor, and the sound of children chattering disappeared into the distance. Then, the two adult figures came into view.

"The hell's this one?" one asked. I could see him now, hair the color of barley and a face that looked more akin to Timperina than a man. His long nose and chin drew down in a dire expression, two buggy eyes staring at me. "Fancies himself an outlaw."

"He did," said the other. "Dead now." This one was totally unremarkable except for the chain dangling from his neck. Looked like a tooth or a talon of some kind.

The horse-face hauled me bodily through the remainder of the house while his buddy took the girl.

"Just like you to take the light one," my conveyor said.

"Shit, she's so bloated, you might've lucked out."

I bounced down a long corridor with doors on either side, through an expansive dining room in the home's rear, the kitchen, and finally, out the back door. What used to be a vast field of crops had been infested by mire and swamp.

"I'm sick of this already. My arms hurt."

A second later, I found myself rolling down stone steps. Apparently, I can still get dizzy—or maybe just disoriented without all the ear fluids, but it's something. The girl and I splashed into a pit of mud at the bottom. The muck got into my mouth and throat. Under my nails. Everywhere.

Before I gained a sense of what was what, or if I could move more than an arm, I found myself being pulled again. By the time the mud shed off my face, we entered the open gate of an old stable.

"Took you long enough," a voice growled. It was deep and throaty and, somehow, familiar to me. "My children are starving."

They placed us down, and there I saw them. The eight children that had dragged us most of the way through the house lying on blood-stained hay. Children—but not. These were pint-sized werewolves.

Youth gave them fuzz that almost confused me into thinking they were cute, but their sharp fangs told a different story. Not baby teeth. The real things.

NINE

Panic hit me in a way it rarely does. I can heal and survive many things, but my body being ripped apart by these adolescent predators? I wasn't sure even Shar could reverse that—or what's more, that she would.

I'd always made a habit of shirking Shar's "suggestions," and who knows, maybe that makes me a fool. But I can't just sit back and watch innocent people die and do nothing about it. Beats the hell out of me how she can.

Even more than my predicament, the young woman beside me didn't deserve to be a goddamn posthumous snack.

"Who is this?" the de facto leader asked.

"Got dumped off with her," my captor said. "No clue. Some hillbilly who won't be missed. Figured they could use the extra meat, growing fast as they are."

"*You* figured." I heard whoever it was stand. This man was huge, that was for sure. And I couldn't see it from how I was positioned, but the one who'd dragged me was smacked hard enough to hit a wall. "What do I always say about unprocessed bodies?"

The man coughed, then sniveled, "They got baggage."

"Exactly. Doubly so in a city this size. Could be the loneliest man alive and still have eyes on him. And you just *figure*?"

"What'd you want me to do—leave him out in the front yard?"

"You should have sent him back with those useless shuckers!" A throat was squeezed. I could tell by the gargling. "I pay for discretion. Otherwise, I'd have the children handle it. Let the Voodoo Queen take the heat, not us. Is that understood?"

I heard only a gag.

"I said, is that understood!"

"Y . . . es!" my dragger managed to squeeze out.

"Good. When we're done here, pay a visit to our partners and shuck out an eye on each of them. They taste better than the gobs those ingrates peddle us anyway."

The man nervous-chuckled. "Y-Yes, boss."

"Now, let's get a look at this stranger." Heavy feet stomped closer to me. As they did, I listened closely. Now, I could hear my flesh and sinew slowly mending and the soft crackle of bones fusing. From what I could see, my whole hand twitched. Then my jaw. Foot.

My reanimation was near complete.

I dared not test any longer and reveal my secret too early. All I did was let my right hand gradually slide toward the grip of my pistol out of sight and bide my time. The leader took a big whiff through a nose that didn't sound quite human.

Then he came around to my front, and I saw his yellow eyes. That was why he sounded familiar. It'd been over a decade since our last encounter, but this was a werewolf. And not just any. Rougarou, ruler of the underworld beneath the *human* underworld of Crescent City, when last we met. Though back then, he made his home in the city sewers by the water and not all the way out here.

Funny enough, he was to be my next visit after the morgue.

We hadn't left things on very favorable terms, so I wasn't exactly looking forward to it. But I guess fate has a way of screwing with me.

Good old Roo belonged to a rare breed of weres known as loup-garou who didn't only rely on the full moon to bring about their horrific transformations. They turned each and every night, which made them far more frightening, though also more reasonable. They had time to grow accustomed to their monstrous, ravenous alter egos, whereas the more common weres turned so sparingly, they usually wound up more crazed for blood and chaos.

Sort of a pick-your-poison situation if you ask me.

Two grotesque, hairy feet with claws dug into the dirt. He hunched a bit, but loup-garou were different from their cousins. More human and upright from the neck down. And even in their faces, there remained human lines to show personality. Shorter snout. More defined neck. Familiar musculature all around.

That, and most wore clothes. With their shifting being more of a routine, they didn't tear through trousers on the full moon. In Rougarou's case, he had a suit jacket and pants custom-tailored for his proportions. Might as well plop a bowler hat on his dome.

He gave me a whiff from afar. "Stinks worse than the French Quarter."

His men forced a laugh.

Rougarou leaned in closer. I waited until the right moment when he was off-balance, then sprang up, drawing a pistol and shoving it right under his furry jaw. One of my legs wobbled—I still wasn't perfectly intact—but my hand stayed true.

"Nice to see you again, Roo," I growled, slurring a bit as my vocal cords sorted themselves.

Growls issued all around. But old Roo's shock dissipated

fast, and instead of anger, he sneered in the best way his wolf mouth could.

"If it ain't James Crowley," he said. "Everyone, settle down. He's as harmless as my pups."

"I got a bit of silver in here that says otherwise," I spat back.

"Do you, now?"

"You wanna find out?" I cocked my gun's hammer. He flinched. Almost imperceptibly, but I noticed. That got his men fussing again. In my peripherals, I noticed the two responsible for bringing me out here.

Roo lifted one of his claws and traced the still-healing gash on my neck. "You know, we always wondered what would happen if you or your kind lost your head."

"You and me both," I said, shrugging. "Lightning bolt from the sky, probably. You know who we serve."

He grunted. "Somehow, I think they'd just replace you. Easier than lifting a holy finger."

My tongue caught. Was he right?

"Did I strike a nerve, Crowley?" he asked.

"I don't got any," I said. "And maybe you're right, but the next 'me' sent here might not be so friendly."

"Friendly? You?"

"You're alive, ain't you?" My gaze flitted to the jagged, pale scar on the right side of his chest, where a silver bullet from the chamber of this very pistol had once struck.

He grew cross. "That was a lucky shot."

I exhaled in frustration. "Look, I ain't here for you."

"You said that last time."

"And you got in the way. It doesn't have to be like that this time. You can help willingly. Gain favor with my superiors."

That got him to perk up. "Oh yeah?"

"Sure." It was a little fib, but I still had cards to play. "Before we get to that, I'm gonna need you to return that girl's body so she can go in peace."

I wasn't ever a religious man—I know, weird to say when I'm intimately aware the other side is actually there. And I was definitely unsure if a proper burial with a priest and all that fliberty jabby would help redeem her for the sin of taking her own life. Or if she had family that would care. Maybe a husband. Babies don't just appear in bellies . . . Well, except for that famous one. Still, I highly doubted we were arguing over the next immaculate conception.

"No can do," Rougarou said. "My children gotta eat."

"So feed them a gator."

He shook his head. "We eat plenty of game, but it just doesn't quite have the same nutrition. Human flesh curbs the bloodlust. You know that. And I suspect we both would rather us eat the newly dead than the still living."

He wasn't wrong there. Rougarou was a power in Crescent City well before I met him a decade or so ago, and still now, after all this time. He didn't do that by unleashing his pack on unsuspecting civilians. He'd worked hard to instill a sense of patience in them. Teach them to operate in the shadows and manage their hunger.

"And I appreciate that," I said. "But not her."

"What's she, your daughter or something? I know she ain't a lover," Rougarou said. "I heard the plumbing don't work downstairs." He laughed. "She's nobody, Crowley! A whore from a brothel who not nobody will care about. And we have to lay extra low with all the feds sniffing 'round these days, what with senators dying."

"Feds . . . Them marshals don't know their assholes from their blowholes."

"That may be, but there's strength in numbers."

This wasn't getting us anywhere. To be expected, really. I'd shot him. And near-death experiences lend themselves to judicious behavior. Also makes things personal, but Roo wasn't as dumb as most of his kind.

"I hear there's a vampire problem in Crescent City these days," I said, shifting the conversation in a direction I hoped would help. "That can't be easy, what with you both having a taste for humans."

"We manage," he grumbled. But I could tell it was me who struck a nerve this time.

"Do you? Or is that why you're stuck picking up the scraps from dead houses? You know, seeing as they're stronger and faster than—"

Rougarou snarled and swung. The back of his thick, furred hand caught me in the chest, sending me flying against the stable wall. My gun went off before it flew from my grasp, just missing his ear.

It was an awful reminder of the day I died in a similar venue amid gunfire.

He stalked toward me, hunching and growing more grotesque and seemingly inhuman with every step. "There's plenty of room in my city to share, Crowley. You come here all these years later thinking you still got a pulse on the place?"

I went for my other pistol. His foot slammed down on my forearm. Before I could reach for anything else, his two men hopped to restrain my arms.

"You think you can tell us what to eat?" Roo slashed my collar with a single claw, revealing the black scar on my chest. "I ought to tear your head off all the way this time." He spread the rest of his claws against my chest and started to dig.

Now would be a good time for that lightning bolt, I thought, channeling Shar. She's never there when I need her, though.

"Be smart, wolf," I said, trying not to show my very real concern. "There are worse enemies to have than marshals. I'm after a vampire lady, not you. As beautiful as she is deadly. Likes to get off while she drains men."

At that, Rougarou backed off me. "Tourmaline?"

"Maybe." Didn't know her name; now I do.

"You're after Tourmaline?" he asked, a slight chuckle in the question.

"Sounds like it."

"Well, *putain de merde*. That'd be more fun to watch than anything I could do to you. You think you've got the balls to run up against her?"

"Sure I've seen worse," I said.

He shook his big wolf head. "I doubt it."

"If you're done posturing . . ."

For all I knew, Roo had made that name up. He lies more than he breathes, and it wouldn't have been unlike him to play games.

"She runs a brothel in the quarter. That was one of her cocottes," he said, nodding toward the dead girl. "Not a vamp, though, clearly. So, the White Throne wants Tourmaline dead?"

I shook my head. "Her maker, I think. But sometimes other people get in the way."

"Don't I know it."

"Would that appeal to you, Roo? Last we met, you had a nice setup downtown. I figure it can't only be the law that's got you hiding out here."

"You think I'm scared of her?" he roared.

I pressed my palms placatingly. "Now, now. I'm just deducing information."

"Well, you deduced wrong, cowboy. It's safer for my children out here."

"Right. And young vamps are simple. Mindless. I've heard what can happen when a highborn lord or lady sets up shop. They get their fangs in everything. Sooner or later, you'll be cattle instead of wolves."

Rougarou took a beat. I struggled to get a read on him, no doubt aided by his less-than-human features. He turned and strode toward the pups, who howled and squealed, eager for meat.

"Let's just rip him apart here and now, boss," one of the thugs holding me said.

"Yeah, you remember last time," barked the other. "We can send him home to St. Louis Cathedral in a bag."

"I don't need your help, mongrels!" Rougarou snarled as he whipped around. "And you." He stuck a razor-sharp nail in my direction. "You couldn't even handle two lowlifes. You think you can take on Tourmaline?"

"I don't get snuck up on twice."

"Or you're getting old."

"I don't age."

Rougarou scratched lightly at the side of his head. "I mean in here."

"Look." I scooted back to a more upright position, attempting to pull free of the thugs. They resisted, but Rougarou nodded for them to allow it. "I can either go in there guns blazing and get more heat on the city. Or you can take me to her for a meeting, and we keep it personal. I prefer the latter."

"And then you kill her?" he asked.

"I do what needs doing. And then you do what needs doing. You'll have a favor from me and my benefactors in your pocket. And in exchange, all I'm asking is for you to find your pups another meal. Leave that girl be in peace."

"And a meeting," Roo said.

"That's implied."

He growled, low and thoughtful. Then he turned back to his pups. They yapped and jumped at him, nibbling on his claws. Wouldn't be long before their teeth were big and sharp enough to tear them off.

"You got yourself a deal," he said.

"But, boss, he—"

"I have spoken. Have her returned for rights. Then slaughter and bring one of the spare horses. If my children can't eat well tonight, they'll eat big."

I swallowed. Save a woman. Damn a horse. I'd have to make sure Timp never found out, or she'd make life on the road a living hell for weeks, bucking and being obstinate.

Rougarou returned to me, picking up the pistol I'd dropped and handing it over. "You're lucky I like you, Crowley. You've got a pair on you that drags in the dirt."

I chuckled. "You're gonna make me blush." I stretched out of reflex, all my parts seeming to work correctly again. Moving to the pups, I stuck my pistol out and let them chew on the barrel.

"So, when do I get to meet their mother?"

TEN

Taking the werewolf's word for it that the dead woman's body would be returned wasn't easy, but I'd done my part. Sometimes it's better not to push it. And that goes for both Rougarou and Shar.

It was past time for me to be done playing the good Samaritan and get on with my mission. People were going missing in Crescent City—Senator Cartwright among them—and all signs pointed to this Tourmaline.

We took a carriage back to the city. Nothing fancy, but not a hunk of junk either. Roo was smart. Always knew that the best way to blend in was to not stand out. Sounds pretty common sense, except the truth is, most folks wouldn't know how to stay hidden if they'd been given a burlap sack in a wheat barn. Roo lurked inside the buggy, still in his wolfish form.

I sat up front with a haggard boy who white-knuckled the reins of a horse. Like his own litter back at the house, Roo always had a tendency to employ the homeless and needy kids of Crescent City. Get his claws in them early. Gave him eyes everywhere.

Swampland whizzed by. The air was filled with the sounds of the marsh—gators hissing, no doubt hungry for some tasty morsel or another to satisfy their insatiable hunger. Mosquitos buzzed, owls hooted, and in the distance, you guessed it, wolves, howling at a moon that sat so low, I would've sworn I could reach out and grab it. And in the east came that faint, purple-bluish glow of sunrise. I welcomed it. Used to be I loved the colder temperatures night brought, but now that I was numb to such things, I welcomed the light. Harder for *unwelcome* things to hide.

"Say, I've always wondered," I said, glancing back. "Your breed turning day in and day out. When do you find time to sleep?"

All Roo offered in response was a grunt. He yanked the drape shut with a loud whoosh that made the crickets quit their song. After a moment, I heard him rummaging around and a few more low grunts. The sun's light bloomed brighter, and it didn't take Nik Tesla's brains to know what was happening.

"What do you think?" I asked the boy beside me. "Dogs like to turn circles, you know, get more comfortable. I think that's what he's doing."

No answer. Just gave the reins a snap, and we turned onto a somewhat paved road.

"Y'all are a friendly bunch, you know that?" I quipped. If he wasn't gonna talk, I was fine talking to myself. "Really, since being here, no one's even asked me if I was hungry or thirsty or tired. Nothing. Just took my dead corpse and tried to make it deader. Guess southern hospitality hasn't made it this far east, huh?"

The boy shifted his frame so—even directly beside me on the bench—his back was turned.

"Fine. Fine. I can take a hint."

Crescent City grew visible through the twisted, drooping boughs of southern oaks. Bram was right when he said the trees around here were strange. Though I didn't see them as praying. Sad-looking things to me. As if they used to stand tall but melted, half their branches scraping through the muck at their proverbial feet.

The carriage drape whipped back open, revealing Rougarou hunched in the space. But no longer was he the menacing wolf. Now in his human form, he actually did wear a bowler hat. I could've laughed under different circumstances. And although his suit was nearly identical, it was smaller, built for a man, not a beast. Behind him, the old one was neatly hung from a clothes rack along the back wall.

Somehow, the ensemble looked stranger with his shaggy beard than when he was shifted. Human Roo had dark skin and Cajun features. Half his middle-aged face was scarred by what looked like too much itching of scabies. Or fleas, maybe. Huh, that's a fun thought. Wonder if he licks himself too?

A monocle sat over his undamaged eye. Always said back in the day that it was tough getting used to human sight after what he had at night. My guess was he could see just as well as I could in the darkest hours, but during the day, I had him at a disadvantage. Something I was sure he was well aware of. I didn't trust him. He didn't trust me. And that was just fine.

He lit a cigarette, pulled in a long chuff, and closed his eyes in ecstasy. He held that breath a moment, letting the feeling linger. I could've killed him right then and there. What I wouldn't give for that feeling once more. The heart race, the slow numbing of my thoughts, all the weight of the world temporarily lifted off my shoulders. I watched—one part disdain, one part envy—as he slowly exhaled the smoke my way. The boy at the reins coughed.

"Best part of bein' human," Roo remarked.

"What's that feel like?" I asked.

"You telling me you never had a quirly at your age?"

I groaned. "I mean shifting. What's it like?"

"Ah." He took another lengthy drag. "For a long time, like being skinned and pulled inside out like a dead rabbit. And then, one day, the pain just numbs, and it's like meeting an old friend again. After a few moments, you forget it's you. Then, you fall back into the old vices, and it's all one and the same."

I watched the embers glow. Between jobs with Ace, when I was feeling uncertain, I used to just stare at it until the light gave way to ashes. That was one good thing about that bastard. He never let us go without a pack or ten of sissy sticks for the road. Said it kept us honest.

Honest . . .

We turned onto the main avenue leading into the city proper, pushing through the rabble who hadn't quite made it home after last night's festivities.

"You ever wish you weren't this way?" I asked.

"What—and be like the sheep?" he scoffed. "Hell no. You?"

"Every goddamned day," I said, almost so low he could've missed it.

He didn't—doglike hearing and all.

He shook his head and clicked his tongue, flicking his cigarette off the road and into a thin stream near the city's edge. "That's your problem, Crowley. You gotta embrace what you are. Wolves don't wish to be sheep, no matter what mama's night tales say."

"I embrace the *choice*. It's either this or Hell, and 'weeping and gnashing of teeth' don't sit so well with me."

"That ain't the same," he spat.

"Says a cursed man who makes a dinner out of folks and just shrugs."

"You see—that right there. That's the difference." He

chuckled and looked around at some locals, fishermen heading down to start their day at the docks. A gaggle of lawmen stood by the main road, watching comings and goings. "You still think you're the same thing as them."

His words reminded me of an earlier conversation with Shar. She hadn't said it out loud but made it plain enough, these people weren't my peers.

Roo tipped his hat to law enforcement while I hid my face in the shadow of my own the best I could. Probably not a good look to be spotted near both him and Laveau so soon after arriving. But they did nothing. Just kept their eyes trained. Wasn't even sure the marshals I'd run into would be talking much with the locals.

"We may look the same. Feel the same. Die the same even," Roo said. "But there ain't any of them who wouldn't lynch us the second they found out exactly what we are. Bastards are more likely to throw us on a table and start poking and prodding to find out what makes us tick."

He leaned out over my shoulder and pointed to an argument being had between a black man and a white shopkeep opening up for business. "They barely get along with their own."

"Sure, sure," I agreed. "But wouldn't it be nice not to have to hide way out there in some dilapidated old pile of barely standing wood every night?"

"Who said I'm hiding? And I'll have you know that home is palatial."

"If you say so."

He chuckled and sat back. "You ain't a city man, are you, Crowley? You been here long enough, you start to appreciate the solace of a place like Mandeville Manor. I accomplished all I needed to, being down here with the sheep. Now, I got people for it. Giving back, as they say."

A beggar inched out from an alley as we passed. A kid. Couldn't have been more than seven. He gave Roo a nod, and Roo sent him back a wink. One of his boys, I gathered.

"You call that charity?" I asked.

"Kids like them'll either rot on the streets or wind up out netting fish or working factory lines 'til their hands are calloused and they drink to forget the aches. So, yeah. With me, they stay safe, and they get their worth."

"Or tossed in a cell."

"This ain't the frontier, cowboy. Too many people crammed in here to even know how to dispose of all the shit. Not enough for men to do worth doing. No marshals giving out land or farms. Y'all from out west don't know what it really means to fight to survive. Gotta eat to live. Gotta live to eat."

"Got that part right," I said.

"There are worse things than wild beasts, natives, or outlaws."

I had my own thoughts as to what he was referring to. Nephilim, demons, even people like him. But I figured I'd heard him out this far. "Like what?"

"Bureaucracy." He laughed.

I wasn't sure what to say. He was right. It was different in these parts. I'd heard stories of the Big Apple—like a zoo of all races, creeds, and colors, most of which hate each other just for being different.

I'd also joined up with Ace and the Scuttlers when I was young and impressionable. When he seemed more heroic than the evil shit-eater he turned out to be. Fighting the good fight for the good of his crew. Took me a few years to see the suffering we left in our wake. And Ace, like Roo, always liked to wax poetic, making grand claims about how magnanimous he was.

Maybe Roo was the real deal. Who knew? But I doubted it. Seemed most anyone claiming to be philanthropic—they hurt just as many as they help. I did appreciate the perspective and the insight. The kids—his eyes throughout the city—were clearly a weak spot I could exploit if need be. Only problem: I don't hurt kids.

"James?" a familiar voice hollered. "James, there you are!"

I swore under my breath. Rosa. Just the person I was trying to avoid after Irish let her tongue go. And to not involve her in any more unsavory business. I'll stick with that excuse.

Why was it that no matter where I found myself, there, too, she would be? She jogged to try and catch up, but the boy kept the horses moving.

"James!"

Roo gave the order to stop.

"She can wait," I said, low.

"A beauty like that?" Roo asked. "Where're your manners?"

The carriage stopped, and Rosa came up alongside it, panting. I'd been used to her dour demeanor for a while now, but she looked damn near excited, inspired by something.

"Mahrnin', Rosa," I said, feigning joy at seeing her here.

"Where'd you get off to last night and . . ." Her gaze moved to the grungy boy driving the carriage, then Rougarou. Her excitement waned. "Who are your friends?"

"Old acquaintances," I said. "I told you I had folk to meet with here. This is, uh . . ." I realized I had no idea what the man went by when in human form. "Jean Luc. He's a local farmer."

"*Was* a local farmer," Roo said, bringing a bit of fear in me that he was gonna tell her something she needn't know. "Now, I am the town's leading purveyor of fine spirits." I gave him a look that he returned. "What can I say? I get more by the barrel than I do the bushel."

He laughed, and I must admit it was a charming sound. Rosa joined in.

Roo opened the carriage door and stepped out. Even in his human form, he was tall without an ounce of fat. Could've passed as an aristocrat, but instead, he was dressed like a businessman with a hobo beard. A walking contradiction.

"How do you two know each other, Jean Luc?" Rosa asked.

"Why, James Crowley is just about one of the most honest men I've ever had the pleasure of meeting." He stuck a hand down toward her. "And my friends call me Rouge, and you are?"

"Rosa Mas—" she caught herself. "Just Rosa."

"A beautiful name . . ." He took her hand and gave it a light peck, pulling just enough to reveal her snake tattoo. She winced, but nothing too noticeable. " . . .for a beautiful woman. Like a rose amidst a trash heap, you are. Now, I turn the question upon you. How is it you came to know this ghoul?"

"A story for another time," I said. "Rosa, if you don't mind, we have urgent business to attend to."

"Mind if I tag along? Marie gave me a list of ingredients that could help with . . . you know. I figure since you know the city—"

"Wait. Marie Laveau?" Roo asked. "Well, how about that? Who'd have thought you were rubbing elbows with the Voodoo Queen herself?"

"Barely introduced," I said before Rosa could reply.

"What do you say?" Rosa asked me.

"I don't mind if she comes along." Roo turned to me, his lips pulling nearly to his ears.

"No," I snapped. Then, regaining my composure, I turned to Rosa. "I'm sorry, but we really gotta hurry."

"It will only take a minute," she insisted.

"Rosa, *please*. This don't concern you. And besides, I thought we discussed letting this thing go. Marie's a fine host, but she can't be trusted with this. It ain't right."

"No, *you* discussed it," Rosa hissed.

I sighed. "I'll see you later, okay? We can talk through it all. Promise. Until then, just sit tight and keep a watch on Bram. This city ain't safe for—"

"For what?"

"I . . ."

Dammit, Irish, and your meddling. Her earlier words had me all up in my head. I could spin a compliment, but that might make it seem like I thought Rosa was weak. I knew she could handle herself, and I couldn't come out and say there were ravenous vampires on the loose. Digging myself deeper than a grave.

"She's got me, ye dryshite," Irish said, catching up seemingly out of nowhere. Speak of the devil. "Typical bloke. Always wantin' fun 'til it's wantin' it too?"

Irish nudged Rosa in the side. She didn't budge. I'd really gone and pissed her off now. Shar would be proud. There was nothing I'd rather do than hop off that cart and help Rosa—keep her safe from whatever madness she and Laveau were concocting. But, unlike last time, I refused to get her involved in White Throne affairs. My feelings would have to wait.

Look at that. Maturity.

Roo, thankfully, came to my rescue. "As much as I'd enjoy having the company of two such stunning women," he said. "I know when to stay out of a lovers' quarrel."

"Oh, trust me, we aren't that," Rosa said, terse.

A dagger to my lifeless heart.

Irish was busy looking down at herself in her loose clothes with nary a curve to be found, mouthing the word 'stunning' in confusion.

"All the same, Mr. Crowley and I won't be long," Roo said. "And very soon, I do hope he'll bring you by my humble home. You seem like you'd make a fine dinner . . ." I caught a glint as his gaze flitted toward me, ". . . guest."

"Don't need these jackeens. Let's you and I scrounge up some trouble of our own, aye?" Irish said, coaxing Rosa along.

"Let's." Rosa set off down the road. She accidentally bumped into a man unloading crates from his wagon. Her glare would've struck him dead if he dared say a thing about it.

"Rosa!" I called after her. Pure reflex.

She stopped and glanced back. But I had nothing to say. We were on separate paths here in Crescent City, no doubt about it. I was here to end the existence of something that didn't belong, while she was here clinging to the desire to do the exact opposite.

She huffed and continued on her way.

"C'mon, cowboy," Roo said, climbing back into the carriage. "Let's ride."

I just stared at her as she left, wishing there was anything to be done about it. In the end, I resolved to shake my head and return to my bench beside the boy.

No sooner had my butt touched wood than the carriage started up again. The boy whipped the reins like he had some vendetta. After a while, Rougarou leaned out the window.

"So, who's she?" he asked.

"She's nobody," I grumbled.

"Liar. There's something about her. Got an aura."

"Nobody. Just human."

"Ah, I didn't know a man in such a state as you needs . . . carnal delights. Good for you, then. She's a looker. Could make a fortune where we're headed."

I stretched back and grabbed him by the collar. "She ain't a whore!" Probably not wise to give him such insight into my feelings, but I couldn't help it. The anger just came burbling up in me like a hot spring.

He raised his hands in mock surrender. "Whoa now. Never said she was. I just meant—"

"She's a friend. Just a friend, all right?" I released my hold on his lapel.

He straightened his jacket. "Lies again."

"Drop it, or you'll be chewing on silver next, Roo. We got our own business."

He grinned wide, teeth yellow like an old hound. "Fine, fine. Now you're gettin' it. Leave the humans to their own devices until we need them."

As we continued on into the heart of the city, we were mostly ghosts, but we caught glances here and there. He offered nods of acknowledgment to both shady-looking folk and legitimate businessmen all the same. Back when we'd met, protection was his organization's most profitable trade. Some things never change.

"We ain't far now. Sure you don't want to go home first?" Roo asked. He got my attention and nodded down a boulevard toward the St. Louis Cathedral. She was a beaut. Plenty of churches and chapels dotted the West, but rarely did I get to see a true monument to the Almighty. Three spires and white stone soaring higher than anything else around it.

Truly, I didn't know how man was capable of constructing such things without the help of giants. And why?

Never understood it, and Shar certainly never felt the need to answer in detail. What'd it matter where people showed their faith, where they bowed their heads? Why waste so much time and money building such extravagant edifices. Was that what God wanted?

My opinion: it was a great way to distract countless lemmings from how shitty the world could be.

"Very funny," I said.

"Can they see me at least?" He reached out the window and waved. "I'd kill to get a glimpse of a real-life angel."

"Bet you've killed for less."

"I'm serious, cowboy. I'm dying to know what they look like."

"Keep dreaming," I told him.

No reason to tell him I was dying for the same. Too mortal to handle Shar's true visage or whatever cock-and-bull she claimed. All the while, she was probably just pissed she wasn't as pretty as the cathedral built in the glory of her and her kin.

The carriage turned down a street alongside trolley tracks.

"Welcome to Storyville," Roo said.

Taverns and inns were joined by less upstanding establishments. Opium dens. Brothels. You name it. A Cajun magician had a crowd building as he performed a magic trick. The boy pulled the reins to keep our horses from maiming anyone, and we were stuck. The street was packed, and we had little choice but to watch until things cleared.

The magician lit a cigarette, took a small puff. Then, with two fingers, he pulled it away. Nothing too special so far, until he let go of the stick, and it kept floating in midair. Everyone cheered. Hell, I wanted to also. He smiled and waved his hands all around the cig, just to show everyone there were no wires or strings. How he did it beats me.

He retrieved it from its place suspended in the air, and returned it to his mouth. At first, I thought he was done. But everyone started clapping again. Upon closer inspection, I saw smoke coming from his nostrils and ears. The cigarette was backward, burning end between his lips. He just stood there as if it didn't bother him at all.

Then, he stuck his tongue out, and the quirly bobbed with it, the fiery tip resting on his tongue like it was nothing more than a peppermint candy. With a curl of his tongue, the whole thing disappeared behind his teeth, and he swallowed, reopening his mouth to show it gone.

The whole crowd applauded, hooted, and hollered.

"Fun trick," Roo said.

We were getting ready to leave when the man raised a single digit. The crowd stopped cheering as he strode forward to a woman whose cleavage threatened to choke her. He gave her a smile, then dug two fingers between her breasts and pulled the cigarette out.

Now that got people going. I shook my head. "Things people do for money."

The street performer bowed, and the crowd cleared the streets as they rushed in to throw greenbacks into the man's tin cup. Our adolescent driver snapped the reins, and the hooves started their rhythm again.

Beggars, cheats, whores, and drunks galore filled the place. As ungodly as Hell to my mind. Ace would've made a fortune if we'd found ourselves here back in the day. Though even he may have had trouble gaining power with weres and vamps around.

"All right, we're here," Roo said.

We stopped across the street from a four-story frame mansion with a cupola on top shaped like an onion. A bronze sign over the entry read: ARLINGTON HOUSE. Might've been nice if not for its location and the corset-wearing ladies with their hair all done up hollering down from every balcony. Though, if there was one thing I'd learned in this life, you can call a fed a fed, a thief a thief, but always call a whore a lady.

Besides, compared to other brothels I'd seen, it was a gem. High-end. The kind of locale that attracts the rich and snollygosters both.

Roo hopped down and stuck out a hand, inviting me to join him. He flicked a coin to the boy at the reins. "Get some chow." The boy caught it deftly and hopped down to scurry away.

We crossed the busy street, and my foot landed on a poster for the missing senator, amongst others deemed less noteworthy.

I was gonna pick it up, when I heard some black folk playing the strangest sort of music I'd ever heard from a bandstand adjacent to the brothel's porch. If you could call it music. Instruments like long pipes with flared ends seemed to be missing notes on purpose, almost screeching. Nothing like I'd heard last time I was here.

"Saints and Elders, what is that racket?" I asked, stuffing my fingers in my ears.

"That sound's the new craze, Crowley," Roo said. "Welcome to the future."

Their fingers moved expertly. Never been much of a player of anything myself. Couldn't sing. But I hadn't ever witnessed something that appeared so extraordinary yet sounded so dreadful.

"I guess my ears are too old," I said.

"You ever think about that?" Roo asked. "What the world will be like when I'm rotting, and my grandchildren's children are traipsin' these streets, and you're still here?"

What a question. To be honest, I hadn't really. Not until that fateful day I ran into Rosa in Dead Acre, all grown up. That was the first time it hit home how long I'd been alive after dying—those twenty-some-odd years. Twenty more, she might've been gray, or remarried with kids, or dead.

I swallowed. "I try not to." That was the truth. Safer that way.

Roo slapped my back. "Man, Crowley, you got no imagination. Though I guess I wouldn't with a leash around my neck like you've got. God's pet. More a dog than me." He laughed, picking up his pace and skirting ahead of me to the doors.

Roo's hand reached for the door when a slipshod-looking man came stumbling out, suit jacket slung over his shoulder, wearing a sweat-stained shirt and pants that'd both seen better days. His eyes were bloodshot-red, and his gaze was . . . empty. Only way I could describe it. Barely there. Loaded up on whatever drugs, booze, and hard-ons. City joints like this made the paltry nightlife of saloons out west seem like schoolhouse play yards.

Though I didn't realize to what extent until we stepped inside.

Looked like a regular colonial château at first glance. Nothing out of the ordinary, but beyond the entry hall, there were more curtained-off rooms than usual. Beads. Doors. Lacy affairs. We had a view of a living room full of golden velvet couches and plush-cushioned seating, dimly lit by red-tinted lamps.

A bar served drinks to men who looked nothing like outlaws. They were upper crust. Their pedantry showed like a cold sore. Wearing suits and timepieces worth more than I'd ever had, even in the glory days of the Scuttlers. And the women—angels be damned, these were breathtaking women. They didn't have that glint of misery behind their eyes that I usually saw in ladies of the night. Well-paid for their efforts here, no doubt, as they hung all over men who acted like they deserved their affections.

Soft words whispered in ears, polite giggles at jokes told, and gentle caresses disclosed the stories. A gorgeous blonde swayed wide but alluring hips on her way to deliver drinks from the bar built into the corner. They didn't perform—no playing music or singing. It was different here.

Men outnumbered ladies in the frontier, so women in saloons had a certain . . . service to provide more than sex. They were female companionship for hundreds of roughriders who couldn't find an old dutch to settle down with. They didn't have to be good conversationalists, or sashay when they walked, or show off leg—they just had to *be*. Doesn't say much for frontiersmen, really.

Here, they were professionals plying men to their whims without them even knowing. Controlling situations even though it was *them* being paid. Exquisite bodices and skirts showed just enough skin, and enough to drive dreams. Yet behind those curtains and doors, anything went. Easy enough to tell that by the older fellow in a top hat being escorted down the hall by three women.

Nah. Men weren't here because they were lonely or needed companionship. This place was pure fantasy fulfillment.

"Rouge! So nice to see you," a woman said, approaching from our side. Judging by her dress and how much it covered, I assumed her to be the establishment's madam.

I braced myself. But as she got close, I realized this wasn't the woman from my Divining. No fangs, no pale skin—not a vampire. In fact, looking around the room, I saw no signs of anything strange or otherworldly. Didn't feel the tingle in my chest of a Nephilim nearby. I figured—if what I believed to be happening in those rooms was true—there'd at least be some vamps guarding the place, blending in.

"As always, Madame Arlington." Roo took her hand, performing the same kiss atop her soft, yellow glove as he had Rosa.

"A friend of yours?" She surveyed me from head to toe and didn't appear pleased. Judging by the patrons this place kept, I wasn't surprised. I looked like trash's trash, covered in soot and grime, with a fresh scar on my neck still healing and bloodstains who knows where. Probably looked like I'd been the recipient of a failed lynching.

"We go back a ways," Roo said. "I do apologize for his state."

"Yes . . ." Her lips pursed, eyes the color of wheat ready for harvest, giving me another once-over. Her nose crinkled like she'd smelled a donkey's fart. "I'm afraid I can't permit anyone looking like this, even for you."

"Don't worry. We're here for downstairs," Roo said with a facial gesture that concealed something.

Her eyes went wide. "Is he . . . ?"

"He's something."

This time, she gazed upon me with curiosity rather than disgust. Made me want to pull my duster closed.

"All right. Get going, then," she said. "And next time, bring the riffraff through the back way, you hear?"

Rougarou retook her hand. "But then I wouldn't get to see you, *mon coeur*." She rolled her eyes, then headed off to speak with the bartender. Why use the back way when he could remind the city folk of his terrifying presence? Ace used similar tricks. There is power in fear.

"Never been to a brothel with a dress code," I remarked.

"The Arlington is what they call a 'five-dollar house,'" Roo said.

I smirked, sparing another glance at the blonde serving drinks. "You get what you pay for."

"Ain't that the truth."

With a nudge, he led me across the back of the living room, footsteps clacking on oak. All eyes were on me—and that was saying something with the other candy on offer. Roo fit in, but I most definitely did not. One man shared my particular standoutedness. He was in the corner without a woman within grasp, just watching the goings-on while he puffed on a cigar. Took me a second to recognize him. Then he lowered his hand, revealing that port-wine birthmark on his chin. The marshal from outside Laveau's cottage, out for a little leisure time, it seemed.

Figures. You find me a man, I'll show you a sinner. It's amazing any of us ever makes Heaven at all. I can just picture God lounging by the pearly gates tapping his toe, waiting for the first man in a millennium worthy enough to step inside. Bet the angels are just waiting with streamers and fireworks.

"Arlington runs a fine business," Roo said as we passed into the kitchen. A few chefs were working hard preparing food that would've made my mouth water. Not a one bothered to look up. "But it's a front. The real money's downstairs. Tourmaline ensures none of it gets touched."

"Can't hurt to have a vamp in your pocket," I said.

"Make no mistake, nothing happens in Storyville without her say-so. Arlington runs this house at Tourmaline's discretion."

"And what *does* happen downstairs?"

He stopped in the pantry, casting a sinister smile my way. "Hell on Earth."

Pulling back a nondescript blanket of sorts, he stepped onto the platform of a dark, hidden lift. My gut told me not to follow. My brain too.

Yet, I'd already pissed off Rosa. And Irish, I suppose. Timp wasn't here to talk to. What else would I do? What else was I but a Black Badge?

And as one, it was my duty to take this ride to the end. No damnation for me. Only if it came in another blaze of guns and glory.

ELEVEN

Chains creaked as we descended into dank darkness. My eyes adjusted to reveal cinder block walls coated with algae. Nothing in Crescent City survives the wet air.

Rougarou hummed that awful music from outside, apparently carefree as a summer picnic. I, on the other hand, kept my palms resting on the pearl grips of my Peacemakers the whole way down.

"Lighten up," he said. "You're going to love it."

"Just remember—"

"I know," he cut me off. "You'll feed me silver."

The lift stopped, and a grate cranked open.

Don't know what I was expecting, but it wasn't this. A large cavern of rough-hewn stone, like a cave, surrounded us.

"What are you playing at, Roo?" I asked, hands drifting closer to drawing.

"Wait," he said, ominous as could be.

Water dripped from all over, streaks of mildew coating every surface. Roo's breathing echoed in the chamber. It brought a chill to my core.

A chill?

Then I heard it—the soft pitter-patter of feet from somewhere. Could've been anywhere the way the sounds reflected in this place.

"Roo . . ."

"Wait."

A figure emerged that looked like another child, but as it drew closer, something was off. What I mistook for the silhouette of unruly hair came clearer into focus, revealing pointed ears and a set of horns. A third set of spikes coming up from the center of its head, I could now tell was a pair of wings folded behind its back. It was cold blue—almost white. The color of Hell itself.

My chest caught fire, the black badge-like mark there burning with a ferocity I hadn't felt in a long while.

The creature came to a stop several yards away. He—and there was no mistaking his naked form—stood about three feet high at best. A potbelly hung over his manhood, but there was still more to see than I would've ever asked for.

"What the fuck is this thing doing here?" the creature asked.

"He's a friend," Roo responded. "Cowboy, meet Fazar, Prince of the Imps."

I started to speak, but the imp cut me off.

"Very fucking funny, you shitty excuse for a fucking dog."

Thing had a mouth on it. One with a lot of small, sharp-looking teeth.

"Gimme your fucking fingers," the imp said.

"Excuse me?" I asked.

"Protocol," Roo explained. "A test to see if we are who we say we are. Humans and Heavenly hosts aren't allowed below."

Roo held his finger toward the imp, and I followed his example.

Fazar waddled closer, grabbing Roo's wrist and dragging his

hand toward his mouth. A long, bifurcated tongue shot out and wrapped around Roo's finger. Then, he slurped the digit beyond his teeth. Blood trickled out of the corner of his lips while Fazar groaned in ecstasy, sucking on it in a back-and-forth motion.

"That's enough," Roo said.

Slowly, the finger slid loose, and Fazar shuddered.

"Your turn," the imp said to me.

"You know, I don't think this is what I signed up for," I said.

"Quit being such a baby," Roo said. "Give the little bastard your finger."

An icy cold grip took my wrist, as if my bones were frosting beneath my skin. I sucked in a deep breath when Fazar's tongue spindled around my finger.

I often long to feel something, but now that I was, I'd have gladly given it up again. Visions of death and despair flooded my brain. Wasn't quite like a Divining, but it had the same feel. I saw Rosa shivering in the bitter cold, and I was too stunned to do a thing about it. I saw Father Osgood, my former mentor growing up, rattling his fist in the air as if calling down the wrath of Heaven. Ace Ryker, eyes like a blizzard, laughing, and finally, my vision was cut unregrettably short by a hacking cough.

My spiritual eyes opened—for my physical ones had never closed—and Fazar hunched over, gagging and dry heaving, puffs of dust billowing out.

"What manner of fuckery is this?" he said between gasps.

Roo laughed. "This is James Crowley, the one and only."

"You brought a fucking Hand of God here?" Fazar demanded. "Are you out of your shit-for-brains mind?"

"Relax, Fazar," Roo said. "I told you he was a friend, and I meant it. Besides, what harm can he do downstairs?"

Fazar wiped his mouth of bile that wasn't there. He gave Roo a look that carried with it the disdain of a million years.

"Just get the cart," Roo said. "Quit wasting my time."

"This whole city might work for you. But I fucking don't."

Despite his words, Fazar walked a short distance before stopping. His wings extended, and it was impressive. Where this little imp stood half my height, his wings covered a distance twice that. Then, with a snapping like a whip, they flapped, and the ground rumbled.

Rock split, and a mining cart and track rose from the newly formed gorge.

I eyed Roo, who just stared with a stupid grin plastered on his mug.

"Well, what the fuck are you waiting for?" Fazar barked.

Roo clapped his hands, looked at me, and said, "Well, what the fuck are you waiting for?" before stomping off toward the imp and his cart.

Well, what the fuck was I waiting for?

* * *

The ride down took forever. It twisted and turned, once nearly flipping completely upside down. When it was through, we stepped off, and Fazar raised his middle finger to us before darting off again.

"Fazar's a bit bitter," Roo said. "Was next in line to lead the imperial forces until his brother, the king, had a child. Fazar got caught trying to smother the babe and was sentenced to exile on the surface. As you can imagine, life above ground for something like him never ended well. Luckily, I found him. Gave him a job. Gave him something worth living for."

"Yeah, you're a real saint," I said.

"You got just the right amount of self-righteous judgment to work for the Throne, you know that? C'mon. Through here."

Roo led me to a massive stone door marked in some language I couldn't read. He stretched out the same finger Fazar had just performed fellatio on, and a sharp claw shot out. With it, he traced a line over a few of the symbols, and the door cracked open.

A wave of noise hit me with the force of an angelic choir—but what awaited us inside was far from Heaven. That burning in my chest never let up, not for a second, like I was surrounded by an army of Nephs.

One look and, it turned out, I was. Rougarou wasn't lying. Beneath the Arlington House was something otherworldly. The room we now stood in was as large as a shipyard. Vaulted stone ceilings, flickering lights everywhere, more colors than a circus. Card tables and roulette wheels filled the hall—a casino for all things not exactly . . . human.

"Been a long time since you've been our way, Crowley," Roo said, stepping off. "We've built a place of our own in the South, me and Tourmaline."

"You're working with her?" I asked.

"Took a few street brawls, but we have an agreement. Was her idea. A place where nobody's got to hide what they truly are."

"You didn't think to mention that?"

"Didn't I?"

Nobody hiding was for damn sure. Vamps sat in booths drinking from chalices filled with blood drained from their cattle—humans who dedicated their lives to being living, walking beverages. They get addicted to the pain and the power, or so I hear.

Something I could only think to describe as a gnome—though I was sure it wasn't—dealt a round to a pack of werewolves in human form. Ain't hard to spot them usually. Their skin was saggier than it should've been at any age, stretched to the point where it'd never return to its former elasticity. A stone gargoyle took sledgehammers to the stomach while others bet on how many hits it would take before he cracked.

Mutants and Nephilim galore. Half-men with horns or four arms. Witches. Warlocks. All the kinds of things Shar had sent me hunting at one point or another—gathered under one roof. Get me a stick of dynamite, and I could earn myself a year's vacation in a second.

Did she know this existed?

I'd never know. As I surveyed the room, I noticed one thing was entirely absent: reflective surfaces of any kind. Even the roulette wheel was made of wood.

I'd never be able to make a move. The power radiating from all around the room was palpable. And just like upstairs, there were dividers and curtains beyond which I could feel raw energy emanating. There were old things here. Things that could erase me with the snap of a finger.

This wasn't good. We Hands of God take extra care not to find ourselves in situations where we are grossly outnumbered.

"Relax, you're with me," Roo said, as if noticing my apprehension. "Besides, see those?" He pointed to an archway carved in Luciferian etchings. "Those evoke the full power of Hell. This place? Heaven couldn't touch it if it wanted to."

So engrossed was I by the upside-down crosses, five-pointed stars, and goat skulls, I bumped into someone. Something clattered on the stone floor. A bone. I followed it up to a skeleton wearing a tattered dress, holding a tray of white cake.

"Watch where you're going!" a man snapped. A necromancer—not in hiding. My least favorite Nephilim, right there and unafraid. And why would he be? If what Roo said was true, I couldn't touch him here.

The necromancer—a short, pudgy fellow with too much cheek and not enough beard—rushed over and replaced the bone on his skeletal pet. He spoke to her in a purr-like tone, as if she was his girlfriend . . . Shit, she probably was.

We squeezed on by, and raucous cheering took over as the primary sound.

"But *this* is why this place really exists," Roo said with a wry grin.

We crossed under the sigil-marked archway to a pit sunken into rock at least twenty feet deep and covered in rows of charred iron spikes. Silver killed most Nephilim and demonic things, but iron—iron was for the Underdark creatures—the fae, the wisps, the banshees, and boggarts. On this level were three tiers of standing room and benches. An arena.

Men, women, and everything else gathered around the edges, and faces stretched into madness as they cheered. Women wearing leather bodices and dull metal chains took bets from patrons while big-ass *gentlemen* armed with clubs stood back to ensure no one took advantage of them.

I stepped closer to the wood railing separating us from the crowd. It seemed Beastboy had also found his way to Crescent City from Revelation Springs. Small world. With the fallout after my battle with Otaktay, many of the city's inhabitants were displaced, and it had a lingering effect on those who made a living off big city shows. No doubt, his performance troupe had fallen on hard times after. It's possible some of them even died when a chasm opened through the town square.

Below, Beastboy faced an enraged vamp. The young ones get like that. Jaws unhinge, and veins grow bright all around their faces. These were the kinds I was used to seeing—no true thought in their brains other than kill and eat. Beastboy took off at a sprint, using the wall as a springboard, and flung himself at the pale-faced vampire.

He was fast. And few things on Earth could move as quickly

as one of the bloodsuckers. A point proven by the vampire's next move. He ducked, lightning fast, gripped Beastboy by his furry tail, and flung him against the wall with enough force to break off chunks of rock.

The crowd moaned blissfully with delight. More money changed hands. Odds keepers hollered while their ladies made their rounds.

"That's one of Tourmaline's children," Roo said, pointing down at the vampire.

"A kid, huh?"

"In some ways," Roo clarified. "Those created by the elders grow in their craft until they can become lords of their own children."

I almost scoffed at the word *craft*, as if he was discussing a woodworker or stonemason. In this case, the craft meant hunting and murdering humans for food.

The vamp dashed forward in a blur and drove a fist into the wall like a bullet. His fist chewed off more rock as Beastboy rolled aside, coming up in a fighter's stance. He had moves. I'll give him that. Recovering quickly, Beastboy went at the vamp with wild swipes, each of which the vamp evaded with ease.

A swift uppercut sent Beastboy soaring high above the gathered crowd. He landed on his neck with a sickening crunch that could be heard even from where I stood. The onlookers gasped, one part horror, one part thrill. Then the vamp leaped just as high and slammed down on him.

By some miracle of God or Devil, Beastboy hadn't died—by the way he slashed with his claws, it seemed he hadn't even been fazed by the fall. However, try as he might, the vamp was too much for him. The bloodsucker caught his arm, pushed his head to the side with the other hand, then sank his fangs into Beastboy's exposed neck.

Blood gushed like a geyser. I winced. I had no love for the

creature. Thing was a Nephilim but seemed to stay out of trouble with the White Throne. That had to garner a modicum of my respect. But my respect mattered little when faced with a nightstalker like this. He had no chance.

He howled as the blood drained, clawing and twisting to try and break free. The vamp pushed deeper, bending Beastboy like a twig.

I saw the move before anyone else. Beastboy arched his back enough to get his ridiculously powerful tail free and around the vamp's neck. He planted his feet and pushed into a flip.

Long fangs ripped from his flesh as the vamp was pried free and launched to the far end of the arena. A nasty iron spike impaled the vamp's chest, eliciting a bloodcurdling scream as his veins ballooned. He wriggled to pull himself off, but before long, those veins burst like new wine in an old skin. He hung there lifeless, dry as a raisin.

The majority of the crowd groaned and booed, making it obvious where the odds were placed. One lucky bettor cheered. A fight broke out across the way. Considering how wagers went in any saloon across the West, this would be worse in spades.

"Well, I'll be. Tourmaline's gonna be pissed," Roo said. "Huge underdog."

"I guess not today," I said.

I moved closer to the edge. The Nephilim was on his knees, panting, blood leaking from his collar where he'd been bitten. A gate I hadn't previously noticed opened, and a giant, hairy man trotted out to drag him out of the arena.

"This is all very exciting, Roo," I said. "But I think we've wasted enough time."

He sighed. "You're right."

When I turned to go, someone bumped into my side. Hard enough to make me wobble. "Hey—"

Fearing a pickpocket in a place like this, I whipped around. It was none too soon either. A boy rushed away, not even looking back. The strap of my rifle had been sliced. I went to catch it, and Roo shoved me as hard as he could. He gripped the gun as I tripped over the ledge. I bounced from spike to spike before landing on my back in the pit, surrounded by a cloud of dust.

TWELVE

Laughter echoed as I pushed off the ground, finding my bearings. Roo stared down, wearing a shit-eating grin that'd rival Ace's. His pals filled in on either side of him, loup-garou and vampires, adults and children. The whole crowd was amused.

"Dammit, Roo, are you insane?" I shouted. I drew my pistols and aimed, but one of the vampires stepped in front of him, wielding a shield welded from nonreflective scrap metal. They were prepared. This was planned. How had I been foolish enough to trust him, especially in a place like this?

I held my fire. "You really want to make enemies with the angels?"

Roo looked around as if searching for the subject of my threat, mockery evident on his aged and scarred face. "I have friends now, Crowley. Powerful friends. And you . . . you seem all alone in a place where being alone ain't smart."

"We had a deal!"

"Which I have fulfilled. You said you wanted to meet my kids' mama. Well, she met an unfortunate end." His lip puffed into a pout. "Guess their stepmama will have to do."

He moved to the side, and the lady vampire I'd witnessed in that brutal memory stepped forward. She wore a form-fitting crimson bodice that left little for guessing. Puffy skirt, flared net sleeves, high collar; she was like something out of a baroque painting. Her midnight-black hair was pulled into a severe bun, a gold hairpin sticking up from it bearing the likeness of a peacock with red jewels for eyes.

She gripped Roo by the chin and kissed him long and hard, her sharp, red nails scraping across his chest. His foot twitched like a dog having his spot scratched. Only in Crescent City would I find a werewolf king and a vampire queen carousing. This was unheard of. Though I had to admit, they made quite the power couple.

Make no mistake, however. It took me only seconds to see that she was in charge. She had him by the balls, figuratively speaking.

"I'm gonna skin you alive, dog!" I barked.

More laughter. Tourmaline released him, and members of her brood placed an elaborately ornate chair beneath her. She crossed her salacious legs, pale, milky skin showing, and watched calmly.

"What a surprise I got for you today!" Roo announced to the enraptured audience. "A rarity. A Hand of God gracing our halls." Loud boos flooded the underground chamber. Food pelted me from every angle, bouncing off harmlessly. Didn't mean my ego wasn't bruised.

"He could've been sent to kill any one of you. Sent by *God*." He spat the word like poison. "But do you see God around here? I see only us. And he would dare come here for our Lady Tourmaline and destroy what we built, in *our* city?"

"I'm only here to talk with her!" I shouted back, but more booing and thrown food drowned me out.

"Well, I say it's high time he knows what it feels like to be hunted!" Roo said, clapping twice.

"Oscar, Oscar, Oscar!" Everyone around the arena began cheering that name, pumping their fists, claws, or hooves in the air. The ground trembled. Then quaked. Chains on the single gate leading into the pit slowly began to crank.

"See you in Hell, cowboy!" Roo shouted.

That same hairy man emerged from the tunnel. Only from down here could I see how big he really was. Wasn't just a hairy man—he was a giant. Nearly two feet taller than me, with knotted strands of brackish hair hanging from every inch of him, intertwined with swamp muck and plants. His face was invisible but for glowing green eyes.

His feet struck the floor—they were webbed. A soft touch despite his size. Which meant it wasn't him causing the whole room to shake.

His arm stretched back, gripping a thick rope dripping with some kind of viscous fluid. The crowd continued to chant "Oscar" as whatever he dragged out moved through the tunnel. I could barely stand straight the ground shook so violently. But there, in the mouth of the tunnel, a shadow loomed. Something enormous.

Then it all stopped—the shaking, the quaking, even the cheers. The hairy giant shouted something, but the rope showed resistance. Like it didn't want to fight. He pulled as hard as he could with both arms, muscles straining. A roar thundered out with salty spit. The giant caromed onto his chest and was dragged toward the tunnel like he weighed nothing. He let go just in time, rolling to the side of the gateway as a monster rumbled out.

Decades doing this, and I'm still shocked by some of the things hiding amongst us. How, you might ask, does a gargantuan, snapping-turtle-crocodile-hybrid hide? By devouring anything who'd tell its tale.

The size of three stagecoaches cinched together, it could swallow me whole. A shell spanned its top, hard-looking as stone but with leaves of seaweeds growing out of the cracks. Its beaked maw opened to reveal razor-sharp teeth. Apart from that, its mouth was croc-like, while its head was mostly chelonian. It snapped at the giant as it went by, giving credence to its visage. That chomp was as loud as a hammer on an anvil. The giant dove and hustled out of the way, just missing getting swatted by the thing's enormous spiked tail before he was through the gate, and it slammed shut.

With the target of its ire gone, the thing turned on me. A sound like a stopping train hissed from its wide-open jaw. Man-sized claws dug into the dirt, and it stretched its neck. Frilly rolls under its snout started to quiver.

"Hey, boy," I stammered, holding my pistols to the side in an attempt to conceal the threat. Slowly, I edged forward. It scraped its feet back, leaving claw tracks as wide as water troughs. "Easy now. You don't want to be here any more than I do."

Something from the crowd pelted its shell. Then again. Its maw unhinged, and it roared, this time spitting something from deep in its throat. I raised my pistols and fired out of reflex as I dove.

The pistol in my left hand backfired, the barrel covered in some greenish liquid I could only assume to be acid. Some of it spattered my duster sleeve and melted rapidly through toward flesh. I yanked it off and flung it aside, leaving it sizzling on the ground.

"End of the road, cowboy!" Rougarou yelled. "We keep Oscar nice and famished."

I didn't have time to think about how ridiculous a name

that was for such a creature. For a turtle, it wasn't slow. It came rumbling at me, mouth gnashing. I glanced left and right, then decided my only real option was forward. I rushed toward the monster, then slid beneath it at the last second. As I drew my silver-dusted hunting knife, I hoped to discover a soft underbelly. Instead, it barely scratched the surface of thick scales.

Dodging a powerful downward strike from its tail, I didn't see it slam into the pit's wall, but I heard it. I spun around and got a view of the dead vamp, pulverized under its weight. Spikes sparked against the armored appendage, but they didn't puncture.

The wall gave way, and those unlucky enough to be close found themselves toppling into the pit with me. Bones crunched as Oscar scooped up a little black cacodemon in his mouth. The thing barely even had a chance to scream. But all the others did. They tore off like bats out of Hell, looking for any way to escape the arena. Oscar gave chase, and the crowd really loved that. Some happy family of Underdark creatures . . .

"Shar, now would be the time for a miracle!" I whisper-shouted to myself. I'd take an earthquake or a catastrophic flood—

That angelic son of a gun. Wasn't sure if it was her or not—seeing as how we were surrounded by Luciferian wards—but from the shattered wall, water started guzzling through. Must've been Oscar's pen back there. It wasn't much, but it was a start. If I could get him to hit it again . . . I'd potentially corner myself but let the gulf come flooding in. Might be my only shot.

"C'mon, you big sack of scales. Come at me!" I shouted as he ran down a pair of hellhounds.

I fired at its face. Silver didn't seem to have any effect, and the bullet bounced off. I didn't watch where the slug went but hoped it caught Roo or Tourmaline in the skull.

My shot might not have done anything physically to Oscar,

but it pissed him off good. Quickly holstering, I gripped my lasso as he charged me. His nostrils flared, almost like a horn atop his jagged snout.

I held steady, feeling every bit the Spanish matador. Only feet away now, he chomped. I dodged, but it was too big to fully evade. The ridge of his shell hit my waist and sent me tumbling up and over the top. Sometimes, it's a pleasure not to feel.

Rolling down its rear end, I looped the end of its tail and pulled tight. My body wrenched back in the other direction, but I was on. No Heavenly judgment from my blessed lasso, not even a twinge of Shar's justice. This was just an animal, after all—oversized and alone—but an animal nonetheless.

Oscar bellowed and thrashed his tail. I held my grip, pulling myself up until I could jab my knife in just enough to get balance. It shook to and fro, hoping to knock me off. The crowd continued trying to pelt me with food and rocks. I freed my lasso and got it around one of the spiky protrusions cresting the front edge of the shell. I dug my boots in and climbed.

The beast snapped backward, unable to bend his stubby head anywhere near far enough. Lucky me, it was more turtle than gator. I scaled it farther, aiming for the spongy flesh at the base of his head. It ran circles around the arena, making each movement a chore. Then it smashed itself against the wrong wall.

Spikes screeched over my head across the shell as I ducked. Chunks of seaweed slapped my face and obscured my vision. I twisted off to the side. Then, as soon as the event was over, I righted myself and tried my best to steer him toward the gurgling water.

With one more tug on my lasso, I propelled myself to the front edge of the shell, right over his head. Down went my knife with all my might into the top of Oscar's cranium. Only went in a few inches, but it stayed there.

Over my shoulder, I glanced up at Roo. His eyes were saucers. We knew each other well enough for him to get an idea of my next move.

"Sorry, pal," I whispered to the beast.

With one hand on the shell, I balanced long enough to kick my heel down on the handle of my knife. A roar split my eardrums. Oscar reared back as far as he could go, spewing acid. People screamed as some reached the crowd, and more splashed onto the arena walls, melting through.

Then he charged, intent on flinging me off. We hit the mud near the gate, and Oscar sank a step. Then, as he flipped and rolled forward, he sent me soaring.

When I landed, I turned to watch the turtle's handiwork. A beast that size and with such rage and momentum? The arena's wall crumbled and cracked from the force and spilling acid. Water erupted, confusing the critter. He reared back again, then butted his head into the same spot.

Crack!

A bullet just missed my hand, pinging off Oscar's shell. Out of my peripherals, I saw Roo staring down the sights of my very own rifle. I swore. That thing was loaded with silver. If he was trying to take me out, he'd do it with that. Not very fair, to my mind.

His next shot caught me in the calf—in and out through skin. Let's just say that while I'm numb to most things, silver is a son of a bitch even when the bullet exits. Bright lines of pain shot up my leg as it sizzled with white steam. Having gone so long feeling so little, it hurt all the more. But he'd made one fatal mistake.

He pissed me off.

I whipped my lasso and snapped it out. He thought I was going for the Winchester and yanked back. But I wasn't. Instead, it caught the back of Tourmaline's chair.

I was going for her neck, but all things considered, under the circumstances, it was still an ace shot. Behind me, Oscar smashed his head into the wall again. The whole room shook, and I used that momentum to pull an already unstable Tourmaline and her would-be throne right down into the pit with me.

The arena's wall spilled open, driving coruscated cracks through the entirety of the hall. Everyone still watching toppled forward under the weight of the beast and falling rock. In an instant, we were swimming, all of us.

It all happened so fast. Tourmaline bobbed in the water in front of me, rage creasing her features. Then someone slammed down on her before she could get a hit in. Vampires are exceptionally strong and fast, among other gifts—especially older ones—but they aren't invincible.

Together, we all went tumbling through the watery abyss, bumping and smashing between broken stone and shell. Not my finest move. Far from my worst.

THIRTEEN

The shelled beast cleared a path for us straight through caverns in a way nobody had ever entered. I tumbled along blindly. No reason to fight it. I gave in to the current, and, in my state, it was actually kind of peaceful in a messed-up way. Could have taken a nap. My weary mind needed a furlough.

Oscar punched through, sliding out across salty marshes and through a mushy slab of peat and grass. We roared through the mud in its wake, a sopping wet mess of skin and cloth and, of course, scales and spikes.

Then came the light.

With my eyes supernaturally attuned to the darkness, I found myself blind, unable to see a damn thing as rocks sloughed around us. But that was nothing compared to the agony Tourmaline was about to endure.

There was a brain-melting shriek accompanied by a distinct sizzle. She quickly retreated into the mouth of the cavern we'd broken through to escape the agony. Vampires and the sun don't get along much. Cooks them like lobsters, only twice as fast. Already, she was crisp and blackened, her elegant red dress in tattered ruins.

All that air of superiority was gone with her unable to reach me. Dark veins twitched on her neck as she grimaced, fangs brought to bear. My Peacemakers remained in their holsters, shoved there just before the chaos ensued. Now I'd get to test if I could outdraw a vampire lady.

Pulling my right hand's iron, I tried to stand. But I'd forgotten the silver that tore through my leg, embedding pieces on its way out. Abnormal pain flashed and I dropped to a knee. She hissed, fangs extending farther, and her formerly beautiful face contorted into something inhuman.

Then she surprised me. Further risking the sun, she lowered her head and dashed at me—a blur.

My gun went off three times. Missed her completely with each, but I damn sure taught the hunk of gray stone behind her a lesson. Before I could blink, she gripped my wrist with one hand and my throat with the other, dragging me back into the shade. I can honestly say I've never seen anyone move so fast in my life. It was like a bolt of lightning: there one second, gone the next. And somehow, as haggard as she looked and after all that swimming and falling, her hair remained neatly pinned.

"This dress is older than you, *Hamsa*!" she bristled. Then she looked up at the ceiling. "Are you listening, up there? You dare come for me?"

"I ain't here for you," I got out, my throat crushed beneath her clawlike grip.

She pulled her already healing face close to mine, eyes wild and fangs begging for blood I wouldn't give. "They all say that. Who's your handler, eh? Ingram? Amael? Don't tell me it's Kjeldgaard."

"It's the goddamn truth. I'm after the Betrayer. Your maker, apparently."

Her head tilted, grip loosened. For whatever reason, that completely caught her off guard. Before I could make my move,

Oscar roared so loudly and stomped with such force that more rocks fell from above. Blades of sunlight pierced the newly formed holes, a direct shot on the side of Tourmaline's face. She shrieked and gripped her cheek as it melted through enough to reveal her back teeth.

She retreated, and Shellhead stomped ever closer, casting us in his enormous shadow and barricading us in the cave with no way out. I raised a flat palm and stood. This time, there was nobody else to antagonize it.

"Calm down, Oscar," I said in a tone I used with Timp early on. "Settle down. I ain't gonna hurt you." I gestured to the surroundings. "See all that light and open space?"

He stomped again, oversized claws digging abysses through the mud. I didn't know turtles could growl, but something guttural rumbled in his throat. Better than another roar, I reckoned. He flicked his head up and back as if he had an itch he couldn't quite reach.

That was when I realized my silver-coated knife remained embedded in his skull. Poor murderous thing.

"That must hurt," I said. "Sorry. Meant nothing personal. Just, we were both stuck in there." Then I poked a thumb back at Tourmaline. "Because of her."

Tourmaline spat obscenities. I've mentioned that most of my experience has been with rabid, feral vampires that barely resembled humanity. She was sounding like them now, a soft click in the back of her throat growing louder as time went on. I limped away from her, closer to Oscar. My leg protested, but I had no time for such trivialities.

Fact is, most animals are the same. They just want to feel safe. And trust me, they can tell when a man views something as nothing but food or fodder. As a man with a best friend for a horse, I've got some experience in these things.

Oscar snorted.

"How's about this: I'll take that thing out, and you can get on out of here. Swim wherever you want. Be free."

Closer still. One dumb move and those massive jaws take my arm at the elbow. The key is to act calm, even if you aren't feeling particularly serene. Animals, they can sense anxiety, and my having a heart that doesn't beat helps.

"Good boy. Easy now."

Oscar lowered his head, and I still had to get onto my tippy-toes to reach. I gripped the knife. "It'll only hurt for a second. Like a big old splinter." The scales were dense, so the blade barely moved at first. I rocked it back and forth a few times to loosen it up while Oscar cried softly.

"You think me a fool?" Tourmaline cried, ramming into my side.

Her attempts to hurt me only yielded the results I was looking for. The knife came free, and the beast roared in fright, scurrying back and away from us. The shelled beast thundered away, finding deeper water in the Mississippi where it wound ever onward to the east. Good for it.

But I had other concerns at the moment. I found myself flat on my back with Tourmaline straddling me. Her hands around my neck again, those long nails were ready to rip out my throat. And would you look at that, her hair finally fell free. Half her face, framed like a hood under those thick locks, still bubbled from the sunlight. Not a pretty sight.

I grinned.

That might have set her off, but she quickly realized I had her. In the chaos, my knife found its way into her belly. A healthy dosing of silver for something as unholy as a vampire lady.

The half of her face she still controlled corkscrewed. Few things worse than a stab like that for her kind if you don't intend on staking them through the heart. Silver has an adverse effect on all supernatural beings, but there's something special about how it interacts with a vampire. Couldn't tell you why, but right now, I wasn't looking for answers.

I twisted the blade. Then I pushed her over, switching places and jamming the knife deeper. Her back arched as the pain made her choke.

"Your boyfriend really pissed me off." Giving Tourmaline my full attention, I wrenched the knife to the side. "So, now that we've all been acquainted, you're gonna tell me what I wanna know."

She groaned first, and then that turned to a blood-filled cackle—a mad, sadistic laugh. The sight of her face full of uncapped joy was only made worse by her burns and pocked skin.

"I ain't joking," I said.

"You must be, if you're going after *him*." More cackling. "You'll end up like all the others. Like me."

"Nah, I'm resourceful. Turned this little mix-up around, didn't I?"

I accentuated my point by redrawing my pistol. Brushing aside a fancy gold pendant on her chest, I pressed the barrel right against her pitch-black heart. She had an old scar down her sternum, a thin line I hadn't noticed in my Divining. Like she'd been opened up for surgery sometime past. Likely before she was turned.

"You think I'm afraid of that?" she asked. "Trust me, *Hamsa*, I have lived long enough to fear nothing."

"Except not living, I'd wager." I looked up toward the beam of sunlight only ten feet or so away. "How about a sunbath? You ain't looking much like yourself. Maybe you should exfoliate."

"Try and get me there," she spat. "See what happens."

I exhaled slowly. "I haven't been asked to kill you, Tourmaline, despite that Hell club you and Wolfman started. I try not to stray when it does me no good. So, tell me where to find your maker, and we can be done here. No blood spilt."

"You don't find him," she sniveled. "And if he were here, I'd know."

"Oh, he's here."

"Why, because your *angel* told you?" she sneered. "To be young and naive again. It's adorable, really. My advice, tell your handler you couldn't get the job done. Move on. Eternity like this isn't worth it."

"Looks a whole lot better than blinking into nothing, don't it? Besides, you seem to have your fun. I saw what you do to your prey."

"*Hamsa*, are you spying on me?" Her lips pulled back into a smile. This time, it wasn't a sneer, like she genuinely found happiness in the thought.

"Wish I hadn't."

"A Peeping Tom? Did you like what you saw? Mmmmm. Well, boredom after centuries does have a way of refining certain . . . tastes."

"Enough." I pressed my pistol down harder. "This city might've changed, but I'm done playing tourist." With my free hand, I removed my lasso from my belt and dangled it over her face. "The White Throne will judge you now."

She snickered. "So many sins; where will they start? Do your worst, *Hamsa*. Make me feel alive!"

Keeping her at bay with silver, I hog-tied her with my blessed lasso, using a special knot that allowed the rope to cross her mouth and shut her up too. Light blossomed around us, the weight of God's judgment coming into effect like a thousand iron bars set on her chest. She groaned into the rope. I could see the strain in her eyes.

Even for all her preternatural strength, she was powerless against it. She clearly had a lot to atone for. The brilliant ray showered like the clouds had parted and nearly rendered her unconscious.

Once sure she wasn't going anywhere, I rolled off her, plopping down in exhaustion. My leg still ached, radiating small pulses of agony I rarely felt. With a pat on her back, I said, "We're gonna have a bit of fun."

I took a deep breath, held my thumb and forefinger to my lips, then whistled. Timp and I had a bond that surpassed most things. I knew she'd come, no matter where she was or what she was doing. She'd find a way. Left me wondering if maybe Shar was up there, playing puppeteer and directing her to me.

While I waited, I took a look at my leg. The sharp pain had become a dull burn which I almost welcomed. It was nice not being numb for a change. But I'd need to be at my best for what came next.

The skin around the puncture hole was dark but not black. Looked like a three-day-old bruise. Luckily, the silver had indeed found its way out, making a clean tunnel through one side and then the other.

Using a plier from my satchel and water from the marsh, I got busy douching out any bits of silver, careful not to let them touch any more of me than need be. A more familiar sensation washed over me. My silent benefactor finally wanted to get back in touch. Also from my satchel, I retrieved my shaving mirror and placed it down next to me. I propped it up against some of the rubble, realizing that my face could do with a wipe. I practically looked made of mud.

"About time you showed up," I said, beating Shar to the first word as she swirled about.

"Do you imagine I have no greater responsibility than keeping tabs on you, Crowley?" she replied.

"I'll be honest. I imagine that's *all* you do. You've always been a little hazy on details."

"*Quite a mess* you've made already, throwing in with those wolf abominations."

Half ignoring her, I used my sleeve to clear some of the filth from my brow. "Really? I think it's been pretty smooth."

"That's always been your problem. Trust in the good nature of others. We do not deal with *good-natured* things."

I shrugged. "What can I say? I'm a man of faith. But Roo got me here in the end."

"You and your pet names," she scoffed. "You would do better to find respect for those who can damn your soul."

"We talking about you or him now, Shar?" As always, it was the wrong time to push buttons.

"You must feel rather good about yourself," she said. "The wrath of the Almighty is not a frivolous tool at your every beck and whim. Look at her. At best, you have exterminated a pest, nothing more. Slay her, and others will rise in her place. She is irrelevant as compared to the Betrayer."

I plucked out the last bit of silver, studying how it glinted in the reflection of that Heavenly beam. All the while, Tourmaline writhed in torture within the light.

I chuckled. "From someone who sits so high above the rest of us, I'm surprised you're missing the bigger picture."

"And you're pushing my patience, *again*. You have tilled this field. I just hope you're prepared for the harvest. Release her and get her to talk. There is a bond between maker and child. She will know."

I sucked through my teeth. I loved when I had a chance to make Shar seem foolish. *All-seeing* as she might be, but she'd never lived on this plane. Human nature is a consistent thing. And Roo was wrong. While we all might be something more than what we were, we all rose from the same dust.

"Waste of time," I said. "You can't coerce someone to talk who ain't afraid. But Ace—bastard he was—taught me a few things in our time together. The best way to draw someone out of hiding is to be a son of a bitch."

"Do you have not a shred of decency?" She never liked when I cursed, which was why I did.

"Hey, you chose me," I reminded her. "I'd have been fine wherever you found me."

"I found you in worse shape than your feeble mind could imagine," Shargrafein said, a new emotion crossing her smoky features. Was that pity? "If I had my way, God's Hands would be left with a glimmer of a memory of the place from which you'd been liberated. However, it is well within my power if you desire to return."

I thought about that. I'd always wondered what happened to me during the years after Ace shot me dead. Had I been in Hell already? Was she telling the truth, or was this just another misdirection to get me to behave?

"All right, all right," I said. "I'll play nice." I shoved myself to my feet, thankful the silver wound in my leg had already mostly healed. "Gonna need to keep that rope on her, though."

Without another word, Shar disappeared, and so did the stream of God's judgment, leaving me and Tourmaline face-to-sneering-face.

FOURTEEN

Timp found us out in the bogs. Took her some time, though. The current had carried us farther than I thought. A good thing, since I didn't particularly feel like being out in the open when Rougarou's goons found us. And no doubt they were searching.

Thanks to my trusty mare, we had the jump on them.

I pulled my sleeping mat out of Timp's saddlebag. During my days traveling with the Scuttlers, we never knew where we'd wind up nodding off. True, I didn't need it now and haven't for a couple of decades, but old habits die hard. Besides, things like this can serve dual purposes.

Tourmaline glowered at me. Her arms and legs strained against the lasso, desperate to pull free. Her face was fairly healed already, and I couldn't help that old sense of wonder at someone so beautiful. Too bad she was a rotten piece of shit.

I palmed her face lightly.

"Wouldn't want to cause any more damage."

She screamed something muffled, a wild look in her eyes. You know what? I was feeling generous. I pulled down the rope gagging her.

"You're going to regret this," she said.

"'You're going to regret this?' Saints and Elders, I was hoping for something more original than that."

"I have an offer," she said.

"You also have an ass, and you can stick it up there unless you've somehow magically remembered where I can find your master."

"Let me go, and I'll make your wildest dreams come true."

"Shit, lady. I haven't had a dream since before Roo was born."

"I have ways of making even one such as you feel pleasure unparalleled."

"I got one thing that'll bring me pleasure," I said before yanking the gag back over her mouth and draping the mat like a blanket over her. I mussed it up a bit and tucked the sides, so it would appear to onlookers as nothing more than a travel bag of supplies. Just an old cowboy far from home. Nothing to see here.

She hooted and hollered like a banshee caught, but she'd wear herself out eventually.

I made sure none of her precious pearly skin was exposed. Tourmaline wouldn't do me any good if the sun turned her into a soufflé, and by moving at daytime, I could ensure that—if she did somehow break free—the sun would keep her down.

With her strapped over Timp's back, looking like a hidden bounty, we trotted back toward Crescent City. A bath would be nice. Fresh pair of clothes and boots. Maybe I couldn't feel how uncomfortable I was, but I knew it in my head. That was just as bad.

A bridge into the city proper came into view. I thought about leaving Timp there and sneaking in, but that wasn't the game I was playing. I wanted every seedy bastard and child spy in Crescent City to see me. Word would spread, and it might bring more foes to my doorstep, but I had a feeling it'd conjure up her maker too.

If the Devil's in the details, I was looking to paint broad strokes.

On our right, the bay shone in the morning light, sparkling like diamonds. Salt-stained buildings rose on the other side of the cobbled street, each unique and reflecting the personalities of their owners. Things were bustling, people out in droves.

A tram chimed by. It was quite the mode of transportation. I figure there might come a day when every city in the world has something similar. A child hung off the side, staring at us. Another boy darted from behind a tree into an alley. It's a city, and cities had children, but it still felt like everyone was eyeballing us.

We stopped at the corner of St. Anne's. Across the street and a few doors down from Madame Laveau's, a shack was empty, with the windows shuttered. It was odd, a patch of darkness amid such liveliness, but I was grateful for it.

Wasn't exactly keen on being so close to where Rosa and the others were staying, but this was a strategic location. Backed up to other buildings so I couldn't get snuck up on, busy enough even throughout the night that Roo couldn't attack in full wolf force without being exposed. And lastly . . .

"Hey, you!" a familiar voice called. I kept Timp walking, not giving any heed. "Hey!"

The Yankee marshal from earlier took her reins, and she damn near chomped his hand off.

"Whoa now, girl! He's with the good guys," I said, though I put a little malice in those words.

Maybe a reminder to him or me.

"Were you born today?" I asked the marshal. "Can't just bullrush a horse like that. Never know which ones bite."

"Yeah, right." He rubbed his gloved hand as if she'd wounded him. The big baby.

"Say, you ever find who killed that fella in the alley? Thought of it's been eating away at me. Couldn't sleep."

"We're still searching. You wouldn't happen to know anything more now, would you?"

"I wish."

A few seconds of awkward silence passed by before he cut to the chase.

"What were you doing in the Arlington House last night?" he asked bluntly.

"Just taking in the sights," I said. "You know, a tourist in a big town."

"Don't lie to me." He walked around Timp, letting his hand stray too close for my comfort. I watched him keenly as he neared my makeshift body bag.

"What were *you* doing there? A marshal in a whorehouse." I whistled playfully. "That's a bad look."

"I got a wife. Kids. What could I possibly want from that filth?"

I made a show of looking at his trousers. "You're a man, ain't ya?"

He stretched a hand toward Tourmaline's body bag. Before I could even yank on Timp's reins, my good girl huffed unhappily and circled away hard all on her own, sending a clear warning.

"People go into the back, invite only," he said.

"And?"

"Some never come out."

"Sounds like they're getting their money's worth," I said. However, I could practically feel the slow creeping of Hell's frost overtaking my insides like little frosty spiders.

"Now, word on the street says it's some weird, circus-freak sex show, but local law enforcement won't even take a gander.

So, tell me, stranger." He stopped directly in front of me. "What *does* go on back there?"

"You said no one comes out," I told him, gesturing to myself. "Here I am. Turns out, I didn't receive the same kinda invitation you're hinting at. Thing about rumors, in my experience. They're usually true."

"I said *some* never come out."

"Potato, potahto." I shrugged.

"You're confirming nothing's going on in there but *freaky* sex?" He pressed a fist against his hip, shoving his jacket aside. He was trying to act like it wasn't a blatant attempt at showing his pistol and badge, but I knew the trick.

"I ain't *confirming* a thing. Now, if you don't mind, I got places to be."

"This isn't a game, you dumb redneck." His face grew stern, brows furrowing. I bet he thought he looked mighty frightening, a man from the north, down here in hick town. "I know the senator frequented that establishment. Now you show up, hanging out with that witch Laveau and strutting into special backrooms with known criminals like Rouge Garrett."

"It a crime to have old friends, officer?"

"Depends."

I sighed. "Is that all?"

He studied me from spurs to Stetson. "What's that you're hauling?"

"This?" I gave the mat a hard whack. She wouldn't dare speak up for fear of having that mat pulled back and facing the oven. "Nabbed me a gator. Fierce one too. Ever try hunting one? I reckon not. They don't have these up where you Yanks come from. Really makes you feel alive. This one almost had me, but now I'll get some new boots. Don't taste half bad either. Like chewy chicken."

He stuck out his tongue in disgust. "I'll take your word for it. First hunting owls, then this? Most men don't visit cities for hunting."

"Most cities don't have this kind of game. Besides, I like a change in scenery, and Madame Laveau has use of the parts for her remedies."

"Remedies," he scoffed.

I nodded. "Staved off a bad infection for me years back. She's a wonder, truly."

"She's something all right."

"I like helping out when I've got downtime."

"What is it you do for a living, Mr. . . . I didn't catch your name."

"Never said it." I spun Timp back toward the road. "Look, I really do wish I could be of more help, but I've gotta get this thing on a spit, lest its spirit come back biting. A lady lets you crash at her place, least you can do is fix dinner for the house."

"I guess that makes you the only gentleman in all of Crescent City, then."

"Could be," I said. "Tell you what, I'll keep an eye out for your missing senator. And do yourself a favor. Go back to the Arlington, get a drink or a smoke, find a pretty girl, and have a good time."

He harrumphed.

I offered a final friendly nod as I steered Timp along. Then I watched him in the corner of my eye, moseying down the street. I'd gotten into his head. Here he was, in a city known for debauchery and dishonest men tucked into the sweaty armpit of the nation. Invisible outside these marshes. Why not stop being a hard-ass and loosen up?

Once he faded out of view, I brought Timperina to a stop in front of the vacant home rather than Laveau's cottage.

"Stay out of sight, okay, girl?" I said as I hopped off. I took her by the snout and pressed my forehead between her eyes. The incident with that turtle-gator had me feeling closer to her than ever, even though in cities, we've never been further apart.

She snorted.

"I know, but you can't stay here. It ain't safe. Go back to Laveau's until I call."

She tapped her hoof.

"Timperina, enough."

I heaved Tourmaline over my shoulder and gave Timp a nudge to trot across the way to the hitches. She did so, still grousing. Then I turned to the entry. With marshals keeping watch on Laveau's—which Roo seemed to know about—I had extra defense here. Where there was one, more were always hiding. The law rolls like pack animals.

I gave the area a thorough once-over, then pushed the door open with my boot and entered, gun at the ready.

FIFTEEN

My eyes gathered all available light, adjusting to the dark, dank, dirty room.

"Hey, who dere?" An old Cajun man sat in the corner on a wicker chair, sporting a beard like Moses. And if cleanliness was next to godliness, this fellow was further gone than me.

"Out," I demanded, pushing inside, and he looked at me like I had three heads. "I said get out!"

"I was here first," the man argued. He curled up to the side and tucked his feet under a tattered rag.

I grunted. His problem, then. He'd be another distraction if anybody broke in, but considering his drunken eyes were looking at two sides of the same room, his presence wouldn't affect me.

"Your funeral," I told him as I set up the stairs, hauling Tourmaline over my shoulder. She tossed and turned now, throwing a fit now that the sun wasn't a threat.

"Hey," the drunk said, starting to rise. "Whatchu got there?"

As I ignored him, he lost heart fast enough and settled back on the chair. Once upstairs, I checked all the bedrooms. No more vagrants. Nothing but spiders and cobwebs. This would do. I brought Tourmaline to the master suite and dumped her in the center of the floor.

"Don't move," I said, though I don't think she found it funny.

She shouted something I couldn't understand, what with the gag and the mat between us.

"Yeah, yeah, yeah," I grumbled, then moved to the windows. They were caked with dust. Using my muddy sleeve, I managed to smear it worse, but I had a street view. Laveau's cottage sat catty-corner to my right. Timp was slurping on water out of the trough. Marie stood on the porch, her front door wide open. She watched the old girl quizzically, probably wondering how she'd run off and returned without me in sight.

I turned back to Tourmaline, walked over, and ripped the mat off her. Her eyes glared fire my way. Something deep down told me I should cut down this snake before it could coil and strike, but she was still useful to me.

I cautiously removed the gag but kept her bound, tossing the loose end of the lasso around a low rafter. After a bit of work, I had her suspended upright. She dangled half a foot off the floorboards.

Once she was secure, I positioned my knife below her, hilt jammed between slats. This way, if she did break free and fall, silver would slow her.

"Now, this is just undignified," she said, spitting and scraping her tongue with her fangs to get the fibers off.

"I saw how you handle yourself," I said. "I ain't taking risks."

She sighed. "I suppose I wouldn't either. Though I am curious what your plan is."

"Ever go fishing, Tourmaline?"

"So that's it, huh? I'm bait? Here I thought I was worth more than that."

"The tastier the worm, the bigger the fish." I returned to the window. Marie was back inside, hopefully finishing with returning Bram back into the world of the living.

Tourmaline laughed. "You're wasting your time, *Hamsa*. My maker is not here. He hates the so-called 'free world.' Lacks vision for a future out of shadows."

"You're gonna have to forgive me for taking your words with a grain of salt. And if your hairy lover comes first, this time, I'll put a silver slug right between his eyes. I promise you that."

She stared at me blankly. "Is that supposed to affect me, child?" I noted the way she said that. Just like Shar always did. Condescending bitch. "You know how many men have fawned over me throughout the centuries? Rouge is a . . . welcome distraction. But I think I've found someone more worthy of my talents." She winked.

Though she couldn't be trusted, I didn't doubt her one bit about fawning men. All her burns were healed now, and, as she hung there, flesh exposed, and memories of my Divining still fresh in my mind, she was positively beautiful. Not just gorgeous but radiant . . . mystical. The surface-level part of my brain responsible for more banal emotions roared with need. Her raven-dark hair cascaded over her shoulders like a waterfall in the middle of the desert. If I hadn't been a Hand of God, my body would have been right there too.

That made me wonder if she was telling the truth about being able to bring pleasure to a Black Badge. It wasn't because of some ultrareligious compulsion to be pure or holy. Being undead, or no longer dead—reliving, I simply can't enjoy those behaviors anymore, much as I may want to. Which just leads to frustration.

And that's when I recognized what she was doing. "Flirting ain't gonna work on me."

She clicked her teeth. "*Quel dommage.* You do look like fun."

"Cut the shit, Tourmaline. How about I tell those nice marshals that've been dancing around town that it was *you* who killed the senator?"

That caught her tongue. It was a relative shot in the dark based on circumstantial evidence, but her reaction was all I needed. Man, if only Pinkertons existed when I was younger, I could've excelled. Or if I'd had a sense of the law. Sheriff Crowley. Has a nice ring to it compared to Black Badge.

"Thought so," I said. "He wanted a good time, and things got a little too rough, huh? Or maybe you got too lazy to do your homework and didn't realize who he was. You still have the body, or did you send it floating?"

"I don't know what you're talking about," she said through her fangs.

"Sure, the hangman's noose would never get you, but I reckon you wouldn't have spent as much time building the club you've got here if you didn't care about the place."

"*Jeune homme*," she spat. "I stood by while Joan of Arc burned. Watched Napoleon's rise and fall. Do you think this foul toilet of a city matters to me?"

"I think you've finally found a place that embraces the weird enough where you and others can hide in plain sight. Feed your vices. Live however you want to." She opened her mouth to speak, but I cut her off. "I don't fault you for it. What you do is monstrous, but I've seen plenty worse. So, here's the deal, plain and simple. If your maker comes for you, help me kill him, and me and my kind won't trouble you any further."

She chuckled. "You do not speak for the White Throne, *Hamsa*. You lack the authority to make that promise."

She was right, but she didn't have to know that. One problem at a time. "My lips to God's ears, I can."

At that, her brow furrowed. "You really don't know what we are, do you? What is it that you're so fervently hunting?"

My chest had been burning so long, I'd forgotten about it. But the question brought it to the forefront of my mind. "A perversion. Some unholy spawn of things hellish and mortal like any other Nephilim. But more importantly, a killer of those who don't deserve it."

A sick smile splayed across her face. As stunning as she was, this was nothing pretty. "Now, this is interesting. I suppose I didn't know either, but it has been quite a long time. Memory fades after seeing more wars than you can count on your fingers."

I stepped toward her. Even suspended by my lasso, our eyes were level.

"Know what?"

"I shouldn't spoil the fun. I'll let you revel in the discovery. As for your offer, *mets-le dans ton cul.*"

I sighed. "And that means?"

"Shove it up your ass."

"Cute."

"I may not care for my maker, but I won't aid you. Not even the Devil himself could kill him."

"You might know the Devil, lady, but you don't know me."

"Such false confidence." Her laugh chided me. "Even your angel must have given up on you to send you on such a mission. It's futile, child. I know it. They know it. Only you are left to acknowledge it."

"Enough." I pulled out the dirty rag I used to clean my guns and stuffed it in her mouth. "When he comes, you can join him."

She stared at me as I moved to the window and relaxed. Her gaze never left—I could feel it burning the back of my skull. I loaded my pistols with silver bullets. A couple of guns against a vampire lady and whatever else. Not the best.

While I had time, I went to the staircase and snapped spindles off the railing.

"Let me borrow this." Sitting cross-legged right in front of Tourmaline, taunting her, I used my knife to carve the ends into sharp spikes. Still, she stared. I was able to stuff six of them in my belt at the small of my back and spread the others throughout the room before returning the knife to below her.

Like back in the fighting pit, a stake through the heart kills a vampire. They'd kill a werewolf just as well, or at least adequately maim them.

Sitting in the corner, I bided my time, a lesson learned by someone who had far too much of it.

Finally, night fell. Dogs barked. Sounds of taverns opening to the rabble and drunkards stumbling around. That same awful music I'd heard with Roo echoed from far off.

Cities have too many sounds for my taste. I'll always prefer the still quiet of the West.

The window creaked.

I was back-against-the-wall, beside it in an instant. Someone climbed through, and I grabbed them by the hair, flipping them onto their back and ready for my Peacemaker to make peace.

"Jesus, feck, Crowley!" Irish had her hands up. "It's me."

I didn't avert my aim. "What are you doing here?"

She leaned into the barrel, forcing herself upright with no fear of me shooting her. "Heard a familiar voice yammerin' up here on our way home. Don't ye worry, I didn't tell the others."

"You shouldn't be here."

"Ye got a bed back there. Why are *ye* here—" The word caught as she must've noticed my guest. There were no candles lit, just a bit of moonlight, but it was enough to see Tourmaline all tied up, eyes closed, and chin against her chest.

"This ain't what it looks like," I defended myself, unsure why I cared about the opinions of a loon from across the pond.

She shrugged. "Hey, I'm not one to be judgin'. Yer business is yers."

She sauntered over to Tourmaline and poked the vampire between the eyes. Tourmaline's eyes snapped open. She hissed into the rag. If Irish was even slightly taken aback, her actions betrayed none of it.

"Deadly lookin' thing, her." She peered back at me nonchalantly. "Need me to bump her off?"

"No. I need you to leave."

Irish shook her head slowly. "Ye know how borin' it is waitin' for a man to get better? And Rosa wouldn't even go for a piss-up with me. Just wanted to go searchin' for strange shit for Laveau. I just wanted one drink. Maybe three. I'm needin' to live. Gotta feel somethin', and this looks a right festival."

I took her by the arm and led her to the window. "Irish, you can't be here."

"Blah blah. I ain't intendin' to stay. I'm here for yer girlfriend."

Hearing that, I let go.

"What happened?" I demanded.

"Nothin'."

"Goddammit, Irish. Quit with the song and dance and tell me what's wrong."

"She's after somethin', Rosa. Somethin' I ain't sure's possible, but you seem to know a bit about impossible things. Things I ain't fond of triflin' with. Ye know her more than I. It's dangerous, wrastlin' with the dead. Ye should be helpin' her, not me."

I exhaled through clenched teeth. "She already knows how I feel about chasing ghosts."

"Then ye better talk sense into her before she does somethin' thick. We got words fer ladies like Laveau where I come from. Don't trust 'em. Not a lightly poured ounce."

I pulled Irish away a bit. "You can't stop her?"

Irish smirked. "I like doin' thick things. I can tell she don't. To her, this ain't so stupid. So, why won't ye help her say goodbye? It 'cause ye really are rosy for her, Crowley? Ye don't wanna share?"

My hand shot out, clutching her by her jaw. Words didn't come. I simply squeezed and glowered. Irish didn't fight back.

"Quit pussy-footin' then," she squeezed out.

"What do you even care about any of this?" I asked.

"I had a fella once, ye know. Married we was. Weren't much to look at, but I loved him at a time. Then he got hold of a bottle. Liked to grab me, like ye are now."

I let her go, my gaze falling to the ground.

"Got off on hittin' me. Loved usin' a belt to show me my place. Prolly had li'l ones by more'n half the ladies in town. One night, he comes staggerin' in, langers drunk and in a right funk. I could tell he was lookin' for a scuffle, so I gutted him. Watched his insides paint the whole feckin' floor before packin' a bag, and I left."

Irish looked over at the vampire, but only for a moment before returning her eyes to me. "Rosa . . . She ought to have somethin' better."

I took a step back, letting the weight I was carrying but couldn't feel rest against the wall. I shook my head. "Rosa had that already. Some miracles only come once. And I'm—"

"Crowley!" a deep voice shouted from outside. "James Crowley, come out, come out, wherever you are."

Pushing Irish aside, I darted to the window and peered out. Roo's carriage sat in the road outside of Laveau's, driven by a different kid holding a torch. From my vantage, I could see Roo's wolf snout sticking out between the curtains, facing Laveau's.

"Feck's he?" Irish asked, squeezing her way beside me.

"You took someone from me, Crowley!" Roo yelled. "Someone that means a lot."

"That voice," Irish said. "Ain't that yer friend from earlier?"

"We ain't friends," I said, then, under my breath, grumbled, "I don't have time for this."

Damn Rosa for mentioning Laveau's name and giving that bastard a lead. I'd honestly forgotten, what with finding that Hell club and giant turtle monsters. But this was why I couldn't have her involved in these things.

"Should I kill him?" Irish asked, licking her lips. "C'mon, lemme gut him."

I barred her with one arm and set my pistol along the sill to steady my aim. Then, I let her rip. The silver round sliced through the canvas, hitting Roo in the flank. He roared, flailing enough to tear through the curtains and fall out into the street. Pedestrians screamed and fled the sound of the gunshot.

"Drop your weapon!" the marshal ordered, running out of a nearby building with three others. Looked like they'd been on a stakeout as well. "On the ground."

The marshals closed in on him, yelling at all bystanders to leave the area. Silver steaming from the wound, Roo's fists pounded into the stone as he pushed off and up. I almost heard the marshals piss themselves as he rose, a tremendous half-man beast. His growl practically made the window vibrate.

"M-m-monster!" the youngest of the marshals screamed and started firing off at random.

The one with the port-colored birthmark had enough wits about him to yell for the kid to stop before he killed someone. Luckily, one of his bullets struck Roo in the shoulder. Unluckily for them, it was barely more than a mosquito bite to a werewolf.

I glanced over at Tourmaline, who was absolutely gleeful.

He must have really had a thing for this vampire seductress, exposing himself like this.

The kid in the carriage snapped the reins, taking off without Roo. Some bit of loyalty there. Before he got far, Roo grabbed it by the back wheel. The whole wagon came to a halt, and everything else seemed to slow down. With a tremendous roar and display of strength, Roo whipped the carriage around and flung it across the road at the lawmen. One—the trigger-happy guy—was crushed. The others dove, barely finding safety.

"Rougarou, how dare you show your true self here like this!" Marie Laveau shouted as she threw open the front door. "Be gone!"

Roo stood upright, not even the slightest bit of concern that he was surrounded. "James Crowley! He in there?"

"He is not," Marie said calmly. Damballah, her snake, raised its head and hissed.

"You!" He looked past Marie to Rosa, standing just behind her. I watched her eyes go wide with dread. Sure, she'd seen bizarre things, but nothing like a drooling were-beast. "Tell me where he is."

"We gotta get down there," Irish said to me.

I kept my arm in place, sealing Irish off from hopping down and blowing my cover. Seeing Rosa in danger brought back too many painful memories, but I couldn't abandon the post.

"You will leave or consider our truce over," Laveau said, stomping forward.

"Truce," he growled. "Your days are done, you old relic."

"Old?" Laveau's face contorted with anger in a way I didn't think her gentle soul allowed. She pulled a vial out of her satchel and spilled its contents over her front porch. Her lips moved with words I couldn't hear, then she blew a kiss. In an instant, the ground in front of her house went up in white-hot flame.

Roo leaped out of the way. As he did, the remaining marshals found their footing and shot at him while they sought cover.

"Get her!" Roo ordered.

He wasn't alone, apparently. Shadows dashed across rooftops, moving on all fours. His pack, big ones and small ones too.

"Feck out the way, Crowley. I ain't standin' around any longer!" Irish bit into my arm hard to get me to move. She must've had quite the shock when I didn't react. Then, when she tasted no blood, her brow furrowed. She grasped my pistol. I elbowed her in the chin. She staggered back, and as I turned, I saw eyes glinting in the darkness of the stairwell.

"Irish, down!"

Young, feral vampires snuck up the stairs behind me to free their maker. Rosa, Irish . . . all the humans I couldn't kick from my life had distracted me. One more second and Tourmaline would've been free.

The vamps bore their fangs and hissed. I didn't hesitate. Hurdling over Irish, I put a silver bullet through the head of the one nearest Tourmaline. They were quick but nowhere near as fast as their maker.

She watched calmly as I slid, grasping one of my handmade stakes and plunging it through the chest of another hard enough to send him flipping down the stairs. Like dominoes, they tumbled backward, landing in a writhing heap at the bottom. Idly, my mind drifted to that poor drunk downstairs. Could only imagine the shape he was in.

As I brought my revolver up to plug one of the vicious devils, another rammed me from the side, and we smacked into the wall. The sucker was huge, and he was on me like flies on shit, swiping and biting—and predictable. Problem with beings of this size, they never really had to learn to fight. They used their size to intimidate and manhandle. But after facing Otaktay the Yeti, I was less than worried.

When he went left, I struck right. His clawed fist came around, forcing me to duck. While down there, I unleashed a salvo of punches and covered him with a score of nasty bruises—fat good they would do.

The back of his fist hit me hard.

Thing about striking wildly is if you can send enough blows, eventually, those chaotic movements pay off.

I went stumbling, toppling over something I couldn't see. When I came to a stop on my hands and knees, two things happened. One, my arm slipped on a pool of blood, sliding out underneath me. And two, my knife broke from my grip.

Scrambling to get into a position where I could pull up my handgun, a swift kick to my midsection stopped the action. I suppose he hoped to knock the wind out of me, but shame on him for not knowing I had none in me to begin with.

I turned, fell to my back and hip-fired. A .45 caliber cartridge exploded from my barrel and buried itself right between the brute's eyes. Then he was no more—just a cloud of fiery dust.

"Crowley, what are these th—"

A scratching, wrenching sound issued above, and a second later, the ceiling crumbled as another vamp fell through. I spun just in time to watch two fleshy hands wrap around Irish's throat. Saliva dripped from gnashing fangs. Irish screamed and unloaded both her pistols into its stomach. There was enough force to knock it off her, but those plums weren't silver. I gripped a stake from my belt and tossed it to her. The vampire rose for a second attempt, and she used its momentum to spear it through the heart.

Then, with a screaming hiss that rose above the range of human hearing, its skin sloughed off, the black, stringy muscles and bones showing through before it erupted into a plume of ash.

"Hell's feckin' bells, Bram was right!" she exclaimed, and I couldn't tell if she was terrified or excited. "Them things're real."

She looked to me, and we exchanged a brief nod. What else was there to say, with proof staring her right in the face.

From behind, a nightstalker screeched and leaped at me like a grunch on wild shrooms, swinging a stake of its own. I whirled, parrying the blow with my pistol. I hated being on the defensive. Irish strafed beside us, unloading round after useless round into the vamp. Just mere flesh wounds.

Outside was more screaming and gunshots. The sound of flesh rending.

Rosa . . .

Marie was more powerful than she let on, but so was a pissed-off werewolf.

"Irish, I have them!" I yelled. "You get down there."

Without hesitation, Irish took off toward the window. Her boot struck the sill, but she was met by a vampire swinging through. Its bare, taloned feet hit her in the chest, and she careened across the room into the wall.

What came next was chaos.

Three more of the beasts followed. I fired, putting one down immediately. Then I turned toward Irish. An unhinged jaw lurched for her, but to her credit, she was scrappy and held it away.

"Irish!" I tried to help, but I was surrounded. The remaining bullet cases from my left pistol hit the floor, their former inhabitants taking down at least two more vampires in their destructive wake. But it wasn't enough. One grabbed hold of me, rooting me in place. We grappled, me being unable to get a good angle with my Peacemaker.

Beyond the biting of my combatant, Irish ripped a shred of wood off the wall and stabbed madly. Blood sprayed in a wide arc, turning her clothes and face crimson. Her scream was primeval—a mixture of rage, confusion, and fear. Like it or not, she was meeting, face-to-face, the creatures her boss had long spoken of. It was a wonder to see, even in the little snippets I'd been afforded. A human—no experience fighting Nephilim or demons—and she was kicking ass. She just kept stabbing, driving the vampire back.

I yanked my right hand free and fired a slug through the soft skin beneath its jaw. Silver, steam, and brain matter spewed up through the top of its dome.

Too late.

Through the cloud of ash, I could see Irish and her vamp hit Tourmaline hard enough to cause her to swing. Loosened by the collapsed rooftop, the beam she was attached to fractured and snapped. Tourmaline dropped, and with her position shifted, thanks to Irish, my silver knife missed her chest and only sliced deep through her thigh. She wailed in agony.

I lunged to scoop up the knife and attack, but the blade stopped inches from her chest when her hand shot out and clutched me by the neck with such raw power, all my momentum stopped. She pivoted to me, eyes burning yellow with rage.

Irish reared back and batted Tourmaline in the head with another stake. Poor girl didn't have a clue. If only she knew how to properly kill them. The wood snapped, and Tourmaline didn't even budge.

"Tragic," she spat. "*Aurait fait une bonne pute.*"

With the flick of her wrist, the back of Tourmaline's hand collided with my chest and sent me soaring bodily toward the window. I snagged the sill before crashing all the way through. Hanging there, struggling to pull myself up, all I could do was watch as Irish gawked at the broken stake.

Leg still steaming from my silver-dusted knife, Tourmaline hobbled forward. She grabbed Irish by her longer-than-normal red hair, yanked her down to her hunched-over level, and plunged needle-sharp teeth into the side of her neck.

Irish's eyes rolled back as—unlike in my vision—Tourmaline didn't take her time to savor her. The last thing I saw before the sill snapped free and I dropped to St. Anne's Street was the spray of red as her fangs tore free.

Irish fell as I did, throat shredded. I didn't even see her hit the ground.

SIXTEEN

There's nothing in this world like an old friend who's still there for you through thick and thin, muck and mire. It's another one of those corny lessons a long enough life teaches you. So what if that friend happens to have four hooves?

At some point during the fracas, Timperina escaped Laveau's side yard, and my rump landed on her saddle instead of the street. Now, I don't wanna oversell it. Falling a couple of stories wouldn't have mattered to me much in the end, but it's the thought. Timp saw me in danger and rose to the occasion as only a friend would.

I clutched her mane to stay on, then looked up. Tourmaline darkened the window with two lesser vampires holding her upright. She sneered, her teeth slick with fresh blood.

"You aren't even worth my maker's time, *Hamsa*," she said. "Enjoy the company of angels."

Timp whinnied and kicked, her rear hooves darting backward. I heard the grunt before turning to see she'd struck a werewolf sneaking up on us. The furball toppled ass over tea kettle, skidding across the stone toward Laveau's. My gaze was torn between there and Tourmaline.

This was mayhem like St. Anne's Street had likely never witnessed. Windows were shattered. People were screaming, swearing, running. Shadows moved like ghosts. I was barely able to register some of it.

In front of me, werewolves attacked the marshals, one being dragged down the street by his leg. One was crouched behind a barrel, aiming at nothing, frozen by fear. I could feel the sharp tingle of Shar's wrath as I weighed my decision.

"Damn you, Roo!" I shouted.

I whipped Timp around. The beast she'd kicked was already back up but dazed. I charged, slashing it with my knife as it tried to find its bearings.

"Stay far out of sight, girl. No matter what. You hear? I'll whistle for you when it's clear," I said as we passed Marie's charred porch. I stood on the saddle, dove from her back, and bounded through the front door with reckless abandon.

Deep claw marks marred the bookcase in the foyer. Tables and shelves were busted, and all Laveau's oddities were spilled all over.

"Come out, Voodoo Queen," I heard Roo's resounding voice echo. "I only want to talk."

"Roo!" I yelled. "It's me you want."

Shadows darted deeper inside. I pressed forward with my knife in hand, checking corners. No time to waste reloading. In quarters this close, I'd risk putting a bullet through anyone. An unfortunate marshal was flat upon the table, eyes still open, a deer antler candlestick poking out of his chest.

I brushed through a beaded curtain and into Laveau's small hallway leading to her main room. Claws raced toward my head, and I ducked, coming up with a backhanded stab into a werewolf's chest. A howl quickly transitioned to a wheeze as the air left its lungs. It wasn't Roo.

"C'mon, you bitch," Roo cursed. "They worth dying over?"

"They are guests in my home, unlike you," Laveau replied, and unlike earlier, Damballah was no longer with her.

The place wasn't big, but there were plenty of nooks and crannies in which to hide or stay unseen. Ripping my dagger free, I rushed into the next room. Rougarou had Laveau cornered between a wall and an armoire where Bram had been healing. The bed was overturned, and he was nowhere in sight.

"Leave her be, Roo," I warned, squeezing the grip of my knife.

He glanced back, snout twitching with anger. "You took her from me!"

"Tourmaline's alive. Whatever you monsters have with each other, it can go on."

"You don't get to tell me what to do, cowboy. That's your problem, no respect."

"This curse upon you shall be nothing compared to what I have wrought for your trespassing," Laveau said. "You shall not know love. Your children will mature frail and lacking vigor."

"Crescent City has moved on from you, witch!" Roo turned his attention back to her and swiped. Yet there was no blood. His claws went right through her and sunk into the wall, causing him to get stuck.

Marie Laveau had a lot of tricks up her sleeve. I'd never seen her illusion magic before, but it was a thing to behold. The apparition of her fizzled away, a watermelon where the visage of her head had been clunked to the floor in its place.

The doors of the wardrobe flung open, and Rosa came out screaming. All that pent-up anger and grief burst out of her with force almost as potent as her gun. She unloaded the chamber of her five-shooter into Roo's back until he was slumped against the wall. By the end of it, she stood there panting.

"Rosa!" I called. "Rosa!"

No answer. I wasn't shocked. Things in Dead Acre happened so fast she didn't really have a chance to grasp what the necromancer had truly done. She'd seen as the dead rose, heeding the commands of her once-friend and simple bartender, Mr. Phelps. All in a haze of confusion that could easily be chalked up to her fear feeding the imagination.

But to witness the existence of a werewolf face-to-face. To see magic and mystery firsthand—that was a thing that could break most mortal minds.

And Rougarou wasn't down and out. So when he inevitably moved, I rushed forward, grabbed Rosa, and spun around, so when he tore his claws free of the wall, they scored my back instead of hers.

Hers pounded the wardrobe as the potency of his strike made me stagger. I reeled on him and brought my knife to bear. The first slash caught two of Rougarou's weaponized fingers and severed them clean off. Laced with silver, the blade cut through like he was made of butter. He howled and came at me, giant paws around my neck, me swinging to catch him somewhere vital.

"Stop!" Rosa's voice cracked like thunder. I don't know exactly what happened, but Roo and I stopped as if winter had dropped. We stared at each other, both clearly wanting to tear each other to pieces but unable to.

Damballah slithered out from under Bram's overturned bed, snared Roo by the ankle, and sank her teeth in. He roared in pain, then roared some more as vines from a wicked-looking plant in the backyard flew through the window. He tried to fight them but remained semistunned as the snake coiled up and around his body, holding his limbs tight in spots so the vines could take hold of his arms and chest.

Then they yanked him against the back wall and straight through in a cloud of dust. Damballah dropped to the floor where he had been. It all made me realize just how prepared Laveau was for such an attack. Good on her for thinking clearly.

"James, Rosa, we must go," Laveau said, appearing in the doorway back to her quarters.

My eyes darted to see her before my head could move. A line of blood was drawn down the center of her forehead. More of it dripped from an open slash on her palm, which she extended toward Damballah. The snake slithered to climb to Laveau's shoulder.

Rosa didn't move, empty gun still raised and hands quivering. When I regained use of my body, I crossed the two steps to her and took her by the hands.

"Rosa, Rosa, stay with me. C'mon!" I stared down the barrel of her Colt. Her finger hadn't left the trigger.

Growling from every direction informed my next move. The deceitful werewolf could wait.

"Gotta move, sweetheart," I said, soft. My thoughts were singular: I had to get Rosa to safety. She shook her head and blinked.

"I-I-I . . ." The shock had her fully.

"Rosa."

"E-Everything I gathered . . . Laveau's stuff . . . I need it."

Her hips pivoted like she was planning to run somewhere and retrieve whatever Laveau had her fetching to contact her dead husband.

"Don't be a fool and join him!" I took her by the wrist. For a second, she resisted, then gave in as I followed after Laveau.

Snarls resonated from outside. We raced through to meet Laveau in the hallway. She stood by the narrow door I'd assumed to be a closet.

"In here," Marie said. She opened the door, and it indeed appeared to be a closet. I felt foolish cramming in there with the two women, but then, Marie moved right through the back wall. Without waiting, I followed, and we, too, slipped beyond the illusionary wall.

Instead of winding up in the backyard as expected, we stood in a four-by-four-foot space. The darkness was near complete, but I could see well enough to spot a staircase before us and a hole in the ground barely wide enough to squeeze through.

"Down we go," Marie said, pulling a lever I hadn't noticed. The ground shook, sending dust billowing around us, and a real hunk of wall shifted into place.

"That should keep us from their claws for a time," she said. "Let me get a look at her." She took Rosa by the shoulders and stared into her eyes for a few long seconds. Damballah did the same. "You will be okay. We can't stay here."

With us blocked in from behind, she took something off the wall, but with her form covering it, I couldn't see clearly what it was. After some low whispers, green light bloomed within a lantern.

"Come," she said, raising it up.

In the sickly light, I saw Bram and Harker already waiting for us at the bottom of the stairs. The former leaned on the latter's shoulder, conscious and upright. A few of Laveau's followers were with them. None of it mattered. I turned to Rosa, who backed up to the wall breathing so quickly, I feared she might pass out.

"Wh . . . Wh . . ."

"Rosa, look at me." I did as Marie had and took her by the shoulders. Her eyes seemed to stare through me. No, around me. Down at my side, where Roo's claws had traced around my back and rib cage. My shirt was torn, revealing deep gashes yet no blood.

"What are you?" she asked softly. Words I never wanted to hear. Not who—*what*—as, for the first time since we'd reunited, all the clues about my true nature merged in her head. Not *exactly* what I was, but the important part. That I, James Crowley, wasn't human. Not like her.

"Now is not the time, James," Laveau said, hand on my shoulder. "We must get to safety." She squeezed by me and took Rosa around the waist, comforting her as they hurried down the stairs.

Rougarou's words from earlier that day echoed in my brain, taunting me about living such a long life, watching everyone around me die. I couldn't care less about that infernal tingling from Shar trying to scold me. I'd barely even realized my chest was burning like hot coals had been poured all over it.

Fuck vampires and werewolves and this Betrayer . . . I had more important things to tend to.

SEVENTEEN

We made our way through the dark tunnels in solemn silence until Bram finally asked the question I'd been dreading.

"Where is Irish?"

I thought back to her swinging that stake like a club, shooting bullets made of regular iron. Helpless in the face of immortal beings. I let about ten steps pass without a response. Then, I had no choice. "Dead."

Bram dragged his good leg to a halt, forcing Harker to pause their march. He looked at me with a lethally severe expression. "How?"

"Trying to protect you, for whatever her reasons. Wasn't prepared for what that meant here."

We stood in solemn silence, each of us afraid to meet eyes with one another.

Bram slowly nodded, sucking in a lung. "Yes, well, none of us were prepared for what befell us in the swamp. She chose this job, and I brought her here. I will carry that guilt for my remaining days. What happened—"

"While I appreciate the sensitivity of this subject," Marie interjected. "We must keep moving."

I glared at Bram, and he gazed back, eyes glistening. I nodded. He had to play strong to keep hope in his dwindling party, but he cared. I saw it. The news pulled at his heartstrings, even if it might never convince him to abandon his mad quest for truth.

Harker, speaking not a word of protest—which was entirely against his nature—followed Laveau as we twisted and wound our way through the tunnels.

Crescent City was home to many secrets. I couldn't guess where this one led. I reloaded my pistols as we walked. My Winchester was gone, lost to Roo back in the arena. Felt such a trite thing to worry about when we'd just lost one of our own. Still, I'd have felt much better knowing I had a rifle.

After a short time, we found ourselves at an impassable stone wall.

"Great," Harker moaned. That was more like it. "The wrong way."

"There are no wrong ways, my friend. Only detours," Bram replied.

Laveau brushed cobwebs off the stone, running her hand along the side until something clicked. Pressing her shoulder against the rock, she started to push. Dust fell, but it barely budged. I squeezed past the group to help. Rosa averted her gaze as I went by, which hurt me more than silver ever could. More dust kicked off as I pushed, making the others cough. The heavy stone swung aside with a groan, and we found ourselves in a torch-lit crypt—a warren of stone columns and low vaulted ceilings.

"*This* is safer?" Harker asked.

"As safe as it gets," Laveau said.

Feet shuffled from somewhere to the side. I whipped around, Peacemaker trained on a man's heart.

"Easy now," he said, his accent thick and Dutch. "I am a friend." He stepped into the torchlight, wearing the robes and regalia of a high-ranking Roman Catholic priest.

"Archbishop," Laveau intoned. She rushed ahead, and they gave each other a light embrace. "Forgive us, this late hour."

He was a man of middle-age and medium build, but a bit thick around the gut. Seemed like the kind of guy who ate well and often. A widow's peak sat atop his head, revealing liver spots. Thick, angular eyebrows made him look dour, though he had kind eyes.

"Never. Praise God, you're alive. The city is abuzz with news of monster sightings and mayhem near your home." He looked up at the rest of us. I'm pretty sure my mouth was agape. A holy man and the Voodoo Queen, embracing?

"Forgive me," he said, bowing his head. "I am Archbishop Francis August Janssens."

"You are colloquial with an archbishop?" Harker took the words right out of my mouth.

"Strange friendships are forged in strange places," Laveau said.

"She is modest," Archbishop Janssens said. "Just as the Apostle Paul suffered from a thorn in his flesh, so too did I. However, the Lord saw fit to send me aid in a way Paul never received. The Madame helped me. A healer. Protector of children. Champion of the Church. If Marie Laveau's are the tools of the Devil, then I am reprobate. Yet, here I remain."

"You simply do not know me well enough," Laveau told him.

They exchanged coy smiles. There was something there. Something forbidden that, in this life, neither acted on. I recognized it because I'd been getting used to the feeling.

"We can use a place to hide, Frank," Laveau said.

"Of course. Of course." He stepped aside, flourishing his hand toward the chamber. "Consider this sanctuary for as long as you need. I will have food and clean clothes brought down from the rectory."

"You are a saint."

"Not yet." He winked. More playful banter that left me feeling empty. As they chattered a bit more, Harker brought Bram to some steps and sat him down. Rosa wandered aimlessly in the other direction. Lost.

"Leave her be, lad," Bram said to me. I stood silently, staring. "What happened up there anyway? Soon as the ruckus began, we were sent to hide. Not my choice, but a bum leg is a bum leg. I'd have only gotten in the way."

"What happened?" Harker bristled. "I'll tell you what happened. Him, her, they all got us caught up in some crazy nonsense! We shouldn't have ever picked her up."

He was talking about Rosa, and I'd have slugged him in the gut if I didn't agree with him.

"Settle down, Harker," Bram said.

"Settle down? I steadied my tongue when we were fleeing, when news of Irish's death meant so little because 'she was prepared.' But *I* have never done more than draw pictures of what I truly believed to be the ramblings of a madman hopeful to write the next great fiction!"

Bram cast his gaze down. Harker remained relentless. "You think I don't have ears? Whatever attacked Laveau's, it wasn't human. That wasn't normal."

"We aren't after the normal," Bram said. "I am sorry you believed me to be full of chicaneries, but I've been nothing but honest with any of you."

"Right, yeah. The *supernatural.* I think it's time we went

home, Bram. We've seen enough here. Irish is dead. Who's next?"

"What's done is done," I cut in. I didn't mean to be so cold about it, but my focus was elsewhere. Not to mention, the itch in my chest from Shar demanding a conversation was growing overwhelming. She was last on my list to talk to.

"But Harker is right," I continued. "Bram, you've gotta see you two are in over your head here. When you seek dark things that shouldn't exist, you can't expect to survive."

"So, it wasn't a man who killed her?" Bram couldn't mask the glimmer of excitement at the notion.

"A woman."

"Just a woman?"

I didn't answer.

He took me by the shoulders and shook. "Her death can't be in vain. If she discovered something here, please, you must tell us."

I pushed him away. "When you can move well enough, take a ship back east. Leave."

"He's right," Harker said.

Bram's lips trembled as he shook his head. "Irish will be missed, but our work is not over."

"Then you'll die with her!" I barked. Silence ensued, my words echoing around the vaulted ceiling, enveloping us.

"That's enough, James," Laveau said. She strolled toward us, stroking Damballah.

"They shouldn't be here," I said.

"Who among us is where we should be?"

That was a loaded question, if ever there was one. Though most didn't know their destinations, I did. Always did. Just never knew for sure why, and I can say with all assurance it wasn't to watch a brave woman die at the hands of some god-forsaken Nephilim.

"Must you help everyone, Laveau? Them. Him. And who knows what you've been filling Rosa's head with." I've always had tremendous respect for Laveau, but I'd had enough. I rose to my full height before her. She didn't flinch.

"Yet my home is in shambles because of you," she said calmly. "And I would not turn you away even now had I known the future. Because there is hope for you still, as is there for all. All there is left to do is pray."

"Praying is for people who leave things to chance," I said through my teeth.

"Praying is for those who understand they are not the one in control," Marie said.

My teeth ground as I growled low, unsure what to say. The itch in my chest grew unbearable. Shar had to wait, but I wasn't sure how much longer I could hold out.

"That's it," I said to myself.

The three of them answered, "What?" but I turned around and stormed down the crypt. Irish probably would've wanted to die just like she had—a warrior's death against a worthy inhuman foe—but nearly everyone else would now join her by being sucked into my world. Enough was enough.

I found Rosa standing near a sarcophagus and yelled, "Rosa!"

She yelped and hopped back, snapped from whatever reflections she was lost in. "Jesus Christ, James. What is wrong with you?"

"Everything you saw in Dead Acre was real," I said. "A Nephilim known as a necromancer killed your husband and summoned the dead to try and kill us. In Revelation Springs, a demon possessed the native man who caused all that chaos and unleashed Ace upon the town."

Her brow furrowed. "What?"

"You asked what I am. I'm a Hand of God. A Black Badge.

It's my duty to hunt down perversions of life such as those and destroy them in the name of Heaven. You're not crazy. I can't bleed 'cause I ain't human. Not anymore. I died that day, long ago, when I saved you and your mama from Ace. Heaven brought me back."

She swallowed, still unable to make eye contact. "From the dead?"

I nodded. I knew what she was thinking. If I'd been brought back, maybe her Willy could be too. I needed her to know that wasn't the case.

"There's more to this world than most people think," I said. "And I may be punished or scorned for telling you the truth, but you've seen enough to know it. And you deserve to know why I didn't want you trifling with things unknown. The dead can speak. Sometimes, sure, they return. But they ain't never the same. And if you keep pushing, I don't know . . ." I paused. She looked up at me, right into my eyes. "You might cross a line you can't turn back from. And it might be you I'm asked to hunt."

I winced and leaned on the sarcophagus to get my balance. Rosa caught me. The itch in my chest became a deep, searing burn. I'd trade silver for it.

"James, I . . ." Rosa's words trailed off. It was no wonder she was speechless. Not every day you learn the swarthy reality of our world.

"You don't need to say anything," I said. "I just wanted you to finally know the truth. I was never trying to control you or keep you from anything *good.* Only to protect you. But you don't need me for that. Facing down werewolves and Scuttlers—you're a finer outlaw than I ever was."

A tear rolled down her cheek.

"Do what you have to. Keep on living, Rosa," I said. "All I wanted was to keep the dead from dragging you down. But what hubris for a dead man himself to say it."

I wiped the tear off her cheek with my thumb and held her gaze overly long. Then I reached into my satchel, scooped a handful of silver bullets, and slapped them down on top of the sarcophagus, letting them roll and clatter to the floor.

"Silver kills things like Roo better than iron," I said. "Keep them loaded. Just in case. I have a job to finish."

I turned to head around the corner and left her to herself. The truth would set her free of any need for me. She couldn't have known, but I did. The moment I got out of here, I wouldn't see her again.

"James." She stopped me in my tracks. "The day before he died, I drank too much and said awful things. I told Willy he was boring me, that he wouldn't ever be more than a worthless cobbler. That was the last thing I ever said to him."

I sighed and glanced back over my shoulder. Her eyes were wet, glinting as torchlight danced in their reflection.

"Liquor has a foul mouth," I said. "He knows you didn't mean it."

She sniveled. "How can you know?"

"You said those vows, richer poorer, health sickness, all that? You don't go through all that for someone who's worthless."

The corner of her mouth lifted in a smile. A frail, pathetic thing, but there, nonetheless. I bobbed my head and spent all the willpower I had left to continue along. Being around her was trouble for me and for anybody else unlucky enough to be with us.

Bram and Harker sat eating stew I guess the bishop had sent down, listening to Laveau as she spoke last rights for Irish. Not in the proper Catholic way, but in her way. Considering her friends, maybe it was two sides of the same coin.

I waved a silent goodbye as I left the crypt to fulfill my duty as a Black Badge.

EIGHTEEN

Chest burning so deep it felt like my soul was unraveling, I climbed the stairs out of the crypt, emerging into the St. Louis Cathedral. The place looked like a goddamn palace meant for a sultan or a sheik. Hard for me to imagine a God who sat in the luxuries of Heaven would care about the platitudes of Earth. A semidomed ceiling soared above me, painted in what looked like a depiction of the ascension of Christ.

Behind the altar, the words *Te deum laudamus te dominum confitemur* were written.

"We praise thee, God. We confess thee, Lord."

Well, I've got a confession. I'm sick to death of the shit. A good woman died because of my hunt for the wicked, and I found it difficult to reconcile the idea of an Almighty God with less than almighty power.

Moonlight filtered through the narrow windows out front. Otherwise, it was all candles set for prayers at the dedicated side altars. Some half burned, others full, others down to the wick, like a field of low-hanging stars.

Other than me, it was empty. Just row after row of barren pews.

Empty. Just the way I liked it.

I stopped by the main altar, where a shaft of light from the windows around its arch illuminated the Virgin Mary holding a cross and chalice. I couldn't help but notice the motes of dust dancing in it. Even here, in this holy place, the scene reminded me of the old saying: *From dust, we came, and to dust, we return.*

The burn intensified, sending me to my knees. Finally, I pulled my shaving mirror out and set it on the altar.

"Have you lost yourself, Crowley?" Shar hissed, her form seeming to drown out the candles with its own whitish aura. "Have you completely lost sight of your purpose?"

"Have you?" I groaned, the burning vanishing the instant I answered her, leaving me hollow and, for whatever reason . . . missing it. "You've got me chasing ghosts in a city full of them. Tourmaline said it. This Betrayer of yours ain't here."

"He is."

"He ain't!" I slammed a fist down, knocking a communion bowl off the altar.

"You are too distracted."

"No, Shar. I'm seeing clearly."

"The things you revealed to that Child. You have doomed her."

"She deserved the *truth*!" I shouted so loud, it repeated back to me three times in the immense chamber.

"What makes her so special?"

"What makes *you* such an asshole that you think only special people deserve honesty?"

The windows all around me shattered into a million pieces, spraying inward like they'd been hit by explosives.

However, Shar's following words were explosive in their own right. "You have forgotten your place."

We stared at each other, me watching what amounted to

steam floating around in the mirror's reflection. I waited for her to say more, but she remained silent.

"Shargrafein, Rosa's no demon," I said. "She's not a witch. She'll do nothing to harm the White Throne. She's good."

"Ah, so now you are the judge of good and evil, Crowley. Is that it? You know what will happen—what always happens. She will dig deeper into the unknown. Get lost in mysticism until the darkness takes hold. She'll never be content with a routine life. Damnation will weave its way into her soul."

"I'm choosing to have faith." The words were soft, strained, and buried under a two-ton pile of doubt.

"No, you chose selfishness. To unburden your grief to her detriment. Did it lighten the load, Crowley? Do you now feel capable of performing your duties?"

My hands squeezed into fists. I glared at the shattered glass all around me and then at the colossal cross hanging above the altar. "You want me to kill vampires, fine. Tourmaline went and made it personal anyhow, but—"

"You were not sent after her."

"What's the damn difference!" I roared. "She's a killer. Confessed to murdering a senator, for Christ's sake. How is she unworthy of your judgment?"

"Because she cannot reveal the location of her maker if she is vanquished."

"I'll make her tell me first."

"In that, you have already failed."

"I never fail twice," I said, standing tall. "That's why you keep me around, right? For what I just did with Rosa, you oughta smite me. But you won't."

"Your overconfidence amuses me, Child," she said.

"Don't call me that."

"Your value is proximity," she continued like I hadn't spoken.

"The Betrayer never stays in one place for long. If it is not you, then it is no one this time. And if you fail—"

"If he's here, I'll find him."

The mist in my shaving mirror went dark. Shar's voice, usually resonant like a church organ, went utterly silent. Considering our eternal battle to get the last word over each other, I found that odd. Then, cold started creeping in, tracking muddy boot prints on the carpet of comfort I'd built, thinking that here, in this place, I was free of Hell's gaze.

My hand dropped to the pearl grip of my pistol.

"Who's there?" I called out. No answer. "I ain't gonna ask twice!"

I went to turn. A *thwerp* preceded a bolt attached to rope puncturing the wrist of my gun hand and pinning it against the altar. A perfect shot. From all the way at the cathedral's entrance, two figures all in black approached wielding crossbows. Their hoods were up, casting shadows over masks with upside-down crosses painted in red.

"Who in the Hell?"

Before thinking twice, I yanked my arm forward, ripping free of the bolt. Another shot aimed to crucify me like Christ, just missed my other hand as I scrambled for a gun. A third zipped over my head. I vaulted over the altar, taking cover on the other side.

Upside-down cross masks? My first thought was Tourmaline's Underdark and the symbols I'd seen there. Nothing else rang a bell. I hadn't noticed anything like these men down there.

"Put those down, and we can talk!" I shouted. Still no answer, just ragged breathing through the slits in masks as they neared. "All right, fair warning."

I grabbed the service bowl I'd knocked down earlier and flung it out from cover. A bolt struck it in midair, eliciting a loud clang.

Hoping their focus was elsewhere, I popped up and fired, catching one of the masked figures below the jawline. He rasped as blood sprinkled the pews like some kind of sacrificial lamb. The masked assailant collapsed to a knee, but there was no sizzling or silver steam, even though my gun was loaded with the like.

Were they human?

I prepared to charge, but all my body managed to do was fall forward. I looked back. Two more strung bolts crossed behind me, having punctured my ankles while I was kneeling. Their ropes were attached to the crossbows held by two more masked individuals crouched on either side high above inside the clerestory windows.

With an irritated grunt, I reached back, grabbed the ropes in one fist, and pulled with all my might. One of the masked men held on, but the other fell, and their ropes crossed, causing both to plunge. They hit the floor hard. I drew my knife and slashed the ropes so I could pull my ankles free.

The bolt in my left one was really jammed in there. Stuck on a bone, maybe. I couldn't jostle it.

The forward attacker appeared around the altar, leaving me no time. He fired another bolt, and I raised my hand to take it through the center of my palm. With my fingers intact, I gripped it and pulled him toward me.

"Who are you!" I growled.

With my leg still pinned, I dragged him down to my level and bashed him in the face with the butt of my pistol. The same sound the bowl had made echoed loudly. The masks were dull plate metal as if we were in the goddamn medieval times.

He clicked something in his hand, and thick smoke poured out around us. I couldn't see anything. Which, since I couldn't feel, was like chopping the whiskers off a cat. My next punch cracked the marble flooring as my foe kicked free.

The smoke didn't stay thick long, and as I raised my gun to put an end to him, another bolt went clean through my arm. Then, from another direction, through my other arm. A third through my right leg, joining the one already stuck in my left. The three surviving masked figures gripped the ends of the ropes and pulled them taut like I was a kebab on a skewer.

"What is this!" I growled. "Did Tourmaline send you?" I thrashed this way and that, but my limbs merely slid on the ropes.

"I heard you were looking for me," spoke a refined voice. It possessed an almost angelic quality. Smooth, resonant, and with the slightest hint of an accent I couldn't quite place—somewhere in the Far East.

"Depends who you are," I replied, still testing what it might take to pull free.

Candles along the aisle went out one at a time, a shadow creeping closer as a presence neared. It stooped over the body of the masked man I'd shot. I could make out little but heard the sound of flesh tearing, then gurgling.

The downed assassin coughed, and the presence whispered something to him in another language. The masked man rose, cracked his neck, then approached me as if nothing had happened. He took the end of the unmanned rope in my ankle and held it tight.

"Nice trick," I muttered.

"Life is no trick," the shadow said.

What could I do but laugh exhaustedly? "You know, I'm getting really tired of things in this wasp nest of a city trying to kill me. So why don't we skip the banter and get to it?"

"Ah, but how many mistakes would have been solved if the culprits had merely decided to converse honestly and plainly? How many wars avoided?"

"Bold to say while you have me here like a pincushion."

"My guardians had to ensure you would play nice," he said. "My apologies. They can be . . . enthusiastic. But you will heal."

"Yeah, people usually just get right up after being crucified," I said, tugging against the restraints. "Pretty sure that's common as toast."

"But you are not so common," the presence said.

I eyed him as he casually approached, and asked, "So you know what I am?"

"I know everything about you, James Enoch Crowley."

That answer caught me. I never used my middle name. Hated it. The name of my good-for-nothing pa.

"Rougarou isn't the only one with a network of eyes," the shadow said. "Only mine is vast and sees so much more. A perk of eternity."

The man I'd shot pulled his mask off to reveal his face. I recognized the port-wine birthmark. I noticed it then, though I hadn't realized it before. His cross necklace wasn't just stuck hanging upside down. It had been designed that way.

I don't generally fall prey to fear. Without worrying I might die, nothing truly strikes me as worthy of such an emotion. However, at the moment, the shadow-man standing before me might as well have been the Devil himself—hell, maybe he was.

A preternatural fog swept through the place in the man's wake, moving like a swift-flowing river. I swallowed hard—another leftover from my old life.

"I've been waiting for you, *Hamsa*," the shadow said, using the same word Tourmaline had been calling me. "I believe you've met Mr. Chapelwaite." The man I'd believed to be a mere marshal stepped forward, a new vigor in his step. He held his mask to the side. The shadow took it from him and held it up. "I don't believe you'll be needing this anymore."

He tossed the mask with the upside-down cross amongst the pews.

"So, what's this—some kind of satanic cult? You its leader?" I asked.

He stepped closer, and the mark on my chest was like a cattle brand searing hot against my flesh. His friends were human, but the shadow definitely wasn't. "Even one such as you only sees that which you have been groomed to see."

"Who are you?" I strained against the ropes, but they'd struck true. The tips had pierced right between the bones in my wrists and ankles.

"In time, *Hamsa*," the shadow said. His eyes shifted to my Peacemaker on the ground where it had fallen. "Silver bullets? I can smell them from here. I hope you have enough."

He laughed, but it wasn't the same kind of sinister sound one expects from an overly confident Nephilim. That said, I got the distinct feeling that although this one reeked of something evil, he wasn't like anything I'd met before.

"I asked a question," I said. "I ain't fond of wasting words."

The man squatted before me. No longer bathed in shadows, I could see him clearly for the first time. He wore dark robes, crimson, the color of blood. He pulled back his hood to reveal a gaunt face—sharp lines for cheekbones. He had a firm chin covered in a thin strap of beard that lined his face upward to long black hair.

Absolutely no emotion in his features.

Like his accent, he had the appearance of someone from the desert lands to the east, if I had to wager. He didn't look particularly strong. Then again, neither do most snakes.

"You seem like a man unused to giving answers," I said. "I'll ask once more. Who are you?"

He flicked one of the ropes, and it twanged like a guitar. "I don't think you're in a place to make demands."

"All I have to do is ask, and an army of angels will be here before you can spit," I lied.

"And where have I heard claims such as these before?" His gaze wandered up to the crucifix, where the Man himself still hung in his underwear. "At least they sent someone with a measure of courage this time. And to you!" He clapped slowly. "Surviving so long on what little information they supply. Gets tiresome, though, doesn't it? Go to this place, travel to that . . . left to deduce the desires of the White Throne, yet expected to share their moral predilections. How often have you strayed from their vaguely lit path? How frequently are you threatened with eternal destruction simply for failing to comprehend their often impotent leadings?"

His words reverberated in my mind like they were my own. How did this man know so much about my dealings with Shar? Had he been listening before making his presence known?

"Nice trick, reading minds," I told him, unsure if it was true. "Or were you just eavesdropping?"

"No trick," he said. "One needs no deception when one has walked upon the same guide stones, Hand of God."

I took a beat. "So, what, you're one of us?" Twenty-so-odd years and I'd never run into another Hand of God or Black Badge or whatever. Was always told they kept us spread out so as to best battle the creeping darkness of Hell.

"Not just *one*. *The*."

As he said it, more men wearing inverted cross masks entered the cathedral, closing in on me. I knew there was a strong chance I wouldn't be leaving this place, but I also knew what I'd been told by Shar a million times before: if he wasn't for us, he was against us.

"In my time, we were called *Hamsa*," he said as four sets of hands gripped me and pulled me to my feet.

I struggled to break free, but it was futile.

"You are only acting upon your training," he said. "I will not hold it against you . . . For now."

"Who the hell are you people?" I demanded again.

"We have much in common, James. I, too, turned upon the One who only wished to save me. And I, too, did it because I was lied to, manipulated. You asked me my name, though I've gone by many." He leaned in, mouth open wide enough so I could see what were undoubtedly vampire fangs. Though his were short—evolved in a way. "You may have heard of me referred to as the Betrayer. Some have called me the Descendant of Cain, the One Who Kissed, though you would know me best by my true name: Judas Iscariot."

NINETEEN

During my formative years—a young boy living with Father Osgood in Granger's Outlook—I dutifully cleaned the church building. I listened to Bible stories since some were entertaining enough. I went through the motions when it came time for prayers. But I never truly believed anyone was listening.

However, I'd be a fool to say I didn't believe in Heaven and Hell. After all, I had a damned angel in my pocket. I just wasn't certain of anyone's true intentions. My confidence in the White Throne's power didn't extend to my understanding of what they truly wanted.

Was it to abolish evil as I'd been led to believe? Or was it simply extinguishing any threat to their seat of ultimate dominion?

None of it truly mattered. The harsh truth was I have been beholden to the One who brought me back to life and will be until the day the other side finally manages to put me down, or I outlive my usefulness. And right now, I was supposed to kill the one before me. The Vampire King. The Betrayer. And so much more than I expected.

The man who called himself Judas Iscariot was still talking, but I didn't hear a goddamned word. I was too fixated on the fact that this man was claiming to be one of the original disciples of Christ. If that were true, every question humanity had about the truth of the gospel could be answered in one interview.

Except, I figured he was just insane. Driven mad by being alive so long. And even if he told the truth, from my recollections, Judas hung himself before the supposed resurrection, which meant he couldn't know the answer to the most crucial question of all. So, to me, he was just another . . .

"Dead man walking," I said, not missing the whole pot-calling-the-kettle-black thing.

"After all this time, you still don't understand the gravity of the life you lead," he replied.

"Guess I can be a little dense. What do you want from me?"

"What makes you think I want a thing?" Judas asked.

"If you didn't, I'd be dead. Tourmaline made that clear enough. Unless I'm reading the room wrong, kill me or tell me why I'm here."

Judas walked over to the pews and motioned for his men to follow with me in tow. "Have a seat, Mr. Crowley."

"I'd rather stand."

Judas gave his men a look, and they forced me into the pew.

"That's better, no?" Judas asked. "Your whole life, you've been nothing more than a dog on someone else's chain, yes?"

"You know nothing about me."

"I know myself," Judas said. "And I know the White Throne."

"I'm my own man," I said.

"Of course you are. Let us see if I can paint a picture, shall we? You grew up in a home filled with turmoil."

"Congratulations, you've lived in the West."

He ignored me. "Your mother had no time for you. Your father was a drunk."

"Yet again—"

"You were forced to devote hours to a man of faith—a reverend? Priest . . . Yes, a Catholic. That much is clear."

It was possible the vampire was clairvoyant—one this old might have extra gifts. I let him continue. Didn't have many choices in the matter.

He placed a hand on my thigh, patting it a couple of times. "You do not believe. Never did. You found your own way. Something your mother never would have approved of. You went from being the lapdog of a drunk to the trained hound of a new man. When you died, probably by the hand that fed you, you were given a new lot in life by Heaven. However, the only thing that has changed is who holds the leash."

In a matter of minutes, this man had read my mail. He'd just encapsulated my whole life in a way I'm not sure I'd have been able to do had he put a gun to my head. One thing was certain, he was something else.

"Look, I don't know who you are, *Betrayer*, but I know for sure you ain't Judas Iscariot."

That proclamation brought something like anger flashing to his pitch-black eyes.

He sneered. "I walked with your Christ. Shared the bowl with him. Broke bread. I, too, suffered at the hands of both gods. I tasted the fruits of Heaven and Hell, and I can tell you, both sour the tongue. I alone can offer you true freedom."

"From one master to another, yet again." I glanced over my shoulder at one of the men holding me.

"These you see around you are not my slaves," Judas said. "They follow because they believe as I do. That we are all caught between the whims of two almighty beings who care nothing about us."

"I've wiped out my share of Luciferian cults," I said. "Follower is just another word for slave."

"Do you not listen? Satan. God. Me, my blood-children, we exist beyond their desires. No matter what your handler tells you. We are our own."

"Funny. I know an angel who calls everyone a child."

Judas leaned in. If he was breathing, I couldn't tell. Then again, I don't breathe either, and I suppose being as old as I am, without having aged a day, should make me at least that much less skeptical of his claims. But Judas Iscariot? Really?

"So, what," I said. "You're a Hand of God?"

"Was," Judas corrected.

"Was," I repeated with a fair share of scorn. "From what I've heard, that'd either put you in Hell or nowhere."

Judas gestured to the room. "Does this look like Hell?"

"Gotta admit, it's more colorful than I'd imagined."

"You think this a joke, *Hamsa*?"

"You know what, *Judas* . . ." I spat the word to make it extra clear I still wasn't buying what he was selling. "I'm not sure what I think about all this. Hard to develop much of a thought while I'm being strong-armed."

Judas flicked his wrist, and my captors let me go. Each grabbed hold of a shaft and pulled it free. Almost immediately, my wounds began to close.

I shrugged, shook out my arms, and straightened my sleeves.

"Is that better?" he asked.

I cracked my neck. "What's stopping me from standing up right now and leaving? Better yet . . ." I pulled my other pistol. The men around me moved to stop me, but Judas waved them off. "What's stopping me from blowing your vampiric brains out all over this pew?"

He stepped closer. Whereas Roo was just acting tough when I placed him under the aim of silver, this guy wasn't spooked. Not at all. Vampires are fast, and I think he knew that even if I pulled the trigger from only inches away, he'd evade it with ease. And if he couldn't, the look in his dark eyes made me believe it.

"I was once just like you," he said calmly. "Bound to a throne whose king was so far removed, I wouldn't have believed him real had I not walked with him."

"You're saying Jesus Himself is on the White Throne?"

"In a manner of speaking," Judas admitted. "I was just as confused as you are now—more so even. Imagine a man you called 'friend' not living up to your expectations!"

That wasn't something I had to try very hard to imagine. I'd known plenty of disappointments over the years. One that comes first to mind is Ace Ryker. We had a great thing going; him, me, and the Scuttlers. All until he took our little crew and turned us into cold-blooded killers over a few greenbacks.

"There are men and women like you all over the world," Judas said. "Some of whom have never heard the name of the Christ. Yet still, they fight for Heaven with the same fervor. The Almighty wears many masks."

I groaned. "You're no different than Shar with all your riddles and skittles."

"Shar?" Judas laughed. "As in Shargrafein?"

My stomach turned at his use of my angelic handler's proper name.

"You know her?"

"Perhaps," Judas said. "The monikers by which angels are known are not so much names as they are titles. Assuming she's not yet been killed and replaced, yes, I know her well. Very well, indeed. I take it she sent you here with little more than a command?"

"Sounds like you do know her." I turned my attention to my darkened shaving mirror, still open on the altar. Wouldn't she hear all this?

"We've had our history. You saw what happened to her when I entered, yes?"

"Completely vanished," I said.

"How would you like such obscurity from her glare? This . . . this is what I offer you. As long as I am near, she cannot see us. She is as blind to us as any other seeking to view our reflection. We are entirely hidden from the White Throne and aim to keep it that way."

I was about to answer, but then something popped into my head. "Wait, what do you mean by *we*?"

The slightest smirk crossed his features. "Ahh, so you do pay attention. My kind. Vampires, as the world has come to know us. Many think our true gift is eternal life, but no, it is anonymity. Born of both Heaven and Hell through me, we are hidden from their gaze. So, you see, Shargrafein wasn't playing games this time. She couldn't direct you because, to her, we are shadows. Darkness itself. Ever fleeting."

That got me rethinking a few things. Back when I first got to Crescent City, I was talking to Shar a block away from a vampire sucking a poor man dry. She wasn't surprised when I found him, but would she really speak so calmly with such a powerful enemy so near? Was this "Judas" telling the truth?

"All right, let's say I bite," I said. "What are you asking me to do in exchange for this freedom?"

"Only what you already wanted to do before our mutual friend spoke her piece."

I thought about it for a moment, then said, "Kill Tourmaline."

"Precisely."

"But why? I thought she was your *child*."

Judas sighed. "There are times when a child becomes so petulant, the only recourse is swift punishment."

"Sure, a lashing. But you're asking me to exterminate her?"

"A lashing is meant to teach a lesson," he said. "What happens when the lesson is never learned? She's received centuries of rebukes. I thought she'd learned, but it seems her desire to flee the shadows will never abate. Butchering a politician is one thing. I have done the same when it suits us. But gathering Nephilim and the scions of Hell, allowing her young brood to graze openly on the streets with no discipline and fight like brawlers . . ." His fists were in balls, and his tone vibrated with fury. "Our youngest are savage until groomed. If we are not purified, then we are the monsters your Shar makes us out to be."

"Look, killing a child is sick even by my standards, even if *child* is a loose definition in this case. But I've got one more objection."

Judas gestured for me to continue.

"Why not kill her yourself? Don't wanna get those ancient hands dirty?"

"Nothing so practical. The truth is, she has a piece of my heart."

"Shit. You're in love with her?"

Judas shook his head. "I'm not speaking metaphorically."

I stared at him like he had a horn growing from his skull.

"See, like us, Tourmaline once served the White Throne. Like me, she longed for escape. Bent the rules. Such as letting an innocent native boy go regardless of the devastation and destruction he'd caused."

I stayed quiet. How long had he been watching me to know about what happened in Revelation Springs?

"And so, when the time was right for the angels to try and send her to her doom against me or finally defeat me, I approached her. The only way to become whole once more, James Enoch Crowley, is to take for yourself a power you do not possess on your own. You must bond a piece of her heart to yours as she did mine and as I did Azrael's after slaying him for the White Throne."

"Azrael—*the* Azrael?" I said. "Angel of Death, Azrael?"

"The one and only," he confirmed. "You see, I said the names of angels are more akin to titles, but not Azrael. He was singular, for he was the one responsible for Lucifer's fall. He was the first betrayer, and I knew if I could harness his power, I alone would defeat death and my ties to Heaven."

Can't say I knew much about angelic pecking orders, other than the archangels ruling the roost, but Azrael was a name familiar to me from my time spent with Father Osgood. The Angel of Death, the protector of the Garden of Eden, and the one who took the firstborn children during the time of Moses.

"Long before man, the angels dwelled in peace and harmony—or so we are told," Judas went on. "But Lucifer had designs of his own. He'd gained a following, built an army right under the Almighty's nose, and when the time was right, he and his second-in-command, Azrael, would strike and claim the White Throne for themselves."

"But that's not what happened," I said.

Judas shook his head. "As soon as Lucifer declared war, Azrael's true colors showed. At first, there was no saying whether it was a loss of nerve or his plan all along, but he drove his flaming sword through Lucifer's black heart. This absolved him of the sin of insurgency and granted him a place of honor amongst the White Court."

"Like Caesar and Brutus," I commented.

"There's a long history of betrayers. Most do it with a blade for power. I did it with a kiss for a mere thirty silver coins."

"Silver . . ." I said, beginning to put the pieces together.

"Indeed. I told you I could smell it. The very sight of it

makes me sick. Part of any Nephilim's curse—as greed is a tool of Hell—and thus, yours as well."

"And wooden stakes? That got something to do with the cross?" I turned my attention to the crucifix.

"A wooden stake to anyone's heart would end them," he said. "I'm afraid that's just the nature of hearts."

That made a certain kind of sense.

"But Azrael too fell from grace. Despite his position, he wanted more. When word of his scheme reached the ears of the Throne, it was I who was dispatched to end the threat."

"To kill Azrael," I said.

"And I did."

"How does Tourmaline fit into all this?"

"It has been written, 'It is not good for man to be alone.' She was my first child, and now, like Azrael, she must be stopped," he said. "She threatens our concealment. She's upset the balance, drawn too many eyes. My firstborn children and I have lived without conflict for many ages. They were all like you, Hands of God. Powerful enough by the grace of the White Throne to receive a piece of Azrael's heart from me directly and survive it. They may then dole out parts of their own to create a weaker brood or retain all their strength—that is their choice."

"Then why not make another kid to take her down?"

"I have no more left of me to give," he said, a hint of regret in his voice. "It is both darkness and light that binds me. Too much of one, and I will fade. Not enough of the other, and I will cease to be. And I'm not ready to forsake the ones I freed."

And there it was. The answer to everything about this Judas. He could talk about how generous and protective he was all he wanted, but the truth was, he didn't want to die. Wasn't ready to, even after thousands of years. And if he killed Tourmaline, my bet was that his other firstborn, bearing their slivers of his angel-infused heart, might think it's time to erase their maker.

Could I blame him, not wanting to let go? I couldn't. Every time I complained about Shar and the White Throne, I could easily just stop and accept the fate I deserved. But I persevered. Nobody wants to leave the game when they've got a hot hand. An immortal, demi-god-like vampire king, equal parts Heaven and Hell—Judas had been dealt a royal flush.

"Would they really miss you?" I asked, making no effort to mask my snideness.

"Her actions jeopardize our peace. Our *only* way out: take her life. Return her heart to me, and you, too, will find true salvation."

"And what if I don't?"

Judas rose. "We are not enemies, James Crowley. Perhaps we can even be friends."

He started off toward the front entrance.

"That's it?" I asked, confused.

"I offer you true freedom. No more servitude to a throne which lacks the respect to even inform you of my true name. Should you decide to travel that path, all you must do is look for me, and you will find me."

"Seek, and I will find, huh?" I asked.

"You're beginning to understand. The heavens are at war, *Hamsa*. Just be sure you're standing out of the way, or you may as well be cannon fodder."

With that, he left, along with all his men. I sat there alone in a room that had once been beautiful, now shattered and broken.

Moonlight returned, and my mirror swirled to life, along with that itch of Shar wanting my attention.

"Crowley?" her voice intoned.

I strolled over, confused, mind in a knot.

"Crowley, where were you?"

Should I tell her? Really get on her good side?

"Sorry. It was, uh . . . another vamp attack," I said. Not yet. I needed time to think. "Got away again."

"Of course it did. One day, I truly hope you cease to disappoint me."

No scolding. No calling me a liar. Did that mean this Judas was telling me the truth, and being in his presence truly did hide me from Heaven's gaze? Or maybe he was playing me too.

"You and me both, sweetheart," I said. "But I need you to trust me on this one. Tourmaline is the key to getting the Betrayer. I feel it in my bones. And if I'm wrong, maybe losing a child will bring him to me one day. At worst, that murderess bitch is gone for good."

The truth, as far as I was concerned. I wasn't sure what I wanted yet. Judas reminded me of Ace in a way, using his generosity as a mask for selfishness. He could have been playing me, so I didn't come after him. Could've been fabricating the whole tale. Vampires, the result of him killing Azrael and merging with angel power? If that's not the very definition of a fallen angel . . . News to me. And I couldn't ask Shar because she'd want to know where I learned it or spin some riddle.

"Then do what must be done, Crowley," Shar said. "Prove me wrong, or don't. At least the question of your usefulness shall be answered."

This time, she wisped away on her own, and it felt like a weight coming off me. Took everything not to ask if the Betrayer was Judas and try and glean the truth from her response.

I took a step back, turned, and there was Chapelwaite, dressed like a marshal again, leaning on a pew.

"What do you want?" I questioned.

"I'm a United States Marshal," he said, feigning shock. "If

what you've told me about this Tourmaline is true, then she must be brought to justice for the death of Senator Cartwright. We can help each other."

He winked.

Help.

More like Judas keeping an eye on me with a follower who'd somehow embedded himself into the highest echelon of US law enforcement. Couldn't say I was surprised.

Nothing to complain about, though. Tourmaline would be ready for me now, and more guns couldn't hurt. Help is a rare thing in this world. I take it where I can get it. Plus, Shar's eyes were always on me anyway. What was another set?

"You know what we're up against?" I asked, playing coy.

"I have my suspicions."

"Hope you've got your affairs in order." I patted him on the shoulder and walked by, back straight, acting all confident—the way you do when you walk into a bank set to rob it, even though your insides are fluttering like fall leaves.

True freedom or loyalty to my benefactors. All I had to do for the former was kill someone I already itched to. Well, that and claim a demon heart. And then spend eternity having to feed on other humans to survive.

Nothing's ever simple for a Black Badge.

TWENTY

Some vices are universal. Living, undead. Taste or no taste. With a bit of time to let my mind settle after everything with Rosa and Judas, and all the vexing shit in this forsaken city, I had clarity—I needed a fucking drink.

I went to the one place nobody would think I was dumb enough to enter. Storyville. Rain had started to patter while we were in the cathedral, so it didn't even look weird, me dipping the brim of my hat to hide my identity.

Ignoring the whispers and flirtation from more women and men of the night than I could count, I found a saloon across the tram tracks and canal from the Arlington with a clear view of it through the window. *And*, it didn't have any infernal jazz playing.

I marched right up to the counter and ordered a whiskey. Chapelwaite joined me but didn't say a word. Congrats to him on being able to read a goddamn room.

The barkeep clanked a glass and filled it with that familiar amber liquid. I shot it back, slammed the table, and tossed down three more. The taste was a hint to my tongue, but the memory remained—that hard bite that made you shiver from the inside out.

"You had a rough day, cowboy?" the barkeep asked, bringing me one more.

A fraction of anger rose at him calling me that, a reminder of Roo's taunts. I shoved it aside.

"Having a rough couple of decades," I grunted.

He laughed. "Ain't we all. Another? On the house."

"Something that lasts a bit longer." I thought for a moment. "How's about a Sazerac."

I remembered that was Rosa's favorite drink back when she used to imbibe. Not sure I'd ever tasted one, but I might as well have a private, silent cheers to her before I made sure I left her life for good.

"Is this helping?" Chapelwaite finally spoke up.

"It ain't not helping." But that was a lie. Heaven had stolen my ability to enjoy drunkenness. I downed the last bit of whiskey and exhaled slowly. Man, did I wish I could get truly shitcanned.

"So, what's the plan?" I asked.

"That's your job," Chapelwaite said, rimming the edge of his glass with a fingertip.

"Damn. Thought maybe you'd come along with one. No good help these days, I reckon. What about the rest of your compadres?"

"The other marshals?" he clarified. "Dead outside of Madame Laveau's. Destined for the ground soon."

"Didn't mean them." I was careful not to get specific. Did I completely understand how much or little Shar paid attention to me? No. But I wasn't in the presence of a vampire lord anymore, which apparently meant she *could* hear. I glanced up at the mirror behind the bar, the one near the back exit, and the plethora of other reflective surfaces within the tavern. She could be lurking behind any one of them—or all.

"Just us, I'm afraid," Chapelwaite admitted.

I clicked my tongue. Just then, the barkeep set a copper cup in front of me. I tipped my hat in appreciation. Once the man left, I asked, "Is this a job or a job interview?"

"Excuse me?"

"You know, for . . ." I didn't dare say it.

Chapelwaite nodded in understanding. "You can speak freely, Crowley. At least with me."

"If only that were true."

"It is." He reached into his shirt and showed me his upside-down cross. It seemed unassuming. Plain, gold, sharp edges. I also noticed Chapelwaite's neck and two sets of fang marks on either side, like a vampire had taken turns drinking from each spot. I kept my mouth shut about it.

"I may not be one of his children," Chapelwaite said, "but there's a remnant of him in these. To shroud us in our service."

My eyes widened. I extended my hand out of reflex to touch it, and he didn't stop me. I'm unsure why I moved slow, timid, but I did. My fingers grazed the very bottom, and in an instant, I felt that burn in the mark on my chest like there was a Nephilim sitting on top of me. I recoiled.

"Protects him from anyone witnessing our meetings with him," Chapelwaite said.

I rubbed my fingers together, reminded of when I touched that cursed harmonica back near Revelation. Unnatural.

"Of course, it's for him," I said. "Nice perk, though. When we're through, I may have to kill you and take it myself."

"When we're through, you won't have to." His gaze flitted through my torn shirt, to where the Black Badge mark scarred my chest, then back to my eyes. "If you make the right choice."

Picking up my drink, I swirled it around. “Right. Wrong. Who decides. If your master is who he claims, it’s just another side claiming their stake in being right.”

“Fair.” Chapelwaite nodded and took a swig.

“You ain’t gonna defend him?”

“I don’t have to. I have the honor of knowing him.”

He said it as I sipped my drink, and my scoff caused me to spit some out. “Oh, please. I saw the scars on your neck. I think you just like the pain.”

His features twitched. “Blood of the living is the cost of his freedom. We count it a joy to sacrifice. Not all of his kind resort to murder and savagery to get their fill. Think of it like opium. The more they quaff, the more they need. The younger they are, the more prone to that addiction. There are no untamed vampires, only addicts and unworthy makers.”

I chuckled. “Like Tourmaline.”

He nodded. “Judas is an ally to the living, whatever it may seem. So yes, I genuinely believe that removing her is objectively *right*.”

“My friend, I’ve been alive a long time. If I’ve learned anything, it’s that there are two things that must never be needlessly spilled: blood and good whiskey. That’s the one part of the Good Book I can’t find fault with.”

“Yet I gather from the look of you that you’ve killed many.”

“One out of two ain’t bad.” I raised my glass.

I’ll be honest, I was just having fun with the guy at this point. Sometimes, I get downright sick of all the supernatural hoopla, and it’s nice to have a drink and tease a fellow into frustration like me and the boys used to back in the day. You gotta grow tough skin, running with outlaws.

He didn’t seem irked in the least.

The doors to the saloon swung open with enough force for

me to reach for my Peacemakers and turn, ready for an attack. Instead, I saw a sweaty, inebriated businessman strutting in. His belly stretched the bottom of his pinstriped suit jacket.

"The Arlington House, closed. Can you believe it?" he moaned to nobody in particular. "They got some nerve. Half the reason I come here."

All eyes fell upon him, and the band quieted. Where we were was *not* a venue for the upscale. Fishermen, shuckers, miners—the kind of salty men who liked some bite in their drinks.

"You don't understand," he slurred. "They have a Messican girl there. She's—" He kissed his fingers, then leaned on a table and nudged a hairy fisherman with arms like tree trunks. "This guy gets it. They taste better down south."

The towering fisherman stood, ready to knock his block off.

"All right, all right," he slurred, stumbling back with his hands raised in surrender. "You're missing out." He made a V shape with his fingers over his lips and wagged his tongue like he was with a woman. Now *I* wanted to rip it out of his mouth—the creep.

He staggered in my direction, but I think my glare nearly made him shit kittens, and he continued to the other end of the bar. As the man ordered, the barkeep raised his hand and snapped his fingers. A curly-haired broad in a corset strode down from upstairs to greet the businessman. Easy prey.

"Do you know why my master turned his back on yours?" Chapelwaite asked, calmly earning back my attention.

"Considering I didn't know he existed, I think not," I said.

"After his first betrayal—"

"Getting Jesus killed," I filled in for him.

"Yes . . . Guilt racked his brain, and the Almighty offered a chance at atonement. Jesus changed things, you see. Roused humans to Heaven and their enemies. And so, for his crimes,

Judas was offered the chance to be the first Hand of God. An opportunity to guard *these people* against Hell." He pointed at the drunk. "Men like him."

"Men like him ain't the only ones," I said.

"Yes, yes."

"Way I see it, what I do is better than going to Hell."

"For a time," he said. "After decades of loyal service, the angel Azrael attempted to invade the mortal realm by opening a Hellmouth. Only Judas stood in his way, and he stopped him, but the energy of closing the Hellmouth caused Mount Vesuvius to erupt. It was inevitable. Thousands below were suffocated by ash. Slaughtered."

"Wouldn't that make Azrael a demon? Sorry, I just get confused when talking about myths."

"A fallen one. Yes. A demon. A war in the spiritual realm in which Judas was forced to be a soldier. He wasn't warned. Wasn't given the choice to stop Azrael differently. And so, he saw things for what they were and chose to take Azrael's power and break free."

I downed the rest of my Sazerac and placed down the glass. "Quite a tale. Were you there?"

"I'm not immortal."

"Right. You're food."

His knuckles cracked underneath the lip of the bar. Finally, I'd gotten his mask of composure to crack.

"I don't know what he sees in you," Chapelwaite said, low and almost in a growl.

"All I'm saying is, if any of that is true—and let me remind you, you weren't there—that don't make him a hero. He may find more Black Badges to free and make them vamps, but then they make more, lose control, and their broods kill innocents."

"Your point?"

"Don't anoint heroes who aren't ones." I stuck my finger in his chest. "Choosing to live *is* selfish by nature. It's human." I took a beat. "And it's the one part of all this that sounds honest."

His shoulders relaxed as he leaned over the bar. "Are you selfish, then, James Crowley?"

"Haven't decided yet."

"This country fought to end slavery. Yet, here you sit, a slave still to another power. Maybe you deserve it for your sins, but they removed choice from the equation. You woke up this way. That is all he seeks to bring you. Choice. Is there nothing you'd want to live for in this world, free of their endless war?"

I stared out the window at the people passing by. Men and women of all sorts, but one stuck out to me. A posh woman in a puffy dress, pushing a buggy with a baby inside, her husband keeping pace right beside her.

A classic family like that wasn't in the cards for me. Never had been. Though I couldn't deny it. Walking side by side with a woman I loved was quite the dream. Quite the reverie to get lost in. Quite a reason to betray my service and be *selfish*.

"That's too big a question to answer in a saloon," I said. "We ain't friends yet, Chapelwaite. Just temporary partners. The way I see it, killing Tourmaline gets me back in front of your boss. Who knows what might happen then."

"I suppose us killing you is another path to freedom."

I grinned. "You mortals think you could take me?"

He sent the expression right back. "Judas wouldn't even have to lift a finger."

We kept up appearances for a second or two, then I laughed. Couldn't help it. "I like you." I squeezed his shoulder, then waved for the barkeep and held up two fingers. "Whiskey."

"I don't drink," Chapelwaite proclaimed as if that's something to be proud of. Easy for a city man to say. I waited for the barkeep to put down the glasses, then slid one across the bar.

"Buck up and have one with me," I said. "Make a toast to being human."

He slowly and gently gripped the glass.

"Oh, it won't bite," I said. "You follow him because you think he's special. But you're mortal. I think the gods envy humans for that. You got a beginning and an end, the way all stories ought to be told."

He raised the glass toward his lips. I pushed on the bottom to get it all the way.

"Down the hatch." I took mine, watching sidelong as he did the same. His eyes squinched, and his lips pursed. For a moment, I got to live vicariously through his reaction and remember my first taste of that holy nectar. Then he coughed.

"Good for you. Let it out." I patted his back. "Enjoy the mortal things, Chapelwaite. Live free, and all that shit. Because look over there." I pointed through the window to the Arlington House across the way. Unlike earlier, there were no prostitutes out on the brothel's balcony. Just hardened-looking men with shaggy beards. Protection. "They're ready for us. Odds are, you aren't walking out alive—"

"Hey, hey, you two!" the drunk businessman hollered over. The prostitute had her face in her palms, totally embarrassed. Working hard for her money, which I can respect. "You didn't invite me? Let's do another."

"Why don't we go upstairs, honey," the lady said, trying to turn him away. He wouldn't.

"No. I want to share a drink with my new friends first."

Before I could, Chapelwaite drew his revolver and aimed it at the man's head. In many places, that sort of behavior could cause a riot. Here, not a peep. The man's eyes crossed, trying to stare at the gun's barrel. He tried to stifle a hiccup.

"I do not share drinks with vermin," Chapelwaite snapped. "Miss, come here." Considering his gun was out, she obliged. I'll admit, I was intrigued, so I kept my mouth shut and watched how a servant of Judas handled himself.

"What is your fee?" he asked.

I couldn't hear her answer.

Chapelwaite dug into his pocket with his free hand, pulled out a couple of greenbacks, and slid them into her hand. "Spare yourself his company tonight."

Her brow furrowed as she looked down at the cash and then at the drunk. Only took a second more thought before she stowed her riches and sauntered away to chat up someone else.

"Hey, where are you going?" the businessman asked, completely forgetting he was at gunpoint. He fell off his stool as he turned. And when he hit the floor, all he could do was laugh.

Chapelwaite flashed his badge to the barkeep and said, "Send him somewhere else." Then he placed his hands on the bar and exhaled slowly. "Got a plan for Tourmaline, then, Black Badge?"

Right back to the conversation. I liked his style. He'd spared a working woman a night to forget and, honestly, probably saved the drunk's life. Acting like that in a place like this, he was bound to get his teeth knocked in. Can't say he wouldn't have deserved it, though.

In the same spirit, I got right to business as well.

"You're really a marshal, then?" I asked. "Like, that ain't just a costume?"

"I am."

"Then yeah, I think I have an idea. Think you can stroll right into the city barracks and get something for me that I've always wanted to try?"

A look of hard consternation came over him. "Depends on what it is."

My smile stretched from ear to ear. You spend a lot of lonely nights lying awake as a Black Badge. Often, I thought about old jobs and how they might have gone differently. Or future ones and what I might use.

I'd always had an idea for a weapon. And let's just say the Arlington House was in for an explosive surprise.

TWENTY-ONE

Eyes on the horizon. You spend a lot of time like that before a heist. Most outlaws never talk about that part. All the waiting.

I always enjoyed the calm before the storm. The way I could feel my pulse in my fingertips. Now I'm not an anxious man by any means, but you aren't sane if you feel nothing before riding out to meet iron with iron.

The man next to me, however, was a dozen shades of maniac. To this day, I ain't sure if Ace Ryker got nervous before a big job or not. He never had a tell.

"There's too many ways for a man to win for a man to lose," he'd always say.

I suppose he was correct in a loose sense. If you planned things right, had enough contingencies in play, you were gonna succeed. At least that's what Ace made us think. We'd always have a Plan B, which should've been a good indication the first one wasn't very good to begin with.

"They're late," Ace grumbled. His eyes went to his gold timepiece then back to the horizon. A dirt road ran around a ridge across a low valley north of our position. An armored stagecoach

conveying all sorts of valuables was scheduled to be skirting around it any moment.

"They'll be here," I assured him.

"Better be. Unless someone ratted." His dark gaze fell upon me. Even though I was innocent, it gave me a shiver. When Ace smelled a rat . . . Woo boy, that was never a pleasant time amongst the Scuttlers. Someone always found themselves at the wrong end of a noose.

"Watch that look, Ace." I stayed stern. I'd found that was the best way to be in these situations. Push back on him. Never act skittish. He often mistook fear for guilt.

Ace kept fixated on me for a few seconds, then sneered. "Nah, you're all right, Crowley. Loyal like a hound." He gave my shoulder a firm tug.

I grunted in acknowledgment. He always had a way of making compliments insults, though I'd gotten used to it. Ace filled our pockets. Kept us fed, sheltered, and most of all . . . busy. There's nothing more dangerous in the West than idle hands.

"Who do you think it'd be?" Ace asked.

"What?"

"You know. If any of 'em was gonna turncoat."

"Hell, I don't know, Ace. I just shoot when you say aim."

"Nah." He clicked his tongue. "You pay attention, Crowley, more than you let on. I can tell. You hear things at night around the piss pot. Men who listen like you have trouble sleeping. I know it."

"I sleep like a drunk baby."

"C'mon, who'd you put your money on?"

I exhaled through clenched teeth. "I ain't a rat."

He laughed. "Fair enough. Fair enough. See, you're smarter than you look."

Everything was a test with him; seemed that way by any rate. Nowadays, I see it for what it was. Ace kept his distance from the rest of us in that way because we were all cannon fodder. Easier to move on from peons than brothers-at-arms when one takes a bullet.

"I'd put a fat twenty on Big Davey," Ace said.

My heart skipped a beat. Did he know something? Of all the Scuttlers, me and Davey were the closest. Joined up about the same time and had the same number of birthdays behind us.

"No way in hell," I replied. "Damn good with a rifle, but Davey's a teddy bear."

"Yeah, true. I just would wanna hear how loud it'd be when he falls." He snickered.

Unsure how to answer, I kept quiet and continued watching the ridge. A bit of dust kicked up and I tensed. Then a deer skittered out and across the brush.

"What's wrong, Crowley?" Ace asked after a short silence. I guess my face betrayed my emotions.

"Nothing," I said.

"You look like you swallowed shit and here we are talking about traitors. Spill it."

"Seriously, it's—"

The hammer on Ace's LeMat clicked. I felt the barrel tousling through my hair before I noticed him aiming at my head in my peripherals.

I swallowed a lump in my throat. Shit, he'd heard something. I'd complained too loudly last time we holed up in a saloon. Ace had gotten too handsy with some locals. I'd imbibed a little too heartily. Referred to him with some foul words I couldn't quite recall.

But was it a crime to voice your annoyance about some of what your boss gets up to?

To Ace, maybe that was enough.

Then he chuckled and lowered his aim to the dirt.

"Don't make me force you, Crowley," he said. "I've known you since you was a runt. I know when something's eating at you."

"It's just . . ." I sighed. Says a lot that he could aim a gun at my head for fun and I could shrug it off so quick, but I did. The truth was, I had been thinking too much those days.

"Where does this end?" I asked.

"Simple. We get some scratch; we spend it however we please."

"No. Not this job. I mean, everything. The Scuttlers. When does it end? When do we cash in all we got stashed and settle?"

"Settle?" He scoffed. "You some kinda fuckin' pilgrim?"

"You know what I mean, Ace. We keep at this, eventually it'll bite us. You can only steal so much. And with these new Pinkertons moving out—"

"I ain't afraid of them Yanks."

"I know, but—"

"No buts, Crowley." He used his revolver like a pointer finger. "You listen to me. They're sent out here in the name of law and order, but that's horseshit. They're coming to muzzle men like us so the rich folk can lay train tracks. Men who take the living they want. Who live free on this here Earth. And you know why?"

I didn't answer.

"Because this, out here? It's primal," he went on. "It's the way we were meant to live. Winner takes all. Strongest at the top. We're predators, Crowley. And that means we gotta eat. It ain't a sin. It's our goddamned nature."

Just then, I saw the glint of an arrow racing up into the air from atop the ridge across the valley. That was the signal. More dust billowed at the edge of the road. The stagecoach was coming.

Ace caught my attention and winked. "Here we go. Time to fill our bellies."

A stick of dynamite handled the rest for us, courtesy of Big Davey. A chunk of the ridge above the trail broke off. Rocks sloughed down. Horses neighed as they swerved to dodge the rockslide. The coach might have avoided crashing, but it tipped over off the side of the trail. Just how we wanted them. Exposed and out of sorts, with all their valuables intact.

Ace put his fingers to his lips and whistled so loud, it echoed. Then he spurred his horse along, gun out and ready to start shooting. All along our hill, the other Scuttlers came pouring out like wild men.

I paused. For a fleeting moment, I thought about getting away. A farm farther out toward the Golden Coast, as they called it. A couple cows. Maybe find a wife. Pop out a few little Crowleys.

Then I took a shallow breath, pulled my Peacemakers, and chased after our fearless leader . . .

* * *

I had to admit, these kinds of hijinks brought back memories of my outlaw days.

Only difference is I wasn't running with a crew I'd known for years. This wasn't a stagecoach. This was more akin to piling into a hideout and shooting a rival crew full of lead.

Sometimes, a job requires more than just kicking down doors and stomping new assholes. Sometimes it requires blowing a big fucking hole in the side of a building—then stomping new assholes.

Storyville was relatively quiet this early in the morning. If you were still in this part of town now, that meant you'd been awake all-night partying or carousing.

I, however, was here for neither such thing. Tourmaline was inside her brothel, feeding off innocents, and with a brood of vampires and werewolves protecting her. Hence hitting in the morning, when the latter weren't turned and the former couldn't risk the sun.

It was time to tear down the kingdom.

If Chapelwaite played his role right, she wouldn't know what hit her.

I stood just off the road. Unlike other parts of Crescent City, here, the streets were still dirt. Storyville was an up-and-coming part of town, the government just now getting their grungy fingertips under the surface so they could tax and levy the bejesus out of everyone.

Just beside me, a smaller structure was filled with pottery and clay artwork. By the size of the place, looked like they did a fair amount of business. And though I couldn't be distracted by such trivial things, they really did fine work.

Across from me, a building that doubled as a telegraph office and a money lender rose three stories above street level. In the alley beside it, a handful of local officers lay in wait. Chapelwaite had rallied whoever he could get to help raid the Arlington House, claiming he had evidence that the senator was there.

Not everyone showed. Not even the district's sheriff. I imagine Tourmaline kept the pockets of many law enforcement officers lined in exchange for turning a blind eye to her dealings. Rougarou too. Which was fine. No doubt one crooked cop would leak news of the coming raid, and I wanted any civilians out of the place for what was to come.

A couple extra guns on our side with a taste for righteousness over bribes? That only helped. They knew what they were getting into—sorta—and unlike my benefactors, choice was all I could offer.

At the corner of the street, diagonally adjacent to the telegrapher's, the Arlington House stood like a four-story beacon of sin, calling all those with bigger dicks than brains to come in for just a little taste. Problem was, anyone answering that call would get more than they paid for.

Running down the center of the road was a set of tracks.

Though these weren't as big and sturdy as the train rails back west, they did a fine job carrying Crescent City's famous trams around town. Was a fun and unique way to see the place or travel long distances in a city where horses were becoming less common.

Come to think of it, where was Timp? Poor girl was probably still waiting for my promised whistle, which I'd been too distracted to offer. She was better off not involved in all this craziness anyway. I owed her a bushel of apples when this was through—and a nice combing.

My position was just beyond view from any of the brothel windows. In the distance, silhouetted against the rising sun, the tram approached. A dark figure hung out the side, waving at me like an idiot.

Foolish-looking or not, it was the sign the tram cart was empty except for the US Marshal.

It neared at a quick clip. Everything was ready. A rapidly assembled plan, but sometimes those are the best kind. You overthink a job and more than likely your brains wind up scrambled from a stray bullet.

Improvisation. That's what keeps the West free and running.

My gaze hovered upon the brothel, watching the human guards. I couldn't help wonder what they were thinking, getting mixed up in this kind of business. Then again, I hadn't thought much about that kind of thing when Ace was handing out gold bars either.

I registered movement behind me. I spun, pistol raised.

"Whoa, there!" Chapelwaite said, out of breath.

As planned, he'd leaped off the tram and hoofed his way to me. I lowered the weapon.

"Don't be a sneak," I growled.

"Did you want me to announce myself?" he asked.

"What the hell is that?" I asked, pointing to a sword hilt where a sidearm should've been.

"You do things your way. I'll do things mine," he said.

I grunted and turned back to the Arlington. The bearded human guards out front—or more than likely, werewolves in human form—were totally unaware of their soon-to-come fate.

"Rails handled?" he asked.

"Whose plan was this?" I replied.

"Don't gotta be a prick about it." He shared a glance with one of his men by the telegrapher's. The lawman nodded, confirming he and the others were ready in waiting.

"Here it comes," Chapelwaite whispered.

The steady rhythm of the empty tram whipped by. Then, with a *kerchunk*, it dislodged from the track, all according to plan—an old trick, slipping a thin sheet of metal on the track. Flipping onto its side, it rolled, catching air before plowing into the ground-floor level of the Arlington.

The two guards didn't even have time to react before getting squashed like summer melons.

"You sure know how to make an entrance," Chapelwaite commented.

Mere seconds passed before screaming people—mostly staff and scantily clad women—started pouring out like a ruffled ant mound. I recognized Lady Arlington with them, urging everyone out, so only nonhumans remained.

Not Tourmaline or her brood, though. Not with the sun making its first appearance of the day.

Just as the chaos of the mass exodus subsided, a portion of the second-story balcony collapsed, sending splinters flying and dust billowing.

Still, no Tourmaline.

That was okay. If she was inside, we'd suss her out. If not, we'd send a message pointed like a dagger.

I stepped out from concealment and strode forward, Peacemakers drawn and at my side.

"Come out, come out, wherever you are!" I sang, using Roo's own taunt.

The bullet chambered in my right hand was standard iron and I pulled the trigger, sending it into the dirt. The echoing boom punctuated my command.

In response, a cluster of pale-skinned vampires came almost literally crawling from the rubble. Others were already skulking within the rest of the Arlington House, cracked open like an egg now so I could see all the way through the first floor. They stayed within the shadow provided by the immense structure. Accompanying them, I recognized some of Roo's pack from earlier in human form. Several perched atop the crashed tram and the others paused not far off.

Then, from behind his men, human Roo himself appeared at the back of the foyer by the stairs. He wore that same pinstriped fitted suit that I'd seen him in earlier. In one hand, he calmly puffed on a cigar. With the other, he gripped my own rifle.

Perfect.

He cackled. "I knew you'd try something flashy, cowboy."

"Fine choice of words," I shouted.

I gave a signal to Chapelwaite's boys. The copper whistled and a small torch lit on the telegrapher's rooftop. Then, it came soaring to land unimpressively beside the tram.

Roo glanced over at the dithering flame. "You plan to smoke us out, Crowley?"

"Not quite," I admitted. I gave him a curt wave. "Goodbye, Roo."

He laughed again, but this time, it was cut short as the shady refuge exploded into a mixture of fire and glitter. Chapelwaite and I ducked behind a feeding trough as a stick of silver-filled dynamite blew.

Chapelwaite had been successful in commandeering a few sticks of the stuff, and the silver I'd gotten from Laveau worked nicely when shaved and packed along with the gunpowder.

"I'll give it to Ace, that sure is a satisfying sound," I said.

Chapelwaite just shook his head.

Once I was sure all the flying fragments had settled, I stepped out and walked toward the scene. Civilians still around Storyville went into a panic and fled. A crash and a gunshot, that was nothing out of the ordinary in a place like this. A deafening explosion? That's a universal warning to get the hell out.

The screams as werewolves and vampires burned alive from the inside were unlike any sound I've ever heard. This would be a fair representation of the torments of Hell if the rumors were anything to go by.

In fact, it sounded like a thousand souls rising up to meet their fates. Couldn't even begin to think of what that would look like.

Werewolves aren't exactly Nephilim. They aren't the spawn of Satan, and clearly, if Judas's story about Azrael could be believed, there was a spark of Divinity in vampires. Sickening to think about, really.

As I approached the flaming wreckage, I saw movement. Then heard a familiar cackle.

"Can't be rid of me so easy, cowboy."

Roo threw aside one of his men who'd absorbed the blast for him. Somehow still alive, he crawled for my rifle, his suit singed off in places and covered in grime. His face so gray with ash, it may as well have been his fur.

I raised my pistol, sight locked right on his black heart.

That was when a brutal, agonized cry pealed through the air. I looked up, just for a moment, to follow the sound. The lawman who'd thrown the torch was airborne and falling fast. Where he'd just been, one of Roo's grizzly men stood, howling even though he was in human form.

But I ain't stupid. I had Roo dead to rights, and when you've got an enemy in that position, you take it. However, when I turned back to put the old dog down, he was gone.

"Goddammit!" I shouted. "Everyone, follow me."

Chapelwaite didn't hesitate, but at the sight of their colleague plastered on the dirt street, the lawmen did.

I was already stomping toward the brothel when Chapelwaite gave the order. "You've got a duty, boys. Don't let this city down."

Footsteps hesitated to start up, but then, more and more, our small army started following.

When we got to the brothel steps, the putrid aroma of burning flesh and metal was bad enough that even I could smell it. Charred corpses littered the front porch. The ashy remains of the vampires fluttered in the air.

But I didn't stop.

"Roo!" I shouted, but no response came. "Tourmaline! This ends now!"

The interior rose four stories high, mezzanine-style balconies wrapping the main lobby on all levels. It was still and quiet but for creaking wood and crackling flames. Where there'd been life just days ago—albeit a despicable excuse for life—now, only death remained.

Smoke filled the room, but sharp movement near the back stuck out. I held up a hand for the others to halt.

Suddenly, as if hit by thin air itself, I found myself flying. I landed behind the bar, some ten feet away, my guns no longer in my grip. Then Chapelwaite went airborne, and the other cops were also tossed around like rag dolls.

All around me, the lawmen found themselves a step closer to the afterlife and I still hadn't seen a single one of our attackers. Gunshots rang out every which way. These ordinary cops had no idea why their guns had been outfitted with such extraordinary bullets, but they should've been grateful for it.

A vampire was struck in the crossfire, bursting into flame and steam from what had to be a direct hit to the chest or head.

Then, it was over. Just like that. Silence.

"What the hell is going on?" one officer asked, reaching for the strange, silvery ash hanging in the air.

Something blurred in front of him. His words were quieted, replaced with a gurgle as his throat was slashed open.

"Crowley!" a voice called out from somewhere. A voice I knew. "You want me. I'll give you more than you can handle."

Tourmaline. I found her standing on the mezzanine of the fourth and topmost floor of her burning brothel.

I rose slowly, taking my time and retrieving my weapons. No one stopped me.

Several vampiric blurs converged on her position to protect her, returning from their onslaught. The lawmen were in a panicked frenzy, but still very much alive. They weren't prepared for anything like this. To their credit, they had their rifles trained on Tourmaline.

She was surrounded by a vampire army. Many had silver lodged in them from the dynamite, missing limbs or steaming. They huffed, in pain, but goddammit, they were ready to fight. Their veins bulged and their eyes went so dark, they barely looked to have ever been human at all. Starved. Feral. Monstrous.

Tourmaline, on her part, was resplendent in a sheer red

nightdress, leaving absolutely nothing to a man's creative faculties. A classic beauty. Her hair was split down the middle with pigtails pulled tight and braided over her shoulder.

To my left, Chapelwaite stirred. Much as I disliked the man, he and his crew were my only allies in this war.

"We're just getting started, honey," I said.

"Looks like you blew your load a bit early," she said. "Don't worry. It happens to every man. I should know."

I raised both pistols and put a silver slug in the two vampires in front of her. They were dead shots, right through their chests like stakes. Together, they exploded into fiery clouds of dust.

Their fellows shrieked, hissing, but dared not move until they got the command.

"You shouldn't have done that," Tourmaline warned.

"Really? I quite enjoyed it."

"Enough. End him!" she commanded.

Now that I knew what I was looking for, following the vampires' movements was easier. However, there were a dozen or so of them, and they were swift as young stallions with much less bulk. Our only fortune was that the explosion had knocked out swathes of the building's front wall, letting in shafts of light they had to evade. And as fire and weakened structure damaged more of the building, more light came to our aid.

Reminded me of the lasso's light, calling down God's judgment. Was this Shar's half-assed show of support in our battle?

Gunfire erupted all around me. Several shouts of "Check your fire!" resounded, but those men kept on shooting, only stopping to reload.

I experienced the first strike as I sent a silver bullet toward a blur I'd targeted. My face swiveled to the left—a punch I hadn't seen or felt. The strike caused me to miss the resulting shower of powdered vampire as I fired, but I knew the shot struck home. When I turned back to my attacker, it was gone, only for another to fill the position. She bore her fangs and let out a loud, shrill cry.

I took two more blows and ducked under a third, using it as an opportunity to stow one of my pistols and pull my silver-dusted knife free of my boot. At such close range against such a quick enemy, I'd have better luck with a melee weapon.

I brought it to bear in an upward arc that would've decapitated the female bloodsucker if it'd been a longer blade. Still, steam poured from the wound like a dam had been breached. Then I shoved a boot into her belly, pushing her out of the room and into the light where she was cooked alive. Saints and elders, did she let out a cry.

Across the room, coppers fired their rifles up at vamps that appeared to be everywhere at once. I would've considered them superfluous if they hadn't been so damn effective. Their efforts had more than a few of Tourmaline's brood chicken-dancing to avoid being shot, and others floating on the air in a macabre burning dance.

Chapelwaite was on his feet again, dazed but now wielding that long sword like a knight of old. The guy sure was skilled with a weapon I'd thought to be out of use for a hundred years or more. His long blade sliced the back of a vampire's neck and its head rolled free. The vampire erupted into flaming detritus before the skull even thumped the ground.

All of this I noted in less than the few seconds it took me to tag my next target. A male vamp that could've been someone's grandfather in his previous life blazed toward me, diving down from the third floor. His jaw was unhinged like a snake set to devour.

I slung my lasso upward at the staircase's second-level railing and used it to pull myself over him just in time. As I landed, I took the liberty of filling the back of his head with a silver snack. The slug bit through his skull like wet paper.

As things go in battles like this, I had no time to gloat.

Another cry rose from my left. I turned to see Chapelwaite on his back, a pair of Roo's goons on top of him, joining the fight. He batted one with the pommel of his sword but didn't have the proper leverage to do any real damage.

They were a tangle of limbs, making it difficult for me to put a bead on either without also risking danger to my ally who was twisting and writhing under their weight. I lassoed one of them around the neck to pull him off Chapelwaite, but a snarl from my side stole my attention and I missed.

I turned and hip-fired, hoping instinct would be with me. It was, but the vampire had picked up a gold platter to guard its heart and the bullet glanced off. For the first time in my undead life, I hoped to see Shar swirling around in its reflection, but with Chapelwaite and his inverted cross necklace so close, I saw nothing but sparks and fire.

The vampire hissed, eyes locked on me. This one was less veiny and terrifying than others. Maybe one of Tourmaline's first born. Chunks of silver were lodged into its arm and steamed everywhere, no doubt causing it immeasurable pain.

He barreled into me full bore and I lost my grip on my lasso. I took the hit in stride, using the momentum to roll in a series of backward somersaults through a wall. That kind of raw power—like a locomotive—would've leveled a mortal flat. While I couldn't feel anything, I had to assume at least a few of my ribs were broken.

As I came up to shoot, my arm didn't respond to the command my brain had given it. Instead, it hung limply at my side, a clear bend at the center of my forearm where no bones connected.

Son of a bitch broke my arm.

It would heal, and probably pretty quickly once I jammed it into place, but I didn't have time for a handicap at present.

As the thing leaped on me, I shoved my knife into its belly. I'd always learned never to bring a knife to a gunfight, but today, I was glad I had.

It screeched like a sick goat, but this one was strong and didn't back down. It ripped out the knife and threw it at me before charging again. Having no other choice, I did what I'd been taught best and improvised. I reached back and broke a candelabra off the wall. Holding the skinny end in front of me, the vampire ran straight through it, impaling itself.

As the body crumbled to dust all around me, I noticed a fat little imp standing at the other end of the hall. Fazar.

His eyes went wide. If he got to his cart, he could ride down to the Underdark and warn enough monsters to turn the tide. Maybe they weren't all loyal to Tourmaline, but enough could be.

"Don't!" I called out.

He didn't listen. He went to run, and I threw the candelabra like a spear, two ends of it plunging through the wall and pinning him by his neck so he couldn't move. He still tried, thrashing around like a fish out of water. His grunts sounded sexual in nature. Vile little thing.

I took a moment to gather myself and snap my arm back into place before turning back to my allies. I scanned the ground for my knife, but a scream caught my attention. The lawmen still near the massive hole in the front of the building held their own as more vampires scaled the building's inner walls down toward us. Reminded me of a scene straight out of an old medieval battle, only in reverse.

Some of the cops smartly retreated back and into the sun, limiting their line of fire as a result.

Chapelwaite, however, was in dire straits. It was his cry I'd heard. One of his two attackers had been thrown to the side, still alive with a back riddled with smoking bullet holes. Even in human form, werewolves can take more than an ordinary man. The other, however, still sat atop him with nothing good in mind.

The werewolf man reared back to punch. I took the shot, turning that hand into a bloody fountain. He howled and glared at me. I hoped Chapelwaite realized the opportunity I'd just presented him with.

Thankfully, he wasn't as stupid as he looked.

With the werewolf man distracted and off-balance, Chapelwaite had room to bring his blade around, and like death himself, he dragged it across the man's chest. Still intent to prove himself as something other than a fool, Chapelwaite crab-crawled backward behind the bar and into relative safety—at least for the time being.

I, too, considered myself somewhat of an intelligent man and fired off another round at the werewolf man's center mass. That was it. That was the killing blow, sending old wolfie to meet Lucifer face-to-ugly-face.

"You all right?" I called as Chapelwaite drove his blade into his second squirming attacker. He bent to retrieve my lasso. When he looked up, ready to respond, his eyes went wide.

"Behind you!" he shouted.

I spun to find myself paired up against yet another vampire. Seemed Tourmaline had pulled out all the stops. I saw her out of the corner of my eye, up high, smiling. Judas was right about her. These were beings she'd made—children of a sorts—pieces of her own heart. She appeared to enjoy watching them fight and die. Like chess pieces on a board. As if she could just whittle more out of their ashes.

The vamp in front of me—this one also a woman in her mortal life—smiled. Where Tourmaline was the vision of beauty and elegance, this horror looked like she'd received the full force of that tram crash.

Her face was flat as an iron, scars from ear to ear. What she'd done to earn those marks was a thought I wasn't willing to entertain. When she grinned, her split lips revealed only the presence of those fanged canines. Apart from them, it was only empty, black abyss staring back at me.

"You look like shit," I told her.

She sneered, only making her uglier.

I brought my pistol up, but she was too fast for it.

She and I traded punches until I found the opening I needed and drove a shoulder into her stomach. We intertwined like love bugs in July until we crashed through the bar. Bottles of expensive liquor tumbled and broke all around us. Staggering backward, I grabbed one and smashed it against the vamp's head. It hardly fazed her.

"I'm going to suck you dry," she said.

From anyone else, that kind of statement would have had my attention.

"Prepare to be woefully disappointed," I told her as I grabbed her throat with my one good hand and slammed my forehead against the bridge of her nose.

Vampires might be immortal and super strong, but that flat schnoz shattered all the same. Didn't stop her. She lurched forward and I was falling under her weight. Perhaps she looked to be ninety pounds soaking wet, but she drove me to the ground with enough raw power that I couldn't stop it.

"I don't know what you are, but you're dead," she said. She pinned my good arm down while the other remained entirely inert at my side.

I was about to make a snarky remark when she raised a clenched fist and there, in her bony hand, was my silver-dust knife in motion toward my heart.

In the two decades since I'd overstayed my welcome on Earth, I hadn't given a ton of thought to my mortality. Guess that's a side effect of not *being* mortal. I'd experienced just about every sort of maiming imaginable, including, most recently, a broken arm and having my head chopped off.

However, as this vampire was about to stab me with my own fucking knife, myriad thoughts flashed through my mind. Heaven, Hell, death, and the inevitable nothing I was destined to face were present among them, but truth be told, above all was Rosa.

Goddamn me, but I simply couldn't get that woman off my mind. She'd been living there free of charge since our reunion in Dead Acre.

What would happen to her if this was it for me? Would she waste the rest of her life searching for a dead husband? And what would she do once she found out that wasn't possible?

Suddenly, my face was covered in blood, blinded by the sheer quantity of it. My mouth, which must've been open, filled with the stuff. I heard a thud, felt my body jerk to one side and my hand was free.

I wiped my eyes with my sleeve and turned to see the vampire was gone, reduced to ash.

"We're even." Chapelwaite flourished his blade, then turned to reenter the fight before the words even fully left his mouth.

I rose, retrieved my knife and guns, and followed. As I ran, I discovered that my broken arm had fully mended itself—thank you, Shar. I stepped through the broken wood and glass, into a disaster zone. Ash from both the flaming buildings and eviscerated vampires was like fog in the air. Cinder and scorch marks marred the floor.

"Tourmaline!" I shouted. "This ends now. Enough have died."

Even as I said it, I knew it wasn't true. I wouldn't be satisfied until every last one of these abominations tasted silver.

She leaped down gracefully, as if she'd just stepped off a buggy and not fallen forty feet. She sauntered toward me through the wreckage, surrounded by the four remaining cops, no fear at all. Her army, though, was all but destroyed—yet there she was, walking as if she had the upper hand.

Until I realized she did.

I hadn't even considered Roo in all the confusion. But as soon as I heard Timp's fearful cry, it hit that they'd gotten me by the short hairs. I slowly turned to see Roo back in the street, rifle aimed at Timp's head. She looked as if she'd put up a hell of a fight, but in the end, she was no match for him.

"Tell what's left of your men to stand down," Tourmaline commanded.

A rifle boomed, the only sound save the crackling fire. Faster than I thought possible, Tourmaline dodged the shot and grabbed one of the deputies. Her teeth sank into his throat and ripped outward, spraying red everywhere.

Blood rose like bile in the young man's throat, then Tourmaline let him fall to the ground.

"Hold your damn fire!" I yelled.

"Finally, something intelligent from you," Tourmaline said. "Now, where were we?" She snapped her fingers in Roo's direction and he dragged Timp forward.

"What's the matter, cowboy?" Roo asked. "Wasn't it just days ago you thought horse was a fine substitute for human flesh?"

"You hurt her again, and I'll—"

Roo stretched out a finger and dragged his sharp nail along Timp's back. I could see the blood mingling with her tawny fur.

"Goddammit, Roo! What's the play here?" I demanded.

"Simple, really," he said. "You surrender or she dies."

Timp whimpered softly. I could tell she had very little left in her. It was a pathetic sound, and it pissed me right the hell off.

"Listen to him, Crowley," Tourmaline said.

I obeyed, sucking my teeth at the thought of being controlled by this whore mother. I didn't put it past her to slaughter Timp after what she'd done to so many humans in this place.

"Now that we understand the pecking order," she said, "I think its high time we have a little discussion. Guns down."

"All right," I said, dropping my pistols and raising my hands. I looked to my companions for them to do the same.

"I must ask, did you find my maker?" she said, walking toward me, hips swaying.

"Maybe. Maybe he's already dead."

She shook her head. "No. I don't think so. You being here tells me one thing."

"Yeah? What's that?"

"He isn't here, or he made you an offer," she said, almost singing the words. "I know what happens to the children he deems expendable."

"You should know by now, I don't make deals with the Devil."

"The truth, Crowley!" She stomped forward and screamed. "Your angels aren't after me, so why else come?"

"Justice, for one," I said.

"I'll give you a choice." She licked her lips, looking around to one of the few remaining lawmen. Poor sap had piss staining his pants and was shaking in his boots. I didn't know his name, but I heard him begging under his breath.

She moved toward him. "Fine-looking man," she said. "*Voulez-vous coucher avec moi, ce soir*?" Her hand slid down to the man's soaking wet privates, and I'm not sure what he was thinking, but his frown turned to a smile.

"That's enough, Tourmaline," I said.

"We're just getting started, honey," she said, repeating my warning. "They'll die one by one, and then the wolves will eat your horse right in front of you, you—"

"Time to die, false-child," Chapelwaite spoke loudly. My eyes darted to his position, now on the second level of the mezzanine. His left hand clutched his upside-down cross against his chest. Tourmaline's eyes went wide.

"So, he is here . . ." she whispered.

Chapelwaite gave me a determined look. I understood. Sometimes you find friends in the most unlikely of places.

He raised his right hand and used my lasso to loop the foyer's grand chandelier. He pulled, the weight snapping the mounting bracket of the chandelier and causing it to plummet.

That was the grand heroic move of Judas's right-hand man. Bringing down a chandelier like a damn cliché. Only took me a second to realize what he was playing at, though. The damage and the fire had done its job to weaken the building, and the weight of his tug brought more than just the light fixture down. A huge chunk of the roof collapsed, crumbling around us. Which caused yet more roof and structure to join it.

Absolute chaos ensued.

Tourmaline rushed away from the deputy in a mad attempt to not get caught in daylight. But it was too late for whoever he was. The chandelier turned him into a bloody pulp.

Timp started going nuts outside, neighing and bucking, and Roo shouted warnings to her as if she understood him.

I took the opportunity to kick my Peacemaker up off the ground with my boot. In a heartbeat, the tables had turned, and I had Tourmaline point-blank. Instead, I fired two precise rounds at Roo. The first hit his hand and knocked my Winchester out of his grasp so he couldn't use it to hurt Timp. The second just missed splattering his brains, and shredded through the side of his face, pulverizing one eye and skinning off a chunk of his nose.

I didn't bother looking to see what happened. Timp was free and Roo was either dead or no longer an immediate threat.

"Get her!" Chapelwaite shouted, already leaping from the second floor.

Choosing to save Timp let Tourmaline get the jump on me. She clutched me by the collar and heaved me into the air. More ceiling gave out and a beam of light struck us.

She wailed and tossed me aside out of reflex. Piano notes chimed as I crunched through the brothel's baby grand.

From somewhere, Tourmaline screamed in pain. I jumped up, spotting her trying to dart out of the light, but Chapelwaite landed beside her and slashed. She caught his sword, its silver burning her hand down to the bone.

"Not even brave enough to come himself!" she screamed. She pulled the sword free and Chapelwaite fell closer. As she fried, her fangs extended.

"You aren't worth his time," Chapelwaite spat. He yanked his upside-down cross free and jammed it into her eye. She roared.

In the meantime, I scampered forward, grabbing hold of her dress, and pulled before she could rip him to pieces. As she spun, I ripped Chapelwaite's sword free of her grip, turning it back on her, and stabbed it straight through her belly. We fell together, like lovers entwined. When we landed, the sword drove hilt-deep, pinning her to the floor in the middle of the sunlight.

Her skin sizzled, bubbling and broiling. She screamed. I didn't care. She'd earned the pain.

"Senators, I could forgive," I said. "The shit you did here? That wasn't personal. But you brought my goddamned fucking horse into this!" I lifted my knife and drove it down into her chest, right above the heart, and sliced down. She groaned, her face literally sloughing off in fiery ash.

"He'll turn on you too," she said, starting to cackle. "This is what he does . . . Freedom . . ." She coughed. "There's no such thing in a world of gods and men."

"You don't deserve it anyway." I reached into her chest and grabbed hold of her demon-infused heart. I pulled, and that was the end of Lady Tourmaline.

After a long second, I rolled onto my back and took a moment. There are more hues of exhaustion than physical, and watching Timp that close to dying had me feeling every shade. I turned my head. Timp was inches away, pounding her hooves and whinnying.

Roo, on the other hand, was nowhere to be found. Just what was left of his eye lying in the street. So much for loving Tourmaline. Wolves . . . only thing they're good at is surviving.

"Yeah, yeah, I'm moving," I said to Timp.

She nudged my head, and eventually, I got to my feet and gathered all my belongings—lasso included—before following her out to the entry stoop where she or I wouldn't be crushed if more of the brothel started falling.

Chapelwaite guided the two remaining deputies out. The terror on their faces would never leave them. Probably drive them to madness.

"Don't scare me like that, girl," I told Timp, touching my forehead to hers. "I'm sorry I didn't call for you faster. Never again, okay?"

She snorted.

"How'd you let a fool like that catch you anyway?"

Hooves tapped.

"Had him right where you wanted, eh?"

My beleaguered laugh was interrupted by Chapelwaite's voice.

"Keep back, everyone! Keep back!" he yelled, flashing his badge. A crowd had gathered around the brothel at a safe distance, civilians drawn to the chaos now that the shooting had stopped. Everyone likes a free show.

"Set a perimeter!" he ordered the two deputies. They blinked, dumbfounded. "Dammit, do your jobs!" They roused into action, though more enforcement numbers would surely be needed as the rest of the city woke up.

Chapelwaite pulled me away from the building. "It will be difficult to explain this to the city officials."

"Went pretty smooth if you ask me," I said.

I glanced up at the Arlington. Most of the front of the structure was in shambles, parts still burning, more chunks cracking off. The back half where private rooms were located remained mostly intact, but God knows for how much longer. A lot of rich men and tourists were bound to be gravely disappointed.

"Scour what's left of it," I said. "Somewhere in that heap, you'll find something that belongs to the senator, I promise. Then you'll be a national hero. That ought to help."

"Indeed, it will. Thank you, Crowley." He extended an open palm. "Now, hand it over."

I held up Tourmaline's heart, blood leaking out and down my wrist. Looked normal, except black veins crisscrossed it all over like a spiderweb. That, and despite it clearly being long-dead, the tissue behind it pulsed a glowing red.

"Just like that?" I asked.

He nodded. "He'll find you, James Crowley."

"Everything on his terms," I sighed. "And what if I decide to do Heaven's bidding and kill him."

"You can try."

"What if I just decide to say no and walk away?"

He smirked, nothing more. Then he took the heart from my hand, and I didn't stop him. He wrapped it in a cloth and stowed it.

"Whatever is to come, take solace that you have ridded this world of a true monster, regardless of how she started," he said.

"I won't," I said. "I'll keep killing them and somehow more will pop up."

We exchanged one last solemn look, then he returned to the aid of the deputies. I took Timp's reins and started walking her away, eager to avoid even more of a crowd. Those cowardice cops who hadn't the balls to fight in the first place were trying to push through and help secure the area.

I stopped to retrieve my Winchester from where Roo dropped it, and noticed Lady Arlington on her knees nearby, distraught as she watched a building either named after her or her family crumble.

"I don't know what you knew or helped with," I said. "But sometimes it's better off having no partners at all than ones you don't really know." She looked up at me, tears in her eyes. "If you get a second chance, be smarter."

Then Timp and I continued on our way. Might have been the blood and soot covering me head to toe and making me look like a zombie, but most everyone got out of my way. I crossed the tram tracks and headed for a bridge over the narrow canal.

I noticed a couple wandering along the waterfront across the water, as if Hell hadn't just broken loose in Crescent City. Ah, to be young and in love and see nothing except the lady two feet in front of you.

It was a pale man and a tan woman, and the man appeared to

have guzzled a bit too much of Satan's tears. He stumbled along, while she appeared lucid as anyone at this hour should've been.

I chuckled to myself. It was that same damn drunken businessman Chapelwaite had cockblocked last night. Looks like he'd finally found his Mexican . . .

I squinted. If I had a beating heart, it probably would've stopped.

"Rosa?"

She was too far away to hear me, even if I screamed. But I had no doubt it was her. What the hell was she up to, hanging out in a place like this with someone soaked in suds?

It was her business, sure, but I just couldn't help myself. I could keep my distance—just make sure she was all right.

Dammit, Rosa. So much for staying away.

TWENTY-TWO

I reckon you can't blow up a building downtown and start unloading bullets without causing a ruckus. The commotion of the city was left at my back. Shouting. Bells tolling. You name it.

A raid to find a senator's body was all it'd ever go down as in the history books. My name, nowhere to be found. Just a list of dead and the heroic deeds by Marshal Chapelwaite to uncover a dark truth. A footnote in a long line of tragedies in a city built on a swamp wherein man was never meant to live.

A thick morning fog stewed around us—Timp and me. My chest stung with Heaven's ire as she stepped out into the wilderness beyond the sprawl, hooves trudging through mud and muck.

I won't lie; it was bad. Almost like silver through the heart, causing me to involuntarily hunch over Timp's back. But I fought it as we followed Rosa's footsteps.

Most men would lose the trail in the muggy swamplands, but in my days, I'd learned a thing or two about tracking from ranchers and my native amigos. Timp's nostrils also flared a mile a minute. She knew Rosa's scent.

Injured as Timp was at Roo's hands, she carried the same resolve I did. Vampires and werewolves be damned. Rosa could be in trouble.

Timp whinnied, like she always did near cliffs. Heights made her uneasy, only, we weren't high. I reckon the threat of falling and sinking had her worried.

What I did next, I wouldn't call a whinny, but it was a groan, at least. Shar's call worsened, my chest feeling like someone poured hot coals down my shirt.

The sound of my pained voice must've spooked Timp worse. Her hooves sank deeper and her pace slowed. Unbidden, my body tilted off to the left. There was a tug at my side, almost as if Heaven's weighty judgment was being transferred through my lasso, pulling me down.

Eventually, it grew too much to bear. Timp really started to panic. Her leg gave out, and she bumped into me. I fell into the supernatural pull—the last little bit needed to send me into the mud with a splash.

"Timp, calm down!" I shouted with as much vigor as I could muster under the current circumstances.

She bucked, hooves pounding mud, getting stuck, then unstuck.

"Timp!"

She bolted. I tried to rise and follow her, but couldn't manage to get upright. So, I crawled, and little by little, my hands sank deeper until I couldn't move. I found myself clinging to a thorn bush so as not to be consumed like it was quicksand.

Timp's noises faded. As I thrashed, I saw a faint orange light. Here in the fog and under the canopy of cypress and southern oaks, it was eternal twilight.

Rosa and the drunkard were at an old campsite. And it looked like they weren't alone either. Hard to see through the fog, but one of the silhouettes had something hanging from around their neck. A snake, maybe.

Laveau . . .

And I could guess the others would be Bram and Harker.

I know, I said I was done mussing up Rosa's life. That I'd be on my way. But things change after you meet the man who got Jesus nailed to a tree, then raid and slaughter the house of his child. Maybe . . . it was just me seeing her again. Easier to make claims about letting go when she wasn't right there in my sights, very clearly up to no good.

Waist-deep in mud, I dug into my pocket and freed my shaving mirror. It was caked in gunk, but I flipped it open to a perfectly clean interior. Gone was the whitish wisp that was Shar's earthly presence. Instead, she raged like a thunderstorm.

"You have *failed me* for the last time, James Crowley!" her voice roared. I'd never heard such an authoritative tone from her before, and it had me concerned.

The ground beneath my knees gave out and I plunged deeper. I dropped the mirror. Thorns dug through my gloves, tearing into skin as I tried to fight it. Was this her?

"I haven't," I groaned.

"Tourmaline is dead. Your plan is forfeit."

"She's irrelevant," I said.

"No. You are."

"It amazes me that an all-seeing angel can be so fucking blind," I snarled. Probably should've chosen my words more carefully. The mud rose to my chest, or rather, I guess I plummeted into it.

The idea I'd be submerged so deep beneath the swamp I'd once again be buried alive started to become clear. Angels sure have clever ways to keep you out of Hell.

"You were right," I said, starting to get frantic. "He's here. The Betrayer."

Stillness. The ground stopped shifting beneath me. Clinging to the thorns until my gloves were shredded and my bloodless hands were gashed to pieces, I heaved myself up.

"You cannot be trusted," Shar said. "You will bend the truth into whatever shape suits you."

"I ain't lying, Shar." Then, knowing better than to push my luck, I added the last part of her name. "He came to me in the cathedral, cocky as a squirrel who'd found a nut. Knew you couldn't see him. He wanted me to get rid of Tourmaline."

Now that gave her pause. "His own child?"

"Some parents get sick of their kids. Heck, most do."

"Get to the point."

"He offered me freedom if I—"

"You?" The storm in the mirror subsided, and there was the calm, judgmental Shar I'd come to know. "Centuries since the last Hand he stole from us, and he chooses *you*?"

"Don't sound so surprised," I muttered.

"On the contrary, I'm pleased. Scraping the bottom of the barrel. How far he's fallen."

"So, it's true, then? He converts Hands of God?" I asked.

"If by 'convert,' you mean transform you into ravenous, bloodsucking abominations who pervert and destroy everything they touch, then yes."

"He seemed happy," I dared say.

"What more proof of their curse do you need than the mess you just crawled out of?"

I scooped up Shar's mirror and brought it closer to my face. Beyond it, the silhouettes of Rosa and those accompanying her stirred.

"Look, I did what he asked. I gained his trust. I found a way to do your bidding, as always. He's gonna approach me now that it's done."

"Why did you not end him when you had the chance?"

I shook my head, still splitting my attention between the mirror and Rosa. "I couldn't. He had me surrounded by his ilk."

"You kept all of this from me," she said. "From the Almighty and from the White Throne. Now you expect me to believe anything you have to say?"

"I'm an honest man," I said. "Lincoln's got nothing on me."

"No." Her form swirled within the glass. "Your service rendered to the White Throne is completed, Crowley. It is time you meet the fate you deserve."

I lost any semblance of composure I still held. "I'm sorry, Shargrafein! I did what you asked! I'm sorry if you—"

"Everyone's sorry on judgment day."

From the direction of the campsite, fire flared on the ground, painting Rosa's form in clear shadow. Only this one wasn't natural—it was green—which could mean only one thing.

"You did all of this for her," Shar said. "To feed your juvenile infatuation. Fine things have been laid upon your table, but you've become determined to grasp only for the things you can't reach."

"That ain't true."

"You would sacrifice everything to become the Betrayer's pawn for her. So that you can sit at her side for the rest of her mortal life, until she's shriveled and old and destined for Hell. For where else do you think a sinner shall go?"

"No."

"No?" Shar's gleeful guffaw could have sent a shiver up my spine if I felt shivers. "I promise, she has sinned in more ways than you can imagine."

"I don't give two shits about her breaking the words in your boss's big book! I meant no. You ain't right. I don't deserve her. No way. Willy probably didn't neither, but a heck of a lot more than I do."

"I see through you, Crowley. Deceive yourself, but you cannot deceive God."

"Then he's blind, because that's the damn truth," I said. "I just . . . she shouldn't do what she's about to alone."

"She isn't alone."

An old coot from Britain with a hard-on for the supernatural. His artist partner who didn't even want to be anywhere near the place. A voodoo witch clinging to what little was left of her power, desperate for an old life with followers and an heir. Not a soul in Crescent City was there for Rosa. Not one of them knew her grief. Didn't make them bad people, just was what it was.

"She is," I said. "And all I did was make it worse, standing in her way. But my head's clear now."

"Then I am glad that before your end you finally have clarity," Shar said. Her tone was soft, pitying. I preferred the harsh edge.

"Give me this, Shargrafein. Let me help her, and I *will* kill your Betrayer for you. I'll serve you for eternity without complaint. Just let me keep her safe."

"I already have you for eternity. And you are incapable of not complaining."

"I ain't asking. I'm begging. And you've got nothing to lose. Either I kill him, or he kills me, and maybe, you get a Black Badge you can tolerate."

"Or perhaps you change your mind in the face of eternal damnation and join him. You Children are so . . . weak, after all."

"Even better. Then, you get the pleasure of hunting me. You'll enjoy it. Heck, we might even find something you get off on. Win-win."

Her form swirled, but she didn't answer.

The eldritch flame near Rosa flashed and grew. Some new ingredient being added to it, I reckoned.

"Please," I whispered.

"Fine," she said. "But if the Betrayer does not come for you, then that is the end. You will be buried so deep, you'll be the foundation of the great cities of the future. Never found. Bedrock."

I exhaled through my teeth. "You're an angel, Shar. Truly."

"As if you have any chance against him," she added.

The ground loosened its grip on me and I felt myself rising fully to the surface.

"Never count out a Scuttler." I went to snap the mirror shut, then stopped. "Oh, one question. Is he really Judas? That's bullshit, right?"

No answer. Not that I was surprised.

One by one, I started ripping thorns away to free myself. Until I heard a snort.

Timp bowed to offer me her mane. I grabbed on and she lifted me free of the mud.

"Found your spine, eh, girl?" I asked, patting her side. She tapped a hoof. "You're right. That one was on me."

I checked to make sure I had my guns and belongings. Still there, though filthy.

Timp moved in front of me and slightly lowered her bleeding back.

"Nah, I won't weigh you down after that. We walk together. And I promise, we'll get you fixed up as soon as this is over."

She huffed and I took her reins and started in Rosa's direction.

God, was I sick of the swamp and this city. Been nothing but trouble since arriving, but this was it. Wouldn't be long before Judas came knocking, and that would be the end.

"Things were simpler when you were the only family I had, weren't they, Timp?" I chuckled. "Yep. I miss simple."

TWENTY-THREE

Timp and I splashed through the swamp until the fog dissipated enough for us to see each other. I heard movement before the voice.

"Who's there?" the voice trembled. A gun cocked.

It was Harker. Where the hell had he gotten a gun? No one should've trusted that man with a firearm. Too squirrelly. He and Bram had taken what appeared to be a guard post several strides from where the campsite was set up.

"Oh, stuff it in your pants," I hollered back. "It's me."

I pushed through the brush. Harker had a rusty shotgun aimed my way, though his hands were trembling.

"My God, Mr. Crowley, trouble sure does seem to follow you," Bram said, slightly out of breath. He sat on a log gripping his thigh, seeming well enough. Guess Laveau's charms had done most of their work.

"Got along fine until I met you," I countered.

Harker rolled his eyes. "Somehow, I doubt that."

"Irish's killer is dead, by the way. You're welcome."

Both men went silent. Bram drew a cross over his chest

with his finger. As I went by, I disarmed Harker in one smooth motion.

"Hey, that's mine—"

"You're gonna hurt yourself."

I tossed the shotgun into the swamp. Harker pushed me with two hands. I could tell he wasn't thinking. It was just reflex. His eyes went wide with fear, and Timp damn near bit his fingers off.

"You, uh . . . owe me for that . . ." he stammered.

My glare leveled on him. "You'd be lucky if that thing still fired. Where'd you find it, a junkyard?" I turned my glare to Bram. "Goddammit, Bram. I thought I told you two to hop the next boat out. Instead, you brave the swamps again. You want them grunches to finish the job or something?"

"It didn't seem proper to leave in such a manner," Bram replied.

"Proper ain't got a damn thing to do with it."

Bram tried to stand. It didn't work. He just ended up falling back on his rump and wincing. "We've come a long way with Rosa, Mr. Crowley. It would be wrong to abscond just as she faces her gravest trial."

I scoffed. "Or a chance to witness the occult. I see right through you, Mr. Stoker."

"A rare occasion, then, that opportunity and the right thing share a path."

Exasperated didn't begin to cover the sigh I let out. Placing my hand on Harker's shoulder, I met his gaze. "Get a new job."

He froze like a mouse caught in a cat's shadow. Didn't even blink.

"And you," I said to Bram. "Find a new hobby. Vampires, séances—I'm telling you, this is how good people die."

"Be that as it may, I have a calling, and I plan to see it through to the end. Whatever that end may be."

"You already almost lost a leg," I said.

"Don't worry. I've got another." He raised his good leg, waggling his foot around in a circle.

"Suit yourself."

The greenish firelight emanated a short distance away, and I clicked my tongue to get Timp moving with me. I'll give them some credit: Bram and Harker were ready to defend against who they worried might be an intruder. Wouldn't have lasted long if I'd had ill intent, but it's the thought that counts.

The campsite was anything but. Hard to classify it, so I guess I'll just call it a shrine to nature. A brass bowl sat atop a tree stump, with strong incense inside causing the verdant flame. Stones were arrayed in a circle around it, unmarked and each a different size. Like something cavemen might have done to beg the sky not to rain. And overhead, two gnarled trees met in an arch, twisting together like horny lovers.

Rosa knelt in the mud on one side of the stump. She wasn't at ease. Uncomfortable looking, even. If she wanted to spring to her feet and flee, she could have done so with ease.

Laveau, positioned across from her, was the opposite. She was right at home, cross-legged, concentrating on putting the finishing touches on sewing a tiny doll made of thread and reeds. Damballah hung around her shoulders and hissed at Timp, getting her to give a bit of ground.

Back against a rotting tree trunk, the drunkard was tied up, facing the stump between them. His black suit was stained brown from dirt. His thick double chin hung against his chest, and he was snoring. Could've started a fire just off his liquor breath.

"If you are here to argue, James, I'd ask that you please leave," Laveau said calmly, not looking up from her work.

I stared at Rosa. Disheveled as she was from the hell we'd

been through, that raven-black hair could fight off any grime. Her sleeves were hacked up, her snake-and-dagger tattoo peeking through the shredded strands. And those eyes. Through a tousle of loose hair, she stared up at me without anger or contempt. Wasn't love either.

What I saw justified what I'd promised Shar. She was a scared woman in need of a friend. That's all.

"I'm not," I said, letting Timp go. She trotted over to nuzzle against Rosa's head. I followed, kneeling beside her like a love-drunk idiot about to propose. "I'm sorry for how I've been and for taking so long to tell you the truth about me." I laughed at myself. "The truth . . . Well, the truth is I just didn't want this life for you. I know what happens when you turn this page, and the story has no happy ending. Doesn't get easier knowing more than we humans should know."

Rosa watched me out of the corners of her eyes now. They glistened, the beginning of some emotion.

"But seeing as how you hog-tied this asshole and brought him out here all yourself, clearly, you know what you want. Only a fool would try to stand in the way. But family's got to be at your side, through thick and through thin. So, that's my dumb speech. And here I am to help however you need me."

A single tear slowly trailed down her cheek, washing away a thin streak of dirt. For a second, I thought we were in for waterworks, but in typical Rosa fashion, her lips lifted to a smirk.

"Family, eh? You adopting me, *anciano*?"

"Very funny." I reached to her clasped hands, taking hold of one. "It's the law of the West. The companions you ride with are family. Because if you don't treat them that way, you'll all need a grave dug sooner than later."

"You're a big softie, you know that?"

A few inappropriate retorts came to mind, but I decided

to be a gentleman. I simply patted her hand, smiled, then took my seat on the stump.

"So." I clapped my hands and rubbed them together. "You planning to puppet him, right, Laveau?"

"That is a degrading term," she said.

"Forgive me for being ignorant of all your voodoo colloquialisms."

"I admit, it is not the simplest method, but thanks to your friend Rougarou, neither I nor Rosa have access to my home, to everything I needed to commune in a more civil manner. And considering the *explosion* in Crescent City, it seems speed is of the essence. Can I assume that was your doing?"

"Whoops." I looked to Rosa and shrugged. "You'll be pleased, though. The city will soon know sure enough that you didn't touch the senator."

Marie nodded. "Until the next issue arises, then."

"Jesus, Joseph, and Mary. Thank-yous ain't easy to come by around here."

"Grow up, James," Rosa said.

I laughed. We wouldn't be traveling companions without throwing insults back and forth during downtime. Big Davey would've fit right in around this fire—may he rest in peace.

"There." Laveau finished the doll and held it up. It bore a striking resemblance to the drunkard, even without proper materials. Laveau didn't earn her nickname by accident.

"That simple, huh?" I asked.

"To perform, yes," she said. "But it's the stain it leaves on the soul that makes methods such as this dangerous. To control another against their will. To own their body entirely. It mars the soul in a way that can never be washed away."

I remembered back in Revelation Springs when I'd used a Nephilim's cursed harmonica to control Rosa and keep her from ruining her life. That guilt still clung to me every time the thought snuck in, and it would never go away. I couldn't imagine how many memories like that Laveau had.

"If you don't feel comfortable . . ." Rosa said meekly.

Laveau smiled. "I have enough blemishes to bear one more in order to help a lost soul, dear. It is you I worry for."

Rosa swallowed. "You said it won't hurt him."

"Not in a lasting way. Memories of your beloved may bridge into his dreams and disorient him. But it will fade in time, and he will go on living never having known of this invasion."

"I did volunteer, you know," Bram spoke up from behind us. They'd left their post to sit on a tree trunk at the edge of the site. "The offer still stands."

"We already went through this," Rosa said. "No."

"Better I choose than it be forced upon a stranger. I'd like to help," Bram argued.

"You just want another experience for your notes," I said.

"Merely an ancillary perk."

"How about nobody does it?" Harker said. "Oh, right. I'm not even here."

"Choose or not, it cannot be you," Laveau said without looking up. "She cannot have a relationship with the man. It will distract her and that is not a danger worth risking to satiate your curiosity."

Bram's disappointment was evident, but it didn't seem like the first time he'd been told the same. He backed down quick, though, with Harker continuing to complain under his breath.

"I, for one, think you made a good choice," I addressed Rosa. "Maybe it'll teach the drunk how to treat a lady."

"You know him?" Rosa asked.

"Not from a hole in the wall, but I got a few minutes watching him at work with the fairer sex. I may not love you doing this, but helping you is probably the only kindness he's ever done a woman."

"He was quite rude to me as well," Rosa said with a small smile. "Easy to get to follow me, though."

Timperina snorted.

"Tell yourself whatever you must to justify this," Laveau said, "but whatever you do, do not take this lightly."

I removed my hat and held it by the fire to dry. "Marie, if I didn't know better, I'd think you were trying to talk Rosa out of it."

Laveau got to her feet and stroked Damballah's head. "Those who trivialize what we do will find themselves consumed by it."

Rosa's cheeks went pale. Mine probably would have too if they could. A grave warning, but probably half the reason the White Throne was content to call Laveau a friend. Witches could be much, much more wicked.

The green light played eerily across Laveau's dark features in a way that made her seem far from matronly for once. She circled it, and when she reached Rosa, she extended her hand without a word. Rosa, clearly knowing what to expect, stretched out her own palm. Then Laveau pricked Rosa's finger with her sewing needle.

Rosa recoiled and sucked on the wound. Her nervous gaze went to me.

My attention was on the blood painting the needle red, dripping down the length of it. A white strand of thread hung limply from the other side, and slowly, it went crimson.

"Last chance," Marie said.

Rosa nodded, and Laveau raised the effigy of the drunk and ran the needle through the heart of the little doll.

Rosa's breath shuddered. She straightened her spine, shoulders pushed back.

"You wanted this," I reminded her.

Laveau continued on around to the passed-out man. She lifted his arm and drew blood from his finger in the same manner, then passed the needle through the same spot on the doll. Once it was through, she bit off the string and tossed the needle into the fire.

Turning back to Rosa, she held out an open palm. "Now, something of Willy's that he cherished, which you now cherish in his stead."

Rosa's stare got lost in the fire. She breathed low and fast. I scooted closer and took her hand, pressing a thumb against the still bleeding prick. Her fingers clasped mine. If the White Throne cared about me at all, they'd have given me normal feeling just that once . . . Imagination would have to suffice.

"Rosa, it is now or never," Laveau insisted.

"Right." The muscles in her hand stretched as her grip around mine tightened. One last breath, then she reached into her pocket and pulled out a ring.

I recognized it. Didn't even know she still had it. Her wedding band, which I'd discovered on Willy's dead and detached finger soon after he was murdered in Dead Acre.

"I'd never seen him as nervous as the day he presented this to me," Rosa sniveled. "He should have walked away."

"He's lucky he didn't," I said.

"Then I should've said no."

"No time in this life for should haves." I gave her hand a squeeze. "Now, go on. Unburden your soul."

She met my gaze, then handed the ring to Laveau. Her fingers fought to maintain a hold on the last thing she had to remember her husband by, but she got it done.

Goodbyes are never easy.

Laveau took it, all business, and placed it around the arm of the little doll. Then she approached the basin and suspended it over the absinthe-hued flames. There, she paused to look back at Rosa. Not a word was shared, but Rosa nodded her approval.

Her throat clenched visibly as Laveau let the bloodied doll and the ring fall. The little idol crackled and gradually caught. Little fiery worms crawled around as the straw burned. The beads Marie had used for eyes melted. Laveau stepped back and sat between Rosa and the unconscious drunk.

"Your hand again," she instructed.

Rosa gave her the hand I wasn't holding. Laveau stretched it out toward the fire, close enough to feel the heat.

"I will act as your conduit," Laveau said. "Whatever you do, Rosa, do not let go. No matter what."

Rosa grunted.

"Say it," Laveau insisted.

"I won't let go."

"Good. Because if you do, this man's mind will sever from our mortal plane, and then something innocent becomes murder."

Harker gasped audibly behind us.

"You never mentioned that part," Bram said.

We all ignored the two of them.

"I understand," Rosa said, voice quavering.

Laveau took a deep breath as she gripped the drunkard's hand.

"Now, wait a bleeding minute," Bram said, doing his best to stagger forward.

I turned toward him. "That's enough, Bram. You wanted to play in the Devil's playground, don't get upset when demons join you."

"But this is—"

"Exactly what you wanted. The supernatural. What did you expect? Now sit down before I sit you down."

He huffed a bit, but listened.

Rosa eyed me, a thank-you in there somewhere.

Her hand was now touching that of this stranger, and a flash of something like anger slithered up inside me. I shoved it down, glancing down at Rosa's other hand, which I still held a bit too tightly.

Laveau settled into her spot and closed her eyes. She spoke some words in French, and her pupils started to dance back and forth under her eyelids.

"Think of him, and only him," Laveau said. "Your happiest memories. Your worst memories. Everything in between."

I didn't have to worry about Rosa letting go of me. Her knuckles were white from squeezing, as she too closed her eyes and dug into her memories. All I could do was watch helplessly. Not a position I was used to, but this was what I needed to be for Rosa. A helping hand.

The fire burned on, the doll little more than shreds crisping beside the glowing ring. I can't say I understood how all this mysticism worked, but I got the gist of it. Things in our world are connected—like giving a piece of sculpted metal intrinsic value, binding two souls together for life.

Laveau's eyes were like scurrying rabbits. She murmured under her breath something that sounded like tongues. No longer French. Total drivel from what I could tell. The drunkard moaned and twitched. He didn't wake.

Must have gone on like that for a few minutes. Loneliest I'd been in a spell. Even Timp kept her distance, knowing instinctually that she shouldn't interfere with witchcraft.

Then I saw it. Rosa's eyes had filled to a point she couldn't hold it in any longer. Tears came freely, her breathing in deep heaves.

"It is you," Laveau spoke softly. It wasn't a whisper, but her voice had an ethereal quality to it, like it didn't belong to her. No accent or anything. "William Cornelius Massey, it is you."

The drunkard inhaling suddenly scared the shit out of me. Rosa too. Her eyes sprang open, and she pulled her hand free of mine to defend herself. Her other hand tried to do the same, but Laveau had it in a death grip.

The drunkard leaned forward, eyes searching from side to side like a baby just born. I turned to Laveau. Her eyes were open now, only they were white clouds. Sort of like mine got when I Divined, and I reckoned this was a similar sort of a thing.

"What . . . is . . ." Like Laveau, the drunk's voice was his but not. I'd heard the man slurring and cursing back at the bar, and this was his tone with none of the timbre. Just cold, emotionless words delivered by a puppet.

"Willy?" Rosa asked, barely able to get the word out.

The puppet turned to her and blinked.

"Willy, is that you?"

The man's eyes were aimed at her, but like the voice, they were lifeless. It was my first time witnessing anything like this firsthand. In my head, it'd been more romantic, where he'd inhabited the body in full and they shared one last loving embrace.

Only real life ain't butterflies and rainbows.

"Rosa?" he asked.

"It's me," Rosa said, swallowing the lump in her throat. Her eyes were puffy. Could barely speak. "Willy, it's me."

"I . . . where am I?"

"I don't know . . ." She nearly broke down at that, but I regripped her hand to remind her she wasn't alone. "At peace, I hope."

"Are you okay?" Willy asked through the drunk.

She nodded. "I am. Better than okay now."

"You do always bounce back, don't you, my love? And Father?"

Rosa chuckled through her tears. "Complaining about something or other no doubt."

I thought I saw the puppet's lips flicker with the slightest smile as well, but I was probably projecting.

"Same as always, then," he said.

"God." Rosa bit her lip to steady her crying. "I miss you, darling. I miss your smell." She laughed again. "Funny how we remember tiny things like that. It was like leather from whatever boot you were fixing in your shop."

"You always hated that."

"No. I hated so many things, Willy, but never anything about you. The world dealt me a difficult hand . . . I—"

"I know it did, sweetheart."

It was hard to watch this drunk who was so putrid in life speaking such kind words. Even harder knowing what it took to get here, and how ephemeral it would be.

"You never pried," Rosa said.

"I never had to," Willy answered.

Rosa gulped audibly. She was on the verge of breaking down, as any normal person with feelings would in a situation like this. I can't quite say how I felt. I'd never known them together. Hearing terms like "darling" and "sweetheart" made me feel queer. Like I was eavesdropping on my parents or hiding under their bed.

A feeling of dread stole over me. Like I didn't belong.

The green fire grew brighter, then lost potency, flickering like a candle in the breeze.

Laveau's eyelids—which had been stuck open all this time—blinked. "I'm losing him."

The desire to let go of Rosa's hand overwhelmed me. Fog

engulfed us so much that even Timperina wasn't visible. Maybe it was darkness. Something didn't feel right. It wasn't just that I didn't belong; something *else* didn't. Like we weren't alone.

"Willy, I need to tell you something," Rosa said.

"You can tell me anything, honey," he answered. His voice sounded different all of a sudden. Deeper.

"Rosa, I think it's time to end this," I said.

She squeezed me harder. I looked down at my hand, and by God, as much as I might have tried to pull free, I couldn't. It was like she'd gained the strength of a minotaur. My bones crunched. And not just mine. Laveau whimpered as her eyes twinkled in and out of the trance. Her fingertips lost all their color.

"Anything cruel I ever said to you," Rosa went on. "Anything at all. I didn't mean it. You were the best thing in my life. It should have been me who died, not you."

"You're right," Willy said, voice even deeper. "Darkness clings to you like a sickness. It chokes you. Guides your every move. You are beyond redemption."

Rosa recoiled. "What?"

"Is that not the answer you were looking for?" Willy chortled. An evil sound. A demonic thing. "They so rarely are. You deserve darkness, Rosa Massey; you just refuse to embrace it."

"No . . . I . . ."

"You have no inkling of what you are, Rosa. But I've found you."

"Rosa, you have to let go," I said. "Rosa!"

Unable to break free of her, I scrambled around in front of her, nearly knocking the bronze basin over into the fire. I tried to free Laveau, but Rosa wouldn't give up an inch.

Laveau whispered her name and started to convulse.

"What are you talking about, Willy?" Rosa said, as if completely ignorant to my presence. "I found you."

"After so many centuries, here you are," Willy said. The body stood, the ropes that bound him to the tree snapped. And when he rose, it was unnatural as hell, no bending of the knees or anything. Just seated one second, and right up the next.

As it strode forward, I did the only thing I could do and stepped over the log to try to punch it. Nothing. It was like hitting stone.

"James! Stop!" Rosa shouted like she was totally oblivious to the strangeness that had begun.

I did stop. Only not because I wanted to. What I wanted to do was put a dozen silver slugs through his head but found myself unable to move. Everything became frozen in time except them.

Willy's puppet stopped in front of Rosa, reached out, and wiped the tear from her cheek.

"Perfection," he whispered.

Rosa could hardly catch her breath as she met that lifeless stare. "Willy, you're confusing me."

His hand moved down her face to her neck. The fingers slowly edged around her throat. "Stop diminishing yourself with remorse for these mortals," he said. "You are finally home, thanks to them."

His eyes darted to Laveau and her head lurched back suddenly. She unleashed an earsplitting scream.

TWENTY-FOUR

Laveau's shrieking echoed all around me. The fire turned from green to blueish white. No, it didn't change colors; it froze. I didn't believe fire *could* freeze, but it did. Just hovered there like an ice sculpture. But not before one of those tendrils lashed out at the puppet-man and engulfed him.

Frost crept upward, starting at his toes and crackling along until he too was blue-white like Hell itself. His skin splintered off in chunks, then the bone, and whatever else. His eyes became piercing sapphires, reminding me all too much of the possessed Yeti I'd met recently.

This was different by spades.

It didn't cause just a tingle or an itch in my Black Badge mark either. This was all-encompassing.

"The portal is open, Rosa. The time has come to step through," Willy said, just before the puppet's head shattered to snowy dust.

Darkness and light inverted. Down became up—more accurately, no direction seemed right anymore. Things just floated without anchor or hold to reality. Everything distorted. The very air before us split in two, like someone dragged a sword through it. My whole body—no longer numb—felt turned inside out. I think I joined Laveau in screaming, and when I stopped, I wasn't sure where I was.

The ground shifted to a murky, gloomy darkness. And though snowflakes drifted all around me, there was no touch of Christmas joy. They didn't dither downward or pile up. Just fluttered on the chill air. Like I said, I don't know how to explain it. There simply was no down. No up. Our whole world spun. Frost clung to my clothes and my hat and beard. Everything.

And the cold. I longed for numbness because I'd forgotten what it was to be freezing, and all at once, I could feel again like a normal human. My very bones chattered.

"R-R-Rosa!" I called out, shivering.

I put my hand in salute over my eyes to see better through the endless snow. What had been a slit in the sky was now an all-encompassing chasm. Things—dreadful, horrible things—moved in the darkness. Shadows large and small, making inhuman sounds and insect-like clicks.

I ignored them until I spotted Rosa, standing across the strange inky tundra with the drunk in front of her. He had his arms wrapped around her. I could make out his face, but it wasn't his. As he held her, he glared right at me and smirked.

"*I should thank you, James Crowley. You brought her right to us.*" That same deep voice filled the air all around me, only now it had more form to it. Echoing deeper and deeper, endlessly inward.

"Get your goddamn hands off her!" I shouted.

"*She no longer has to hide.*"

"Whatever you are, I'll kill you. Let her go!"

His laughter kept getting louder and louder in my ears. Familiar laughter. And that was when I realized exactly who I was dealing with. What a damn fool I'd been, tempting fate with the eyes of the unholy upon me. The eyes of the Devil.

Not Lucifer. He was too lazy and fat on his throne to handle anything himself. No. This was the same demon I'd thwarted back in Revelation Springs. A master of mischief. Chekoketh.

"You," I spat.

"*I told you I would see you soon*," Chekoketh replied. "*Welcome to my domain*."

I wasn't exactly sure what that meant. This couldn't be Hell . . . could it?

"You son of a bitch! Let her go!"

"*I think not*."

"You have me here. So let's dance, demon. If you can take me."

"*I have no interest in you, Hand of God. Only her. But your despair will be a welcome addition*." Icy air gusted against me, like it was his breath. I could almost sense him reaching out to choke me.

I squinted against it. The air choked my lungs as I spoke. "What do you want with her?"

Again, his callous laugh rattled me to my core. "*All this time with her, and you still have no idea. Shargrafein is right about you*."

That was it! Shar could help. I dug into my pocket and pulled out the mirror. My hand shook, fumbling to flip it open. When I did, despair became my bedfellow. No reflection or light. Just more of the same void. Totally black. Lifeless. Hopeless.

"Good-for-nothing angels!" I shouted, shoving the mirror away.

I looked back to Rosa. The demon mirage posing as Willy released her from his embrace, stepped back, and extended a single hand, like a gentleman encouraging his woman to go on ahead.

Bastard, lying piece of shit. If it ever really was Willy, Chekoketh intervened to send her right to her doom.

She glanced back, looking past me, through me. There was longing in her eyes.

"Rosa, get away from him!"

She took his hand.

"No!" I shouted.

They started to walk together, hand in hand. I charged like a battered mule. The snow turned fierce, balls of ice and sharp shards whipping around and stabbing at me. The gust twisted into a gale. I fought against it with all I had, taking the cuts and bruises in stride.

A screeching creature leaped at me from within the rift. The hellish blizzard and tenebrosity caused by the demon made it impossible to discern much, but there were plenty of scaly legs and gnashing teeth.

I pulled my pistol and put a bullet through those very teeth.

"Let her go!" I shouted again.

Something else swooped down, digging talons into my shoulder. My feet lifted, and I fought, managing to tear my knife free of my boot. I slashed up at a bat-like wing and the sinuous appendage severed from its body. But that didn't relinquish its grip. Together we toppled, the thing unable to find balance. I slashed again, and again, until we crashed hard to the ground. My face hit first, and again, I felt it. I felt every damn bit of it. Tasted blood in my mouth.

I rose, one word ravaging my mind: run.

That was something I'd always been good at. Whether it was running from trouble, or into trouble—the physical action all the same.

Except I couldn't. Not this time.

Rosa and Chekoketh kept walking, though I could tell she was hesitant. Rosa was too smart to fall for tricks. A part of her had to be resisting.

"James!" Her voice reverberated in my head, but I didn't see her lips move. "James!" it called again, reminding me of how much I liked hearing it from her mouth.

"Rosa, you can beat this," I called out. "You can move on!"

I pushed toward her while more scions of Hell came for me. I unloaded every bullet I had. Stabbed my knife dull. So long yearning to feel human again, and now I had that awful pleasure. Be careful what you wish for.

My body was battered and bruised. Gashed, cut. But like a barreling freight train, I never slowed. Gained ground on them too.

Shouldering a beast out of the way, I grabbed my lasso and lashed out. The loop swirled through the air, a perfect toss right for Rosa's waist. Then, I was suddenly yanked back, and it fell just short.

My feet flew out from beneath me and I fell flat. Rolling over quickly, I saw an icy chain around them, wielded in one hand by something truly awful. In its other, it gripped the staff of a scythe too large for any mortal to wield.

Its tattered black cloak billowed in the storm, draped around skeletal limbs. A hood rose to a sharp point above its head, only there wasn't a head . . . Just pure blackness.

A reaper.

"*It's futile*!" Chekoketh bellowed. "*She is ours. She will be our champion.*"

"She don't belong to nobody!" I spat.

I was all out of bullets. All out of words. All out of moves. I tried to get my feet free, but the chain tightened, making my foot go numb. Then the reaper started to wind it around his wrist, dragging me ever closer. The storm either died down or I got used to it enough to see. Behind him, grotesque creatures and beasts of all sizes and types amassed. All of Hell had shown up for this party.

Only, that wasn't all.

Until then, I'd been too much a fool to look back. Beyond all the monsters was a gateway to the swampy shrine right where I'd been before.

I hadn't been transported to Hell. Somehow, through Rosa and Laveau, and maybe me, Chekoketh had used our power to open a Hellmouth while we contacted another realm and created a portal-rift between realms. The Hellmouth all around us, I was caught between worlds, stuck in a sort of purgatory.

The air rippled and whirled. Flying demons swirled by the dozens.

"*Eternal damnation is not enough*," Chekoketh said. "*No. I have a special torture reserved for you, James Crowley. For you and all the Hands of God. We have wallowed in the dark too long.*"

"You'll unleash this nightmare upon my kind?" I replied as the reaper dragged me closer and closer.

"*The White Throne's favored Children will be like lambs to the slaughter.*"

"Where's the sport in that?" I barked, desperate. "No wonder your master lost."

"*You cannot goad me, human*," Chekoketh said.

I was mere feet from the reaper now, its scythe extended. I expected the worst, but instead, the curved blade dug under my back and scooped me up until I found myself face-to-face with the faceless hood.

"*The White Throne has its servants like you*," Chekoketh said. "*We have ours. That is your fate, Crowley. To be my reaper. To gather all the souls that fall at Rosa's hands after I unlock her true power.*"

Suddenly, the chains loosened, and I dropped to my feet. A face began to appear in the hood. My face.

"*My slave. For eternity . . .*"

"I'll fucking kill you!"

Close enough to use my knife, I brought it up and lunged. The blade stopped in front of the reaper, my whole arm going board-stiff. All my muscles burned with white-hot agony like I can't even describe. All I could do was scream until my voice went raw.

Chekoketh's laugh boomed like thunder. And just then, something else stole my attention. The hellish beasts started to panic, groaning and screeching. Some fell, others ran. Still others sought refuge deeper into the swirling rift.

A pack of hellhounds started to stampede over each other and only the ones that could fly were safe.

The reaper, however, held its position while I kept roaring in pain until, out of nowhere, the cloak ripped in half and the ghostly thing vanished in a wisp of black smoke. My body came free, and my knife plunged forward, where it was promptly caught.

"What have you done, *Hamsa*?" Judas asked, wearing a loose, billowing black robe strangely similar to the reaper.

Black blood trickled down from his lips and that air of dignity from earlier was replaced by his more feral nature. Blue-black veins sprawled all over his face. Long, sharp fangs glistened with that same dark fluid. And his dark eyes were tinged like fire.

"This wasn't me," I said.

"Yet here you are, *Hamsa*." He took my arm. "The beasts pour through. We must depart."

"Not without her." I pulled free and pointed back at Rosa. Though she was barely visible through the fog and snow now. Almost gone.

Judas stepped past me and looked through the rift, back at our world.

"Which of you is it this time?" Judas said calmly.

Then, Rosa stopped. Everything stopped.

"*You*?" Chekoketh spoke. "*It can't be you*."

"Mammon? Moloch? Ah, no. I know that voice. Chekoketh."

"*You would dare show yourself here*?"

"Azrael never was very fond of you."

"*Enough of this. Destroy him, my pets*!" Chekoketh's command was obeyed without hesitation. Regardless of the fear clearly raging through the demonic army, they all turned and crashed upon us. Wings slashed from the sky. I swung blindly as the snow swirled, but if I'm being honest, I was pretty much useless in this fight. I blinked once, and Judas stood exactly where he had been, calm as ever.

A dozen or more monsters dropped dead around us. Judas licked his lips.

"Get her!" I barked.

He nodded, then zipped across the tundra in a blur. More beasts stirred in the distance. Growls and roars rang out like a chorus and the storm got so intense, I was blind. Could barely stay upright against the driving wind.

Calling out for Rosa, I squinted to try and see anything. Before I knew it, Judas was in front of me, Rosa's body slung over his shoulder. She looked to be unconscious, and her skin was deathly pale.

"*Betrayer!*" Chekoketh bellowed. "*Deceiver! It could have been you to stand as our champion!*"

Judas glanced up. "I am no one's servant."

"Is she al—" Before I could get my words out, Judas took my arm and pulled me toward the Hellmouth's exit. Creatures slashed and bit at us but found only air. He moved so fast, it was dizzying.

"Judas!" I shouted, but it was buried amid the roaring wind.

TWENTY-FIVE

Pain. That's what it feels like when you're transported through a Hellmouth, from one realm to another. Like your lip being stretched back over the crown of your head.

Judas led me through the open rift toward Crescent City and the tangible world. Frost scraped my flesh, excruciating like nothing else. Then, the roaring of wind, the whipping of snowy ice, the bellowing of Hell's worst creatures ceased. We were back in the swamplands, in the real world, back from Hell, and all the damage I'd taken within went away and I was a numb Hand of God once more.

I'd never been more grateful for it. Though now wasn't the time to count my blessings.

I desperately tried to get my bearings. Where the small, green fire had been, now stood a faint portal of sorts. In it, light was inverted, and ice spewed out. The muck surrounding it was totally frozen, all the creepy trees covered in snow.

Laveau stood before the rift with her hands outstretched, chanting in that same language I couldn't understand. Damballah clung to her neck, maybe a little tighter than was safe.

Judas's knights encircled her. Most fired their crossbows at the monsters pouring out. Chapelwaite stood close as could be, defending her with his sword in one hand and a pistol in the other.

It was surreal. All of it. Unearthly, otherworldly, supernaturally surreal. I've seen a lot of things as a Black Badge, and nothing compared. Nothing came close.

I spun. Timperina neighed and kicked a hellhound with her back hooves. It slammed against a tree trunk and slid down to remain unmoving at its base.

Bram and Harker had their hands full with a flying beast, both men screaming in terror. It had dozens of eyes, multiple sharp-toothed mouths, and barbed wings that slashed at them. Harker had found his shotgun and fired upward without aiming. Sure, the thing worked, but it was clear he'd not so much as pulled a trigger in his whole pitiful life.

I reached into my satchel, digging for rounds, and found it empty. The flying beast continued scratching and gnawing at them.

"The witch holds the rift at bay," Judas said. He still had Rosa over his shoulder.

"Put her down," I demanded, needing to yell over all the chaos.

"There's no time," Judas said.

"I need to see if she's breathing!" I shoved his chest until he obliged, relinquishing her to my outstretched arms. I cradled her there, wiping the rime from her cheeks. People as pale as she looked didn't live long, but raspy breaths snuck through her hoarfrosted lips. She was close enough to death to count the stitches that held it all together.

"Timp!" I whistled.

She reared up, swatting her hooves at another beast to get it off-balance, then trampled over it on her way to me.

I raised Rosa and carefully placed her over Timperina's hind. "If I say run, run."

She snorted.

A shriek drew my attention back to the rift. Another of those multi-eyed monstrosities lifted one of Judas's knights with its talons and dropped him from high enough to break his neck on a rock right beside me. Without hesitating, I grabbed the knight's already loaded crossbow, whipped around, and sent a bolt right through the neck of the one harassing Bram and Harker.

Smoke poured out and it landed at Bram's feet. However, the threat wasn't over. Something grotesque crept across the foggy swamp beyond them.

"Harker, down!" I shouted.

He listened, just as a grunch bounded for the back of his head. I was reloading a weapon I'd never used, hoping to shoot the grunch dead when Bram roared and snatched it by the tail. In a feat of strength I didn't think him capable of, he smashed it down to the ground. Its head cracked hard against the tree stump the two had been watching guard from.

"That's for my leg," he said.

The grunch twitched, but it wasn't going anywhere.

More things behind them fled toward Crescent City. Another went into the wilderness. Who knew how many other invading Hellbeasts did the same.

"Bram, Harker, it's time you went home!" I shouted. I couldn't bring Irish back after getting her killed, but I could save them. A final courtesy to a couple of men I'd called companions for a short time.

Bram wiped the black ichor from his face, eyes gaping. "Yes, I-I believe you are correct, Mr. Crowley."

"Oh, *now* it's time?" Harker squeaked, tossing his shotgun my way. "I've always hated guns."

The fools.

Judas was facing away from them, though now that he was out of Hell, his refined nature had returned. They wouldn't know what he was just by looking at him—probably hadn't even noticed him amidst the calamity. Wouldn't know they stood only twenty or so feet from the father of all vampires, the descendant of Cain, and the one who betrayed their Christ. After everything that happened in that Hellmouth and Chekoketh's words, I believed it now too.

That he really was *the* Judas Iscariot.

Bram had gotten a look at plenty of other supernatural things, though. Enough to write a hundred novels and fill a dozen of Harker's art books. Well done for him.

"Don't look back!" I yelled.

For once, as they started running, they listened. Didn't steal a single backward glance.

I returned to Rosa, peeling back an eyelid with my thumb. If there was a light behind her eyes, I couldn't see it. Not even a single damn floating mote of it. I wasn't sure if it was hypothermia or something else the demon did to her. Couldn't know. Only thing I could be sure about was that she was alive, because if she wasn't, I'd be Divining her horrid final moments.

"Laveau, she needs you!" I called.

Judas's hand fell on my shoulder. "She can't help."

"Like hell she can't." I stormed around Timp toward the Voodoo Queen, my only hope.

The knights continued defending her and she kept chanting. Now that I was settled, I noticed her hands. They were deathly black. Energy coruscated out from them, darkness and light swirling, as if she were absorbing the Hellmouth itself.

"This was unwise," Judas said, stepping up beside me, hands folded behind his back. How could he be so relaxed?

"Yeah, no shit!" I barked.

"We can't hold them for long!" Chapelwaite yelled, slashing an imp in two.

Horse hooves drew my attention, thinking Timperina had gotten spooked. When I turned to calm her, I saw it. A black-armored rider with glowing blue eyes atop a horse that was nothing but bones. His lance, a thing that appeared to be made of black, smoking ice, pierced through the head of one of Judas's knights.

With no transition at all, Judas stood next to me one second, then in a puff of smoke, he had the rider off his horse and tore him apart with his bare hands.

Laveau shrieked and fell to her knees, everything in her keeping her hands raised toward the Hellmouth. Her arms shook like she was holding back the weight of an entire world. I reckon she was.

"*You cannot halt me, witch*!" Chekoketh's voice echoed, though it was distant compared to earlier. "*The end has begun*."

"I knew she was . . . different," Laveau groaned. "I should have stopped myself." With a primordial scream, she pushed her hands forward. The edges of the rift vacillated. Frost turned to mist. Then she sank back a bit more, huffing for breath.

"*I will devour you*!" Chekoketh roared.

"I only wanted to help a lost soul . . ." Laveau lamented.

A giant hand with sharp claws burst through the rift and clutched Laveau by the waist. Chapelwaite rushed in and slashed at it, but the skeletal horse, now riderless, bowled him over.

From the Hellmouth, a Nephilim I recognized stepped through. A goat-man as big as one I'd fought outside Revelation, with curled horns the size of wagon wheels.

It lifted Laveau by the chest, squeezing so hard, I could

hear her ribs cracking all the way from where I stood watching, unable to do a goddamn thing about it.

"Laveau!" I shouted. I tried to run to her, but Judas barred me with his arm.

"Leave her," he said.

The goat-beast opened its mouth to devour her, when suddenly, her body vanished. Damballah plopped down onto the goat-man's arm, slithered upward onto its face, and bit its single eye. The Nephilim howled, flinging the snake across the swamp.

One last illusion from the Voodoo Queen. Laveau remained on the ground, arms outstretched and crackling with energy.

"Do not abandon her, James," she said. "No matter what." She looked back at me and smiled warmly.

My mother was a callous woman who'd practically abandoned me with Father Osgood in Granger's Outlook. Made believe it was for my own good. I knew better. Barely knew her before she kicked the bucket, and that was fine with me. However, I couldn't help wondering what would've become of me if I'd had a mother like Marie Laveau. Probably wouldn't be anywhere near here.

She turned back to the Hellmouth. "Be gone, demon!"

Screaming from the bottom of her lungs, she slowly crept forward, hands still up, bracing against the storm of energy. The rift continued to waver, then shrank. Monsters fled out, desperate to escape. The knights slaughtered many of them.

Laveau's powerful vociferation echoed across the swamplands as the Hellmouth shut all around her in a wave of black distortion. The goat-man was caught in it and got sliced clean in half, his guts pouring out like pig slop.

In a flash, it was closed.

Frost radiated out from the epicenter of where the Hellmouth had been—a tiny region of winter in the hot, mucky swamps. It would melt soon enough without Hell fueling it, though it only served to make the silence more eerie as snowflakes flitted about.

Laveau was gone. But her voice continued to echo.

In my mind, it always would.

TWENTY-SIX

I stared at the spot where Laveau had been. Demonic creatures skippered away, abandoned here in the mortal realm by the closing of the Hellmouth. It could've been far worse, but there were still many loosed upon Earth to terrorize this area and beyond. Enough future work to keep a Black Badge busy for centuries.

I'd known Laveau was powerful. Being able to singlehandedly close a Hellmouth put things in perspective. Living in a city and serving as little more than a healer was far below her talents. She could've owned the entire place with such ability. And now none of her city would ever know what she'd sacrificed to save them from a complete demonic invasion, though I think that's how she'd have wanted it.

Timp neighed and nudged me with her snout. I must not have noticed a few times, because she was insistent. Downright irritated, honestly.

"Rosa," I remembered. I checked her again, and her state hadn't changed. I patted her cheek. "Rosa, wake up."

"Crowley."

I whipped around. Judas and Chapelwaite stood side by side, watching, the former's black robes billowing.

"Can you help her?" I asked Judas.

"Traveling between realms is not a task meant for mortals," he replied.

"I didn't ask that. Can. You. Help. Her?" Each word was punctuated with half the urgency I felt inside, but I was tired, and my undead heart had suffered as much strain as it could handle.

"Perhaps," he said after long contemplation.

"Will you?"

The corner of his mouth rose in what I might've called a wicked sneer. "That, James Crowley, is the right question. And one I cannot answer here."

I got right in his face. "She's hanging on by a thread, you son of a bitch. Where else?"

"Someplace safer than a swamp surrounded by demonkin. Do you think this went unheard? Mortal officers will be on their way, if they aren't already. Soldiers next. Anonymity is my peoples' resource."

"More than her life?"

"More than any life. You are not in a position to argue. But, you did deliver Tourmaline's unworthy heart." He touched his own chest, the self-righteous son of a gun. "And so, our affairs are not concluded. I did not place myself in Chekoketh's cross-hairs for nothing."

I swallowed, then spit off to the side. "You know him well?"

"I know them all, on both sides of their veiled war. Now come, we will go someplace only the dead can hear."

He pulled his hood up over his head, the only part of him not already protected from the sunlight by heavy robes. Thick as the fog was here, and with the canopy of trees above, he was safe from it, but once we entered the city . . .

I had to wonder if he was less concerned about human lawmen, and just worried about the sun, like Tourmaline. Too proud or whatever to admit to how great a weakness he carried. Either way, it didn't seem like I had much of a choice—again. So, I followed him.

Chapelwaite gave me a slap on the back. "Trouble clings to you like shit on a stick, Crowley."

"Yeah," I grumbled. "Sure does."

I took Timp's reins in one hand and walked her. The other I placed on the small of Rosa's back. She kept breathing, which meant there was still time. But, as we started off, I couldn't ignore my predicament.

Judas practically floated in front of me, unafraid. An easy target. I could stab him in the back with my silver knife since I was all out of ammo. I could wait until we hit sunlight and rip his hood down. Fulfill my promise to Shar.

Only, I couldn't yet. Not with Rosa's life hanging so precariously in the balance. Luckily, Judas being so close kept my actions hidden from curious angels.

And I suppose Judas was aware of all that. It explained his leisurely pace, like we were in an old English garden and not some frost-bitten swampland now infested by demonic beings as much as mosquitos.

I heard a hiss and looked down. Timp sidestepped and stomped. I held her back. Damballah lay on top of a fallen tree trunk, gazing up at me.

"You did good, snake," I said.

It rose, half its body upright and swaying. She tilted her head.

"I'll miss her too." I looked around. "Might make a better home for you out here, though. You can find a mate."

She hissed again.

"I'm sorry."

I stepped over the log and clicked my tongue to get Timp moving again. Damballah slithered down the trunk and followed along beside me.

"All right. I guess you're coming too, then."

A grumpy old horse, a house-trained snake, and a Black Badge . . . We were one odd fellow away from forming our own circus.

TWENTY-SEVEN

Crescent City had descended into even more madness than when I'd left. At least this time it wasn't my fault, necessarily. I couldn't have known what would happen when Rosa tried to commune with Willy . . . though I had warned her.

Still, it was something witches and covens of all sorts had been doing for ages. Never resulted in a Hellmouth tearing through the fabric of reality. Not that I know of. What was it about Rosa? Chekoketh, Laveau, even back in Revelation—people kept seeing something in her.

I forced it out of my mind when I caught a glimpse of her pale face. All she was now was a helpless, dying young woman caught in a feud between Heaven and Hell.

I'd heard it said when elephants fight, it's the grass that suffers.

Guess it's true.

Judas and the others stuck to covered walks and storefront awnings—as distanced from sunlight as possible. His long cloak and hood seemed to do the trick of protecting him, though it couldn't be comfortable wearing only wool between skin and agony. Luckily, it was a cloudy morning.

Citizens fled the city, unable to be controlled by a police force I'd spread thin with my actions. Inhuman roars and human screams rang out from within. Some of the straggling beasts which poured out of the Hellmouth weren't wasting any time hunting.

Gunshots went off. Fires blazed. All accompanied by yet more screaming. Terror, everywhere.

There'd be no hiding the existence of monsters after this. The cavalry would be called in to kill the stragglers and the bodies would be found. A peek for all mankind behind the curtain of an Underdark I dealt with daily.

Maybe. The government would probably cover it up and spend decades studying the remains, only to never understand a goddamn thing. Might be for the best in the end. Make people more afraid of trifling with the unknown.

Probably not.

People are, by and large, two acres dumber than dirt.

Still, it made it easy for us to traverse the city without anyone shoving their noses where they don't belong, odd a group as we were.

Glass shattered to my left as a man burst through carrying boxes, while the shopkeep fired at him with a shotgun.

"Flee! Flee for your lives! The devil comes!" someone yelled.

People hollered crazy shit all over. Looters had their fun. Homeless preachers spouting the typical "The end is near" or "Jesus is knocking on this or that." That's the thing about the darkness. When we don't know what we're seeing, all logic goes out the window. We revert to our primal selves. Hunting and gathering.

Another time, I might have set the lot of them straight, but I kept on with Judas and his followers. We crossed the main throughway, a straight view down at St. Louis Cathedral. A stone gargoyle had descended from his perch and now stood on the steps, chomping on a disemboweled priest.

"Jesus Christ," I muttered.

Judas stopped in his tracks and glared back at me.

"Sorry."

"Mr. Crowley!" a voice shouted, having clearly recognized me. The archbishop burst up through a cellar door on the east wall of the church. "Tell me—Blessed Mother, what happened to her?"

I didn't stop, and he kept pace with us. "She's in bad shape. Laveau is dead. But thanks to her, this is better than it could've been."

He said something in Dutch or German, then crossed himself. "Who are your friends?"

"You wouldn't believe me," I said. "Look, Padre, we're in a hurry."

"Yes, yes. Right."

I handed him Harker's shotgun. "Stay safe."

He looked down at the weapon, then expertly cocked it, and gave me a nod before turning back toward the gargoyle and blowing its head off in an explosion of chunks.

"I can see why Shargrafein can't tolerate you," Judas remarked, eyeing me with contempt.

"Excuse me?" I said.

"The best Black Badges walk the path they're instructed to, never erring. You walk the path, but your eyes remain elsewhere. You still see yourself as their peer."

"What is it with you ancient things and riddles?"

"Humans. You don't look past them."

I grunted. "And I never will."

"Time will tell."

Judas led us into the city cemetery. Odd thing about Crescent

City cemeteries, nobody's buried underground. Standing crypts and mausoleums littered the place, arranged in sweeping paths almost like a corn maze. Baroque, marble decorations were everywhere.

"You're not planning on entombing her, are you?" I asked.

He ignored me.

I kind of preferred this to grass and crosses made of sticks. Even tombstones. It's prettier, for one. Less maggots for another. And, if some necromancer's gonna bring the dead to life, better they come at me from straight on than below.

Though graveyards do make it easy to see your enemy. In this warren of stone, there could be an ambush around every corner. Good thing my companion was the king of vampires who'd just taken on Chekoketh.

We wove our way through all the honored dead. The place was devoid of life—literally. In the practical sense, I mean to say there was no one running around. I suppose a cemetery wasn't somewhere anyone wanted to be during a citywide crisis. Also, not anywhere anybody would look.

Judas stopped in front of an unassuming mausoleum with Grecian columns out front. Those on either side were far more impressive, with a bit of gold filigree and veiny marble.

Not this one. The gray stone was stained and cracked all over. Fitting for someone like me to be buried in. The only ascribing feature was a fleur-de-lis engraved into the solid stone at its front.

Within the symbol, using its own lines so as to be nearly impossible to perceive, was an upside-down cross.

Judas ascended the dais a bit slower than time permitted.

"C'mon, c'mon," I whispered under my breath.

A shriek nearly made me back-step, then something darted from behind a column. Judas's hand jutted out, caught the small flying imp by the throat and broke its neck without even sparing it a look. The bloated little blue body tumbled down to our feet, eyes still open and tongue lolling to the side.

Judas calmly placed his hand on the fleur-de-lis, closed his eyes, and offered an Aramaic phrase. Stone shifted. Dust kicked off, and an arched door formed as a chunk of the stone sank back and rotated out of the way.

"Come," Judas said. Without another word, he stepped through the opening into the dark.

I glanced at Chapelwaite, dumbfounded. "What does he have—hideouts all over the world?"

"Wouldn't you?" he replied.

I grunted, taking Timp by the mane and putting my face to hers. "I'll take her from here, girl. Thank you," I said, talking about Rosa.

She snorted and tapped her hoof twice.

"I'd love for you to come, but see that door right there? You won't fit. Crazy old girl."

I rustled the top of her head, then moved to take Rosa off her back. Chapelwaite gave me a hand, but I wouldn't sling Rosa over my shoulder like a carcass. I cradled her across both arms like a groom holding his blushing bride, crossing the bedroom threshold for the first time . . . Some dream.

I carried her toward the doorway. No footsteps followed.

"You coming?" I asked Chapelwaite.

He shook his head. "What happens beyond this point is up to you."

I sighed. "Ain't it always."

Four of the knights had accompanied us, not including Chapelwaite, and they each took positions in front of the mausoleum.

"Watch them, Timp," I hollered. She blew out her nose. "I

know you can take them." I gave her a nod. Then, Rosa and I entered the crypt.

"Wait, not you—"

Damballah slithered through just before the stone shut behind us, leaving me in near total blackness. My enhanced vision let me make out some shapes and walls, but I needed at least some light source for me to see any more. Vampires, on the other hand, could see in any light.

"Apologies, I forget sometimes what it was like," Judas said. A torch bloomed to life, and he angled it my way. "Careful of the steps."

Looking down, I saw that we were at the top of a tall staircase. Rough edges made waves, creating a disorientating effect. Not the best option for steps in my estimation, but this was an old place. Ancient.

Damballah coiled at the top landing, staring up at me.

"All right, up you go," I told her. "I don't want any funny business."

As if she understood me, she slithered up my leg, around Rosa, and up to my shoulders. Judas then led me down. Unlike the stairs, the stone walls were impeccable. Not a crack. No cobwebs. Just smooth surfaces like polished marble. Even the air lacked that stale rankness death often toted with it.

We leveled out and the space opened like a great hall. It wasn't ostentatious, still all stone, but dozens of paintings hung upon the four walls. They all had a classical feel, like ones you might find in a church. Many depicted Jesus, of course. The famous Last Supper of him and his disciples was straight ahead. The crucifixion beside it.

To the right, taking up most of the wall, was a painting of a lone tree. A noose hung from it, barely visible in front of a dark sky. To my left, Romans cowered in the face of a volcanic eruption. I found myself drawn most to this after hearing Chapelwaite's story.

"It is important we remember our history," Judas said. "To embrace our mistakes. To learn from them. To understand our true selves."

"Yeah, and which do you consider your mistakes?" I asked.

"My considerations are mine alone."

"No judgment. I'm just trying to wrap my head around all this."

He waved the torch over a closed sarcophagus right in the center of the space. Could've been a table. On one side of it lay a heart. Didn't take long for me to realize whose. Black veins crisscrossed over it, a soft glow of dull, dark red flashing between the spokes.

Tourmaline's demon heart.

"Was she one of your mistakes?" I asked as I hauled Rosa over and gently laid her down. Her head came to a rest right by the heart. Felt wrong to me, so I reached out to move it.

Judas snatched my wrist. "You mustn't touch it." He took it himself and moved it into an unlit fire basin.

"I've handled worse," I said.

"It would distort your thoughts, and you must have total clarity here."

"You didn't answer my question."

"And I do not have to." He paused for a breath neither of us took, then said, "Though I will. When I presented her with freedom, it was not a mistake. She was kind. Altruistic. Brave. Even after being burned at the stake by men she had helped—simply for being who she was. The last person I would imagine to be selected by the White Throne. Perhaps that is why they did."

"Now, betrayed by her maker," I noted.

In a flash, Judas had me by the jaw and lifted me off my

feet. Veins went dark around his eyes. Damballah hissed and bore her fangs. Judas's glower whipped toward her and her jaw snapped shut.

"Not everyone is suited for eternity, James Crowley," he growled, glaring back at me. "She lost her way. Lost her spark for life and turned to chaos."

"Says you."

"Do not presume it easy to take the life of one's child." He let go and circled around behind me. "Death was a mercy. And necessary. I have all my children to consider, and I weigh none above the others."

"Parent of the year." I placed my hands on the sarcophagus and leaned over. "Look, I don't care what you've done with you and yours. I'm here for Rosa."

"Yes, the girl." He said it like he'd almost forgotten she was right there in front of us. He blinked once, then looked down. "I am no healer, but I have been around a long time. I have seen every ailment there is, natural and unnatural."

"So, you can help her?"

He placed his hands on either side of her head and bent over, putting his ear to her forehead. "Perhaps."

I punched the stone. "That ain't good enough!"

"The truth rarely is." He walked across the space to a bookcase set within the stone. There, he started to thumb along the spines.

"If this is some sort of test of loyalty or whatever, just tell me," I said. He ignored me, opening one of the tomes and flipping pages rapidly with his eyes darting side to side. Could he really read that fast?

He deposited that tome, then opened another and did the same.

"Would you hurry up?" I demanded.

"Patience is a worthwhile companion."

"Yeah, and whiskey makes a poor shot," I barked back. "I'm getting sick of proverbs. She's dying."

He acted as if I'd said nothing. I squeezed my fists. What else could I do but wait? A man who could read that fast would know more than I could imagine. He was her best chance at surviving this.

I moved to her side and knelt, taking her hand in mine. I couldn't feel how cold her skin was, but I knew it. We'd left Hell, yet somehow, Hell wasn't done with her. She shouldn't have tempted the other side like this. It usually felt good to be right. That was no comfort this time.

"Damn you, Rosa," I whispered to her. "Damn you for having a heart." I craned my neck over her and pressed my head to her chest. I rested there an overly long moment. This, with her so near death, was the closest we'd ever been or possibly would ever be. The thumping of her heart was slow, barely perceptible.

"Why couldn't you just let go?" I asked. "Why couldn't—" My words caught in my throat. My tear ducts had been clogged ever since I was reborn, but I still have memories of crying. Even when Big Davey died trying to protect me—trying to protect Rosa, I hadn't shed a tear. Albeit I didn't have much of a chance while dodging Ace Ryker's bullets before finally taking one to the chest.

While I rested my head against her chest, my mind raced, considering those I'd lost and those who'd lost me. I still remember the day I got the news my mama had died. We were never close, not really. Weekends and most nights were spent at that church in Granger's Outlook. She told me I was better off there, that I'd get fed and not have to worry anymore. I didn't know what she meant at the time—I was just a kid.

Then one day, I left. Didn't say goodbye. Didn't leave a note. Just gone—off to follow Ace into a life of boozin' and floozin'.

I went back once. Don't know why. We were in the area, looking to score a hit probably. Stupid as I was, I was kinda excited to see her. Though I thought I was a grown man, I was just a teenager. I stepped up onto that old stoop, knocked—but no one answered.

Figured I'd give Father Osgood a visit, see what he knew. Maybe they moved? Who knew.

He was an old man by then. Wasn't pissed I left. Even his smile at the sight of me was real. When I asked about my mama, he told me the truth, hard as it was for him. I could remember the man, used to delivering sermons and speaking with poise, stuttering over his words when he told me my pa beat her to death for forgetting to pick up a bottle of gin from the market.

Wouldn't tell me what came of Pa—probably thought I'd just seek revenge. He was right.

Didn't cry then either.

Last time I remember crying, I'd just come home from a long day of hunting. Empty-handed. Pa was waiting for me, bottle tight in his grip as always. My dog—a mutt called Juniper—she was glad to see me. Stood on the porch barking, just waiting for me to join her. My pa had had enough and kicked her hard down the stairs. When I came running to collect her, he met me as if nothing happened.

Poor girl broke her leg stumbling down them steps.

I gave him lip, and he swelled mine. Still didn't cry. Wouldn't give him the benefit of seeing it. When he asked me where dinner was, I told him I had no luck. Fury raged in his eyes. He bent over and scooped up Juniper. Told me we'd eat her. That was when Ma came out and distracted him. They went inside, and I don't wanna know what for, but that gave me a chance to get away.

I don't remember what we ate that night. All I remember

was trying and failing to help my dog get better. She died a couple of weeks later.

Phantom tears rolled out of my eyes then. A relic of overwhelming sadness. Damballah stretched out her limber body, holding it there so that her head was above Rosa, watching quizzically.

"If only you had some of Laveau's gifts," I said to her. "Maybe it's good you don't. She lost control. Let Hell in."

Damballah hissed softly.

"Relax. I'm not blaming her. Rosa did what she wanted and that's that. It was me who introduced them."

A fact I'd have to live with for eternity if Rosa wasn't able to be saved from her supernatural coma. My attention returned to Rosa's hand, which I squeezed a little harder.

"That's why you can't die like this," I said. "Don't put that on me, Rosa. I'm too weak for that. But you're stronger than Hell. You have to pull through."

A gust of air blew her clothing as Judas reappeared, standing by her head. He had one hand on either side of her temples and his ear to her forehead.

"Learn anything?" I asked.

He didn't answer, just shifted his hands to feel under her chin.

"You want me to promise I'll join you?" I said. "Done. I don't care what happens to me. Let Heaven come."

He climbed onto the sarcophagus to listen directly to Rosa's heart. "You cannot promise that," he said without looking up.

"I can."

"Promises only bind the weak."

Words caught in my throat. I'd heard that before, recently, from Laveau.

"How'd you know?" I asked.

"About your private talks with the Voodoo Queen, or that

you already promised your angel you would kill me?" He glanced up with a smile. "I have ears everywhere, *Hamsa*. I served the angels for a long time, James Crowley. I know they would not have wanted you helping her, and yet you did. Oh, the things we Hands tell them just to get a hint of balance. I do not blame you."

"Then you know what I said was bullshit."

He put his hand on Rosa's stomach and pushed gently in a few directions. "I am not going to issue you an ultimatum. It is your choice. But I fear . . ."

"What?"

He just moved back toward Rosa's head and felt beneath her neck.

"What!" I demanded.

"I fear what you will do when I tell you the truth," he said, almost a whisper as he stared at Rosa.

"I'm all out of bullets," I said. "Ain't much I can do to something like you. Though I suspect you know that."

He exhaled slowly and shook his head. "I cannot help her."

"Can't or won't?"

"Whatever happened placed her in a supernatural rest. The very energy of Hell overtook her to open that rift. Her life is in the hands of fate now."

"Don't tell me about fate!" I barked. "You and I existing breaks the laws of nature. Now you help her, or I swear to God."

I drew my silver-coated knife. He didn't even humor me by trying to place more distance between us. Like I was nothing to him but a gnat.

"Perhaps the White Throne could, but you have already broken your oath to them," he said calmly.

My grip tightened. "I can still kill you."

"No. You cannot."

I didn't even see it happen. One moment, the knife was in

my hand. The next, he had it by the hilt in front of his face, studying it. Even Damballah didn't get a chance to hiss.

"Such a barbaric tool," he remarked. The blade started to vibrate in his hand, and only a second later, the metal shattered into countless pieces, drifting to the floor as dust.

"I . . ." Despite all I'd seen this day . . . hell, despite all I'd seen period . . . I'd never been left so speechless.

"Eternity teaches us many things, James. You are an infant in the grand scheme of things. Threats and posturing . . . you will learn they can only get you so far. Being brash may win the American West, but it is not true power."

"What do you want from me, dammit?"

"A decision."

"I'll do whatever you want if you just *help her*!" I was damn near begging, and I hated the sound of it. Just couldn't stand the thought of losing her.

"And I already said I cannot. Your choice must be independent of her. For she is mortal, and you are not."

"You'd have made a damn fine angel," I said. "Useless when it matters."

"Some truths are inescapable." He paced the length of the sarcophagus, letting his finger trace a line along its edge. "You see, you can choose to become one of my children. Then you will be free to travel the world, searching for someone who can give her aid. Though that could take a long time and it is impossible to say how long she has left. Or you can try to kill me. Most likely, you will not succeed. But if you do, then perhaps you could beseech the White Throne to save her as a courtesy to you. They might listen. They might not.

"The angels are many things, but fools they are not, and this woman's very existence cripples your ability to serve them. Which they would know, so they would not help her unless it meant cutting your service short. Of course, you would agree to that for her. But you are far more valuable to them than a mortal over which they have no control. Which means . . ."

"They won't help her." A chuckle slipped through my lips—couldn't help it. "Are you done rambling?"

"I do not see the humor in your predicament."

I jutted out a finger. "It's not that; it's you. You talk about freedom, yet your daughter got out of line, so you killed her. You talk about freedom, while you outline every reason why my only good choice is to tuck tail and serve you."

"I do not ask for your service."

"Just my good behavior." I laughed again. "You're as much a hypocrite as they are. I'd be trading masters for a prison warden. What kind of choice is that?"

Judas closed his eyes. His chin sank to his chest. Looked like he'd just lost a poker hand even though he'd had an ace up his sleeve.

"I hoped you would be different, James," he said. "What great things we could have accomplished together."

"Oh, I am different." I stepped right on up to him. "You see, you left one option off the table."

His glare hardened. "And what's that?"

"Take Rosa."

TWENTY-EIGHT

Judas didn't answer at first. His attention went to Rosa, and I'll be honest, so did mine. She looked like a child's doll. Her face was like pale china without the rosy cheeks. Her hair, though still pin-straight, was somehow lifeless.

"'Take her,'" Judas repeated.

"You heard me," I said. "Give her Tourmaline's heart or whatever it is you do to make her one of you."

He took another moment to analyze her. "Impossible."

"Why?"

"That much of Azrael's power would overwhelm her. Even if she survived the transition, a mortal like her would be unable to resist the bloodlust. Perhaps if she were turned by one of my children, with the power diluted . . ."

"I've seen what that looks like," I said. "Young, feral vampires. She'd be a monster. No." I shook my head. "She deserves better."

"It will not work."

"I may look like a dumbass cowboy, but I pay attention. A necromancer fell for Rosa at first sight. Laveau saw something special in her. A goddamn demon lord tried to take her to Hell to serve him. I heard what he said. Chekoketh didn't want me. He was after her."

I tilted her face toward me and stared at her soft features. I don't know why it took me so long to realize.

"I watched her calm a monstrous grunch with but a look. Freeze a werewolf with a word." I looked up at Judas. "She may be mortal, but she ain't normal and she ain't weak. I was just too blind to see the truth of it."

Judas's brow furrowed. I caught something there I hadn't seen since we'd met. Curiosity.

"Chekoketh was merely torturing you by hurting her," Judas said. I didn't buy it.

"As a dumb cowboy, I can smell shit a mile away. And I smell shit. He said it plainly that they wanted her. I was collateral. Said she'd be their champion or something or other."

His features darkened. "You are certain of this?"

Maybe it wasn't curiosity in him. He began walking along the walls, studying the paintings, and muttering under his breath like a madman.

"What is it?" I asked.

"Could it be I was all wrong?" He was talking to himself.

"Heaven forbid."

"How could I miss it?"

"Miss what?"

"Yes . . . perhaps I see it now."

"Dammit, man, what are you on about!"

His eyes met mine, wide as barrels. That expression—this wasn't curiosity at all. It was fear. But what could an immortal vampire king possibly fear down here in the darkness apart from the sun?

"He wants this," Judas said.

"Who wants what?"

He grabbed the painting of the noose and smashed it on the floor. "Chekoketh. He played us all!"

Zipping back to Rosa like lightning, he pushed me out of the way. I was too confused to react with anything but a slack jaw. His entire demeanor had changed like the flip of a lever.

Pulling up Rosa's sleeve, he ran his fingers along her snake-and-dagger tattoo. Then he put a palm over her chest and closed his eyes. When he'd touched her earlier, it seemed medical. This was something else.

"We were both deceived," he said.

"Speak for yourself."

"This is not a game, Crowley! How did I not see it? They finally found her, after all this time."

I grabbed him by the arm. Whatever had him spooked, he twisted it and wrestled me to my knees out of pure reflex. Didn't seem like he'd even realized he'd done it until after he let me go. And Damballah, she didn't hiss, but cowered behind my head.

"I will not turn her," he said plainly.

"Wait. You're saying it *would* work?"

He heaved me to my feet and held me by the shoulders. "You said you have seen her do things that should be impossible. Sway the minds of monsters, for instance?"

"Maybe, I—"

"When was the first time?" He was ravenous, rabid even. His face contorted from human to something else, back and forth like he'd lost control.

"I'm not sure," I said. "It all happened fast. Could just be coincidental."

"Nothing is coincidental with Chekoketh involved. He is a trickster, a deceiver. A player of minds."

I shook, and he was so distracted by his thoughts, I got

free. Probably could have even killed him then too . . . if I had a weapon left that could do the job.

"What the hell would a demon want with her?" I asked.

"You were right, *Hamsa*," he said. "She is mortal, but she is far from normal. She would be a weapon to sway the war between Heaven and Hell. And with Azrael's power . . . Oh, it would not be like us. Hell would already have their claws in her. His full power, reborn."

"Would you shut up and talk plain?"

He paced frantically again. "Chekoketh *wanted* me to save her after you led her here to open the Hellmouth. Wanted us here. Wanted you to face this impossible choice because he *knew* what the solution would be. But how could he know your heart?"

"Judas!"

He stopped and gasped. "Shargrafein . . ." He whipped back around toward me. "James, you cannot trust her."

"Trust doesn't play into our relationship," I said.

"I am no longer sure what side she is on."

"I thought you don't care about sides."

"I care about *balance*! In a war, only this realm will suffer. They will not bat an eye. Crowley, you must take Rosa. Far from here."

"Not until you help her," I said. I wasn't sure what all the fuss was about, but he wasn't seeing things as they were. She was dying, and I couldn't have that.

"Are you listening?" he said. "It cannot be this way."

"Then—"

Rosa vanished from the table, and next thing I knew, she was back in my arms, cradled like a baby. The speed at which Judas moved was staggering. Made me realize how vulnerable I was to his attacks, and I didn't like it.

"You have to take her somewhere safe. Somewhere far from the gaze of Heaven or Hell. Wait . . ." He reached into the folds of his clothes and pulled out a cross with a black gem in the center. With his other hand, he lifted Tourmaline's heart, closed his eyes, and recited words in Aramaic.

The blackness around the heart faded and it stopped glowing. At the same time, the gem on the cross acquired a red aura. He placed it in my hand supporting Rosa's neck. "To shield you from your masters, I sacrifice raising a new child."

Now it was my time to furrow my brow. Chapelwaite had explained to me what the inverted crosses were. However, all of Tourmaline's power in one would mean mine was what—extra strength?

"Why not just turn me?" I asked.

"There is no time," he said. "We must go. Now."

He zipped up the stairs and out of the room, the speed of his motion extinguishing the torch. Few things are as perplexing as waking up after having died, but this took the cake. My expectations only a short while ago were that either I would leave this crypt a vampire or Rosa would. Either that, or one of us, me or Judas, would be dead for good. Now, none of that had happened.

Damballah's eyes shone in the darkness, and we exchanged a queer look before I hurried up the stairs.

"What are you hiding, Rosa?" I asked her, clutching tight to her head so it didn't jostle too much. "What are you?"

TWENTY-NINE

The mausoleum's stone door was already open. Judas stood right outside under the overhang, fully protected from sunlight. And unlike his mood, the clouds had parted, and the day grew bright and crisp. Heaven to most people. Hell to his kind.

Sounds of terror continued to ring out across the city. However, I could also hear the sweet notes of a well-played harmonica. Better than that jazz crap. Some cynic was out putting music to the apocalypse.

"Can you just slow down a damn minute and explain?" I asked.

"Were you not paying attention?" Judas said.

"Maybe your mind works as fast as your legs." I took a breath. "Judas, what *is* Rosa? You're saying Chekoketh played us? Talk to me."

He ignored the question and shouted to his knights in his language. They hovered on the steps of another mausoleum across the way, killing time however unholy knights did such a thing. I looked left and right. Timp must have moseyed off, chomping on some grass. Impatient as ever.

"Is he with us or against us?" Chapelwaite asked. He and

the others approached in unison, loaded crossbows in hand, ready to defend their leader if need be.

"The situation has changed, my friend," Judas said.

"Yes, it has," Chapelwaite replied.

The twang came first. Four bolts flew out of their crossbows without warning, each one piercing Judas's legs just as they'd done to me in the cathedral. I spun to protect Rosa, though if they'd been aiming at me, she'd already be dead.

As fast as Judas was, the betrayal caught him completely off guard. Neither of us had noticed the ropes tied to their ammunition, and with the bolts securely in his flesh, they yanked. In an instant, Judas went from the protective cover of shade to dragged out into the open.

His cloak stretched down and ripped in places. Sunlight hit his skin and affected him no different than it had Tourmaline, despite his power. Maybe even worse.

He howled, scrambling toward shelter. The knights kept him pinned as best they could while Chapelwaite jumped on his back and wrestled to tear the rest of his cloak off.

"Get off him!" I yelled. "What are you doing?"

"Killing two birds, so to speak," someone said.

The voice didn't belong to Chapelwaite or any of the knights. It came from around the mausoleum. Spurs jangled, and a shadow stretched out from its corner. And once more, I heard a harmonica playing, only the tune was somehow familiar to me.

I laid Rosa down. "Guard her," I told Damballah, and the good snake coiled up on her chest, ready to strike.

I found cover behind a column, and though I had my pistols, I had no bullets. With my knife turned to sand, only my lasso remained to my name. I gripped one end and prepared myself for anything. Who knows what might have spilled out of the Hellmouth.

Like an omen of bad things, the harmonica playing stopped. I readied myself to toss. Then my entire body froze. Not supernaturally this time. Just plain old shock.

It couldn't be.

An outlaw stepped toward me, holding the harmonica and wearing the very same patchwork coat Ace Ryker used to. He looked exactly like him even. Dirty beard, sandy hair, same cold blue eyes, same damn boots. A noose was tied around his neck, sliced at the rope so it hung like a necklace.

I blinked. Was this another goat-man, getting into my head and making me see things? Did some doppelgänger climb loose from Hell? Ace Ryker was dead. I'd watched him hang with my very own eyes. Though, he'd have said the same about me. In fact, he did.

He stepped closer, calmly playing another note. His eyes were half-closed—placid—as if we were sitting around a campfire swapping stories in our early Scuttlers days—before I saw his true nature.

Judas and the others continued to struggle, the sun weakening him enough that he couldn't kill them all in the snap of a finger. Though killing former friends is never easy.

I kept my focus on Ace, my mind seizing, seeing him here. I was paralyzed.

He stopped right in front of me, lifted the brim of his hat, and grinned. That same shit-eating grin that'd been my nightmare for so long.

"Mahrnin', Crowley," Ace said.

He clutched my wrist, flesh on flesh, and my head snapped back as the Divining took hold. Though before it did, his head snapped back too and his eyes glowed pale blue . . .

* * *

"Will you repent and find God's forgiveness?" spoke the Reverend of Revelation Springs. My eyes darted from side to side—Ace's eyes. A rope tightened around my neck as I stood on a wooden stage, looking out at a crowd of angry citizens out for blood.

"Yeah, I'd like to pray," I said. "If you'll allow it."

The words threw the crowd into an uproar that took the Reverend raising his voice to bring quiet. People do so love their hangings. God forbid anyone gets a word in to slow the proceedings.

I closed my eyes. This was the end, and Ace Ryker sure as shit wasn't gonna die like some pansy, talking to a God that don't exist. Forgiveness for what? Surviving in a dog-eats-dog world? Wolves don't seek forgiveness after they slaughter the cattle.

"Dear God," I said through Ace's mouth. My eyes opened, and I stared across the whole crowd, straight at James Crowley—myself. "Fuck James Crowley and the horse he rode in on."

The crowd booed. The lever dropped. And in that second before the floor fell out from beneath him, all Ace could do was wonder how the hell James Crowley survived being shot up. And why he hadn't cut the body to pieces just to make sure he was dead . . .

* * *

I snapped back into my present. Ace's eyes returned to normal too.

Unlike most Divined deaths, there was no pain with this one. The way he'd been hung—his neck broke clean. No struggle. No suffocation. Too merciful a death for him.

But that wasn't where my mind was. I'd been there in Revelation Springs watching Ace die, which meant this was him. And if this was him and he'd technically died, yet still walked, that meant . . .

My gaze fell toward his chest where a breeze blew open his lapel. There I saw it, the blackened, five-pronged scar I'd come to call the Black Badge. The very same marking I bore. The one which indicated that I, James Crowley, was a Hand of God.

"No . . ." I whispered.

His grin stretched wider. If I'd seen his death, that meant he'd just reexperienced mine, when he shot me dead for daring to stop him from raping Rosa and her mother. Unlike me, he seemed to enjoy the heck out of it.

"I knew I should've put you down worse back then for turning on me," he said. "Burned you to ashes. But the Lord is good and his mercy endureth forever! I do say he's given me a chance to rectify that grave error."

Ace always had been a fast draw. Still was. He pulled his revolver and aimed it right in the center of my chest. Not that there was much to do about it, unarmed as I was. My eyes darted to my lasso.

"Try it. I dare you," he said. "You betrayed the White Throne, Crowley. You'll find it don't work so well anymore."

I gritted my teeth. I hadn't fully betrayed my vow to Shar until I let Judas step back outside, yet here was another Black Badge, sent to take me out? It was like she knew I'd fail her before I even did. Hell, maybe she wanted me to.

"They gave me a tool too," Ace said. "But you're the one to thank for it, ain'tcha?" He winked and held up his harmonica. Now up close, I saw it for what it really was. The cursed instrument of a goat creature, its sound able to turn minds. The very same I'd buried in Revelation with him, hoping it'd remain lost forever.

"Still works," he said. "Turned those fools on their master easy enough."

Judas's sizzling skin met my ears. More grunts from him struggling with his own followers. Of all the weapons Ace might've wound up with . . . an instrument that could charm him a crew even easier. Get them to do anything he wanted.

Heaven had to be toying with me. Hell, even. Is that what this was? I'd never left the Hellmouth back in those woods, and this was all in my head?

A hiss snapped me out of it. Ace and I looked down, and Damballah clung on his ankle with her fangs dug all the way in. He rolled his foot to twist her limber body and get his boot over her so she couldn't let go.

"New pet?" he asked. "Fits you better than that ancient horse. A snake for a traitorous snake." He chuckled. "So the Lord God said to the serpent, 'Cursed are you. You will crawl on your belly and you will eat dust all the days of your life. And I will put enmity between you and mankind; he will crush your head, and you will strike his heel.'"

Ace lifted his boot. Damballah flopped to the dirt. Then he stomped down hard on her head with a sickening crunch. The fangs snapped. Brain matter spurted out.

"Whoops," he said, kicking her limp body off to the side. "Probably should've warned it that I'm as numb as you are now."

I growled. "I'm gonna—"

He slid his gun up under my chin and pushed my mouth shut to silence me. "Do nothing. That's what. I killed you; you came back. You killed me; I came back. The scales are even now, Crowley. But Heaven wants you gone."

"You belong in Hell."

"So did you. Yet here we are. You've turned your back on another boss and it's time you were punished."

"The great Ace Ryker, a servant. What a joke." I spat in his face.

His grin didn't fade as he wiped it off and flicked it back at me. "Only joke here is you. James Crowley, the righteous outlaw. Yet, here I stand, an agent of Heaven, and you, damned for eternity. Guess it'll only be me left to take care of your girl." He licked his lips. "We'll get properly acquainted soon enough."

I clenched my jaw and stared right into his rotten eyes. All those years working with him flashed through my head in an instant like they were only yesterday. Not a man in the entire West had sinned as much as him. None of this seemed right.

And as I weighed my fate, something came up in my peripherals. Took everything in me not to grin. I kept my best poker face, holding his full attention.

"So, go on, traitor." The hammer on Ace's revolver clicked. "Will you repent and find God's forgiveness?"

"Fuck you." I finally smiled right back at him. "There's the horse I rode in on."

Timperina rammed into Ace's side at full speed, sending him flying across the dirt. He'd been too focused on his resentment for me to notice her. His gun went off, a silver bullet plunging harmlessly into mausoleum stone.

"About damn time!" I shouted to Timp.

I hurried over to Rosa and hefted her onto Timp's back. She stomped her hooves agitatedly, waiting while I pulled myself up onto her saddle.

Ace found his footing and fired. I clicked my tongue and Timperina swung around, knocking him back again with her hindquarters. If Ace was made a Black Badge, it was very recently. Which meant he wouldn't know the extent of how he could push his new, feelingless body yet. Advantage, me.

I couldn't kill him, though. Wasn't sure how to die myself, and I didn't have the armaments. I just had to get Rosa as far away from him as possible.

Judas howled in pain. I peered through the dust to see him. One of the knights was injured, his own bolt shoved through his eye. The others still wrestled Judas down, sunlight having scorched his skin so bad, it was all blackened and crusted like an overdone steak.

Spurring Timp along, I barreled into all of them, knocking the knights away from Judas.

"They're bewitched!" I shouted.

He rolled onto his back. Steam surrounded him, eyes burning with hate.

"Run, *Hamsa*!"

The injured knight recovered first and dived at him. Judas caught his arm, twisted around him, and sank his fangs into his neck.

Fresh skin formed in patches on his face, the human nectar healing him a bit. Though he didn't feed long. His teeth tore out in a gruesome spray of red, and he fled around a mausoleum, into the shadows.

"Go, Timp!" I kicked her sides just as a gunshot barked behind me. The silver zipped over my ear, and Ace emptied his entire barrel as we raced down the cemetery row, bullets cracking off chunks of stone all around us. He never was half the shot as me or Davey.

"You're a damned coward, Crowley!" he shouted. "That's all right. I always enjoyed the hunt! And trust me, Crowley. Heaven's coming for you, and I'm their goddamn right hand. You can't hide!"

I pulled on Timp's reins to spin her so I could get one last look at the bastard. Ace sneered, with the bewitched knights around him—his newest gang.

"Keep on coming, then!" I called back. "I'll be ready."

A snap, and Timp and I were away. I didn't look back again, just kept her hooves pounding the pavement across Crescent City. My hand went to the cross Judas had gifted me. Then I pulled Shar's mirror. Man, did I have a few choice words for her. Ace's handler or not—everything she knew about him . . . How could they bring him back?

The mirror remained completely black. As promised, I was hidden from Heaven's gaze. A good thing, considering my circumstances. My list of disloyalties to the White Throne was a lengthy one. Ultimately, I'd failed to kill Judas and I'd chosen Rosa over service.

Now I was Heaven's most wanted.

But sending Ace? They were more vindictive than I'd ever fathomed. Was I that much a threat? No. I stroked Rosa's hair, longing with all my soul to feel each strand.

It was her. Always her. Whatever she was, whatever Judas realized back in that crypt, I had to keep her away from Heaven and Hell. Which gave me an idea of exactly where to take her, and who might be able to help bring her back.

"Stay with me, Rosa," I whispered. "It's just you and me now."

EPILOGUE ONE

Kjeldgaard, Ace Ryker's handler, hadn't been overly enthused that he'd let Crowley get away alive. Ace didn't mind. From the start, he'd had a feeling the White Throne only wanted him for this sole reason. That after Crowley was dispatched, he'd be sent barreling toward Hell. Can't say he didn't deserve it.

And sure, the thought had crossed his mind to string the angels along for as long as he could, just so he could guarantee more time on this here Earth. But he didn't want that. He didn't care about eternity. No, he wanted Crowley to suffer. To be on the run, fearing for his own life and the life of that woman he loved.

And that damn horse.

It'd been too easy. Heaven sending him here to discover Crowley just after his betrayal. That wasn't any fun. Ace wanted to relish the hunt, to put the fear of God into his old compadre turned rival. He wanted to stare straight into Crowley's eyes while he destroyed everything the bastard cared about.

Then, the angels could do whatever they wanted. Ace wouldn't go down without a fight, of course, but he wouldn't feel slighted.

He puffed on a cigarette as he stood in the entry drive to a rundown old plantation house. Smoke went in, smoke went out. No burn or tingle in his throat. No little dance in the heart as the tobacco filled his lungs. No peace for his brain. Nothing. He was only starting to get used to the numbness, and it sure as hell didn't make staying around on Earth worth it.

Things moved in the shadows as he approached. His guns were loaded up with silver, but he didn't even bother reaching for them. This was business. You pull iron too early in a dealing, and it's sure to go south.

Vines crept up every inch of the facade. Shattered glass from countless windows peppered the grass, porch, and awnings. The kind of get-up he'd bring the Scuttlers to when the heat was on. As he reached the top of the front steps, nobody inside made a move. Though the shadows remained.

A stinging sensation bloomed in the center of his chest, behind the mark the angels bequeathed upon him without his say-so. Meant something not intended for this world was nearby. Neph—something. He wasn't quite caught up on the lingo yet, and when that angel droned on through mirrors, it was hard not to doze off.

What did he care about a war between above and below? His war was here.

He adjusted his collar, then rapped on the big wooden door a few times.

No answer.

"Nothing's ever easy," he grumbled.

Restraint could wait. He was immortal. Pulling his pistol, he gave it a twirl. It came to rest with his hand around the barrel, and he used the butt as a hammer, banging the door with it as hard as he could.

"You gunna make me come in shootin'?" he hollered.

"Try it," came a voice on the other side, deep and guttural. "Walk away while you can, cowboy."

"I ain't no cowboy."

"No. You're dinner."

Wolves growled and Ace spun, gun flipped back and ready. Only they weren't wolves. Two of the things closed in on him from the driveway, lean, towering beasts that were half man, half wolf on two legs, with fangs as long as hunting knives. Saliva glinted in the moonlight. They were hungry.

"Well, I'll be," Ace said, grinning. "You things are real. Uglier than I imagined."

They growled and moved closer. As a sign of good faith, he slotted his pistol back into his holster, raised his hands halfway, and turned his back on the approaching monsters.

"I reckon your pack ain't as big as it used to be these days!" Ace said loudly, so whoever was behind the door would hear. "I'm supposin' I know who the cause of that is."

"You chose the wrong house," one of the werewolves snarled behind him. His big nails scraped across the bottom step. Ace couldn't feel its foul breath, but it was enough to make his collar flap.

"Nope. I'm right where I ought to be," Ace said, standing firm.

The beast stepped between him and the door and leaned in, its giant, angry maw stretching open right in front of his face. He ignored it, strafing to one side so he could speak through the door unhindered.

"I hear you have a bone to pick with James Crowley," he said. "I've got more than a few too."

The wolf didn't dare get any closer. First, there was silence, then the pattering of small feet. The front door unlocked and swung open with a pained whine.

"Move," the newcomer said to his pack mate.

The creature obeyed without question. Now standing before Ace was a refined beast, if it could be called that. Regal-looking, even though one eye was badly damaged, half of it missing and the rest shriveled up in a deep socket. A thread hung from it as if he were in the middle of having it stitched up.

Ace palmed the dog's nose and turned its head so he could look square into its good eye. He winked, then backed up a few paces before turning on his heels. "Thought so."

The werewolves at his back blocked the stairs. Turned out, monsters get to posturing just like men when they're in a weak position. And gangs don't live in a place like this if they're strong. Hideout, sure, but not this. He couldn't help but be disappointed.

"Where do you think you're going?" the werewolf asked.

Ace looked over his shoulder. "Oh, so you wanna talk? Good doggie."

The werewolf growled. "You cowboys are all the same."

Ace turned slow. The rest of the pack closed in, forcing him into the home. Inside was as shitty as the outside. Glass broken everywhere, the remnants of a one grand hall now in ruins. Little shadows darted out of the back doors as he entered. They cackled like children, though the sound rang a tone more beastly. He, however, was focused on the werewolf who'd answered the door. At first, he'd thought it would be one of the lemmings, but no. The man himself had received Ace like royalty.

He was bigger than the others by a foot, his coat grayer. There was more expression in his face. Thought himself something special, he did.

Some fat little demon sat on the railing, nothing but his belly covering his cock and balls.

The werewolf marched toward the demon and sat down on the stairs, obviously returning to his former activity. The demon grunted and set back to work sewing sutures over the pup's eye socket. Sharp claws dug into the wood of the stairs each time the needle went in.

"Who are you?" the werewolf asked.

"Does it matter?" Ace said.

"I'm trying to decide if I should feed you to my children or not."

"Not sure the taste would suit them."

The wolf's laugh become a howl, and his nails dug in deeper.

"Quit moving!" the little demon barked, losing his grip on the needle.

"Enough, Fazar!" The werewolf clutched the imp around his oversized waist and squeezed.

Fazar gasped for words until he was released, toppling off the railing and landing with a thud.

The werewolf rose back to his full impressive height and cracked his neck, thread still hanging from the gash around his missing eye—an endless chasm juxtaposed against his remaining eye, yellow as a hunter's moon.

"You're not afraid, are you," the werewolf said, more statement than question.

"Don't take it personally," Ace replied. "Fear's always been a stranger to me."

"You're one of them," Fazar said from behind the railing posts. The little creature was smart, hiding like that. "Two in a week. This is too much. Angels used to be lazy."

The werewolf stomped closer and used a single nail to stretch aside Ace's shirt to reveal his Hand of God marking. A low, angry growl resonated from deep down his gullet.

"You really shouldn't have come here," he said.

"I come in peace. You have my word."

"Just get rid of him, Roo!" Fazar said. "They ruin everything."

"Roo, huh?" Ace stepped to the side and examined an old silver candlestick. "Sorry, I'm still picking up the pieces of what went down. What exactly did Crowley ruin?"

"What do you want, cowboy?" Roo asked.

"Only what you want," Ace said. "The end of James Fuckin' Crowley."

Roo smiled. "Well, now. Perhaps we could talk."

"Tell me, Roo. What did that piece of shit do?"

Roo snarled. "We had a place here, just for things like us. Out of sight. Underdark's mostly empty now except the few who don't feel like running. Army crawling all around the city after what he did down there and above. Not safe for us anymore."

"What a pity—"

Roo ripped the candlestick away and shoved Ace against the wall, pinning him between two claws. His breathing was ragged, savage. His eye went dark with pure rage.

"He took something more personal from you, didn't he?" Ace said calmly.

"Kill him," Fazar said.

Ace leveled his gaze on Roo's single eye. "Something more than an eye or a chunk of flesh. Some*one* dear to you."

Roo roared loud enough to rattle the broken glass. He let Ace go and stormed back in the other direction. "You don't know nothing about it!"

"And I don't need to." Ace wiped the slobber from his nose. "But he's made himself an enemy of the White Throne. My enemy. The way I see it, you got no reason to stay here. You *do* got every reason to help me end that son of a bitch for good."

"He'll poison you with lies," Fazar said to Roo. "It's what they do."

"Quiet!" Roo snapped, causing the little demon-thing to retreat even farther behind the stairs. Then he came to face Ace again. "My children will eat his beloved horse in front of him. I will dine on the woman he loves."

"Great minds." Ace snickered. "So, we're square?"

Roo turned his head so only his grisly wound showed. "You should have asked before you opened the door."

"One or two, I like to look a man in the eye before I agree to partner up."

"Oh, we aren't partners, Black Badge. Just two hunters on the same trail."

"Fair enough." Ace's lips split into a wide grin. "Then let's get to hunting. But one rule . . ."

"Don't test me," Roo warned.

"Only one." Ace stuck a finger up, then strode right up to Roo and used it to poke him in his hairy chest. "You can have his horse. His lady. But when we catch him, I get to put him down. And if you so much as think about getting in the way of that, I'll shove silver so far down the throats of all your children, your ancestors will shit it out in Hell."

EPILOGUE TWO

Abraham Stoker didn't want to leave the Americas. Everything he'd seen in Crescent City only bolstered his belief in a supernatural world beneath the surface, led by immortal vampiric royalty.

He was also no fool. The less settled western regions of America had led him and his friends into far too many scrapes with death in such a short time. Wild was no exaggeration.

Leaving was no longer a choice. It was a requirement in order to keep Harker by his side. He'd already lost one companion on his mission of madness. Losing another wasn't in the cards.

"I shall miss this place," he said, staring out at the smokestacks of Crescent City. Some fueled industry. Others were the result of burning homes in the chaos of monsters being unleashed.

"I won't," Harker said flatly.

Bram sighed, laying a hand on his shoulder. "It just feels like we were so close."

"Close to death," Harker said. "Wasn't everything we saw proof enough?"

"It proves the hypothesis. Yes." Bram nodded. "The experiment, however, never ends."

"It has for me." Harker turned on his heels and followed the line of civilians roaming down the docks. US military directed people onto a ship. They'd set up posts throughout the city, marching in to clean up the mess caused by James Crowley.

"We killed a man," Harker whispered.

"We did no such thing," Bram argued. "That man was merely in the wrong place at the wrong time."

Harker's face blanched. "Wrong pl—*Bram*, we helped lure him out there to be . . . what?"

Bram shook his head. "What happened was inevitable, my boy. Such is the way of things. When dealing with unknown variables, we have to expect unknown ends. No one intended for this outcome."

"Yet it happened all the same," Harker said, bowing his head as he continued toward the ramp.

Bram let a few moments pass in suitable solemnity before saying, "At least I'll have a permanent souvenir," and motioning to his bum leg.

"I don't know how you jest about such things," Harker snapped.

"One must find the lighthearted, even in the direst of things."

Someone ahead of them got out of line and was roughly corrected by soldiers with rifles. Harker watched with terror.

"You two, move along. Let's go." An officer signaled them up the ship's ramp. Bram had to give his friend a nudge to get him moving.

"You just need a rest," Bram said, using the rail for support.

"I need a lifetime of it," Harker replied, twisting his corncob pipe. "And a warm shepherd's pie. And decent tea."

Bram chuckled. "All of that and more." Bram squeezed his arm and gained his attention. He stared for a few seconds. They were refined, educated men. Even he admitted it was uncomfortable seeing Harker caked in grime and dried blood.

"Thank you, my dearest friend, for sharing the adventure of a lifetime with me," he said.

Harker's eyes glazed over. "I only wish we weren't returning one short."

"She always said she'd die young."

"She always tried hard at it too, the loon." They shared a laugh, exchanged a sober nod. Harker wiped his eyes. "I'm starting to wonder if we're the crazy ones."

Bram smiled. "Madness and genius are strange bedfellows. Now, let's get you that rest."

They made their way down into the cabins. Harker lent Bram a hand on the descent, but Bram refused to allow his injury to become a hindrance.

They were tight quarters, which had been an issue on the ride over from Ireland after leading such a posh life, but not anymore. Bram had slept in far worse conditions since. Their bunks were in a common space. Most of their belongings had been lost or destroyed, though what they could rummage from Laveau's house remained. Some clothing and other effects, but most importantly, Harker's sketch journals documenting everything they'd seen.

Months ago, Harker had dragged both their trunks. Now, Bram and he stowed only small bags under the beds together before sitting to catch their breath.

"You know, some time back home might be good," Bram said, wincing as he pulled his leg onto the cot. He barely got the sentence out before Harker climbed up to the top bunk. "Sleep well, my friend. Remind your nightmares of the time you sent a minion of Hell back to the Devil's arms."

Harker leaned over to gaze down at Bram. "Quiet with that."

Bram chuckled. "As if anyone would believe it! You . . . using a shotgun." He scoffed in playful mockery.

"Very funny," Harker said, shifting back. The upper bunk bounced as he made himself comfortable.

Bram scooted to the edge of the bed and looked up. A man lay in the bunk across the corridor, far to the inside where mostly only shadow could reach. He wore bloody rags and a hood over his head.

"Heading home?" Bram asked.

No answer.

"Sir?"

The hooded man turned, and Bram swallowed the lump in his throat. His face bore the sign of burn marks, like he'd been caught in a fire. Even his hair was singed away, leaving a scaly, bald head.

"Are you all right?" Bram asked. No doubt this was the result of the chaos in Crescent City. Poor fellow.

"I'll heal," he muttered.

Bram leaned in. "Is that a Syrian accent I detect?"

"Similar."

"Where from then?"

"You wouldn't remember it."

"Try me."

He rolled his head back the other way and grew silent. Which for Bram, only intrigued him more. Unending curiosity was his blessing as much as his curse.

"Are you headed to Ireland?" Bram asked. "As you can surely tell by my accent, it's home. Though I prefer to think of myself as a child of the world."

"It's a stop on the way," the man said, still facing away.

"To where?"

Again, the mysterious man went silent. And nothing made Bram Stoker itch more than a lack of answers, no matter how mundane the question.

"It's a long ride ahead of us as neighbors, good sir," Bram said. "We might as well get along."

The man exhaled low, almost like a growl. Then he shifted, dark eyes boring right through Bram—as if into his soul. In a way, that made him both deeply uncomfortable and confoundedly intrigued.

"I have a child to visit," he said. "In Transylvania."